1521

No
More
Bugles
in
the
Sky

Books by
Richard
Newhafer

The
Last
Tallyho

No More
Bugles
in the
Sky

No More Bugles in the Sky

By   Richard Newhafer

 THE NEW AMERICAN LIBRARY

To three women
who have always
been on my side.
My wife,
my mother, and
my sister.

No
More
Bugles
in
the
Sky

Chapter
I

The wind was moist and warm and it blew up from the west, coming past Barbers Point air station and along the expanse of Waikiki Beach in the direction of Diamond Head. It brought the smell of gardenia and frangipani to the surfers and the beach parties clustered in antlike groups on the whitened, sun-bleached sand.

It entered through the open windows of the paneled barroom of the Moana Hotel, stirring the still air and bringing a breath of coolness to the noon heat. Manuel Ortiz, the wizened little Mexican bartender, grunted softly with relief as he felt the breeze on his brow. Now he knew it was high noon. Manuel had spent twenty-three years behind the Moana bar and the fragrant breeze had yet to fail him at this hour. He finished mixing the martinis, poured them expertly into three glasses, dropped an onion into each, and delicately ran a lemon rind around the edge of each glass. Then he carefully placed the drinks before the three sun-browned men standing at the bar.

There was a warm regard in the gaze Manuel bestowed on the three men before him. He thought to himself: They are of a kind, these three. The years have not diminished them in any way. Each of them is worth the second glance of any man. But this Dan Belden, he is *mucho hombre*.

Watching Belden, the dark, big-boned man in the middle, Manuel remembered the first time Belden had walked into this room. The year had been 1944 and Belden had been a young man then, just twenty years old, his eyes bright and dancing at the prospect of war and combat waiting somewhere over the western horizon. Well, Manuel remembered, Belden had headed west to meet his God in a new dimension, and when he had come back a year later, some of the laughter had gone out of his eyes. Too bad, Manuel shrugged, but it had happened in a like manner to all the others who had gone west in those times.

Now Manuel picked up a bar rag and began slowly to polish the glasses arrayed before him. His eyes moved to the man on Belden's right, a big bear of a man with a balding pate and huge, capable hands, now folded peaceably on the bar. This one was Bates. He, too, had fashioned a magnificent record in that war of twenty years ago. Manuel smiled briefly to himself as he remembered the night Belden and Bates had, by themselves, taken on the entire personnel of a rival fighter squadron from another aircraft carrier. It had been a battle to remember.

He moved his glance to the man on Belden's left, a hard-looking man with curly brown hair and incredibly blue eyes. Aiee! Manuel remembered this one too. Cortney Anders was the name and he had become a legend in Pacific skies and later in Korea, too.

Now Manuel placed a glass on the back bar and turned to Belden. "It's been a long time, Dan. We grow old, eh, *compadre?*"

Belden pointed at Manuel's sagging paunch. "*You* grow old, Manny." He turned to Bates with a pained expression. "How can a skinny guy like Manny get a paunch on him?"

"You grow old," Bates said. "Your muscles atrophy and sag and first thing you know you've got a skinny little bartender who looks like he's pregnant." Bates shook his head. "Too bad."

"Like Bates's hair," Anders said. "It sagged right off his head."

Bates ran a big hand over his sunburned pate. "For a number of years," he said slowly, "I thought my hair covered a reasonable amount of brains. Of common sense. Right now I realize how mistaken I was. Who"—he spoke to Manuel—"in his right mind would up and leave a partnership in a charter flying service in Palm Beach, Florida, and come halfway across the world to get into a fight that doesn't even belong to him? And this, mind you, at the exact same time that a gorgeous divorcée with *eight million dollars* had avowed

2

her undying and eternal love for him. I must have gone out of my skull."

"Ah, no," Belden murmured. "That's not it, Batesy. You came because you wanted to prove you were still a young man. This is a fallacy in your thinking because all you have to do is count your birthdays. Forty-one isn't it? But you had to try once more. We all do."

"And what was *I* trying to prove?" Anders asked. "Since you're so omniscient today, suppose you tell me. I was chief test pilot on the X-20A at Edwards Air Force Base. I made fifty thousand dollars a year; I've flown faster and higher in a winged aircraft than any man alive. Now what the hell did *I* have to prove?" There was no rancor in Anders' soft words.

Belden laughed gently. "You were flying with ghosts up there at two hundred and fifty thousand feet, Cort," he said. "Ghosts of guys who went before and guys who will come after. There's no fun in fighting and flying with ghosts. You came back again because you want to fight other men, not shadows or records or headlines. That's why you're here." He straightened up from the bar and placed an arm around his friends' shoulders. "And I'm damn glad you're both here."

"Then buy a drink, if you're so happy," Bates said.

"Three more doubles, Manny," Belden said. As an afterthought he added, "Damn good martinis. Even at this time of day."

"The martinis never change, Dan," Manny said. "Neither do you. Any of you. The years have treated you lightly."

"Except for Batesy's hair," Anders opined.

Belden chuckled. "We're all going downhill, Manny. Someday soon we'll all have to quit pretending we're twenty-five years old again."

"Like you said." Manny grinned. "Not enough exercise." He eyed Belden a moment. "I read where you were in the Congo?" He posed it as a question.

After a time Belden merely said, "I was there."

Belden stared into the mirror behind the bar without seeing his reflection. What is it, he wondered, that has gone out of me? Twenty years ago, standing at this very bar, I knew the greatest happiness in my life. Since that time it has been all downhill. Things

3

lose their taste, little by little, year by year, though a man would think it should be the other way around. There's no anticipation in anything any more. What happened to the boy who was so bright and shining in his youth? He shook his head. Perhaps, he thought, what he had lost was innocence.

Dan Belden was forty years old and exactly twenty-one years of his life had been spent flying airplanes under one circumstance or another. He was an easygoing man with vast patience and gentleness belied by his hard, craggy face and his big-boned frame. In the first month of 1944 he had come west to a war he coveted. No doubt ever entered his mind then that he would become anything but the best, and no doubt had ever entered it since. He had learned well the business of flying, and more important he had learned the art of remaining alive in the sky, which is an altogether different thing. The survivors, he had realized, were usually one of two types: They were men who respected their airplanes and their adversaries or they were cowards who did not want to fight anyway.

When the war ended, Belden honestly admitted to himself that he could never go home again and pick up his life where he had left it. The years that followed had taken him to strange places, but always there were the airplanes, the smell of grease and hot engines, the feel of the stick in his right hand, and the throttle held loosely in his left. There were the clear mornings on the flight lines and the first surge of the blood as the mech kicked the chocks away and the slight touch of the throttle started the wheels rolling. High in the sky, over lands that were not his, he climbed for the cloud tops and the position of advantage out of the sun.

In the years after that war there had been other wars waiting. He had found them and slowly, somewhere along the way, the thrill had become dulled and in its place had come a calm, unemotional proficiency that was true professionalism. The business of fighting in the sky had become his life, and he had flown and fought under many flags and as many names.

He came back to the Navy and spent the Korean War years flying jet fighters from carrier decks. He was glad to be back, but somehow things were not the same. Perhaps it was because he was years older; perhaps it was the fact that flying had become a profession to him and professionals rarely take the enjoyment of a thing as do the ama-

4

teurs. When the shameful treaty was signed at Panmunjom and the free world bowed its head, Belden made a sound of disgust and shed his uniform for the last time, and went back to the life he knew and understood.

It was a simple matter of existence: high, white clouds and hot suns; and the quiet thrill as the throttle was eased back and the plane flared out and then gently settled to touch, feather-light, and begin the long roll-out to the hangar. It was an uncomplicated life as long as a man realized what he was hired for and had no expectations that he was going to live forever. There were good friends and laughter at night over the whiskey, with talk of the day's flying loud on every tongue. The names came and went and he forgot the faces until sometimes he intercepted a radio transmission from somewhere out across the sky and the voice would bring back a name and a face. And so the years piled one upon another until one morning Dan Belden awakened and realized he was forty years old. He had thought about this for a few minutes and then shrugged fatalistically. What the hell could he do about it, anyway? He turned over and went back to sleep.

That had been a month ago and since that time he had been in La Jolla, California. For long days and nights he had lain in the sun, drunk good whiskey, and taken to bed the best-looking women available. All in all a delightful vacation and it might have gone on indefinitely had not the phone call come from the Old Man.

Belden smiled to himself as he remembered that granite-hard old man with the flinty eyes, the rasping voice so accustomed to command, and the heart as soft as a baby's cheek. The Old Man was retired now, gone from the Navy with his three stars and his medals and his reputation. When the Old Man went, the last of the great legends went with him. Bull-voiced, intemperate, irascible, the Old Man had clawed his way to the top of the naval ladder with a rugged disregard for naval proprieties. He was a man who could not dissemble, who would rather crash right through an obstacle than go around it. Consequently he had suffered many a headache before he pinned on the third star. Belden had followed his career the past few years as the Old Man served a term in Congress and then accepted the call to head the Central Intelligence Agency. Things were sure as hell going to be hot in the CIA if the Old Man had the helm.

And now, thought Belden, because of Vice Admiral Ryerson, USN retired, I am standing here with the ghosts of twenty years ago and drinking excellent martinis at high noon with two of the three men I love most in this world.

Manuel placed three more drinks before them. "You'll get us drunk, Manny," Bates said equably.

"What's wrong with that? You're in Hawaii. Hula skirts and soft music. You waste time standing here."

"You running a whorehouse maybe?" Anders asked.

"It is not necessary here." Manuel shrugged.

"Tell me, Manny," Belden said. "Do any of the old guys pass through here? From the war, I mean?"

"Admiral Dusane came through. He was on his way west to take the Seventh Fleet."

"I read about it," Belden said. "A hell of a man."

Anders spoke musingly. "He had the torpecker squadron on the *Concord* during the war. We were boot-assed ensigns in the fighters."

Manny nodded. "We spoke of you. All of you. We wondered where you were."

"I'd like to see Dusane again. Cut up some old jackpots. Christ, that man could fight!" Belden said.

"He said the same about you," Manny said.

"He took that torpecker squadron in at the Battle of the Phil Sea." Bates spoke softly, his voice warm with the memory. "We watched him. He took them in on the deck, under the guns of that whole goddam line of battleships. Creamed the Jap First Fleet. He went out with forty and came back with eight." He looked at Belden and raised his glass. "To Smoke Dusane and the Seventh Fleet."

Manny made a project of polishing a glass while the three men drank. Then he looked at Belden with a tiny smile. "I'd like to tell you about a girl, Dan."

"I'm positive Manny owns a whorehouse," Anders said.

"This is a young girl. Very beautiful. Long blond hair and very light gray eyes. Long-legged; she walks like a queen. Teeth like pearls when you gaze on them at midnight by the light of the full moon."

"Wow!" Bates said. "She's rich too, of course?"

Manny nodded. "Extremely rich."

Belden laughed. "Would you say we were her type?"

"I don't know," Manny said. "The only reason I mentioned this at all is because she's sitting over there at a table and for the past thirty minutes she has been staring holes in your back, Dan."

"Oh?" The three voices spoke simultaneously. Very cautiously all three turned, taking great pains not to be obvious.

They saw her then. She sat at a table with an older man, a man with a thin mustache and horn-rimmed glasses. The first thing they noticed was the way the sun came through the open window behind her and threw golden glints across her hair. She wore it pulled back behind her ears in a fashion that accentuated the gray of her eyes. She wore a white sweater and a blue skirt. Belden found himself staring into her eyes for a long moment and then she blushed and turned her head away.

"She blushes, Manny," Anders said. "How old is she?"

"She and her father, the man with her, celebrated her twenty-first birthday here last night."

"It must be wonderful to be twenty-one years old," Bates remarked.

"Yeah," Belden sighed. He looked at Manny. "You should have done this for us twenty years ago, Manny. We're that much too late."

Manny watched Belden with a genuine affection. Then he turned to the cash register, took out a dollar bill and placed it on the bar.

"Cover it," Manny said.

"What's the bet?" Belden asked.

"I am part gypsy," Manny said. "I have a hunch. I do not think it is too late."

Belden laid two dollar bills along the bar. "You've got two to one on that, friend."

"Why don't you ask him to the table, Papa?" she asked. She spoke with only the slightest trace of a French accent and put the emphasis on the last syllable of Papa.

"I think perhaps now is not the time, my dear," her father answered. "You will meet him before we leave." He paused to watch his vibrant daughter. "There is a reason?"

7

She answered with an easy impudence. "Since when do you and I need reasons for what we do, Papa?"

Robert Morlaix sighed. "I thought when I sent you to that fashionable school in New York they might ingrain in you some of the womanly qualities I seem to have neglected. You are"—he spoke lightly—"entirely too much like your father."

He watched this lovely girl with great appreciation. He thought how wonderful it must be to be twenty-one years old, possessed of great beauty within and without, looking forward eagerly, with anticipation, without trembling and doubt. He hoped the years would not disappoint her and that she would never be other than the laughing, flashing girl he saw now. She had her mother's beauty, the gentle loveliness he had missed so much these past fifteen years. He found it hard to understand and admit that she was a woman now, with a woman's longings and desires.

His wife had died when Lori was still a child; had faded away with the fever before she had a chance to see the great plantation form and take shape. Those had been times of peace, before the unrest and the fighting came, when the most important thing a man had to do was insure the steady flow of rubber from the pierced trees and try to raise a daughter thrust solely into his care. Well, he thought, I've done the best I know how. I am satisfied with the result. Immensely satisfied.

"A penny, Papa," the girl said.

"Hmmm?" he asked, bemused for a moment. "Oh, I was thinking how much I am going to miss you when you return to France next week."

She sipped her drink. "I'm not going back to France, Papa."

He stirred the contents of his tall glass with apparent unconcern. "So? Where are you going then?"

"I'm going home with you."

The man shook his head. "No, my dear. That is quite impossible. You know that."

"We Morlaixes are quite adept at accomplishing the impossible. You told me that yourself."

"I once told you many things, Lori. You must realize that times change and our considerations, our values, necessarily change with them."

8

"You sound stuffy."

The man laughed. "Perhaps. But I think for the present you'll find much more to occupy your time in Paris than you will in Saigon." He was suddenly grave. "You've been away two years. It is not the same any more, my dear. It is no place for a young woman."

She leaned over and kissed him lightly on the cheek. "I'll make arrangements."

"To return to Paris?"

"Of course not. To go home with you."

He knew better than to pursue the argument now. He followed her glance as she turned to look at Belden, standing talking to his friends at the bar.

"Are the things I've heard about him true?" the girl asked.

"Possibly," her father answered. "What have you heard?"

"I remember when you let me take the flying lessons that summer in Maine—my junior year I think it was—I remember the instructors talking about him. They said many things. All of them good. I wonder about any man when I hear only good about him. I don't think they even knew him."

"He's a strange man," her father said. He looked at her slyly. "You notice I said *man*. He is no longer a boy. He is forty years old, therefore you may forget about him. He's too old for you."

"What do you know about him?"

"Very little," her father said. "Only what Admiral Ryerson has told me. He has great faith in Mr. Belden. When Admiral Ryerson places great faith in a man, then I must consider the man to merit that faith."

"I love the Admiral," she said. "He reminds me of a friendly panther."

"I'm sure the Admiral would be pleased," Morlaix said wryly.

The girl took a deep breath. "We'll ask Mr. Belden and his friends for cocktails tonight," she announced.

"We will not," her father replied equably.

"At seven-thirty," the girl said. "You can ask him now or call him later."

"I'll lock you in your room."

"I'll climb out the window. We're only on the second floor."

"So we are," her father agreed. "Well, we shall see." He rose to his feet. "I'll make a sporting wager with you. I'll race you for it. We'll swim to the markers and back. If you win, we'll invite those large men with the brown faces for cocktails. Have we a bet?"

Since she had been beating her father in swimming races for at least ten years, the girl said, "You have a bet, Papa." Almost as an afterthought she added, "I think I will cultivate a taste for martinis."

Belden watched the girl and her father move across the room. At the door the girl paused and looked back at him and Belden thought he saw a fleeting smile pass over her lips.

"What's her name, Manny?" he asked.

"Morlaix. He owns most of the rubber trees in Indochina."

"There is no more Indochina. It's Vietnam now. Laos. Cambodia."

"Wherever or whatever it is, he owns most of them."

"I don't mean the old man," Belden said. "I mean the girl."

"Lori. Lori Morlaix." Manny said.

"Ah," Belden murmured. He poked at the onion in the martini. "What are they doing here?"

"He's on business of some sort. She flew from Paris to meet him. He's had her over in France since the trouble started in Saigon."

"Trouble never started in Saigon," Belden said. "It was always there." He tasted the name on his lips. "Morlaix, eh?"

"You heard of him?"

"I've been in Saigon. If you've been in Saigon, you've heard of Robert Morlaix. I didn't know he had a daughter."

"Well, you do now. Do I win my bet?"

"Not yet, old friend. Not yet," Belden said.

Belden stood at the window of his suite high in the Moana and looked down at the curving line of beach that swept toward the Royal Hawaiian. Behind him in the room Bates and Anders lay sprawled on twin divans, their shirts open to the cooling breeze and half-empty whiskey glasses in their hands.

Belden reached down to a table and poured some rye whiskey over two ice cubes in a glass. He sipped the drink and watched a Navy jet fighter scream low over the water a few hundred yards offshore.

"Dan?" Bates's voice was drowsy.

Belden turned from the window. "Yeah?"

"What about Hawk? Is he coming?"

Belden frowned. "I'm not sure. He said he'd let me know."

"Good old Hawk," Bates mused, his eyes closed. "They don't make them like that any more."

"You can say that again," Belden said.

Anders swallowed the last of his drink and propped himself on an elbow. "Why the hell does the vice president of an aircraft company, a guy with a wife and kids, want to come out here and get his ass shot off? It doesn't make sense."

"For the same reason that you gave up the X-20A and Batesy left that heiress back in Palm Beach." Belden sighed. "We're all crazy."

Anders was refilling his glass when the knock came timidly, the knuckles rapping very gently on the door. Belden crossed to the door and opened it.

The man outside was tall, slender, with the look of a middle-aged athlete about him. He carried a brief case under one arm and in his eyes there was a look of wry amusement.

"Mr. Belden? I am John Conway."

"Come in." Belden stood aside. "Mr. Bates and Mr. Anders."

Conway nodded a greeting and placed his brief case on a table. He took a handkerchief from his breast pocket and wiped his forehead before he said, "You've spoken with Admiral Ryerson?"

"Not since he called me in La Jolla," Belden said.

Conway nodded with a certain weariness. "He will meet you in Saigon. In the meantime you are to sign these contracts of employment." He took a sheaf of papers from the brief case.

"A cover?" Belden asked.

Conway nodded. "You will be employees of the Morlaix Company. Mr. Morlaix is here in the hotel now."

"What kind of employees?" Anders asked.

Conway shrugged. "Who knows. It's only a temporary thing." He walked to the window and stood a moment in concentration. Then he turned and rubbed a hand wearily over his face.

"I'll tell you as much as I know," he said. "It isn't much. The Admiral isn't a hell of a talker." He moved to a chair and eased himself into it. "I presuppose you are acquainted with the situation in Vietnam?"

11

"I know we're getting the shit kicked out of us," Bates said.

"That's one way of putting it," Conway admitted dryly. "No one likes it, but also no one seems to be doing anything about it. The Vietcong have all the best of it right now. We don't have the planes, the guns or the men to do much about it. Admiral Ryerson intends to remedy this situation. To do this he will, of course, need the backing of the Administration. He hasn't got it as of now."

"What *has* he got?" Belden asked.

"He's got Senator Ralph Yeager on his side. Yeager is the Minority Leader and swings a lot of weight. When the time is ripe and the Admiral wants to make his move—well, that's where you come in."

"What's his move going to be?" Bates asked.

Conway shook his head. "I can only guess. There have been rumors going around the department that a possible Chinese offensive is being planned for sometime next year. I guess the Admiral is the only one who knows exactly when." Conway's voice took on a note of urgency. "If we don't manage to break this thing open over there, to get men and planes and armament committed, then if the Red Chinamen come down we won't stand a chance in hell. Damn it!"—Conway pounded a fist into his palm—"we've *got* to escalate this war in Vietnam before it's too late."

"So?" Belden said softly. "How do we fit into all this?"

"The Chinamen will make a mistake," Conway said. "The Admiral is certain of this. Sooner or later they'll make a mistake. Maybe their planes will come down over the Seventeenth Parallel. Maybe they'll move in battalion or even division strength, and once they commit themselves, there won't be one damn doubt about who is behind Hanoi and the Vietcong. It's that one mistake we're waiting for. Christ, we don't even have to prove anything. All we need is enough evidence to convince the President that *something* has to be done. When they make their mistake, and they will, the Admiral will have you and your men, none of you bound by a uniform or by military regulations, to hit back, surreptitiously maybe, but to hit back and draw the Chinamen out, make them come down and violate air space, make them overtly commit themselves. Then we'll have the incentive to fight back, to send over the men and guns and planes that we'll need when the fighting escalates. Hell, right now we're so screwed up over there we're like a bunch of whores at a Salvation Army picnic."

Belden grinned at Bates and Anders as he filled a glass with whiskey and handed it to Conway, who drank it down.

"The Admiral," Conway continued, "above all things is a fighter. We don't have too many of them around right now. Everyone in the high places seems paralyzed by indecision. Ryerson wants to fight because he knows that until we do, until we commit ourselves in force—and now I'm speaking of a hundred thousand men, maybe two hundred thousand—we're going to keep right on going down the drain over there. If the Chinamen recognize this indecision, they'll pour half a million men over the border and what happened in Korea will seem like a Girl Scout outing compared to what will happen south of the Seventeenth Parallel."

"I'll have fourteen men if they all show up," Belden said mildly. "Can fourteen men handle this?"

"I don't know," Conway replied. "The Admiral thinks so." He grinned. "The Admiral is of the opinion you can do just about anything."

Belden shook his head. "That's just like the Old Man. He expects me to take fourteen men and break this war wide open. On the face of it, it's ridiculous." He glanced across the room at Anders and Bates who were studiously noncommittal. He handed each of them an employment contract.

"Sign them," Belden said.

Bates's face held a pained expression. "This is like signing a contract to walk across the Sahara Desert backward in my bare feet. Makes about as much sense too."

Conway accepted the signed papers and put them in his brief case. He handed Belden an envelope. "Your tickets to Saigon and suitable expense money. Your salary starts when you arrive at the Morlaix plantation."

Conway offered his hand to the three men, then paused at the door as he was leaving.

"Something bothers me," he said in a puzzled voice. "None of you are kids any longer, but you're going out there to fight a kid's war. You make your living this way." He shook his head. "How do you end up like that? How do you make a profession out of fighting wars?"

Belden smiled and then spoke very gently. "You get lost, Conway. Somewhere along the way you get lost."

Conway thought about this a moment and then threw a half-salute and was gone.

With a visible effort Bates got to his feet. "Well," he said, "now that I've assigned myself to disaster, I think I'll go over to Kaneohe for a swim. How about it?"

"Sounds good," Anders said.

"You two go ahead. I've got some things to attend to," Belden said.

"Call you when we get back," said Bates.

After they had gone Belden refilled his glass and settled himself comfortably in the chair by the window. There were things that must be done but for the present he was satisfied to shut his eyes and let half-forgotten moments pass across his memory. It was as though a force entirely outside himself was maneuvering the pieces of his life, bringing into startlingly clear focus events, faces, and names that he thought had long ago marched away from him. He could remember now the beginning and the middle; all that remained obscured was the end, and he contented himself with a hazy picture of an old man, browned by the sun, sitting in the lazy time of old age with a lifetime of recollections dimming in his mind.

He remembered Conway's words about the Old Man and smiled to himself. There was between Belden and the Admiral something that only a few men find in their lifetimes. Belden knew how fortunate he was that it had come to him not once but several times. It was a warmth and understanding under a brusqueness that could never conceal the love of one strong man for another. Men hide these things, but the love is there and is understood by those who feel it. It is shown in little ways—the clap of a hand on a shoulder, the extra pressure in a handclasp, a meeting of glances when the chips are down—but the knowledge is there that you are not alone.

Belden finished his drink and shook his head as he remembered for the last time this day how great his good fortune had been. He was considering the telegrams he had to send when he was interrupted by the strident ringing of the telephone.

"Belden here," he said.

The voice on the phone was gentle and softly modulated. "Mr. Belden. My name is Robert Morlaix. I don't believe you know me."

Belden smiled to himself. "The hell I don't, Mr. Morlaix. What can I do for you?"

There was humor in Morlaix's voice. "I'm not exactly sure, Mr. Belden. I seem to be taking orders from a rather imperious young lady. I would be honored if you and your friends would have cocktails with my daughter and me this evening. I promise I shall put her on her best behavior. And incidentally," Morlaix added, "I believe we have a mutual friend in Admiral Ryerson."

"We do, sir," Belden said. "I understand I may be selling rubber for you in the near future."

"Ah!" Morlaix said. "Then you have met Mr. Conway?"

"This afternoon. I think cocktails would be a good idea, Mr. Morlaix. What time?"

"Seven-thirty? In the Banyan Court?"

"Fine. I'll see you then, sir. One thing. My friends are tied up this evening." Belden grinned at his perfidy.

"That is unfortunate. You will recognize us?"

Belden laughed. "Mr. Morlaix, a man who could fail to recognize your daughter in the Banyan Court could miss a trolley car in the middle of the Sahara Desert. Seven-thirty, sir."

Manny, my old friend, he thought, I may lose that bet yet.

Belden stepped out of the elevator and almost immediately saw Morlaix and his daughter sitting at a table overlooking the Banyan Court. The evening was warm and a small combo was playing on the bandstand in the corner. Below, in the Court itself, a buffet dinner was being served.

As Belden approached, Morlaix got to his feet and offered a hand. Belden glanced quickly at the girl and found her watching him with an amused expression.

"Mr. Belden? . . . I am Robert Morlaix." He turned toward the girl. "May I present my daughter, Lori?"

"Lori." Belden nodded his head politely, regarding her with a quizzical expression. He took a chair facing her.

Robert Morlaix signaled to a waiter. "Your drink, Mr. Belden?"

"Rye and soda, please. And the name is Dan." He watched Lori Morlaix as the waiter took their order. She had an extremely gentle beauty, he thought, a beauty she wore lightly, almost with unconcern. Her teeth were a flash of white in her tanned face as she smiled at him.

"Of course you would look like this." At his expression of humorous perplexity she continued. "I had you pictured in my own mind, you know. Girls do that. It's a game with us. We amuse ourselves by drawing in our mind an exact picture of the man we know we will meet someday. Some people call this dreaming, but I don't."

If Belden thought the girl's directness disconcerting, he concealed the impression. "You are fortunate to be able to dream," he said softly. "Dreaming is for the young." He paused a moment. "It has been a long time since I have dreamed."

"Mine has come true," she said with evident satisfaction. "Even to the color of your hair and the crinkles around your eyes."

Belden was aware of the sound of laughter from Morlaix. "Please excuse my daughter," he said. "I fear it is all my fault. I should have taken to the strap when she was a child."

"I'm still a child," Lori said. She looked directly at Belden. "At least Mr. Belden thinks so. Don't you, Mr. Belden?"

Belden shrugged. "I haven't given the matter much thought."

"You will, Mr. Belden," she said softly. "You will."

"I am sorry, Mr. Belden," Morlaix said. "But this is the way my daughter is. I would be foolish to try to change her at this—as you Americans say—late stage of the game."

"I think," Belden said gravely, "that you would make a great mistake if you tried to change your daughter at all, Mr. Morlaix."

"You are learning quickly, Dan Belden." Lori spoke as if the two of them were alone.

"I learn most things quickly," Belden replied. "There's never very much time." He found himself speaking with no trace of lightness in his voice. Something about this lovely, vibrant girl stirred him and he was totally oblivious of the disparity in their ages.

"I shall be unladylike," Lori announced. "Would you care to dance, Mr. Belden?" She was laughing at him. He looked at Robert Morlaix.

"You can't win, Mr. Belden." He sighed. "You children dance and I will order our dinner." He glanced at Belden. "You'll join us?"

Belden was on the point of refusing when he felt the slightest of pressures on his arm from Lori's hand. He nodded at Morlaix. "I would be delighted, sir."

They danced effortlessly, moving slowly to the soft strains of the Hawaiian music. Belden could smell the fragrance of her hair and he felt her breasts pressing against his chest.

Abruptly she pulled her head back to study him, her eyes brightening with some inner amusement. "I was all right until you came along, Dan Belden."

"You'll be all right again," Belden said.

She nodded, as if in serious agreement. "Probably, but not in the way you think."

"For a very young lady you can be extremely devious."

"You sound like Papa."

"I like your father. He seems to be a hell of a man."

"He is a hell of a man."

"He must want the best for you."

"He does." She was faintly puzzled.

"Then content yourself with a nice young man you will find somewhere along the way. Much of the world is violence, Lori. Your world should be sunlight and laughter and bright things to amuse and interest you." He frowned. "There is nothing like that in my world."

"Then you will move into my world, Dan." It was the first time she had addressed him familiarly.

"No," he said. "I guess not. But things will work out for you, Lori. Things will work out."

"They will now," she said contentedly. Her arm tightened around Belden's neck. "Be on your guard, Dan Belden. I'll fight dirty."

Belden spoke lightly. "You've picked the wrong target, young lady. You're a generation too late."

Lori said nothing, merely snuggled closer to Belden, her lips nearly touching his cheek.

Forty-five minutes later Robert Morlaix wearily signaled the waiter and ordered the two untouched dinners taken away. He wiped his mouth with his napkin. He had enjoyed his dinner even if he had had to eat it by himself. He watched the dance floor where his daughter and Belden still moved slowly to the music, and a small smile of understanding touched his lips.

Chapter
II

It is 0530 hours.

In less than sixty minutes the first light will play along the crests of the mountains to the west, and once again death will move over the land.

The young man stands motionless against the tree waiting for the last of his watch to pass. He has been standing here for nearly four hours, and the time has gone slowly. But he is a soldier, and this is one of the least annoying of his responsibilities. From where he stands in the last darkness he can smell the fetid odor of jungle growth and the dead smell rising from the rice paddies. He wears only a dark cotton shirt and cotton knee-length britches tied around the waist with a knotted rope. He wears no shoes and he is probably one of the few civilized men in history who has gone to war in his bare feet. From his right hand a .30-caliber carbine dangles carelessly.

His name is Xuan Nonh and many years from now men may look back and remember him as the ultimate infantryman.

He wears none of the scientific accouterments of war. He wears no flak vest, no arch-supporting boots, no back-pack with medical supplies and morphine. He does without these supposed necessities of war. He fights in his bare feet with his skinny arms sticking out of the sleeves of his worn cotton shirt. He is a Vietcong guerrilla, and

19

when the last war is over, when everyone alive has destroyed every-one else alive and only the last two men are left to face each other in the final slugfest before oblivion, Xuan, or someone like him, will be one of the antagonists.

He has no sense of his own importance or his place in history. If you were to ask him why he fought, he would tell you because he did not have enough rice to eat. When a man has nothing to begin with, then, he has nothing to lose—no matter in which direction he goes—except his life and all of us lose that ultimately anyway.

Now Xuan moves restlessly a few yards nearer the mud hut he is guarding. He rubs his hand along the barrel of his rifle almost sensu-ously. He cocks his head and listens intently for a moment and he can hear the muted voices of the men within the hut. He nods to himself and moves back to lean against his tree again.

A few yards away from Xuan two young men sit with their backs resting against the mud wall of their prison. They are both wearing orange flight suits, grimy and torn, and their faces show the effects of the forced march they completed the night before. They are Ameri-can fliers and in this moment of early dawn they are at least ten thousand miles and a year away from home. The taller of the two men, slender, with a deeply boned face is named MacKellar. He is a lieutenant in the United States Navy and he is twenty-six years old on this first dawn of his captivity. Sitting next to him is a stocky little man, his face already showing the first tracings of fear. His name is Miller. He is a lieutenant (junior grade) in the Navy and he is twenty-two years old. Both are pilots of AD-1 Skyraider aircraft, al-though their flying proficiency, which is considerable, is of little use to them now. They have been silent for a long time, each concerned with his own thoughts and with his own chances for survival. Now Miller turns his head to MacKellar. "What time you got?"

"Why?" MacKellar replied. "You going someplace?" In the dark-ness he smiled privately at his own joke.

"The bastards took my watch," said Miller.

"Mine too," said MacKellar. "And everything else I had that would come off."

After a moment, Miller asked, "Mac, you think they'll be out look-ing for us this morning?"

MacKellar's frown was lost in the darkness. "I don't know, Joe.

How the hell would they know what happened to us? Those bastards came down behind us so fast we never got off a radio transmission." MacKellar rubbed his jaw reflectively and wondered if the whole mess had occurred because he had his head up and locked.

Their mission had been simple enough. A force of Vietnamese infantry, accompanied by certain American Special Forces men, were to be dumped off at the village of Lao Bao near the Laotian border. MacKellar and Miller, on detached duty from the aircraft carrier *Concord*, were to fly from Danang and bomb and burn off the sagebrush in the area the ground forces were to occupy. They had launched at 1430 in the afternoon and, once airborne from the runway at Danang, had vectored northwest to the town of Hue and then had turned west toward Laos. There had been a light overcast and MacKellar had overshot Hue by four minutes.

Thinking about it now, he realized a strong wind had sprung up from due south and his overshooting of Hue had been compounded in such manner that when he turned west he had been much closer to the 17th Parallel, the border between North and South Vietnam, than he had realized. On his west leg the south wind had drifted him farther north until he must have been flying over or very near the border itself.

They had passed the overcast by that time and the afternoon was clear, ceiling and visibility unlimited. Below, MacKellar watched the heavy terrain, the treacherous mountain gorges, and he knew that underneath that heavy blanket of concealing foliage and tangled growth, lay the trail the Vietcong used to come down from the north. They called it the Ho Chi Minh trail. He looked over on his left wing and saw Miller give him a "thumbs-up" and a quick, flashing grin.

"Keep your eyes open, Joe," he called on his radio.

MacKellar turned to his instrument panel, checking power settings, prop controls, gas gauge, oil pressure, all the incidental little things that could suddenly turn on you and send you fluttering helplessly into that goddam jungle waiting so patiently five thousand feet below.

"Let's start down," MacKellar called. He nosed over gently, rolled a little forward trim on his elevator trim control, reduced power settings, and slid down the sky toward the green blanket below him. Miller moved in close, a few feet off his left wingtip.

MacKellar was looking through his windshield, searching the terrain ahead, looking for the first sign of the twin hills, which would pinpoint the target, when the four MIG-17 jet fighters streaked out of the sky from above and directly behind. They had chosen their initial position with great diligence and MacKellar would have had to have two heads to have seen them flashing down behind him. The first he knew of the MIGs was the distant *pom-pom-pom-pom* of their cannon. Then a tracer winked past his starboard wing and disappeared ahead of him.

Miller's voice roared into his earphones. "Jesus Christ!"

The MIGs had made their attack from altitude, coming down swiftly and leveling off behind the Skyraiders, so that when they came up on their target they had far too much speed. They had miscalculated the lumbering air speed of the ADs and as a result they had time on their initial pass for only a short no-deflection shot; then they had overshot and were climbing steeply ahead and to the side of the American planes.

"Reverse course!" MacKellar shouted as he threw his stick hard to the right and eased on rudder pressure, tensing his stomach muscles as the g-forces pressed him down into his seat. The two ADs swept around in a tight reversal turn.

"Down on the deck," MacKellar shouted. They pushed forward stick and headed for the treetops, throttles pushed forward to the stop and prop controls rolled to full low pitch. Within the cockpits the engine roar rose to a shrill whine as MacKellar and Miller charged their guns and switched on their gunsights.

MacKellar looked back over his shoulder and saw the MIGs split into two two-plane sections and bracket them, one jet section ahead and out to either side. He looked over at Miller and motioned to him. "Move out, Joe," he called. "Hold this heading and weave."

In this moment of ultimate peril the names of other men flashed briefly through MacKellar's mind. Jimmy Thach, Harry Hill, Dave McCampbell, Dan Belden, the men who had fought and learned and then had passed on to others the means for survival in an alien sky when all the odds had turned against you. Never let them make their attack unhampered, so the thinking went. Turn into them. Always turn into them so at least there was the threat of your guns. Maybe you couldn't hit a bull in the ass with a shotgun, but if they didn't

know it, their aim might be thrown off just a little, merely by the fact that your guns were there and were turning into them. This was the manner of thinking that had been ingrained into MacKellar and in this moment he prayed fervently that it would work.

"Watch them, Joe," he called. "When they come down, we'll criss-cross. You watch my ass. I'll watch yours." And that is the way Mac-Kellar and Miller went to war. Watching each other's asses.

MacKellar now reached down to switch to his emergency radio frequency. With a horror he saw that his entire radio panel had been shot away by one of the MIG shells. He had not even noticed.

"Joe," he shouted into his mike. "Get an emergency channel and sound the Mayday."

"Will do," replied Miller.

But before the call for succor could reach across the sky the MIGs were down again and this time they came with their throttles re-tarded and their dive brakes extended. They came slowly and did not overshoot their target. MacKellar saw them coming and he watched them carefully, judging his time precisely, straining to turn his head as he saw them sliding down from behind and slightly to either side. When he judged them to be almost within firing distance, he called out, "Break, Joe." The two Americans turned sharply to-ward each other in vertical banks, each turning his guns to cover the other's rear. Joe Miller, fighting to control his plane, straining against the g-forces, striving desperately to turn far enough toward the enemy to bring his guns to bear, never had time to get off his emer-gency radio call.

MacKellar flicked his eyes to his rearview mirror as he turned and he saw the two-plane MIG section coming in behind him. Even from this distance he could see the fan-shaped dive brakes extending from the bellies of the MIGs. God damn, he thought. The bastards are good. They know what they're doing.

It was at this point in his flying career that MacKellar dropped the ball. Had he throttled back, dropped his own dive brakes, possibly his own flaps and wheels too, perhaps he might have slowed his speed to an extent that would have precluded the MIGs bringing their guns to bear. But he did not do this; neither did Miller and so the MIGs opened fire from either side with a 45-degree deflection and both American planes were shattered by the enemy cannon.

MacKellar swore as the shells thudded into his plane. He glanced quickly over at Miller and saw parts of Miller's plane tearing away in the wind, shot away by the MIG shells. Below him the treetops loomed a few feet under the belly of his plane. The entire structure of the aircraft shuddered under the attack, and MacKellar heard the solid *thunk* as a shell entered his engine housing. A split second later the cockpit was filled with smoke and the smell of hydraulic fluid. He quickly opened his canopy and called to Miller, "I'm clobbered, Joe. I'm going in."

He heard Miller's voice. "I'm with you, Mac. The bastards got me too."

The MIGs had overshot by this time and were pulling up and away. Both American planes were streaming smoke as they flew at treetop level and MacKellar searched desperately for a clearing in which they might set down. He found none and suddenly the fall afternoon became a time of desperation.

They had set down into the treetops at nearly stalling speed. This is a thing that may be done with fair chance of success provided the pilot is ready, knows what he is doing, has his plane under control, and his shoulder harness pulled tight. The trees broke the force of their landing and both pilots got out of their planes safely, but they were prisoners before their feet had touched the ground.

Now, in their mud prison, MacKellar spoke reflectively. "Joe, I guess I goofed yesterday. We might have made it if I'd used my head."

"Balls," said Miller. "Two ADs are never going to beat four MIGs in a fight." He sighed. "We did the best we could, but it wasn't good enough."

"We could have dropped our flaps and wheels. That's one way we might have made it."

"What difference now? Stop chewing on it, Mac."

Miller got to his feet and crossed to the small opening that served as a window in the wall of the hut. He looked out at the sky and the first tracings of morning on the mountain crests.

"Mac," he said, turning back to MacKellar, "what do you figure they'll do with us?"

MacKellar thought about this a moment. There was a faint premonition far back in his mind, but he was afraid to deal with it right

now. "March us north," he said. "Maybe make us look stupid. March us through their villages at the end of a rope or something. Christ knows what these crazy bastards are liable to do. Use us for propaganda one way or another."

"Well," said Miller, "it's better than being dead."

So it is, thought MacKellar, and finally faced the thing that truly worried his mind.

He knew the MIGs had crossed the Vietnamese north-south border—perhaps only a mile or so, but they had crossed nevertheless. MacKellar was sure of this because just before the attack he had seen the Ben Hai River just across the 17th Parallel. So the MIGs had come down for the first time, and he and Miller were the only two men alive who could prove this violation that would have international repercussions if it became known. Even as MacKellar admitted to himself that this made their position far less than alluring, he still could not get that picture of yesterday afternoon out of his mind.

They had marched for three hours after their capture. The Vietcong had not treated them roughly. They had been searched and their papers and valuables had been taken from them. Then, surrounded by Vietcong, they had started the slow journey north. MacKellar figured they must have been fifteen miles or less from the 17th Parallel. The fight had taken only that long.

Seen from the air the terrain had appeared mountainous and crisscrossed with deep gorges. From the ground it was a twisting, tortuous maze of tangled undergrowth, interweaving vines, and fourteen-foot elephant grass. They had made about five miles when night had fallen. Just before dusk more than half the enemy party, about nine men, moved swiftly ahead and disappeared into the jungle. Fifteen minutes later MacKellar and Miller heard the sounds of firing in the distance. The spatterings of rifle fire grew louder and finally one of the advance party returned and spoke heatedly with the two leaders of the group. MacKellar thought he heard the sound of a scream somewhere ahead. As they moved on, the rifle fire began to die out and finally it stopped altogether. MacKellar swallowed with some difficulty, and strained to pick up the sounds of jungle dusk. He looked at Miller and Miller turned suddenly and looked back at him, a frown on his face. Had Miller heard the scream? Were there friendly forces ahead? MacKellar listened again and heard only the cheep-cheep of some night bird waking. Then bursting out of the thick growth ahead came a piercing scream that struck at MacKellar's ears in a shrill crescendo of pure agony. It rose higher and then dropped off, muting to a loud sob and then to a hoarse, animal-like groaning. MacKellar felt the sweat break out on his forehead.

His captors moved ahead, now pushing him and Miller, and they came out into a small clear area of a tiny village. The smell of gunpowder was the first thing MacKellar noticed; the second was the smoking ruins of a small church, the wooden crucifix still atop the smoldering ruin. Several of the Vietcong were dragging bodies into the bushes on the edge of the clearing. At the far end were several dark, shapeless bundles of what appeared to be rags, gathered into heaps on the ground.

They approached the bundles of rags at the end of the clearing and MacKellar's eyes widened in horror. The bundles of rags were the bodies of three nuns, impaled on sharpened sticks planted in the hard ground. The women's bodies were in a jackknifed position, so that they had died kneeling. The bodies must have been forced down on the razor-sharp ends of the poles as the nuns knelt in their final moments. The heads were bared, but the bodies were still clad in long black robes. Through the backs of the robes the ends of the sharpened poles protruded like some unseemly skin growths.

It was lighter now in the mud hut and Miller sat down again with his back against the wall. Somehow he sensed what MacKellar had been thinking.

"Mac," he said. "Yesterday . . . Why did they do it? What had those nuns ever done to them?"

"Tried to help them, I suppose," MacKellar replied.

Miller was silent for a few moments. When he spoke, his voice was puzzled. "Mac?"

Here it comes, thought MacKellar. What do I tell him now?

"Yeah?" MacKellar said.

"You really think we'll get out of this?"

"Sure," MacKellar lied. "We'll get out of it all right."

"Mac?"

"Yeah?"

"I was thinking. You know those MIG fighters came down over the border after us yesterday."

26

Well, here it is, MacKellar thought. He's got it figured now.

"So?" he said.

Miller took a deep breath. "So what if they don't want anyone to know they crossed the border? There aren't too many people around who could say they did or they didn't."

"Not too many," MacKellar agreed. For Christ's sake, Joe, answer your own question. Aloud he said, "I suppose we could give them our scout's honor we'd never say a word. Think that might work, Joe?"

Miller refused to be amused. "If you were in their shoes, Mac, what would you do?"

Let's get this over with, MacKellar thought. "I'd shoot us, Joe. I'd stand us up against a tree and shoot us."

He heard the sound of Miller's breath sigh past his teeth. "I thought so," Miller said. "I guess I thought so all along."

"Don't worry about it," MacKellar said. "We'll be all right."

Miller turned from the window. "Mac," he said softly, "I'm scared. I'm not supposed to be, but I am."

"You're not alone, old buddy. I'm scared shitless myself." Then MacKellar added in a flat voice, "But remember this. No matter what happens, we laugh at them. Remember. We laugh."

From across the room he heard the sound of Miller chuckling.

"What's so funny?" he asked.

"I'm practicing," Miller said.

Approximately one hundred and fifty miles east by south from the village where the American fliers were imprisoned, units of the United States Seventh Fleet steamed through the muddy waters of the South China Sea. The flagship of the fleet was the *Concord*, massive, impregnable, her great flight deck canting out from the island structure at an angle. On the forward end of the deck two heavy-bodied RF8A jet reconnaissance fighter planes were spotted on the catapults. The F8 was a 1,000-mph fighter, but certain of them also had been rigged with photographic equipment and served as the far-flung eyes of the fleet. Around the two planes the deck crews clustered, plugging in the auxiliary starting units which would be used to give added electrical boost during the starting procedure, checking the catapult fittings and attachments. In the cockpits the plane mechanics made last-minute checks of battery and generator units. Over the bullhorn came the announcement, "Recco flight will launch at 0615."

Slowly the great ship began heeling, turning into the wind. Across the broad expanse of ocean the other elements of the task force followed her, their white wakes frothing and streaking the ocean's face with circular white markings. The beating of the propeller blades and the action of the rudders disturbed the first citizens of the deep and all across the water there were the streaks of flying fish, darting for only a moment as they flashed once and then were gone again beneath the waves.

Three decks above the flight deck a group of men stood around a table map on the Admiral's flag bridge. Two of them wore the orange flight suits of the pilots. Another man wore the eagles of a naval captain. He was a hard-looking man, heavily bearded, and he wore a baseball cap. His name was Tom Landry and he was captain of the *Concord*. To his left stood a tall, spare man with a shock of snow-white hair. He wore the three stars of a Vice Admiral in the U.S. Navy and his name was Dusane. He was sucking on a dry pipe and his eyes clouded with anger as he spoke in a low, harsh voice to the men around him.

"We know they took off from Danang air strip at 1430. They were due to fly direct to Hue and then west to Lao Bao near the Laos border. They never got there. No radio transmissions—no nothing. They just disappeared and planes don't just disappear. Somewhere in here"—his finger traced the area between Hue and Lao Bao—"something happened to those two boys. Perhaps we'll never find out what it was, but by God we'll try."

"Were they on a combat mission, sir?" The question was asked by a round-faced intelligence officer named Barkalow.

The Admiral's eyes held Landry's for a moment and a small smile played briefly on his lips.

"Just between us girls, gentlemen, they were. But that is not for dissemination. As a matter of fact it's top secret. The two pilots were on TAD at Danang to instruct Vietnamese pilots in close-air support in the AD-1. They were not supposed to engage in any activity against the enemy, although if you ask me why they weren't supposed to engage in any activity against the enemy after having been sent halfway around the world to fly a military combat aircraft, I probably couldn't tell you." The Admiral frowned and scratched the back of his head. "You mustn't pay much attention to me, gentlemen. I get carried away sometimes by the absurdity of some of the decisions I'm forced to make. Getting old, I guess."

Captain Landry gestured at the map. "Admiral, we know they have MIG-17s at Hanoi. You suppose they might have come down?"

"I don't suppose anything, Tom," the Admiral replied wryly. "They won't let me. There is a possibility they came down. But to do that they'd have to come well across the border, and I don't think the Red Chinamen are ready for that yet. When they're ready, they'll come. But why would they sneak? They'd want us to know because you can bet your sweet ass when they *do* come, they'll have a reason behind it all."

The senior of the two pilots, Lieutenant Larson, spoke deferentially. "We just take pictures of all that foliage, sir? We won't get much."

"No," said the Admiral. "You won't get much. But you might get something that will give us an inkling of what happened to those men. It's worth the try." He looked at Landry. "Tom, someday they're going to let us go in there and defoliate that whole goddam country. Burn out all that rubble and forest and jungle and denude the whole countryside so the commies won't have one good goddam place to hide. Then maybe we can get somewhere."

Landry nodded with mock-seriousness. "Defoliate in 'sixty-eight. I'll write a poem about it, Admiral."

The Admiral smiled and turned back to the pilots. "Fly that course from Danang to Hue to Lao Bao. Take pictures all the way. I want a strip of film covering that entire route. Understood?"

The Admiral nodded and returned the salutes of the two pilots. After they had gone, he moved to the porthole and watched for a moment the activity on the flight deck as the pilots manned their planes. The Admiral was not a young man and he had been watching flight decks, or flying from them, for most of his adult life. He looked up as Landry spoke softly at his side.

"Why won't they let us hit them, Admiral? This is a hell of a way to fight a war."

"Tom," the Admiral said facetiously, "we are a defensive force.

Not offensive. Don't ask me why. We know they're coming across the border from Laos. Hell, we can watch them move out from their bases there. We could hit them out in the open, hit them day and night. But of course we won't. That would be offensive and it might not set well with some people back home who have never heard a gun go off in anger." He sighed tiredly. "Well, maybe they're right. Maybe it's better this way." Suddenly he pounded his fist against the bulkhead in a gentle anger. "But I don't think MacKellar or Miller feel that way about now. I don't think so at all."

Down on the catapults the pilots were in their cockpits, their jet engines whining over the noise of the rushing wind. The seat belts and shoulder harnesses were fastened, the multitude of instruments had been checked. Tail-pipe temperature—okay. Fuel—okay. RPM percentage of power indicator—okay. Radios checked and working. Controls free and easy. Airplane in launch configuration. The pilot of the port F8 looked out at the flight-deck officer standing just forward and to the side of his plane. He nodded and then placed his head back against the headrest. The Fly One officer waved the index finger of his right hand in a circular motion and the pilot slowly advanced his throttle all the way to the stop. Quickly he tightened the throttle quadrant screw, insuring a tight hold on the throttle itself. The jerk of the catapult launch could conceivably retard his throttle unless this was done. The engines were roaring now with a great, ear-splitting scream, the blasts from the tail pipes expending themselves against the shields behind the planes. The pilots checked again to insure full 100-percent power, nodded again, and then the Fly One officer's arm dropped and the port plane leaped down the catapult in a giant cloud of steam that was quickly dissipated in the strong wind. From a dead standstill the planes reached 150 knots in less than one hundred and seventy-five feet. As they cleared the bow, they swung slightly to the right and joined up in a two-plane section. Turning toward the northwest, they climbed steeply and were soon lost to sight.

As the planes disappeared, the Admiral turned to Captain Landry. He spoke with a smile. "Think you could still hack it, Tom?"

"Hell, yes," growled Landry. "I'm not that old yet."

"Where have they gone, Tom?" the Admiral murmured. "Where have they all gone, the guys we flew with twenty years ago? Do they ever remember how it was, as I do and as I think you do? Do they feel regret now that their youth has gone? Or do they pat their fat bellies and thank God that they made it through alive? Can you tell me that, Tom?"

"No, sir," replied Landry. "But I'll tell you what I can do as long as you feel so old this morning. I can send down to sick bay and get a wheel chair brought up here. Would that help your aging bones?"

"Perhaps it would," the Admiral admitted ruefully. "But I often wonder where they've gone. The Harry Hills and Dan Beldens. Harry Hill's bones, I know, have been in the mud at the bottom of Truk Harbor these twenty years. He was a great one. And Dan Belden flew an airplane like no other man I ever knew. They were the true professionals. Where do men like that go when wars are finished, Tom?"

"They're probably sitting in front of a television set this very minute, Admiral. Their belts are loosened and their stomachs sag and they're holding a beer bottle in one hand as they try to find out if young Doctor Murphy is going to let Miss Morrow have her baby aborted or if Ben Casey will find a cure for the young boy with hemophilia." He laughed quietly. "What got us on this depressing train of thought. Let's have a cup of coffee. It may clear our heads."

At 0625 the small candle in the hut at the far end of the clearing had burned almost down. The tall Chinese sat at his small field desk and wrote with great concentration in a plain notebook. His pen flew gracefully, precisely, the intricate and delicate figures appearing as if by magic from the point of the pen. His brow furrowed from his efforts. His name was Lee Cheng and he was a colonel in the air arm of the Chinese People's Republic. He was no longer a young man, but in the manner of Orientals his age was indeterminate. He was large for a Chinese, nearly five feet ten inches tall, slender, but with a hint of steely strength underlying the frail bones. He wore the tattered cotton garb of the guerrillas, but there could be no mistake concerning the air of authority he also wore. Colonel Lee had been fighting as long as he could remember. First it was against the Japanese when he was a boy. He had watched his mother and father burn to death in the flaming ruins of his village and, alone, he had buried the blackened bones by a river side. He had shed no tears then and he was never to shed one as long as he lived.

After the Japanese had gone, he had tried briefly to pick up the threads of his life again. There were the years of hunger; the memory of loud promises of the good things that were to come but never came; the years of change, during which something hardened within him until at last, when the Communists took over, he was ready to pledge himself to almost anything as long as he could strike back at a life that had been denying him all his years. He had flown jet fighters in Korea and had disproved the age-old belief in the supremacy of the white man. He had shot down sixteen F-86 Sabrejets in combat high over the Yalu River. He had done this with no great passion and with no overwhelming hate for the enemy. He had learned quickly what the true fighter pilots know; you are fighting the other airplane, not the other man. His political beliefs were hazy within his own mind, but his loyalty to his oath and his allegiance to duty were undeniable and unassailable. He considered himself a soldier. Nothing more and nothing less.

The Colonel finished the last of his reports and threw the pen aside with a gesture of disgust. He stretched prodigiously and then looked at the man sitting across the desk from him. Captain Tran Minh was many years younger than Lee. His hooded eyes concealed the icy stare and the unblinking gaze of the killer. Lee had been with Minh five weeks now, and he would be glad to be rid of the man. The Captain headed the small group of guerrillas that had taken Lee south to scout enemy airfields and installations and to make a quick survey for suitable airfield sites for future construction. In return Lee had taught Minh's men all he could about spotting enemy aircraft. He taught them configurations and speeds, altitude estimation and direction. Minh's men would be used as forward spotters when the real war started, relaying vital information north to the jet strips above the 17th Parallel.

Now Lee watched Captain Minh carefully. The younger man, not at all abashed by Lee's rank or reputation, stared back. Lee thought he saw a flash of derision in the other man's eyes.

"That thing you did yesterday," Lee said coldly. "It was unnecessary. Those women did nothing to you."

Minh shrugged. "I have orders to intimidate the enemy. They were the enemy as far as I was concerned."

"I'm in charge here, Captain."

"Certainly, Colonel," Minh agreed equably. "Until today. Today I take over and we part. It has been nice knowing you, Colonel." Minh did not take the trouble to hide a small smile.

Lee allowed himself a smile of derision in return. He took considerable time to fish a cigarette out of a beaten pack and to light it from the dying flame of the candle. He exhaled the smoke with appreciation.

"One of the minor luxuries I permit myself, Captain," Lee said.

"We have no time for luxuries in my country." Minh spoke shortly.

"You will have," Lee said. "After a while. After you learn." He was pleased at the flash of anger that came to Minh's eyes. "We are allies," he continued, studying the tip of his cigarette carefully. "We are allies as long as you realize who is in command. I speak not of you and me. I speak of our countries. Without us, you are nothing. You will gain nothing and you will win nothing."

"And with you?" Minh's voice held a note of mockery.

Lee shrugged. "With us, who knows? You may yet wear a pair of shoes. You may yet earn a right to the authority you wield with such relish."

Minh leaned forward, his face hard. "Is it possible, Colonel, you have never met a man without ambition?" Minh breathed a short sound of disgust. "I need no shoes. I need no warrant for my authority. I need nothing from you but guns. The rest I will take for myself. You speak of the women I killed yesterday. You who come from a land where death means less than nothing. Where your leader exterminates thousands without reason. Who are you to give me lessons in humanity?" He sat back and studied Lee for a moment. "We will win here in Vietnam with or without you. And for a reason. We will win because to my people one government is much like another. *Che Do Nao Cung Vay,* Colonel. All regimes are alike." Suddenly Minh smiled genuinely. "Why do we argue, Colonel? We are two men who have met, fought together for a short time, and now we part. Argument will solve nothing between us."

Lee nodded. He gestured toward the notebook containing his report. "I have mentioned your services in my report. My comments are laudatory. Now there remains one question between us."

Minh stood up and moved to the window. Despite his brave words, he knew that Lee held the authority here. He stood for a moment watching the first shadows from the rising sun move across the village clearing. He glanced at his watch—0630. He turned as Lee spoke.

"The American pilots, Captain. What had you planned for them?"

Minh heard and understood Lee's use of the past tense. "We will take them north of the Parallel. They will wear rope chains around their necks and they will be paraded through the villages until they are too tired to walk. Then they will be dragged. My people will see the vaunted American 'tigers' on their knees. When they get to Hanoi, they will be exploited. They will sign pledges to acts they have never committed and the world will learn what manner of men come unbidden to this country."

Lee paused before he spoke. He honestly asked himself if he felt regret at what he had to do. He could not truthfully answer himself in that moment, and so he shook his head at Minh. "Your plans make good sense, Captain. I'm sorry they cannot be implemented."

"You have other plans?"

"I have."

"My men and I took the Americans. They are our prisoners, not yours."

"Perhaps," admitted Lee. "But that cannot be helped. The Americans cannot be used for propaganda purposes. They must be disposed of quietly, quickly, and no one must ever remember them again."

"I have my orders, Colonel. I'm sorry——"

Lee interrupted. "Let me tell you something, Captain." His voice lashed out in a flat, driving tone, and for the first time Minh caught a glimpse of the steel-hard core of authority that lay within the Colonel. "Your wishes are of no importance here. These Americans are going to die. I am telling you so and that is the way it is going to be." In a softer voice, he continued, "Those jet fighters that shot them down were my men, and under my orders they were not to come below the Seventeenth Parallel. They will be dealt with on my return. But they came down below the border, and for reasons that need not concern you it is imperative that no one realize this. There are political and military exigencies that would be gravely compromised if the world should know that Chinese jets came down into South Vietnam and shot down two American planes. Is it too hard for you to understand this, Captain?"

Lee held Minh fixed with his gaze. Minh could feel the driving force, the razored will of the other man. Reluctantly he shook his head.

"Good." Colonel Lee was pleased the matter had been settled so easily. He rose and moved to a small kettle suspended over a bed of still-glowing embers. He put his palm against the kettle.

"The tea is still warm, Captain. Will you join me?" As he poured the tea, Colonel Lee permitted himself the slightest of smiles. "It is the second of the luxuries I permit myself," he said. "Enjoy it, Captain, before you make preparations for my departure."

Miller turned away from the window. "Sunrise, Mac," he said. "We'll be starting soon, I guess."

MacKellar had tried not to think of what might happen when the sun had risen. There were too many contingencies and his brain was tired from trying to sort them out according to logic, desire, and probability. Strangely, for the past few minutes, he had been remembering how other men he had known and had read about had died. If what he suspected came to pass, he wanted to do it well. He did not want to foul up on this one.

"You know something, Mac?" Miller tried to laugh, but his voice caught in his throat. "If this was a TV show or a movie, we'd be standing here with cigarettes hanging out of the corners of our mouths, saying bright things to each other." He smiled at MacKellar, then abruptly turned away. "But we don't have bright things to say this morning, do we, Mac?"

"Take it easy, Joe," MacKellar said. "We're only going for a walk. Just a long walk in the sun."

He moved to the window and when Miller faced him again, he saw the tracings of a tear in the corner of Miller's eye. The poor bastard's scared, he thought. Well, so am I. I often wondered what it would be like to know you were going to die some bright morning.

Now I know. It sucks the wind out of your guts and leaves you feeling weak in the knees. You look at the trees and the mountains in the distance and you think how lucky you'd be if you could suddenly find yourself over there. Free. Free to get the hell out of here and go on with your life for all the years left to you instead of dying here in this stinking village this morning. You remember little things you wanted to do, little kindnesses that you would do now if you had any time left. But you don't. And yet you go on hoping. Maybe they're going to take you on north. Maybe you'll live through this yet. You keep on hoping because I guess the human spirit is indestructible.

At this moment Xuan Nonh entered the hut and gestured with his rifle.

"Time to go, Joe," MacKellar said.

Suddenly there was no more time for pretending. Miller took a deep breath and smiled at his friend.

"We laugh at them, Mac. No matter what, we laugh at them."

MacKellar grinned and clapped Miller on the shoulder. The two men, together, walked out into the village.

They saw the two officers standing together in the center of the clearing. The other men were grouped off to one side. Xuan Nonh prodded the pilots with his rifle toward a large tree on the edge of the cleared area. It was an old tree, bent and gnarled with age, the trunk massive with bulk and dignity. As they stopped in front of the tree, Colonel Lee spoke in a loud voice. "Six men will be enough, Captain."

From where they stood, MacKellar and Miller watched six of the ragged Vietcong move out in a line to face them. One of the rifles caught a ray of the sun and flashed briefly in the light.

"Ah," MacKellar murmured.

Miller said nothing. The two men watched as Colonel Lee left Minh's side and approached them. He spoke in English. "There is not much time. Do you care for a cigarette?"

MacKellar's eyes unflinchingly met Lee's. "I think not."

Lee looked at Miller. "It might give me lung cancer," Miller said. The faintest of smiles passed across Lee's face. He nodded.

"It's time to laugh now, Joe," MacKellar said softly.

"I'm all out of laughs, Mac."

Unconsciously their shoulders straightened as the rifles came to the ready. MacKellar and Miller looked down the relentless rifle barrels under the warming sun. There was no other sound in the village. Time slowed itself and crawled along and MacKellar thought: Christ, but this is going to be a beautiful day!

Lee gave the order to aim.

Dimly, from a distance, the sound of a jet engine came on the morning air. It was only a whisper at first and then in a brief second it was upon them, rising to a roar. MacKellar knew they had come looking for them.

Lee watched the two jet fighters sweep along over the treetops, skimming the roof of the jungle growth, then pass swiftly out of sight. The sound of their passing hung on the still air.

At the last moment, just before Colonel Lee gave the order to fire, MacKellar looked directly into Joe Miller's eyes—dying—at 0640 in the morning.

Chapter
III

OCTOBER
1964

In his office on the fifteenth floor of the Marshall Field Building in Chicago, a doctor studies the report lying on his desk. He frowns at the import of the words and shakes his head tiredly. He does not want to believe what his eyes have revealed to him. Finally he flicks the intercom button and speaks quietly to his secretary in the anteroom. "Have Mr. Hawkins come in, please."

He forces a smile to his lips as the door opens and a striking-looking man enters.

"Have a seat, Hawk," the doctor says.

Ray Hawkins is a lean man with a face marked by suffering. Lines of pain touch the corners of the mouth, and back of the eyes there is a hint of sadness. Along the line of his jaw the muscles bunch rigidly at intervals of time. But also there is a calmness about the man, an air of acceptance, almost of dry humor, as if the predicament in which he finds himself has some special jest within it.

The doctor hesitates a moment. "Well, I have the last report here." He pushes at the papers on his desk.

"So?" Hawkins speaks carefully, treading along the edge of the truth.

"You're loaded with it, Hawk. We cut out all we could and hoped for the best. But it came back again." He let the breath whistle past his teeth. "You've got more cancer than the law allows. You're loaded with it."

Hawkins reflectively rubbed the back of his neck, where the pain came. He smiled. "Why the hell does cancer in the lung hurt you in the neck?"

"We could go in again," the doctor said slowly, "but it won't do any good." He tried to keep pity out of his eyes. "I'm sorry, Hawk."

"How long?"

The doctor considered this. "Six months. Eight. Maybe a year, but no longer."

"How long can I get around?"

"Until the last six weeks perhaps. The pain will get worse. You'll lose strength. Your appetite will go. But it will be the pain, mostly. I'll give you drugs for it, but at the end there won't be much we can do." Suddenly he said again, "God damn it, Hawk. I'm sorry."

Hawkins rose and walked to the window. Below him the lights of the Outer Drive sparkled against the darkness of the night. He could see the headlights of the cars as they passed Monroe Street and moved toward the bridge crossing the river. He turned back to the doctor.

"You know, Doc? I've had a philosophy ever since I was a kid. I got it one day in September, 1943, when I was nineteen years old. I came back from my first mission in the South Pacific. It was at a place called Mille Atoll in the Marshall-Gilberts. When I landed aboard the *Yorktown*, my mech found a hole in my tail, in the ass-end of the fuselage where a forty-millimeter shell had passed through. I didn't even know I'd been hit. That shell missed the control wires to the rudder section by about a quarter of an inch. A quarter of an inch closer and I would have been dead at nineteen. I'm forty now, and every minute, hour, and day since that time has been a bonus. Every breath I've had, the good times and the bad times, all of them have been a bonus because by all rights I should have died on a September day in 1943. How the hell can a man gripe after a break like that? I've had twenty-one years given to me that I might never have had at all. I wouldn't have met Janet and my kids would be somebody else's kids. No, Doc. I've had all the best of it."

The doctor felt the sting of tears in his eyes and turned his head away. What the hell do you say to a man like this? he thought. I wish I had that kind of courage.

"Doc," Hawkins said quietly, "there is a thing I want you to do."

"Janet?"

"I don't want her to know, Doc. Not ever."

The doctor frowned. "That's impossible, Hawk. She won't have to be told. She'll be able to see for herself. Quite frankly, in a few months you are going to start looking like hell warmed over."

Hawkins repeated, "I don't want her to know."

"For Christ's sake, Hawk. You can't keep this a secret. What about your job? You're the vice president of an aircraft company. You'll have to tell them, won't you?"

"I resigned this afternoon," Hawkins said bluntly.

"Resigned? But I——"

Hawkins interrupted. "I thought maybe this would be the way the ball bounced." He rubbed his neck again. "It's hard to fool the guy who owns it."

As his hand passed over his neck, Hawkins wondered if he was doing the right thing. Did Janet have the right to keep him and nurse him and weep over him as his body wasted away until there was nothing left but an ugly sack of bones in a wrinkled skin? Did she have the right to tear her heart out as she watched him become a useless, moaning hulk, lying in a soiled bed waiting for death to come? Perhaps she did, but Hawkins didn't think so. He had seen others die from this thing and at the end they had resembled nothing so much as withered mummies, staring at the world at the last out of drug-deadened eyes. He would not have it this way.

"What are you going to do?" the doctor asked.

"You'll go along, then?"

"If you have a way out of this."

Hawkins grinned and suddenly the pain went out of his face for a moment. "I do," he said almost joyfully. "I'm going west, Doc. As far as Janet is concerned, it's a business trip. The only difference is"—his voice sobered—"I won't be coming home from this one."

"California?" the doctor asked.

"Way past that," Hawkins said. "I'm going to meet a guy named Belden in Saigon."

"What is that supposed to mean?"

Hawkins might not have heard the doctor's words. "Christ. I'm not getting one damn thing to say about *how* I die. A man ought to at least have a say about *where* he dies." A sudden thought came to him. "What about"—he hesitated—"toward the end, Doc? I'll need something then, won't I?"

The doctor nodded. "I'll write you enough prescriptions to carry you through." God damn it, the doctor thought. We're sitting here talking about this thing as though he were going on a fishing trip to Wisconsin. I'm not sure myself if he's doing the right thing. But it's his life, what's left of it, and he's done well with it up to here. I think he'll do well all the way to the end. He reached for his pad of prescription blanks.

Later that night there will be the last tender parting for Hawkins and his wife. The final love-making that will give both of them so much true joy and so much to remember. He will kiss his wife gently while a terrible crying sounds in his heart. He will look down at his children just before he says good-bye to them for the last time.

"You'll play with us when you come back, Daddy? You promise?"

"Yes, my darlings," he will say. "I'll play with you forever when I come back."

"That's good, Daddy. We love you lots, you know."

"That's wonderful, my babies. I have to go now. Sleep tight."

"All right." The words come with a yawn. "You'll come back later?"

"Yes," he will murmur. "I will. Sometime I will come back to you. From wherever I am. Good night, my darlings."

He kisses them with finality, and the terrible crying will not go out of his heart.

Thousands of miles west of Chicago the sun is still low in the morning sky. The tower operator at the airfield at Lungchou waits impatiently for the arrival report of the flight of new MIG-21s coming in from Canton. The tower man is understandably nervous because beside him in the ramshackle tower stands a man with hooded eyes and the cold, implacable air of command. He is a small man with tiny hands and a smooth, beardless face. His name is Soohoo Mu Thik, and he is a General in the Air Force of the Chinese People's Republic. He stands now, his face inscrutable, his eyes probing the horizon, only the clenching of his fists betraying his impatience. There is no sound in the tower but the static coming over the radio receiver.

He awaits Colonel Lee Cheng, who is leading the flight of new jet fighters across from the acceptance base at Canton. General Soohoo himself had arrived late the night before. He had come down from Peking under highly secret orders.

The slightest hint of a derisive smile touched his lips as he thought of his superiors at Peking. He had talked to them for three hours, trying to impress them with the wisdom of his plan. They had not accepted it. There was the matter of relations with Moscow, they had said. Soohoo shrugged mentally when he considered the rift that had been growing between Peking and Moscow. It was a little thing. A thing to be blamed on the passions and angers of men, not on the soundness of ideologies. The General was certain that the Russians would back the Chinese if total war broke out in Southeast Asia. They would have no choice. Soohoo's superiors were of the opinion that, as long as the Americans were not unduly antagonized, they would hesitate to escalate the war in Vietnam. Then next year, when the secret attack was ready, fifty divisions of Red troops would thunder over the border and that would put an end to it. The General scoffed at this manner of thinking. He wanted the fighting to start now because he felt absolutely certain that by next year the Americans would be fully committed in South Vietnam. The time to strike was now, while the enemy was weak and disorganized.

Soohoo had commanded the MIG squadrons which had fought above the Yalu River in Korea. He had witnessed the benefits accruing from the possession of a sanctuary near the area of battle. He wanted a like condition to pertain here on the Sino-North Vietnam border. The stupidity of the Americans, he thought. They send men to fight with one hand tied behind them. Such men start with the odds overwhelmingly against them.

He was interrupted in his musing as a calm, precise voice came over the radio loudspeaker.

"Lungchou tower. This is Eagle One. I approach from the east at six thousand feet. Twelve MIGs for landing."

"Eagle One," the tower operator said. "The area is clear, sir."

"Eagle One acknowledges," came the reply.

General Soohoo went below to meet Colonel Lee. There was the whining sound of the dying jet engines as the planes taxied into the chocks and the throttles were yanked back into idle cut-off. Soohoo entered a small office on the main deck of the building and ordered his aide to summon Colonel Lee Cheng.

What would the Americans do when General Pham marched into North Vietnam? The Americans could not contain Pham for long. Soohoo almost sympathized with Pham because he knew that unless Pham did march north, the war would be lost to him. It was probably lost anyway.

Soohoo was fingering the envelope containing his orders when Colonel Lee knocked softly on the door.

"Come in, Colonel," Soohoo called. Lee entered and inclined his head in a polite bow. The General regarded Lee for several moments and then waved him to a chair.

"Your planes are safely landed, Colonel?"

"They are, sir," Lee replied.

"Colonel Lee," the General said. "Your new planes. They are what you expected?"

"More than that, General," Lee replied respectfully. "Much more than that. They are the best I have ever flown."

"Can you fight the American F-102s and 105s?" Soohoo asked.

"I can fight anyone, sir."

"Ah then. That is good." He waved an envelope at Lee. "I have received these secret orders, Colonel. I am going to disclose to you what they are, although it is contrary to regulations. You understand?"

"You do me great honor, General," Lee said quietly.

"No," said Soohoo, "I do not. You are the best I have. Without you, I doubt if I could accomplish what I have in mind. I had hoped that we would be sent down to base out of Hanoi. They have suitable facilities there. However, we are to remain here at Lungchou." At the expression of dismay that crossed Lee's face, Soohoo added, "For the time being. I have little doubt we will move south when the situation dictates. Tell me, Colonel. When do you think General Pham will march north?"

"It is hard to say, General. The Americans are against it. But soon Pham will have no choice. His people will demand it. Either that or throw him out of office."

"Becoming an ex-Premier of South Vietnam is becoming quite an avocation with a great many people," Soohoo commented dryly.

"Sir," Lee said in a serious voice, "why don't they let us attack in Vietnam? The Americans are flying the T-28s and the helicopters. Their jets wait on the runways at Saigon and Danang. This situation is no different than the one we faced in Korea. What holds us back?"

"Patience, Colonel. You must have patience. We must have the provocation. We must be able to say we are moving in to help the North Vietnamese people withstand an invader. No. As long as the Americans stay south of the Seventeenth Parallel, we have no choice but to remain passive."

"And if they cross the Parallel?" Cheng watched the General carefully.

Soohoo allowed himself an overt smile. "That is another thing." He leaned forward and slapped his open palm on the desk. "And you and I will see to it that they *do* cross the Parallel. My orders"—he gestured at the envelope lying on the desk—"are to assume a defensive posture in North Vietnam. Peking labors under the delusion that the Americans will not escalate the war. I disagree. I firmly believe that we must force the fighting *now*, while the odds are in our favor. But also we must not provide the provocation. The Americans must do that. In this way we can force Peking to agree to retaliation whether they like it or not. And you, Colonel, will be the instrument by which I shall implement my thinking. You see, Colonel, the situation favors us. Exactly as in Korea, the Americans will not violate the Parallel much less the Sino-North Vietnam border. We again have a sanctuary provided us by the enemy's stupidity." Soohoo made a sound of disgust. "Their great Navy clutters the China Sea and their Mach Two jets spend their time attacking puny PT boats in the Gulf of Tonkin. The Americans refer to this as a bold decision. Imagine, Colonel. Jet fighters against PT boats and they call it a bold decision. So in essence, this is our plan. Lure the Americans north if we can. Bring this fight out in the open. Force Peking to change their thinking. When the planned offensive takes place next year, we will find the Americans with their backs to the wall just

44

as they were fourteen years ago at Pusan in Korea. Who knows? They may not have even so much as a seaport through which to disembark their troops and supplies."

The General rose, terminating the interview. "A last thing, Colonel. In the next few weeks you will conduct a strenuous training session. I want you to teach your pilots all that you learned in the skies above the Yalu River. I want them to practice gunnery and air-to-air combat and I will want to see a daily report on your progress. You will also fly patrols along our border. Later you will fly farther south, not landing at Hanoi but covering the area between there and the Seventeenth Parallel. You are not to look for trouble yet, but you are to familiarize yourself with terrain and weather conditions."

Colonel Lee nods at the cold figure of his general. How are Lee and Soohoo to know that far across the world tonight other men are setting out on the long journey that will culminate at last in mortal combat high in the contested sky over twisted jungles and stinking rice paddies? How can they know that other men have made plans and resolutions and have dedicated themselves quite as completely as have Lee and Soohoo to the utter destruction of a detested philosophy of life?

Dusk is falling as the giant Boeing 707 jet leaves the runway at the International Airport outside Honolulu. The plane shrugs itself into the sky and heads westward into a setting sun.

Dan Belden sits forward in the plane, his seat next to the window just aft of the engine nacelles. In the seats across the aisle Bates and Anders are already asleep, snoring off the effects of a monumental binge at the Moana Bar. Belden watches the air station at Barbers Point pass below the starboard wing and then he looks ahead and can see the faint outline of Kauai on the horizon. He notes that the warning sign is out and lights a cigarette as his eyes squint against the glare of the dying sun. The loud roar of the engines, laboring under full power take-off, surges with tremendous power and then quiets and suddenly mutes as the pilot retards his throttle, brings his wheels and flaps up, and the aircraft is in a clean configuration for the long flight to Hong Kong.

He fished in his pocket and pulled out a crumpled cablegram and read it for the fifth time:

And so the last of the three men whom he cherished most in the world was on his way. Belden had not been too sure of Hawkins. The man had an executive position with a leading aircraft company; he had a delightful wife, two adorable children, and a future that beckoned him to the heights. Belden wondered briefly what was bringing Hawkins halfway across the world on a lonely trip that might well end in disaster.

He sensed a body in the seat next to him and then his nose wrinkled as the delicious scent of some faint, delicate perfume came to him.

Without opening his eyes, he said, "That perfume is interrupting my dream."

"Is it private?" Lori asked.

He opened his eyes and squinted at her. "It concerns a young lady I once knew in Saigon. Her name was Cho and I was remembering the delightful curve of her belly when your perfume intruded."

"You'll have to do better than that to shock me," Lori said, her eyes dancing. "I'm not at all what you think I am."

"No? Then what are you, Miss Morlaix?"

Her brow furrowed in mock concentration. "Well," she said, "when I was twelve I was raped by a French sailor on the Saigon docks. He was from a ship called the *Golden Arrow*, which always seemed to me a pretty dumb name for a French ship. His name was Emile."

"Emile?"

"Yes. Emile Le Tourneau."

"Did you enjoy it?"

"Well," she said judiciously, "not exactly. You see, he cornered me in an alley outside of a saloon where I was in the chorus. He was hiding there and after work I . . ." She looked at Belden. "What are you laughing at?"

"You," he said. "You and your easy virtue. I presume"—he spoke lightly—"that you are a virgin."

"Is that bad?"

"Not always," he said.

She was silent a moment. "Do you know many?"

"None that I can think of right now."

"Well, now you know one."

He inclined his head. "The pleasure is all mine."

"Is it important to you?" She spoke in a serious tone.

He feigned surprise. "Why should it be important to me? I have never considered myself an arbiter of morals."

"I think it is important to you and you won't admit it. You're holding me away from you. Why? Because I'm twenty-one years old?"

He nodded equably. "Perhaps." He turned to look at her. "I'm nineteen years older than you."

"You're treating me like a little girl. I'm not a little girl, Dan. I don't think like a little girl and what I want little girls don't want. I want you, Dan."

"Well," he said, "all your life you've had what you wanted. Perhaps this time you might fail. And for your own good, too."

"I'll fight, Dan. I can fight for what I want as well as anyone else. I can be a bitch too, if I have to. You'll see."

Belden grinned. "You begin to frighten me. What happened to that gentle, convent-bred girl I met not so long ago at the Moana?"

"She's been out of the convent a long time. And she didn't ask you to walk into her life. You did though, so the blame is yours. You're stuck with it. *And* with her." Lori spoke musingly. "You'll get used to the idea after a while."

"I may have to call your father," Belden said lightly. "I'm sure he wouldn't approve this trend in the conversation."

Lori glanced back over her shoulder toward the rear of the plane. "Poor Papa," she said. "He's poring over his accounts back there. He still doesn't know what to do with his five hundred acres."

"I'd like five hundred acres I didn't know what to do with," Belden said.

"He cleared them to sell," Lori said. "But now, with the fighting, he can't find buyers. I hope he can't sell. I was brought up on the plantation. I'd miss it."

Belden sat up with a show of interest. "Five hundred cleared acres. Where?"

She did not understand. "Why, on the far edge of the plantation."

"I mean, how far from Saigon?"

"Fifty or sixty miles, I guess." She watched him, puzzled. "Why, Dan?"

"There are roads leading to this place?" Belden asked thoughtfully.

"Of course." She turned to face him in the seat. "You're serious all of a sudden."

He smiled at her. "Just thinking, Lori." He put his arm around her and she snuggled close to him and laid her head trustingly on his shoulder.

They were silent then for a time as the muted hum of the engines sounded softly in the cabin. He listened to the rhythm of her breathing and assumed she was asleep.

Suddenly, without raising her head, she said, "Dan?"

"Yes, Lori?"

She said with a gentle fierceness, "You *will* be the first one, you know."

The two old men sit comfortably in the ornately furnished suite in the Mayflower Hotel in Washington, D.C. They are of an approximate age, nearing sixty. The man sitting in the heavily upholstered chair and holding a brandy glass is Storm Ryerson, Vice Admiral, USN (retired). He is a stockily built man with a face seamed by heavy ridges, the skin rough and creased into hard lines. His eyes are a fierce blue and stare unwaveringly out of the brown face. He sips at his brandy and watches his friend of many years, Senator Ralph Yeager, pour coffee from a gleaming pot into the two cups on the tray.

"Do all Senators live this well?" Ryerson asked innocently.

"Only the rich ones," Yeager replied. "I also have oil wells, you know."

"I know." Ryerson emptied his glass and let his gaze move around the room, noting the rich carpetry and the exquisite paintings on the wall.

"I remember twenty-two years ago," Ryerson smiled. "It wasn't brandy in the glass and Picasso on the wall then. It was grapefruit juice and torpedo alcohol in a tiny cubicle on the *Yorktown*."

Yeager spoke facetiously. "We have to better ourselves, Storm."

The dinner had gone well, with the unrestrained conversation of old and good friends. There was much to be said between these two men, but in the manner of trusted acquaintances, when an unpleasant subject had to be dealt with, the moment of truth was postponed.

Finally Yeager said, "Storm, did you see the President today?"

"I did," Ryerson said solemnly.

"And you got nowhere as usual," Yeager said. "I suppose he was upset about that new bomb the Russians claim can destroy humanity."

"The hell with the Russians and their bomb," Ryerson said curtly. "We've already got sodium bombs and cobalt bombs and californium bombs and lasers and nerve gases." He scoffed. "What the hell does another doomsday mechanism mean? Not a goddam thing. The Russians aren't any more anxious to blow up the world than we are. It's the Red Chinamen who scare me. There are about *eight hundred million* of those bastards. What the hell do they care if we kill off half of them? That still leaves too many." Ryerson flicked the ash from his cigar. "And it seems like half the people in Washington are afraid of them. Well, if they don't get up and do something soon, they've got good reason to be afraid of them. You saw that report my people turned in. We have every reason to believe that the Reds are planning a blitz offensive sometime next year. They'll pin us with our backs against the sea and then we'll be in a hell of a mess. I only wish to Christ we could learn the date they plan to move down."

"We couldn't stop them anyway," Yeager said.

Suddenly Ryerson grinned. "Maybe not. Maybe yes." He took an envelope out of his coat pocket. "I've been waiting a long time for the Chinamen to make a mistake. I knew that sooner or later they'd leave the door open for me. Well, they have. I showed this to the President this morning." He handed Yeager a photograph which he took from the envelope.

Yeager studied the picture. It was a blown-up photo of a small clearing in the jungle and he could clearly make out the two pilots in orange flight suits standing against a large tree and a line of Vietcong facing them with rifles at the ready.

"That picture was taken by a photo reconnaissance plane from the carrier *Concord* last month. They were two Skyraider pilots from the same carrier." Ryerson's voice grew angry. "The bastards executed them in cold blood. But why? They usually tie a rope around their necks and drag them through the villages. They've never resorted to this kind of thing before. Why this time?"

When Yeager did not reply, Ryerson continued. "I'll tell you why. Because they *couldn't* let those boys live. They knew too much. They knew the Chinese MIGs had come down below the Seventeenth Parallel for the first time. Those two kids were the only witnesses to the first overt provocation the Chinamen have made in this war. I think they made a mistake. The MIG pilots must have disobeyed orders because the Chinamen aren't ready to open up yet. But they made the mistake and I caught it and I showed it to the President and for the first time he gave me a limited go-ahead."

"Go-ahead for what?" Yeager asked.

"I was hoping you would ask me that," Ryerson said with evident satisfaction. He got to his feet and paced restlessly. "I'll tell you for what. To bring this mess out into the open. To hit the bastards where it hurts and bring them down to fight, to step up the tempo of their operations."

Yeager spoke in amazement. "Damn it, Storm. We're already getting clobbered out there."

"Sure we are," Ryerson agreed. "And the only way we can *stop* getting clobbered is to generate a will to fight. To do that we have to get the Commies to come out in the open. Get the Red bastards to open up. Get our side good and goddam mad. Mad enough to escalate this war. A year from now, Ralph, we *have* to have a tremendous commitment over there or the Chinamen will wipe us out of Southeast Asia. I won't see that happen."

"It isn't our decision to make," Yeager said softly. "Not yours or mine."

Ryerson was silent for a time. Then he threw his cigar into the fireplace. "I talked to General Pham in Saigon this morning. You want to know something? He's getting damn good and ready to march into North Vietnam. He's sick and tired of our procrastinating. He wonders whether the hell we want to fight or not."

"And what did you tell him?" Yeager asked carefully.

"Christ. I told him there were some of us who wanted to fight. And

I told him I knew how to get the Red MIGs to come down and commit themselves. To blow this thing open."

"Storm," Yeager said slowly, "Air Force and Navy planes are not going to go against government directives, no matter what the provocation, and start a war on their own."

"No," Ryerson admitted slyly, "but a bunch of civilians might."

"And you have these civilians?"

"I do."

"And would their names be Belden, Bates, Anders, and Hawkins by any chance?"

"What do you know about Belden?" Ryerson's tone was outraged.

"As much as you do, old friend." Yeager was smiling. "You may be the head of the CIA, but don't ever forget that *I'm* the guy who approves your budget."

"Well I'll be damned!" Ryerson said.

"That's why I'm flying to Saigon with you tomorrow. I have a great many things demanding my attention here but none"—Yeager chuckled—"as important as keeping an old friend from putting his neck in a noose." Suddenly serious, he added, "You could be destroying yourself, Storm. You know that."

Ryerson was quite as serious. "I know it. But, Ralph, a man has to go down the line with what he believes. There's no other way. I truly believe that we have to make our stand *now*. We've got to get this mess in the open where we can attack with air power. Hit their lines of supply and communication. Then later we'll come on with the infantry. We have to do this. We've simply got to *start fighting*. I've got the greatest men in the world helping me; they'll do the dirty work and they'll do the dying. God help us, Ralph, if we let them down."

Yeager's voice was very gentle. "Let's hope we don't have to let them down, Storm."

Ryerson poured the brandy glasses full. His face creased into a grin. "So tomorrow we go west and meet Dan Belden."

Yeager watched his friend with a great affection. "You love him, don't you, Storm?"

"In a fashion," Ryerson said. "They don't make them like that any more." He shook his head. "Christ, Ralph. The stories I could tell you."

"Go ahead," Yeager said. "It's early and we've got half a bottle of brandy left."

They sat there in the suite, two old men of great power, a half-empty bottle of brandy between them, and they took their memories back fifteen years to a time of trial.

Chapter
IV

And this was what the two old men remembered.

The wind came down from the frozen valleys and over the ice-crusted plains of North Korea and spent itself in the vast wastes of the frigid sea. Task Force 77 steamed majestically in the late afternoon sun. Four large carriers and their escort of cruisers and destroyers prowled angrily a hundred miles west of Wonsan.

It was 1951, only six years after the most recent of the war-to-end-wars had been finished. The bomb had been dropped at Hiroshima, and yet the world was at it again. Men were dying in the cold fields of Korea and men were flying and dying from carrier decks—men who had fought their fight once and won it and figured they had done what had been asked of them.

The ready room of Fighter Squadron 23 was on the deck directly below the flight deck. It was a relatively small room and seemed entirely inadequate for the ebullient young men who swarmed into it. Adjustable-back chairs were aligned in rows of three and stretched from the rear bulkhead nearly to the forward. There was a constant babble of voices and the occasional snatch of a rude curse as the pilots discussed the upcoming mission.

Along the bulkheads were cluttered the assorted items of flight gear that the pilots wore whether they liked it or not. There were the heavy rubber suits that fitted a man snugly from his feet to his neck.

They were excessively uncomfortable, but it had been proven that, without one, a man could remain alive approximately thirty seconds in the frigid waters off the Korean coast. If he were so unfortunate as to find himself floating in the icy sea, his only chances for survival lay in the rubber suit and the diligence of the helicopter pilot flying patrol. Under the rubber suits they wore the regular flight suits and under those heavy woolen underwear. After they had managed to cram themselves into all this, they donned a Mae West life preserver, a gun and a cartridge belt, certain single items of survival gear such as a flashlight, a hunting knife, shark repellent, medical kit, and compass. When they were finally ready to fly, they resembled the ancient knights who had to be hoisted aboard their horses with a winch.

Forward, on a blackboard in the front of the room, the mission data was carefully written in spaces marked off by yellow lines. Here the pilots learned the ship's position, wind information, expected weather over the ship, enroute and at the target. Below the weather line was the time of the launch and type of mission coming up.

The hum of conversation muted as Lieutenant Commander Dan Belden entered and walked to the front of the room.

"Knock it off," someone yelled. "The Skipper's got a few pearls of wisdom."

"The Skipper usually has," Belden agreed in a loud voice. He lit a cigarette, waiting for the last of the voices to still.

"I have just come," Belden finally said, "from a meeting with the Admiral. It was not at all a pleasant get-together. The Admiral is pissed-off. Three more planes went down yesterday under the guns around Majon-ni. Two from the *Essex* and one from the *Lexington*. The Admiral just told me he wants those guns knocked out. Today. By us." He looked around the room. "Are there any questions so far?"

"Hell, Skipper," said a young ensign, "we can't even *see* the goddam guns. All we do is hear them. How the hell are we supposed to knock out guns we can't see?"

"That does present a problem, gentlemen." Belden spoke in a quiet voice. "That is why the Admiral has chosen the best fighter squadron in the fleet to do the job. And of course there is the matter of the flight leader. He wanted the best Navy pilot alive for this job. So naturally he picked me because I happen to be the best Navy pilot alive. Is all this clear?"

"You tell 'em, Boss," a voice yelled.

"So I will now tell you what we're going to do today. We're going to take off in this ridiculous weather and if we don't freeze our balls off before we rendezvous, we'll go in at ten thousand feet. Feet dry at Point Oboe." Point Oboe was a projecting finger of land on the Korean east coast, which was used as a landfall by the pilots of Task Force 77.

"It will be 1600 when we get to the target and the sun should be lowering back of Majon-ni. What does this suggest to you, Henderson?" Belden nodded at a chubby pilot sitting in the front row of seats.

"Why . . . well, I guess we ought to circle back and come out of the sun, Skipper."

Belden nodded judiciously. "Excellent, Henderson. Keep thinking like that and you well may live long enough to see your wife and child again."

Belden moved a few steps to a large wall map fastened to the bulkhead by the side of the blackboard. It was a large-scale map of the area around Majon-ni. He picked up a crayon and encircled the area about the town.

"Majon-ni is a rail and highway center, a junction for all communications lines in this area of North Korea. It's a lousy, miserable little town and I doubt if any of you would care to live there for any length of time. I certainly wouldn't. But it is a rat's nest of AA fire, machine guns, twenty millimeters, forty millimeters, and anything else you can think of. They've got them all at Majon-ni. As a matter of fact the newspaper guys are calling it 'The Graveyard.' We've lost more planes around there than we care to count. This is a preposterous state of affairs because we're not even at war. This is a police action and nobody ought to get shot down in a police action. This is my private opinion, of course. Anyway, we are going in there in a few minutes and we are going to find these goddam guns, pinpoint them, and knock the bastards on their Communist asses. Is all this understood?"

"Somebody sing 'Anchors Aweigh,' " a voice hollered.

"I'll sing it for you myself if you get those guns," Belden said. He turned to the map again and pointed to a tiny island in Wonsan Bay. "There will be a helicopter standing by for rescue on Yo-Do Island. Let's hope we don't need him. We'll be carrying rockets and full ammo in the twenties. Rendezvous southeast of the task force. Any questions?"

"Yeah," a voice called. "When do we go home?"

"MacArthur said we'd be home for Christmas," Belden said. "He said that a year ago. So your guess is as good as mine. Get dressed, you heroes. Launch time coming up."

Belden watched them as they climbed, with considerable difficulty, into the cumbersome winter flight suits. There were muffled curses as the bodies twisted and squirmed into the snug rubber outfits. Some of them were veterans from the last war, Belden knew, but now they were fighting a war that was different from anything they had known before. They were fighting an enemy they seldom saw, an enemy that killed without ever revealing himself. And they did not know *why* they were fighting. They knew the MIGs were coming down over the Yalu and the Air Force Sabres were tangling with them in the thin air at 40,000 feet. Christ! The Grumman F9F Panther jets the Navy flew could barely climb to 40,000 feet and those that could had little maneuverability when they got there. What a shitty war!

Now a voice called out, "What if the MIGs come down, Skipper?"

"I would suggest you turn your ass and hightail it for home," Belden answered wryly. "You have as much chance against a MIG as I do of becoming Chief of Naval Operations. You haven't got a chance in a Panther. As a matter of fact there's probably only one man alive who can whip a MIG in a Panther. Despite the fact that I detest adulation, I must admit *I* am that man." Belden grinned at the raucous laughter which greeted his remark.

With a strenuous effort Belden shoved his head through the watertight neckpiece of the flight suit. "By God, if the guns at Majon-ni don't get us, these flight suits may well choke us to death."

The pilots looked up as the teletype screen began banging out the Pilots-Man-Your-Planes.

Here we go again. Belden stuffed his maps into a shin pocket of the rubber suit. Look at the young men, Belden, he thought. You're supposed to say something heroic to them. They think you're some-

56

thing special and you're supposed to keep them thinking that way. What the hell do you tell guys that are going out in that godawful cold to fly from this pitching flight deck to a land a hundred miles away where a lot of people they won't even see are going to try to kill them? What the Christ do you tell men at a time like this?

He said, "One moment, you glory hounds."

The pilots stopped their shuffle toward the door and turned to Belden. "We all know it's contrary to naval protocol and procedure to have whiskey aboard ship. This law was written a long time ago by someone who must have had dust on his brain. However—and this is top secret—someone must have played a joke on me because I found to my great surprise this morning that my safe was full of Old Granddad. I've no idea who put it there, but after this mission, on which we will destroy those guns at Majon-ni, we will have a wetting-down party in my quarters. You are all welcome."

Belden heard a scattering of applause and then they were moving down the narrow passageway that led to the flight deck.

Rear Admiral Storm Ryerson, Commander Task Force 77, watched the unwieldy figures emerge on the catwalk and lumber toward their planes. He stood on the outer flag bridge of the carrier, muffled in a parka and hood, his eyes watering from the bitter slash of the icy wind. He watched the cumbersome figures struggle into the cockpits and then he turned to his Chief of Staff.

"Good Christ. How can men fly in this kind of weather?"

"It beats me, Admiral. And going after the guns at Majon-ni is the next thing to suicide." Almost to himself, the COS murmured, "You'd think a man could at least die where it's warm."

"You've got a point there, Bob."

On the deck the starter units were plugged in. Within the cockpits the canopy levers had been actuated and the canopies closed, shutting out the eternal wind. Now the pilots watched with great concentration the small dials in the center of their instrument panels—their RPM indicators. The starting units whined and on the dials the needles quivered and started to move. At this moment they flipped the battery switches and pressed the starting switches to "on." The whining grew louder and the needles moved. When they reached 12 percent the throttles were moved "around the horn," shoved forward from the locked position at the bottom of the throttle quadrant around the bulge in the quadrant track and up into the idle position. The starting units were unplugged as the needles moved of their own accord up to 32 percent, idle power. The engine blast was relatively gentle now and would remain so until the throttles were advanced.

The launch flag was placed in its slot on the operations platform and on the forward catapult Belden nodded his head to Fly One and shoved his throttle all the way forward. He opened his canopy now because only a fool elects to take off with a closed canopy and risk going into the drink sealed in his cockpit. He placed his head back against the rest and waited for the kick in the ass that would hurtle him down the catapult and on his way to Majon-ni.

The jolt came and, as he screamed down the cat track, he felt as if someone behind him were tugging at his eyeballs, trying to pull them through the back of his head. Then he was past the end of the deck. He flipped his wheel lever and as his speed reached 150 knots, he raised his flaps.

Behind him the other planes lifted off the deck and turned sharply to intercept Belden's lazy circle and thus effect the rendezvous.

Five minutes later Belden straightened out on course 280 and called the ship: "Jehovah Base from Jehovah One. Rendezvoused and vectoring two eight zero. Estimate feet dry at fifty past the hour."

Belden was informing the ship he expected to be over dry land at 1550 hours.

They were on their way then. Twelve Panthers on the prowl over frigid and unfriendly seas. Twelve men flying out to silence the guns at Majon-ni. Others had tried before them. They had suffered defeat with its sour taste or they had died there.

Fourteen minutes after assuming his vector, Belden made his landfall.

Admiral Ryerson, on the inner bridge, heard Belden's voice come across the hundred miles of freezing ocean: "Jehovah Base from Jehovah One. Feet dry at ten before the hour. Passing Point Oboe. Will report over target. One out."

In his mind's eye Ryerson could see them. They were inland now and already the coastal guns had picked them up. The deadly black puffs appeared as if by magic in the sky. Belden was no longer flying a straight course. He weaved through the sky, changing his compass heading every twenty seconds to throw the enemy gunners' aims off.

"Test your guns," Belden called to the flight. The planes spread out in loose formation. The guns were charged and for a brief moment the sky was lashed with tracers. Then all was silence again.

Through his windshield Belden could see the mountains rising in the distance. Majon-ni lay at the eastern base of the range. Quickly he consulted his map, pinpointing the outlines of the town in his mind. When he looked again through the windshield, the mountains were looming up before him. He swung to the north to circle and come at the town from its rear.

"Right echelon," Belden called and the planes swung under him and assumed a stepped-down formation off his right wing.

They had come down to 8,000 feet now and were swinging wide of Majon-ni and the AA had stopped. Belden could see the ground was covered with a blanket of heavy snow, obliterating any landmarks that might have aided him in planning his initial attack. They came into Majon-ni at five hundred miles an hour and the wind whistled past the sides of their cockpits over the sound of the engines' roars. They were still holding their altitude when Belden called his flight: "Jehovah flight from Jehovah One. Stand by and circle. I'll go down and draw their fire. Watch for muzzle blasts against that snow."

Belden waggled his wings, touched his head, and pointed a finger at his wingman, signaling him to take over the formation. Then he peeled off, shoving on full throttle and trimming the plane for a dive. He went down accelerating, swinging around to pass over the town from west to east at low level. He watched the ground come at him and then he was skimming over the deck, watching the treetops and the tiny, snow-covered huts on the outskirts of Majon-ni. As he flashed past the rail intersection, his air-speed indicator nudged 600 knots. Very nearly the speed of sound. Then he could hear the faint sound of the enemy guns. Fifty calibers, he thought, as the *ratatata-tatat* sounded somewhere below him. Over this came the sound of the heavier guns, the twenty millimeters and the forties. Then he was past the town and he pulled up in a tight wingover roll, reversing his direction and coming back down again. They were ready for him this time, and he grimaced at the volume of enemy fire that bore-sighted him along his flight path. He heard a solid *thunk* as an enemy shell struck somewhere in his plane. His heart skipped a beat and then rage came over him. God damn them, he muttered to himself.

He spoke into his lip mike: "Jehovah flight. Did you see the bastards? The sonsabitches are all over the place."

From high above came his wingman's voice: "I spotted them, Skipper. They're along the north edge of the town. Right where the ground hits the mountains."

"I'll make one more pass to draw fire. Then come down and rocket the bastards," Belden called.

He came again, this time almost on the deck. He saw them this time. He saw the winking muzzles north of the town, camouflaged in white shelters back of a clump of trees. He saw the red line of tracers working out at him and the guns followed him as he swept by. The gun noises were louder as Belden passed the positions only a few hundred feet away. Then he was past them again and pulling up steeply as his altimeter wound up until he leveled off at 8,000 feet and watched his flight go in with rockets blazing and twenty millimeters chattering.

Below them on the ground the enemy knew they had been spotted and every gun in Majon-ni opened fire. The sky was crisscrossed with lines of tracer and the black puffs stood out starkly against the white background below. The whole sky was inundated with shells and the sound of the firing grew to a muted thunder.

"Good Christ!" a voice yelled. "There must be a million of the bastards."

"A daisy chain," Belden called.

And so they went at the guns of Majon-ni in a daisy chain, a continuous chain of attacking aircraft peeling off, making their attack, then climbing to altitude to initiate another attack. The enemy guns were continually under fire. The rockets *whooshed* from the wings of the Panthers, flared only for a moment in the cold air, then struck with a great mushrooming explosion of snow and dirt and debris.

Belden came down in a 45-degree dive. At 3,000 feet he let his rockets go and saw them boresight in on a heavy gun position. There was a blast of flame and he knew he had hit an ammo pile. From the rising smoke cloud he saw several figures scurry, racing for cover toward a wooded area a hundred yards away. He was at 500 feet when he dropped his dive brakes, slowing his plane considerably despite its great speed, and he opened fire with his four twenty-millimeter cannon. He saw the shells march across the barren ground and into the group of running figures. He held the trigger down and the shells centered and held on the group, now sprawled in various postures of death on the frozen ground.

Behind him he heard the voices of his pilots:

"Behind that railroad shed on the north edge of town, Jack. There's a whole battery of the bastards."

"I see 'em. Let's come from the south across the open field."

"Yeeooowwww! I creamed that lousy Gook but good."

"An ammo dump. Two hundred yards from the intersection toward the hills. Let's go, Mike."

Belden was circling for another attack when he saw one of the Panthers abort his run. Ensign Henderson had had good luck that morning. He had destroyed two heavy and one light gun positions that he was sure of. He was contemplating the bright bit of ribbon that he would certainly earn from this morning's work when a seventeen-year-old North Korean named Lee Chul Woo rose to his knees in a small .50-caliber machine-gun emplacement in the middle of the village of Majon-ni. Lee had not participated in the attack as yet. He had remained obscured in his carefully camouflaged gun nest until an opportunity presented itself for a no-deflection angle on one of the attacking planes. Ensign Henderson afforded Lee his no-deflection angle.

Henderson came down in a flat angle of attack, his attention focused on a line of gun positions a mile behind Lee. Henderson had no idea that Lee was between him and his intended targets, so he flew directly at Lee's machine gun, flew down the barrel and into the gunsight of the .50-caliber in the concealed foxhole. Lee waited until Henderson's plane filled the entire gunsight, then he squeezed the trigger and held it down, filling with solid lead a chunk of the sky, through which the Panther had to fly.

Henderson knew he had been hit bad when he heard the shells pound into his plane, shaking it like a dog with a bone. A split second later he heard a loud grumbling in his tail section and then the plane trembled as the turbine blades roared in wounded anger. The bastard hit me in the turbine, Henderson thought, even as he pulled back on the stick and pointed his nose for the sky. The trembling became more pronounced and he watched his RPM and tail-pipe temperature needles fluctuate wildly.

"This is Jehovah Three," Henderson called. There was a trace of panic in his voice. "I took a hit in my tail section!"

Belden, circling above, saw Henderson and the stream of smoke trailing from the tail pipe of the F9F. He added throttle and headed for Henderson.

"This is Jehovah Leader. How bad are you hit, Three?"

The engine of Henderson's plane was surging now, revving up and subsiding alternately. The needles on the gauges were fluctuating wildly and within the cockpit there was the smell of fire, although as yet Henderson could discern no smoke.

"They got me in the turbine," he called. "I'm fluctuating badly and this engine sounds like a Model-T."

"Hold straight and level," Belden said. "I'll come up under your tail pipe and check." To the other members of the flight, he called: "Jehovah flight. Continue the attack."

Now Belden inched up behind Henderson. He carefully manipulated his throttle and he slid in behind and below the other plane's tail pipe. Through the emerging smoke Belden could see tongues of flame licking out. He cursed bitterly as he spoke: "You've got a fire aft, Hendy. You'll have to shut down."

They were at 5,000 feet, heading toward the ocean, when Henderson yanked his throttle all the way back around the stop and into the cut-off position. The rumbling subsided and the brutal buffeting ceased. The aircraft glided without power through the inimical sky. Henderson glanced at his altimeter.

"I've got forty-eight hundred feet on the gauge, Skipper. I'll bail out."

"You will like hell." Belden's voice was calm. "You've got mountains under you. You haven't got the altitude."

Henderson was silent for a moment as the import of Belden's words struck home. Then he asked, "Is the fire out?"

"Negative," Belden replied. "You might be burning leaking fuel."

Henderson looked ahead through his windshield, aware of the precious time element which governed his continued existence. If that fuel exploded, he was going to be nothing more and nothing less than a charred hunk of bone tumbling through a sky near the town of Majon-ni on a freezing winter afternoon.

"Jehovah flight," Belden called. "One of you climb to altitude and sound the Mayday. I'll give you the co-ordinates when I get them."

As one of the Panthers started to race for altitude, Belden consulted his grid map. All of North Korea was marked off in north-south, east-west lines, each of which had a number. In addition various areas were denoted alphabetically. Thus a man could pinpoint his position at any time by marking the general area he was in and then tracing the co-ordinate lines to an intersecting point within that general area.

"Skipper," Henderson called, "there's a clear area up ahead."

Belden saw a small clearing, perhaps a half-mile long, about five miles in front of them.

"It isn't much, Hendy," he said. "But it's the best you've got. Put her in smooth, boy."

Even before the Mayday call flew across the sky, Admiral Ryerson aboard the *Phil Sea* had picked up Belden's transmissions.

"God damn it," the Admiral muttered. "Get that chopper from Yo-Do Island in there."

"It has been attended to, Admiral," the Officer-of-the-Deck replied.

On Yo-Do Island the chopper blades turned slowly, then revved up, and the ungainly craft left the ground and headed southwest.

Ryerson paced the bridge nervously as he listened to the drama being played out more than a hundred miles away.

Henderson dropped his flaps at 3,000 feet. At this altitude he was only 600 or 700 feet over the high ground. He judged his distance precisely and turned his plane at a right angle to the landing area. When the altimeter touched 2,500 feet Henderson banked sharply and lined up straightaway with the clearing. It was only a minute patch of cleared ground surrounded by tall trees, but it was all Henderson had this afternoon. He watched his air-speed indicator carefully because a jet aircraft is a heavy piece of equipment and, without power thrusting in the engine, it will stall at high speeds. He kept the air-speed needle steady on 150 knots as he swept down for his landing.

Henderson made an exemplary dead-stick landing, considering the landing space available and the circumstances. It was to his credit that he managed to get his airplane in the field at all. It was no fault of his that the field was bisected by a drainage ditch three feet deep. His plane landed on its belly and skidded several hundred feet, throwing a great spray of snow and dirt into the air. When the Panther hit the drainage ditch, it was still traveling at more than 100 knots. The shock threw Henderson forward in the cockpit, but his shoulder straps held. The nose of the plane, however, rammed with great force into the far edge of the ditch and buckled the nose section inward in such a manner that the sharp edge of the instrument panel in the cockpit was driven back and down and deep into Henderson's leg just above the knee joint. When the plane had skidded to a stop, Henderson was trapped in the cockpit, unable to free his damaged leg.

"Jehovah Leader," Henderson called, his voice weak. "I've got the instrument panel jamming my leg. I can't get out."

"The poor bastard," Admiral Ryerson breathed. "Trapped in that cockpit in this ungodly weather and in the middle of enemy territory. It's all up to the chopper now."

The Admiral was mistaken. It was not at all up to the chopper. As Belden circled the stricken plane, he could see Henderson in the cockpit, struggling feebly to extricate himself. Belden dropped his wheels and flaps, slowing his plane down to its limit, and then flew a tight circle over the downed pilot.

Belden had traced his position on the map, carefully marking out the co-ordinates. Henderson's life could depend on the accuracy of his calculations.

"Jehovah Leader here," Belden called. "The position is Easy Victor four nine five three. I say again. Easy Victor four nine five three. The pilot is down in a clear area, trapped in his plane. Jehovah Two. Do you have the chopper in sight?"

"Negative," came the reply from the Panther circling high above.

"This is Angel One." The helicopter's call was weak. "I am three miles inland. Heading full balls for Easy Victor four nine five three. Estimate arrival in plus fifteen."

Even before the chopper pilot's transmission was completed, Belden saw the enemy. They were moving through the trees a thousand yards from the downed plane. He saw them plainly as they streamed across the broken ground and into cover again.

In that instant past decisions flashed across Belden's mind and he sorted out and discarded the various avenues of action left to him. All of this took the approximate time of a heartbeat. He watched the enemy narrowing the distance and he knew he did not have much time. With a grunt of disgust he actuated his canopy-ejection lever and the canopy tore loose in the air.

"All Jehovah planes," Belden called. "Set up a pattern around the downed aircraft. I'm going down after him."

There was a moment of silence as the pilots tried to disbelieve what they had heard.

"Jesus Christ, Skipper. You can't crash land down there. You haven't got a chance."

"Neither does Henderson," replied Belden. He flipped the landing gear lever and retracted his wheels. "Just keep those bastards off my neck until the chopper gets here."

A hundred miles at sea the Admiral heard the transmissions. He looked at the stupefied face of his Chief of Staff. "Belden's going to crash land and try to save that boy." He spoke unemotionally, almost as though Belden did this sort of thing every day.

"Good God!" The Chief of Staff groaned.

Belden was already in the groove, slanting down toward the field, when he saw the enemy break from cover eight hundred yards from Henderson. Looking above, he saw his flight sweeping down, dropping their wheels and flaps, preparing to set up over the downed men the protective circle that would present at least one set of guns at the enemy continuously.

Belden had seen the drainage ditch and had elected to land along the far side of the field where the ditch was only a few inches deep. Suddenly he was there, hurtling past the row of trees and dropping his nose and chopping off his throttle simultaneously. He eased back on the stick and held the plane a few inches off the ground, waiting for his air speed to dissipate. He felt the plane sag as it stalled, then there was a grinding bump as the belly hit the first time and bounced. A split second later the plane was on the ground and he heard a grinding, tearing rumble as it skidded and burrowed at the icy earth, slewing sideways and finally coming to rest facing the direction from which it had come. Belden was out of the cockpit and sprinting across the field almost before the plane had come to rest.

Henderson smiled weakly through pain-rocketed eyes as Belden climbed up on the wing of the broken plane, wincing at what he saw. The jagged metal edge of the instrument panel was embedded at least halfway through Henderson's knee. Silently, Belden reached in and tried to pry the panel upward, away from the wounded leg. Henderson groaned and the blood spurted around the wound. The panel, however, was wedged tightly and would not move.

Both men looked up as one of the Panthers opened fire with his twenty millimeters. At the far end of the field they saw several enemy soldiers dive for cover. Belden took out his .38 pistol. Then he looked hard into Henderson's eyes, trying to tell him the situation without using words. Belden was not at all sure he had the words available for this particular message.

Henderson read Belden's eyes and tried to smile. "Skipper," he murmured weakly, "you're never going to get me out of this goddam airplane. Not if you take all afternoon." Henderson turned his head in the direction of the enemy. "And you haven't got all afternoon."

Belden nodded. He spoke in a low voice. "You know what I've got to do, Hendy?"

Henderson took a deep breath and let it expel slowly. "Yeah, Skipper. Don't mind me. Go ahead."

Henderson turned his head away as Belden reversed the pistol in his hand and then brought it down in a swift, slashing blow that took Henderson under the left ear. He sagged unconscious in the cockpit.

The enemy were closer now and the Panthers overhead tightened their circle, one plane always firing in the direction of the Red troops.

Under that flat expanse of dull gray sky, Dan Belden took his knife and sawed through the flesh and muscle of Henderson's leg. He did it with his jaws clenched tightly against the nausea that climbed in his throat. He did it with the sound of pounding guns in his ears and he did it without expert knowledge and with only the feel of the knife to guide him. When he had finished and the distasteful bundle had been tossed aside, he injected an ampule of morphine into the unconscious man's arm and fashioned a tourniquet with his cartridge belt. The enemy were within firing range now and the bullets were spanging off the sides of the plane.

Henderson lay unconscious, his face grayish blue and his breath rasping in his throat. The jagged stump at the knee was oozing black blood which ran freely along the metal foot rests on the cockpit floor.

Then skimming across the treetops came the helicopter from Yo-Do Island. Belden hoisted Henderson out of the cockpit, slung the inert body over his shoulder and climbed down off the wing of the plane. Later Belden would never remember how he ran across the two hundred yards of open field to the clump of trees behind which Angel One landed. Nor would he remember much of the flight back to the ship.

But he would remember always facing the Admiral in the silence of the flag bridge. Belden looked a million years old and a dismal knowledge was in his eyes as he watched the grim face of the older man.

"Henderson?" the Admiral said. "Is he all right?"

"Depends on how you look at it, Admiral," Belden said. "He died in the chopper on the way back. Never regained consciousness."

"That was a brave thing you did, Dan."

"It's all relative, sir. You do what you have to do."

The Admiral nodded. He paced to the porthole and stood a moment watching the play of sunlight on the angry sea. He turned back to Belden and said, "I'm God damned if I know whether to give you a Congressional Medal or court-martial you."

Belden was silent. He lit a cigarette as he waited for Ryerson to continue.

The Admiral shook his head. "God damn it, Dan. You had no right to put that plane down in that field. For Christ's sake. You'd think we had jet fighters to throw away."

"What would you have done?" Belden asked softly.

"That's not the point. The point is, what you did is actually a court-martial offense. But I think it's also worthy of a decoration."

"I've got all of those I need. Forget it, sir."

"What do I say on my report?"

"You really want to know, sir? You really want to know what to tell the brass back in Washington? What to tell the politicians and the taxpayers whose half-million-dollar airplane I creamed today in a field in North Korea?" Belden's voice was harsh and angry now. "You really want to know, sir?"

"I do," Ryerson said.

"Tell them to go fuck themselves," Dan Belden said.

The level of the brandy in the bottle had dropped appreciably when Ryerson finished speaking. There was a momentary silence in the room as the two old friends brought their memories back from another time.

"Did Belden really say that?" Yeager chuckled.

"He did," Ryerson said. "And he was right. I often wonder, Ralph, why the people of this country are always so damn slow to anger. We always wait until somebody gives us one hell of a kick in the teeth before we get mad enough to fight. There was World War I and Pearl Harbor and Korea and now Vietnam. Why do we wait so long to wake up?"

"Well," Yeager said in a chiding tone, "we always seem to win."

"We could lose this one," Ryerson said frankly.

Yeager smiled. "Somehow I can't see you on a losing team, Storm."

Ryerson drained the last of the brandy from his glass. "You said something a while ago, Ralph. You said I might be destroying myself. It doesn't bother me. What can they do to a retired Vice Admiral? They can't take my pension away and the medals they gave me have long since turned to rust. So to hell with them. But you're in a different boat. You're a politician. A United States Senator. The people elect you and therefore you have to give some thought to the people's wishes. You're the one who might be destroying himself."

"Perhaps," Yeager said softly, "I'm rather tired of being a United States Senator. Maybe I'd like to go back to my oil wells. It doesn't bother me either."

"Well," Ryerson got to his feet, "we'll see what we can do about this mess out there." He offered his hand. "I'm glad you're coming along, Ralph." The Admiral grinned. "When the axe falls, perhaps it won't bite so deep if it has to cut through *two* necks instead of one."

Yeager shook his head. "There'll be no axes, Storm. I happen to be the Minority Leader at a time when the Administration isn't at all sure what course to steer. I'm not sure myself. But I agree with you that *something* has to be done. Let's hope we're picking the right compass heading to steer by."

"We are, old friend," Ryerson said. "We are."

Chapter V

Belden paused for a moment to study himself in the mirror in the suite in the Caravelle Hotel. Outside the harsh blaring of the horns and the screeching of brakes sounded from the cluttered Saigon streets.

Bates sat on the arm of a chair, a whiskey and soda in his hand, and watched Belden with a derisive smile. He turned to Anders, who lay stretched out on a divan.

"Suppose Dan is looking for wrinkles?"

Anders shook his head somberly. "Nope. He's checking the firmness of his jaw line. This is a thing many middle-aged people do."

"In my case," Bates said ruefully, "I study the line of my hair." Almost as an afterthought he glanced at the glass in his hand. "It's too early in the day to be drinking whiskey."

"Well"—Belden turned from the mirror—"enjoy it because in a few minutes we're all going to work."

"So?" Anders grunted as he sat up.

"Two things to do today. I'll handle one. You guys handle the other."

"We await your orders, General." Bates finished his drink and set the glass aside. "Good booze," he admitted.

"I'll go to see General Pham," Belden said, dropping into a chair and draping a leg carelessly over the arm. "We have to get some

70

airplanes if I'm going to carry out this ridiculous idea I have."

"Would it be asking too much," Anders inquired politely, "to let us in on this ridiculous idea?"

"The idea?" Belden was thoughtful. "I think you know what the idea is. We are going to make a carrier deck out of a slice of jungle. You guys will go to the Embassy this afternoon and try to locate a portable arresting gear."

Bates and Anders exchanged pained glances. "He wants a portable arresting gear," Bates said. "There isn't a portable arresting gear this side of Barbers Point."

"You're probably right," Belden agreed. "So you will arrange to have one flown out here from Barbers Point. Within a few days."

"How do we manage this?" Anders asked.

Belden shrugged. "I leave that up to your ingenuity. You have some ingenuity, don't you?"

Bates got to his feet. "We'll get that arresting gear, Dan. You get the airplanes." He glanced at his watch. "You're forgetting something. It's twelve-thirty."

"I didn't forget," Belden said as he rose. "Let's go down to the bar and have that drink."

They walked down the single flight of stairs to the lobby and paused before the entrance to the bar. They stood a moment and smiled at each other with some deep pleasure. Then they moved across the tiny, deserted dance floor and took their places at the bar next to a man who was quietly nursing a tall drink.

"Funny thing"—Belden spoke as a man in deep concentration—"you always can tell the hawks from the doves. Something happens to a man when he puts away the wings and plants his ass in an upholstered chair. Something goes out of him. Leaves him soft. Weak. No marrow in the bones any more. Age gets to him and pretty soon what was steel in his youth has turned to rubber." He shook his head sadly. "Too bad what a man will turn himself into just to make a few lousy bucks and have it safe and soft every night in a clean bed."

"You're right, Dan," Anders agreed. "And I've been wondering. Why did you get some of those people over here? What good will they be to us?"

"I had no choice, Cort. I tried to get some cadets out of Pensacola, but they wouldn't come. Then I asked some retired airline pilots, all of them past sixty of course, but they were too tired. Then I tried the 'Ninety-Nines,' that all-woman flying club, but even they wouldn't have any. At the end I had to scrape the bottom of the barrel and take whatever leftovers I could come up with. Sometimes this is the best you can do."

The lone man standing next to him beckoned to the bartender. "I have a complaint to make," he said in a quiet voice.

"There is something wrong with your drink, sir?" The bartender was solicitous.

"No," the man said. "The drink is fine. But don't you smell something around here?"

"Smell?" The bartender sniffed, plainly puzzled. "No, sir."

"Sort of like mold," the man said. "Dust, perhaps. Like very old people smell when they are too old to live any longer. Like a mummy smells."

The bartender shook his head. "I smell nothing, sir." These Americans are all crazy, he thought. He turned to the back bar and switched on a small fan. "Is that better, sir?"

The man nodded. "Much better." He pushed his glass forward. "I'll have another rye and soda."

"Make that four rye and sodas," Belden said.

Not until the drinks had been placed before them did the four men turn to stare at each other. For a moment there was no play of expression on their faces and then suddenly all four were grinning with undisguised delight.

Belden lifted his glass. "Welcome aboard, Hawk."

Hawkins nodded and they drank. Then they were shaking hands with the wordless camaraderie of men who had shared the ultimate danger together. For a few brief seconds they were four ensigns again, standing in the hot sun at Corpus Christi, Texas, as some forgotten admiral pinned the gold wings on their breasts.

An hour later Belden stood by the window in a severely furnished office off Dunong Tu Do Street. He watched the flow of traffic outside for a moment and then he turned to face the man seated behind a large mahogany desk.

"General, you'd never know there was a war going on."

General Tran Dan Pham was putting his signature on a number of papers before him. He finished with his writing and tossed the pen aside with a sigh of relief.

"They try to forget, Dan." General Pham's voice was very soft and held only the faintest trace of an accent. Large, liquid eyes looked out with composure from within the hooded lids. The General stood five feet in his boots and weighed one hundred and twelve pounds. His hands were dainty like a woman's, but held the finely honed strength of a surgeon's blade. There was respect and affection in the glance he turned on Belden.

"They are confused," the General continued. "But then, I suppose we all are."

"Read your own papers, General. They say we're winning."

"Of course they do," the General agreed wryly. "But that is because I tell them to say that."

"So what's the answer?"

General Pham sat forward in his chair. "We fought together in Korea, you and I. You remember how it was then." His voice grew hard. "We gave them a sanctuary across the Yalu River, so a victory was never possible. Never at all. We who fought there knew that. But your State Department didn't know that. They still don't. They expect the Vietcong to disappear when they yell 'Boo,' if I may be permitted a figure of speech. The Vietcong is laughing at them. There's a thing, Dan, that your people don't understand. We've been fighting here in my country for twenty years. Fighting is a way of life with my people. A war of attrition is a thing to laugh at as far as they are concerned. You'll never win this war by trying to outlast the Vietcong. You will have to overpower them until they see that you are fully committed to remain here. You will have to carry the war to them in the air. *I* will carry it to them on the ground. This is the only manner in which to fight this war. This is *not* a place for political maneuvering. That time is past. As it is now"—the General spread his hands—"we have our hands tied. Your people have tied them. It looks very much as if Red Chinese are running a successful bluff on your people."

"It's been tried before," Belden said. "It doesn't work."

General Pham nodded. "We can hope so. As a matter of fact"—his childlike face broke into a smile—"I sincerely believe that this state of affairs will not pertain too much longer."

Belden snuffed his cigarette out in a tray before he looked at the General. "Are you going to march north of the Parallel?" he asked bluntly.

After a pause, the General said, "Perhaps. When the time is right. Only when the time is right. I must have some indication that the people will be behind me. When I have that, then I will march north."

Belden nodded, aware that General Pham had already revealed more to him than he would to any other man. "One more thing, General."

"The matter of airplanes?" At the perplexed look on Belden's face, the General laughed. "I talked with Admiral Ryerson in Washington yesterday. He places a great deal of trust in you, Dan."

"He ought to, considering the money he's paying me."

"What type of planes do you seek?"

"AD Skyraiders. With bombs and napalm."

"We have the Skyraiders," General Pham said, "but I doubt that they will do you much good. We have found that bombing the jungle does little to impede the Vietcong."

"I'm not thinking of bombing the jungle," Belden said.

"No? . . . Well, perhaps I'd better not know too much about it right now."

"Perhaps not."

The General got to his feet. "I have several Skyraiders in overhaul. Perhaps they will fit your purpose, whatever it is. Let's go to the field and inspect them."

"I'll need gas trucks and fuel, General."

"Everything you need has been attended to by Admiral Ryerson. He is an exceptionally thorough man."

"It'll be good to see the Old Man again," Belden mused.

"He arrives sometime tomorrow morning. There will be a small social gathering at the home of a dear friend of mine, Robert Morlaix. I have no doubt you will be invited."

"Hell, General," Belden said, "I made out the booze list myself."

❖   ❖   ❖

74

The girl at the reception desk in the United States Embassy building was named Eileen Riley. She was a lovely girl, with blue eyes and a spattering of light freckles across her nose. She looked up from the log she kept of visitors to the Embassy and saw three formidable appearing men bearing down on her. She greeted them with a practiced smile.

"Good afternoon, gentlemen. Is there anything I can do for you?"

The three men said nothing, merely stood and stared at her out of expressionless eyes.

"Whose?" Bates asked.

"Mine," said Anders.

"I said, is there anything I can do for you?" Miss Riley repeated.

"We'll flip," Bates announced.

They took out coins, flipped them, and examined the results with a great display of interest. Miss Riley frowned.

"I win," Bates said. He turned to the girl. "Do you really mean that?"

"Mean what?" she asked.

"About doing something for me," Bates said.

"Of course."

Bates smiled. "That's very kind of you. Where do you live?"

"Why"—she was flustered—"the Hotel Meurice off the Rue de Lubec. But why——"

"That's quite all right," Bates interrupted. "I realize you're nervous. This doesn't happen to a girl every day."

"What are you talking about?"

"Why, moving in with you," Bates said with evident surprise. "I've been looking all over Saigon for a place to stay and——"

"Now see here . . ." Miss Riley said, getting to her feet.

The three men exchanged commiserating glances.

"She so excited she's becoming irrational," Hawkins said.

"It happens to some of them that way," Anders added.

"It's known as the Bates Syndrome," Bates explained. "It starts with a curtailing of sexual activity. After a while the nerve ends become dehydrated or something and all of a sudden it results in irrationality. It happened to my grandmother once." Bates watched a small smile creep over Miss Riley's lips. Then he added, "But she was eighty-four years old."

The girl suppressed a chuckle. "What do you want?"

"Two things," Bates replied. "First, I'll pick you up at the Meurice at seven tonight. Second, we'd like to talk to the Navy liaison officer around here."

"That would be Lieutenant Cormier. He's in that second office down the hall."

"Seven o'clock?" Bates asked.

She watched him for a moment. "Try me," she said.

Bates nodded and the three men walked down the corridor to an open door. Inside sat a short, dark-haired full lieutenant who was, with great diligence, paring his fingernails.

He looked up with an expression of total boredom. "Yeah?"

"Did we wake you?" Anders asked.

"No. Not really," Lieutenant Cormier replied.

Bates leaned on the desk and stared at the wings on Cormier's chest. "You're a flier, I see."

"What? Oh, of course. Have to be you know. Air Attaché."

"It sounds exciting."

Cormier shrugged. "It's a living."

"Well," Bates said, "as long as you're a flier, I suppose you know what a mobile arresting gear is. We're looking for one."

Cormier did his best to swallow a yawn. "Not a chance. The closest one is back in Hawaii."

"Then we've got to get it out here," Bates said.

"Not a chance," Cormier repeated. "No need for one out here."

Bates was interrupted by the sound of voices in the corridor outside. Then a stern-looking man with a shock of white hair thrust his weather-beaten face in the door.

"Cormier!" the man roared. "How the hell am I supposed to——"

He broke off as he saw Bates and the others in the room. A frown of annoyance passed swiftly over his face, to be replaced by a look of puzzlement. "Wait a minute," he said. "Don't I know you men?"

"You ought to," Anders said.

"We saved your ass enough times," Bates added.

"He was much better-looking twenty years ago," Hawkins joined in.

"Good God!" Admiral Dusane shouted. "Bates! Hawk! Anders! I'll be goddammed." He strode across the room with his hand out-stretched.

Lieutenant Cormier looked on aghast as he watched a vice admiral pound the backs of the three strangers without partiality. This was the first time Cormier had ever seen Admiral Dusane smile. It would be something to remember.

"I heard Belden was coming," Dusane said. "I didn't know you guys were coming with him."

"Somebody has to take care of Dan," Bates said.

"Even money it's the other way around. How is he?"

"Same as the rest of us," Anders said. "Older."

"What are you doing here at the Embassy?" Dusane asked.

"Looking for a mobile arresting gear."

"What the hell for?"

Bates shrugged. "Who knows? Maybe Dan wants to arrest something."

Dusane looked at Cormier. "Well, you heard the man, Cormier. Get him a mobile arresting gear."

"But, Admiral," Cormier said helplessly, "we haven't got one."

"What do you mean, haven't got one? You mean to tell me in this whole goddam Navy we don't have a mobile arresting gear?"

"Yes, sir. I mean, no, sir. I mean, the closest one is probably at Barbers Point. That's in Hawaii, sir," Cormier added hopefully.

"I know goddam well where Barbers Point is, Cormier," Dusane roared. "Get them on the phone. I want to talk to ComFairHawaii. We'll fly that damn thing out here tonight." He clapped Bates on the shoulder. "Sometimes it pays to wear three stars. Come on in my office. I've got some good rye whiskey and we'll tell each other a few lies."

At the moment Admiral Dusane was pouring whiskey in the Embassy, an event was shaping up several hundred miles to the north which ultimately would reverberate in the highest echelons of command.

On that afternoon at 1400 hours two Chance Vought F8 jet fighter planes had taken off from the runway at Danang on the north coast of South Vietnam. They were planes from the carrier *Concord*, but had been temporarily based out of Danang while the pilots underwent a short special training course conducted by the Air Force. The planes also underwent a minor overhaul and this flight was an engine test run-in hop prior to the return flight out to the task force.

The pilot of the lead plane, a certain Lieutenant (jg) Robcke, was an intent young man of effervescent spirit, who had been flying these big jet fighters for approximately six months. He considered himself as adept as the next man and secretly at night he dreamed of the bright rows of ribbons he would wear on his chest when this tour of duty was over and he went home again to Coronado and the lovely young girls in the Mexican village. He looked over at his wingman, Ensign Joe Dowdle, also a laughing young man with even less time and experience than Robcke, and gave him the ubiquitous "thumbs-up." Dowdle responded with the age-old signal consisting of the middle finger of the right hand held upright, the other fingers being held close to the palm. Through several wars and elsewhere, this gesture has been rudely construed to mean, "Go screw yourself," or words to that effect. Robcke nodded at Dowdle pleasantly and returned his attention to his instrument panel.

They had leveled off at 40,000 feet when Robcke called to Dowdle on the radio, "We've got to run these bears in for an hour, Joe. Might as well head up along the Parallel."

It was a brilliantly clear afternoon with the only cloud formation far to the north, well over enemy territory. Robcke settled himself as comfortably as possible in the cramped cockpit and watched the landscape move below him as he considered his good fortune to be at the controls of this grand fighter plane, flying in a sky where he could not possibly run into danger of any sort. He was ruminating on this happy state of affairs as he approached the Parallel, moving nearer to his confrontation with destiny.

They passed over Hue at 42,500 feet, 90 percent power on the RPM indicator, all engine instruments reading normal. Robcke tilted his rearview mirror slightly and grinned at himself in the glass. He squinted and wondered how long he would have to wait before the wrinkles began to appear around the corners of his eyes. The oxygen mask hid all of his face except the area round the eyes as he reached over and flipped the gunsight switch to "On." He peered through the sight rings and imagined an enemy weaving and twisting in front of

78

him, trying desperately to get away from the guns spurting flame from his nose section. *Ratatatatat*, he murmured, and the enemy fell through the sky in flames. He switched off the sight, sat back with a contented sigh, and began to hum a ballad the fighter pilots sang aboard the carriers:

> He came to the ninety,
>   With a cool roger pass;
> Flew into the locker,
>   And busted his ass.
> Now he rests in Milpitas,
>   In a vault cold and damp;
> He got slow in the final,
>   And smacked in the ramp.

In the distance he could see the Ben Hai River and he swung more to the westward to parallel the border. Far below him he could see two tiny specks flitting over the terrain at a low altitude—T-28s on a close support mission, he supposed. He looked over at Dowdle again. Dowdle had moved out to the side an appreciable distance and was flying lazily, enjoying the fine afternoon and the feeling of contentment at the great power resting under his gentle hands.

Eight miles below Robcke and several miles to the north a young Chinese lieutenant named Hao Tseng Huao peered diligently into his radar scope. The carefully camouflaged radar site was located atop a prominent hill three miles north of the 17th Parallel. Hao felt a stir of excitement as he identified as enemy fighters the two blips flying at great altitude. There was no identification signal emanating from the blips. He estimated their course and a few moments later their speed. Course 260, speed approximately 600 miles per hour.

He reached for his transmitter mike: "Eagle One from Dragon. Your position, please?"

After a moment a voice broke through the static: "This is Eagle One. I am at forty thousand feet south of Ha Tinh."

Colonel Lee Cheng had led his flight of six MIGs from the strip at Lungchou approximately thirty minutes before Robcke and Dowdle had taken off from Danang. Unfortunately, General Soohoo's plans for intensive training had been curtailed temporarily due to fuel shortages. Colonel Lee admitted to himself that the rift with the

Russians had created certain problems of logistics. Thus even this flight to acquaint his pilots with terrain features had been granted reluctantly. Now Lee heard the radar controller's voice in his earphones: "Eagle One. I have two blips on my screen. They are paralleling the border at forty thousand feet. Over."

"I will investigate," Colonel Lee replied.

He banked sharply to the south and advanced his throttle. A plan was already shaping in his mind. A few minutes later, as he approached the Ben Hai River, Lee called to his flight: "Eagle Four. Take your division and circle behind that cloud formation to the west."

Several miles west of the MIG formation a towering bank of clouds reached to nearly 50,000 feet. The front was moving southeast slowly and behind it the weather was clear.

Eagle Four tapped his head in reply to Lee's order and the last four planes of the formation peeled off and swung westward. Lee and his wingman continued on a steady course for the border. Lee scanned the sky, his eyes narrowed against the sun's glare. He let his eyes pass freely over the sky, never funneling his vision to one particular spot, but sweeping the area ahead of him with broad, scanning glances.

"Eagle Two," he called to his wingman. "Fly tight on my wing. Do not allow yourself to get separated."

The wingman slipped in closer, nestling a few feet under and aft of Lee's starboard wingtip.

Lieutenant (jg) Robcke had flown as far to the west as he dared. He did not wish to cross the Laotian border. Now he reversed course, sweeping around in a tight, reversal turn. Dowdle slid down and under him, and they took up a reciprocal heading to the eastward. This maneuver put Colonel Lee ahead and to Robcke's left a few miles as the two elements flew on courses that would intersect near the border and about thirty miles west of Hue.

"Eagle One from Dragon," Lieutenant Hao called. "Vector one nine zero. Your bogies at forty thousand feet. Twenty miles."

Lee turned 15 degrees to starboard and pushed his throttle all the way forward, nodding his head emphatically as he did so to indicate to his wingman that they were adding power. As he sped south, Lee started a shallow climb toward 45,000 feet. He flicked on his gun switches and called his wingman: "Eagle Two. You will not fire your guns. I say again. You will not open fire. Is that understood?"

"I will comply," Eagle Two replied.

Lee turned his gunsight full bright and smiled in the confines of his cockpit. The memory of a hundred other battles in the sky passed through his mind, leaving behind only a certainty of his abilities and a calm confidence in himself and his machine.

He spoke again into his oxygen mike: "Eagle Two. When we attack the enemy we will go into afterburner."

Lee referred to the device on the tail of his plane which enabled the engine to burn excess gases that would otherwise have been expended uselessly. It was, in effect, an extra engine which utilized escaping gases to provide additional thrust and power.

Lee still did not see the enemy. He eased his stick to the left and banked to a new compass heading. His eyes were alertly probing now and he could feel the beat of his heart under the heavy flight clothing. The roar of his engine was lost behind his plane, left dying on the wind as the swift jets split the sky in the high, thin air. From the wingtips, contrails traced across the heavens, marking the path they flew.

Robcke spotting the MIGs' contrails before Lee had made his tallyho.

"Tallyho," Robcke called, not at all alarmed. "Two bogies. Eleven o'clock high." He watched them closely. Perhaps Air Force jets from Danang or even Saigon. The two unidentified planes turned to starboard. The bastards, Robcke thought. The Air Force wants to play games today. Well, that's quite all right with me.

It was not an uncommon practice for Air Force and Navy jets to tangle in mock dogfights in the high skies over South Vietnam. The young pilots were eager to prove to themselves and their comrades that they had mastered the planes which had been entrusted to them. At night the mess halls echoed to the brave stories of this or that pilot who had taken on three of the Navy jets at this or that place in the sky. Many of the stories were embellished by the dispensation granted to young men who made their living in such a manner, but this in no way detracted from the air of bravura that attended the telling.

Now Lieutenant Hao made his last vector transmission: "Eagle

One from Dragon. Bogies at your nine o'clock position. Three miles. Down."

Lee saw them then. Two dark specks at his nine o'clock position. From this distance they appeared level with him. But he knew better. Altitudes are tricky at great heights in the sky. He started a medium bank to the left.

"Afterburner, Eagle Two," Lee called.

The two planes went into afterburner with a great roar and Lee felt the additional thrust as the plane lurched ahead and he was pressed backward for a moment against the seat.

Robcke and Dowdle saw them coming. Well, hell, thought Robcke. I'll let them make their initial pass. They'll pull up and ahead and I'll go into burner and be on their asses. He grinned to himself and switched on his gunsight with a feeling of anticipation.

Lee was swinging down and from behind the two Americans when he heard Lieutenant Hao's voice in his earphones.

"Eagle One!" There was a note of anxiety in Hao's voice. "You have passed the Parallel. I say again. You are over the border."

Lee did not answer. His attention was riveted on the two F8s flying along straight and level and looming larger in his sights as he swept down and came in on them from astern and slightly to the port, affording an excellent 15-degree deflection angle.

Looking back over his shoulder, Robcke saw the two unidentified fighters swinging in behind him. He waited patiently for them to pull ahead so he could take up the chase.

As Lee closed, he deliberately banked slightly to pull his point of aim to the left of Robcke's plane. When he had assured himself that his shells would miss the F8 on its port side, he pressed his trigger and the shells erupted from his guns and laced a red line of tracer across the sky. The tracers flashed by Robcke's cockpit and alerted the young man to a basic fact of flying. You never take anything for granted.

Before Robcke was fully aware that he was being shot at, Lee and his wingman streaked by only fifty yards on Robcke's port. Robcke saw the markings on the MIGs and the singular tail assembly that made that plane so easy to identify.

"Jesus Christ!" Robcke bellowed. "They're MIGs."

There were, at this particular moment, several courses of action which Robcke should have followed had he adhered to the fighter pilots' handbook, which had been written by men with far more experience in the sky than he. He should have sounded a Mayday. He should have contacted his base for orders. He should have more diligently pinpointed his exact position relative to the 17th Parallel. He did none of these things. Robcke was a young man of vast courage, which is a fine thing indeed, but no substitute for foresight. Robcke was goddam good and mad. When people shoot at you, it is a natural reaction. He had no way of knowing that Lee had missed deliberately and so he flew into the trap Lee had so cleverly set.

Robcke banked steeply to the north. He threw his plane into afterburner. Dowdle needed no orders. He was with him all the way. The two F8s flashed after the MIGs, flying due north now and crossing the Parallel into North Vietnam.

"Let's get those bastards, Joe," Robcke called. His gunsight was on now and he fired a short burst from his guns, testing their efficacy at this frigid altitude.

Lee watched them in his rearview mirror. He nodded to himself as he called Lieutenant Hao: "Dragon from Eagle One. Confirm my position and that of bogies."

"You are ten miles north of the Parallel."

"Report to Hanoi that American fighters have crossed the Parallel and violated North Vietnam air space," Lee directed.

"Will comply from Dragon."

And still Lee led them on. Deeper into North Vietnam Robcke and Dowdle flew, totally unaware that they had violated air space, intent only on closing on the goddam MIGs. Lee finally started a gentle turn, allowing the Americans to turn inside him and thus close the distance. Then he sprang his trap shut.

"Eagle Four," Lee called. "We are at forty thousand feet over Ha Tinh. You are cleared to attack."

Lee watched Robcke closing on him and smiled to himself. They are young, these fliers, he thought. This is probably their first battle in the air. It will be their last. There are things a man learns after years and countless hours in the sky. The first thing he learns is that it is an unforgiving place. These men have not learned that first truism of the fighter pilot. But they are Americans and it has been my experience that Americans usually feel they cannot be beaten. Sometimes this is good, but often it proves their undoing. Above the Yalu River I learned to respect my adversary and his airplane. That is why I have survived. Now I will get down to the business at hand.

Lee allowed Robcke to close within firing range. Just as Robcke's finger tightened on the trigger and his shells spewed forth, Lee threw his stick hard to the opposite side of the cockpit and pulled back tightly on the stick. The MIG screamed into a high-speed reversal turn and Robcke's bullets flailed harmlessly through the air.

Then Eagle Four and his division came down like deadly falcons and barreled in behind Robcke and Dowdle.

The Americans heard the *pom-pom-pom-pom* of Eagle Four's guns before they were aware of the presence of other planes in the sky. Robcke saw tracers pass on his starboard side and then there was a smashing sound aft of his cockpit. His plane lurched momentarily and his eye noted briefly the fluctuation of the tail pipe temperature needle, but he was so intent on turning far enough inside Lee's radius to bring his guns to bear that he did not take notice of his gradually decreasing air speed. The tighter a turn, the greater the decrease in air speed. An aerodynamic law even the fledgling cadet memorizes. But in the heat of battle Robcke forgot and it cost him his life.

Lee maintained his vertically banked turn and Robcke's air-speed needle quavered near the stalling mark on the indicator. Tighter and tighter Robcke pulled on the stick, holding his nose level under the force of g-pressure pushing him down in his seat. Then the air speed fell below stalling and the F8 shuddered violently and fell off on the right wing. Robcke, immediately aware of the trouble now that it was with him, took remedial action, but too late. He jammed the stick hard forward and kicked left rudder to the floor boards. But the heavy fighter fell down the sky in a spiral, its control surfaces unable to respond because of the stalled condition.

It is altogether possible to bring an F8 out of spin if there is sufficient altitude and an absence of a MIG on your tail with a no-deflection shot. Lee saw Robcke stall through his mirror and executed an immediate wingover roll, culminating in a dive and reversing his direction. As his nose came into the dive, he found Robcke's helpless plane 2,000 feet below him in a spin. Lee came down on Robcke, all guns flaming.

Robcke cursed as he realized his foolishness. He reached for the mike button to call Dowdle and tell him to head for the deck and try to make it back across the border. Only now, as he saw the Ben Hai River on a southerly heading from him, did he understand what he had done.

"Joe, this is Jack," he called. "Head for the deck and . . ."

It was as far as Lieutenant Jack Robcke ever got. The shells from Lee's guns took him in the mid-section at 30,000 feet and he died there. He was already dead when the shells found the fuel tank and the plane erupted in a great ball of billowing flame. Lee smiled and swept up in a high Immelman turn and back into the fight.

Joe Dowdle was flying by instinct. There seemed to be MIGs all over the goddam sky. Out of a corner of his eye he saw Robcke's plane accept the tracers and explode. God damn it to hell, he thought. Just then his windshield shattered as a shell entered from behind him and splintered the top of the canopy. The pressurization was gone in an instant and the oxygen mask was torn from Dowdle's face by the screaming wind. He reacted instinctively. He actuated his ejection control, firing the cartridge that hurtled him and his entire seat out of the plane and into the 600-mile-per-hour wind at 35,000 feet.

Dimly, in the back of his mind, the manual for ejection procedure asserted itself. At the top of the ejected seat's arc, Dowdle hazily fumbled with his safety belt, released it, and tumbled away from the seat in a free fall through the freezing sky. He had not breathed as yet since he bailed out and now, when he attempted to do so, the thin air seared his lungs like a tongue of flame. He gasped for breath as his body tumbled through the air like a poorly spun top. He kept repeating in his mind, "Don't pull the rip cord. Don't pull it. Free fall down where you can breathe again. Leave the rip cord alone."

He felt consciousness leaving him. With the last of his ebbing strength, his fingers reached for the metal handle extending from the supporting strap on the left side of his chute. He was distantly surprised at the amount of effort he expended pulling the metal ring free. Then he passed out as his body twisted down past 25,000 feet.

Dowdle regained consciousness in the heavier air below 20,000 feet. He opened his eyes as a great wave of pain washed over him and then seemed to settle in his left leg. He looked above him at the broad expanse of white silk with the intermittent slits in the canopy. The pain came again and he screamed in agony. He craned his neck to look down and his eyes squeezed shut in horror as he saw that his left leg below the knee was missing. The wildly spurting blood sprayed out into the air and was whipped away by the wind.

"Good God," Dowdle moaned. "Dear Christ." The excruciating agony came again and again as he swung helplessly in the parachute straps and then he retched violently and vomited into the wind.

He raised his head weakly and through pain-fogged eyes watched a MIG fighter appear before him, its guns winking at him. Then he knew how his leg had been destroyed.

The bastards. Oh, the dirty, lousy, mother-fucking bastards!

Colonel Lee found it impossible to hold the swaying figure in his gunsight, so he sprayed the area under the parachute canopy with shells by gently easing alternate pressures on his rudder. The nose of his plane swayed to and fro and the tracers licked all about the body held captive in the parachute harness.

Dowdle was consumed by the awful pain, but he saw Lee's MIG flash past him and pull up and reverse course and come down again. He tried to twist the risers of the chute, but found that his strength had gone, had pumped out through the stump of his leg. His eyes dimmed and he felt the erratic beat of his heart. He looked down and the ground seemed a million miles away. It began to come closer now and for a brief moment he thought he was back at Pensacola in the springtime of his life. He saw the MIG coming again and he knew he was not at Pensacola and this was not the springtime of his life. It was the winter and he was dying at 15,000 feet with one leg missing.

Lee opened fire again, holding the trigger down and walking up his tracers to Dowdle's helpless body.

"Good Christ," Dowdle prayed. "Let somebody even up with this dirty sonofabitch. Let somebody make it up for me."

Lee grinned in his cockpit as he saw Dowdle's body buffeted by the shells. The body jerked like a dog hung up in intercourse.

Dowdle felt the shells hit him, but he no longer cared. The pain was gone now and he felt nothing as he stared at his middle and the great hole that had been torn through him. He twisted in his harness and his eyes kept dimming, as though he were looking at something very far away, something hazy in the distance. Then his eyes closed forever and shortly thereafter the blood stopped pouring from his wounds and he was only a dry shell twisting slowly at the end of the risers as the parachute let him gently down through the sky.

Chapter
VI

OCTOBER
1964

The meeting between Dan Belden and Storm Ryerson had not been effusive, as might have been expected between two men who had known and admired each other throughout their adult lives. Ryerson had come to Belden's suite early in the morning, and they had spent five minutes talking in quiet voices about men they had known and other places they had been. Then they had picked up Ralph Yeager and Robert Morlaix and had driven to Tan Son Nhut airfield where the helicopter waited to take them to the Morlaix plantation near the village of Hon Quan.

There had been a minimum of conversation during the forty-minute flight, each of them busy with his private thoughts. Now, as the pilot started his slow descent toward the plantation, Ryerson turned his fierce face to Belden.

"How did you and General Pham hit it off?"

"We're old friends, Admiral." Belden paused a moment. "He's going to march north one of these days."

"Yeah." Ryerson grunted softly. "Well, we've got to help him out along that line of thinking."

"That's why we're out here this morning," Belden said.

The helicopter was approaching the lawn of the plantation as Ryerson laid aside the sheaf of papers he had been reading. "You read the report on those two F8s that got creamed yesterday above the Parallel?"

Belden nodded. "They were north of the Parallel. They weren't supposed to be there."

"They were suckered into it." The Admiral's voice was puzzled. "And that's why something stinks around here. Our radar people watched them decoyed. Now why would the Chinamen want to do that? Unless they were trying to do the same thing you and I are trying to do—escalate this mess. But we know Peking isn't ready for that yet. This is the second time they've blundered. The first time was with those two kids they shot. It looks like somebody on their side wants to bust this wide open as much as you and I do. But who?"

"Colonel Lee, maybe," Belden said. "He led those MIGs yesterday."

"The bastard." Ryerson grunted. "I sat across a table from him at Panmunjom. Hard sonofabitch. Cold-faced. It would take a cold, lousy bastard to do what he did."

"He's got a job too," Belden said mildly.

Ryerson snorted loudly. "You don't know, I suppose. The body of one of those pilots, a kid named Dowdle, came down behind our side of the border. He bailed out and they strafed him in his chute. Blew his leg off and shot a hole in his middle you could drive a truck through. When we got him there wasn't a drop of blood left in him. That's your Colonel Lee doing his job."

Belden spoke in a whimsical tone. "You never strafed anyone in a chute?" When Ryerson did not answer, Belden said, "Lee hates us just as much as we hate him. In a fight the object is to destroy your enemy. What was Lee supposed to do? Let Dowdle get away to fly another day? Hell, no. This is war, Admiral. The days of the white scarfs and the gallant gestures are long gone." Belden's voice grew mild. "If I ever catch Lee in a chute, he'll get it the same way."

"Well, let's hope you do." After a moment Ryerson said, "How many men have you got?"

"Four of us here and ten on the way."

"Can you take out that base in Laos with fourteen men?"

"Hell, yes," Belden said. "Besides, it's not important whether or not we wipe it off. You want to get the Chinamen mad enough to make some more mistakes. This may help. And we can do it without embarrassing the Administration."

"That'll be the neatest trick of the week." Ryerson hesitated a second. "How?"

"Let me worry about that," Belden replied with a smile. "We'll take it out when the whole area is socked in solid, when every plane in South Vietnam is grounded. The Chinamen will know who did it, but they won't be able to prove a goddam thing."

"How the hell can you attack *anybody* in zero zero weather?"

Belden grinned. "That's why you're paying us these outrageous salaries."

Ryerson nodded. "There's something you don't know, Dan. We may not have all the time in the world to accomplish our mission out here. We have reports from reliable sources that the Chinamen are planning a blitz offensive for next year. No date on it yet. I suppose when they can afford fifty divisions along the border up there. I'm hoping it won't be before next summer. And Dan"—Ryerson's tone was urgent—"we've *got* to have massive intervention from the States by that time. It means survival."

"One thing I learned in my business, Storm," Belden said. "Never make promises. You'll get the best we've got. That's all I can promise."

"It's good enough," Ryerson said.

The helicopter threw great clouds of dirt into the air as it lowered gently onto the ground in front of the main house of the plantation. A group of Vietnamese Army troops was waiting, all of them armed with automatic rifles. Morlaix's holdings were within an area held in considerable force by Arvin troops.

Belden, the last to disembark from the chopper, walked a few yards to a slight rise that jutted out of the flat ground surrounding the main house. It rose to a height of perhaps fifteen feet and afforded an unobstructed view of the outlying terrain.

He lit a cigarette as he studied the cleared area sweeping away in front of him for a distance of less than a mile. On all sides of the clearing heavy growths of rubber trees stood in thick proliferation, affording a natural perimeter to the area of open ground.

90

"Do you know the dimensions of that open area, sir?" he asked Morlaix.

"Perhaps three thousand feet long. Three hundred feet wide. We intended to erect new barracks buildings on it at one time."

"You've got a problem, Dan," Ryerson pointed out. "The field slopes downhill into the wind."

Belden nodded as he estimated the degree of inclination of the field. "It won't bother me. I'm getting a mobile arresting gear from Smoke Dusane." He turned again to Morlaix. "How about the weather, sir?"

Morlaix did not understand. "You'll have excellent flying weather, Dan. I can assure you of that."

"That's not what I mean. How many *lousy* flying days a month can I expect?"

"At this time of year?" Morlaix shrugged. "Not many. Perhaps one or two days a month."

Belden thought a moment. "There's another matter, Mr. Morlaix. Our being here could bring down the Vietcong. Retaliation. You're sticking your neck out."

Morlaix inclined his head. "I've considered that, Dan. Let me worry about it."

As the party walked to the main house, Belden mentioned to Ryerson, "I'll need a good chief mech on the line, Admiral."

"I've got one for you," Ryerson said. "An old friend of yours. Larry O'Toole."

"O'Toole! I thought he was still in the Navy."

"He retired three days ago aboard the *Concord*. Thirty years."

"I couldn't ask for a better man," Belden said. "He was the mech on my Hellcat twenty years ago."

Ryerson said, "That's why he took his discharge out here. He remembers too."

"When can I get him?"

"You already have. He's at the airfield in Saigon with your Skyraiders now."

"Admiral"—Belden spoke in a thoughtful tone—"if we bring this off, if we get something moving around here and we get a chance to really fight, there will be the matter of new airplanes. I don't mean

Skyraiders. This is a one-shot deal. I mean jets. You don't fight a MIG in an AD-1."

"That problem occurred to me. I have mentioned it to Smoke Dusane. Don't worry about it."

In a reclining chair by the pool where the sun danced on the sparkling water, Lori sipped her morning coffee with quiet pleasure. Her hair was damp from the recent plunge and now she daintily blew a drop of water from the tip of her nose.

After Dan and Admiral Ryerson had picked up her father early that morning, she had busied herself with household chores. There had been the servants to instruct regarding tonight's party, the checking of the liquor and fine wines that had been delivered the day before. She had spent a few minutes with the young Vietnamese captain in charge of the security detail. He was understandably nervous; when General Pham attended such a function, there was always the possibility of an attempt at assassination.

She sipped the last of the coffee and set the cup aside. She lay back in the chair and turned her face to the sun, letting a sense of well-being spread over her. She was, she decided, the happiest she had been thus far in her life.

She was well aware that she had irrevocably decided to become Dan Belden's woman. She admitted the problems that confronted her but, in the manner of the very young and indestructible, she was certain of overcoming them.

Could she, a young girl with a vast ignorance of life, move into his world, break down his defenses, win his love? He had always been gentle with her, perhaps too gentle, almost to the point of condescension. But this, she thought, might be the barrier he had erected because of her youth, because he knew what he was and what she was and what had made each of them the way they were.

The first things she could remember were broad, tree-lined avenues in Paris shortly after World War II. Dimly she recalled the lovely expanse of the Champs Èlysées and the grandeur of the Arc de Triomphe. Her parents had lived in England during the war, and Lori had been only two years old when they returned to France in 1944.

She remembered her mother only as a gentle, secure presence with soft, tender hands and a lilting voice that hummed to her at night when she went to sleep. They had returned to Indochina, to the plantation and the large pink townhouse in 1949. Her mother had died short months later, wasting away in silence in the big bed as the fever slowly killed her.

The French came back to Indochina when the Japanese left and the trouble was the same as before. The natives were in revolt against the French as much as they had been against the Japanese. At first the trouble had been sporadic, and to Lori it was only some distant, unpleasant business concerning the grownups.

Then one night all that had ended. Lori and her father had returned after dark from a friend's home. The house was silent and there was no sign of the servants. Papa had drawn a pistol he always carried under his coat and they had entered the main house.

They had found Lori's *amah*, a gentle creature who had looked out on the world with trusting, dispassionate eyes, staked out on the floor in the main salon. Both of her legs had been fastened to the floor and her hands tied above her head and nails driven through the palms. Other things had been done to her that caused Lori to turn away, violently and physically ill. Outside in the barracks they had found the other servants, huddled in a bloody pile, murdered in a wild, senseless flurry of machine-gun fire.

Later a message had come from the guerrilla chieftain, a man who had looked upon Morlaix with respect. There were regrets and apologies for the unfortunate occurrence. After that, for a time, there were no more raids on the plantation, but it was too late to give any satisfaction to the *amah* who had died in screaming agony with the stigmata wounds in her hands.

By the time Lori was sixteen, she had matured into a quiet, self-contained girl of deep, gentle beauty. If she possessed the impetuosity of youth, she held it deep within herself and from this calm self-containment developed a strength of character lightly touched with humor and an underlying exuberance. Dien Bien Phu had long fallen, and with it the myth of French supremacy. The Vietnamese were autonomous, although divided into separate governments, north and south. Robert Morlaix's relations with the Vietnamese were excellent, and the plantation prospered despite the increasing Communist insurgence from above the 17th Parallel.

For two years Lori attended Rosemont College in Philadelphia. She left with a sense of unfulfillment because she never truly touched or understood the other young girls at the school. There was something missing; she was searching for something, but exactly what she did not know and would not find until some years later at a bar in Honolulu. She took a job with a fashion magazine in New York and for a time resisted with an amused tolerance the sophomoric advances of the young men on Madison Avenue.

In 1963 she went to France when the fighting in Vietnam precluded her return to Saigon. There were relatives there and the time passed pleasantly enough. But all the time she knew she was looking for something.

Had she been older and wiser, she would have realized she was looking for a man, not a man-child. She needed someone in the image of her dreams, a man of honor and of courage who could laugh lightly and walk the earth like a prince. Most girls dream of such a man at one time or another. In the privacy of their dreams at night they fashion this image in the form of their desires. More often than not the image remains only in the dreams and never invades reality.

But now a man had come into Lori's life who filled the image of her dreams. He was nineteen years older than she, but somehow this disparity in ages did not seem real. Perhaps there were brief moments when she regretted the years that Belden had lived before she had even been born, but she shrugged these moments aside with displeasure and then forgot them.

Since she had met Dan Belden, her life had changed, even her dreams had changed. What had been the hazy, ephemeral hopes of youth, trusting in youth's own invincibility, had become a certain and positive knowledge to her. She would follow Belden, with honor or without it, wherever she must. Suddenly, in a matter of weeks, her life had taken Belden's unto itself and, without him, there was only desert and wasteland and desolation.

At night she lay unsleeping, staring sightlessly at the ceiling as she imagined Belden in his youth, before she had been born. The bright and laughing girls he had known and loved and touched with his strong hands. It became harder and harder to shrug these moments

94

aside and she could feel his body on hers, gently insistent, and sometimes she moaned in the last hours of the night.

Now she smiled to herself as she lay in the warm sun by the pool because she had convinced herself that her dream was not at all an impossibility. She thought: I have seen something back of your eyes, Dan Belden. I have seen a longing there, perhaps a mild puzzlement that you have found something lacking in this violent life you live. Perhaps you are wondering if you have forgotten something.

"Have you forgotten something, darling?" I will ask you.

"I don't know," you will say. "Have I?"

"Of course," I will reply. "You have forgotten me. How silly of you!"

"Oh?" you will say. "And why shouldn't I forget you?"

"Because you need me," I will say. "Because you need to reach back to your youth again, to all the bright and smiling girls you knew. Well, I am a bright and smiling girl and now you can reach for me."

"I am far too old," you will say.

"It is relative," I will answer. "When you are ninety I will be seventy-one. Convince me if you can that seventy-one is too young for you."

"Hmmm . . . !" you will murmur, and then you will smile and my world will be all right again.

Satisfied that she had successfully settled the major problem of her life, Lori got to her feet, her splendid young body supple and graceful in the brief bikini. She ran her hands slowly over her abdomen and then down over her loins and a tiny smile of anticipation came across her lips.

A few hundred miles north of the pool in Saigon, two men sit at a table in a bare room and study a map on a slatted wall. There is a small bottle of rice wine and two tiny cups before them. General Soohoo holds a sheaf of papers in his hand and watches Colonel Lee through slitted eyes. Overhead they can hear the faint whine of jet engines. The General smiles briefly.

"Your action, Colonel, against those two Crusader aircraft was magnificent. You are to be complimented."

95

Lee, his face expressionless, inclined his head. "They were mere children, General. Without experience. It will not always be so easy."

The General nodded. "You will be alert to execute that plan again should the opportunity present itself. But remember, the Americans must violate air space. It must be they who cross the Parallel. When they do, you will fight them over friendly ground and in addition you will have sanctuary over the Chinese border." The General smiled again. "They are playing the Korean game all over again."

"Fools," Lee said shortly.

The General poured the wine cups full. "We have reports from Saigon, Colonel. We have a man high in General Pham's cabinet. He reports that certain men, Americans, have arrived in the city. Ostensibly as businessmen, but these are not businessmen. There is a man named Belden. You know of him." Soohoo did not phrase it as a question.

Lee narrowed his eyes. "I do, sir. Many years ago we spent some interesting times together. Over the Yalu. There was a moment in 1952 when I thought my career had come to an end. Fortunately"— Lee's lips turned up at the corners—"I had the sanctuary over the river." With a strange lack of bitterness, he added, "It is the closest I have ever come to defeat."

"These men are not to be taken lightly?"

"They are professionals, General. There are not many men who make a living fighting in the sky." Lee sipped his wine gravely. "To make your living in such a manner you must be among the best at your trade. No, I would not take Belden lightly."

"You know him by name. How did this come about?"

"Your question brings to mind a matter that has long needed my attention," Lee said. "This man Belden and I met one day above the Yalu at a town called Sinuiju. He shot down three of my division. The American press made much of his feat and in that way I learned who he was. He flew a Sabrejet with the number 17 painted on the tail. We met again after that, but somehow we never fought to a finish. Someone or something—destiny if you will—always intervened. Lack of fuel, out of ammunition, weather conditions. Something always prevented us from testing each other to finality. Perhaps"—Lee's voice was wistful—"this time we shall resolve this impasse that has lasted twelve years."

The General studied Lee's face for a moment. A lean, hard face, unrelenting, demanding, the face of a man dedicated to duty and responsibility, the final coinage of a soldier.

"The fuel shortage," Soohoo said, "has been alleviated. Your men are conducting training exercises?"

"Night and day, General. They need it. There are few of us down here with combat experience."

"The Americans also have few combat-experienced fliers."

"Let us hope so," Lee said.

"Do I detect a note of apprehension, Colonel?"

Lee smiled. "No, sir. Not for myself. I fear no man in the sky. This is my greatest asset. To fight without confidence is ultimately to be killed. I have learned this over a good many years."

"I understand," Soohoo said. "Now I have some news which I know you have been awaiting. The new MIG-21s will arrive in a few days. You have time now to train your men. Perhaps before long you will no longer have that time. Make the best of it, Colonel."

"I will, sir."

"You will continue to maintain surveillance along the Parallel. To-morrow, or within a few days, we may have a plan in effect that will provide your men with more than target banners to shoot at."

They watched each other with grave eyes and touched cups before they drank the sweet rice wine.

Belden stood with a glass of champagne in his hand and listened to the many-keyed hum of conversation. With him were Hawkins and Anders. Bates had gone to pick up Miss Riley with whom he admittedly intended to conduct improper relations later in the evening. Belden, watching his two friends as they considered the constantly shifting scene on the patio, felt a surge of affection.

"I wonder," Anders said, "what the hell we are doing here." He glanced at Belden. "Ambassadors. Prime Ministers. Generals. Admirals." He shook his head. "And a few old beaten-up fighter pilots. It doesn't figure."

Belden did not answer. His eyes passed over the groups of guests which were gathering, breaking apart, and re-forming with others. The medals on the dress uniforms glittered under the hanging lanterns as the owners spoke politely, warily, inquiring as to this or to that without any real intent or purpose. Grouped at the long bar at which three bartenders worked furiously with amazing dexterity, the young Air Force and Navy pilots segregated themselves and their voices, young, animated, came clearly across the patio.

"We'll get a crack at the bastards. Mark my words. Did you read about Dowdle getting it in his chute? Christ. They'll get nothing but the same from me."

"Go slowly, friend. You may end up nothing but a statistic in the 'loss' column."

"Hell. We can take anything they've got in an F8."

"Can we? Who's tried it up to now?"

"Screw you, buddy. I'll take any MIG going in an F8. Spot him the advantage too."

"Well . . . based on your recent gunnery scores, it seems probable that you could shoot at a MIG standing on the flight line and miss the sonofabitch with a goddam cannon."

Belden smiled at his friends. "We used to talk like that."

"A long time ago," Hawkins mused. "They're all indestructible."

"We can hope so," Anders said.

They knew the talk was always the same with the young pilots. It had to be because the young men harbored a secret, nagging doubt concerning their invulnerability. It was a well-camouflaged doubt, but it was there, and speaking in light, boasting terms served in some manner to overwhelm it. Some of them would win this private battle; the doubt would disappear in the hard school of combat experience and so they would find glory in the skies above them. Others would go down early to the inevitable defeat.

"We're in demand, it seems," Belden said. From across the patio Admiral Ryerson was beckoning to them.

They moved slowly through the clustered groups toward Ryerson, Smoke Dusane, and General Pham.

Belden lifted his glass slightly in salute. "Good evening, gentlemen."

"Join us, Dan," Ryerson said. He introduced Hawkins and Anders to General Pham.

"I was telling General Pham," Ryerson continued with a broad grin, "that he looks like a neon sign tonight."

Pham glanced down at his bemedaled chest and sighed. "It is to

remind some people that I am of *some* importance around here."
There was humor in the remark.

"Hell," Dusane grumbled. "If they forgot, you would march them down to that wall of yours and shoot them. It's not a bad idea in many cases, either."

General Pham smiled, his face appearing much younger as he revealed strong white teeth. "You make me sound like one of those evil Caribbean dictators. I kill only to preserve myself, Admiral."

"That's as good a reason as any," Belden agreed.

"Dan," Smoke Dusane said, "those mobile arresting units are on the way. Coming out by MATS tonight."

"Thanks, Smoke. Can you truck them out to the Morlaix plantation for me?"

"I'll attend to that, Dan," General Pham interposed.

Belden nodded his thanks. "General," he said to Pham, "do we have possession of high ground near Lao Bao at the Laotian border?"

General Pham thought for a moment. "Sometimes," he said. "We have patrols up there and we can take a certain piece of ground and hold it for a given length of time. Why?"

"I'll need men up there with a portable radio transmitter within the next few weeks. Possibly sooner."

"It can be arranged."

"I'll also need a transmitter at Ban Me Thuot, a hundred miles northeast of the Morlaix plantation. And another at the plantation itself. Can do?"

General Pham's eyes held a speculative gleam. "Can do."

Dan is handling this well, Ryerson thought. General Pham is not overtly committing himself, nor are any of the rest of us who wear these shackles of politics.

"Smoke," Ryerson said to Dusane, "you have several squadrons of Chance Vought Crusaders aboard your carriers, do you not?" Ryerson was perfectly aware that Dusane had eight squadrons of Crusaders under his command.

"Yeah," Dusane replied warily.

"Well," Ryerson said contemplatively, "I remember, back during the Korean mess, when I had Task Force 77, we once had to survey several Grumman Panthers. Some sort of mechanical malfunction.

As I remember, all we had to do was fill out some papers surveying the planes. Then we flew them to the beach and that was all there was to it. Now, I don't suppose you have any Crusaders in such a condition?"

"You'd like to see me court-martialed? Or maybe reduced to seaman second class?" Dusane's tone was wounded.

"Or perhaps make that fourth star," Ryerson said.

"As a matter of fact," Dusane said, "I think I do have several Crusaders in pretty bad shape. I'll see what I can do."

"Dan"—Dusane turned to Belden—"you know this bastard Lee who got those two kids of mine yesterday. How good is he?"

Belden paused to light a cigarette before he answered, "Not as good as I am."

Perhaps an idle boast, he thought, but they know what I mean. The book tells you how to fight, how to maneuver your plane in the air under a given set of circumstances. But the book is read on the ground and has been compiled from the reports of other men who do not always remember clearly what transpired in the heat of battle. Experience is better than any book and the recollections of past victories more important than any resolution or anger. All the courage in a brave man is useless unless the tempered skill is there, the skill that comes after a man has eaten up his own mind with remembering other fights until the mind is worn down like a fine old knife blade and all that is left when the battle is joined is a calm appreciation of one's own ability and the sure knowledge that the enemy is second best. When this confidence has settled deep into the bones, then experience becomes the greatest asset the fighter pilot has.

"The bastard," Dusane said. "I hope he gets his."

"He will, Smoke," Belden said. "I'll see to it."

The others watched Belden as he continued, "We met over the Yalu in nineteen fifty-two. I was on TAD to the Air Force. Lee was a major then, a squadron leader at a base a few miles past the river. He must be a vain man because he had a special paint job on his tail. Some newspaper reporter had named him the Dragon of the Yalu, so Lee had a dragon painted on his empennage. You couldn't miss it. I think he still carries that insignia. I'll find him." There was a dead certainty in the words.

"Yes, Dan." There was no levity in Ryerson's voice. "I think you'll find him."

Past Ryerson's shoulder Belden saw Lori and her father coming across the patio toward them. Hawkins followed his glance and whistled in soft astonishment.

"You're a lucky guy, Dan."

"Good evening," Robert Morlaix said. "Are you enjoying yourselves?"

"I am now, sir." Belden smiled.

Without embarrassment, Lori took his hand. "I'm going to borrow Dan for a while. There's something I want to show him."

"It's Dan's good fortune," Ryerson said.

"Be careful, Lori." Anders was faintly mocking. "I can tell you things about Dan Belden."

Lori looked up at Belden. "Oh, no," she said lightly. "I know all there is to know about him."

"I think you do, Lori." Hawkins said quietly. "I truly think you do." He turned his glance to Belden. "Walk lightly, Dan. Perhaps you will get one more chance at salvation."

Belden understood and nodded. "Perhaps, Hawk." He made his excuses and left the others talking about the effect of synthetic-rubber production on Morlaix's considerable holdings.

Outside the patio there was a garden with a small bench at the end of a flowered arbor. The night was fragrant and the sound of a night bird came on the delicate air. Lori and Belden sat together and she laid her head on his shoulder.

"Dan," she said softly, "why do you have to do this?"

"Do what?"

"You know what I mean." She drew back to look at him. "Papa told me about that Vietcong base in Laos."

"It isn't important."

"It is to me."

He sighed. "All right. I honestly believe that if we Americans are still here in Vietnam a year from now, it will be because we have a couple of hundred thousand men in the rice paddies and a few thousand airplanes on the fields around Danang and Hue. That's *if* we're still here. If we haven't been pushed into the China Sea.

There may well be a Chinese offensive next year and unless they start moving back in the States it will be too late. A lot of people are talking truce, negotiation, pull-out. Well, there may be a truce all right, but not unless we get the stuff over here to make a truce the only way out for the enemy. So how do we get Washington to escalate the war? We bring the Chinamen into it, get them to come down and fight. Our people back home don't openly go along with this thinking, but some of them are beginning to sweat a little. I'm going to take out that base in Laos for a couple of reasons. One is because it's there and it's ridiculous to watch those Reds move from that camp and do nothing about it. So I'll take it out and the Chinamen will know who did it, but they won't be able to prove it and even if they could, what the hell can they do about it? Washington may rant a little, but we're civilians and not the military, so there will be no court-martial. But even if there were, we'd still have to start the ball rolling someplace, and the base in Laos is as good a starting point as any other." He looked down at her. "Does that make sense?"

She nodded wordlessly and he felt the pressure of her fingers on his. They were silent for a time as the moon rose higher in the sky. Finally she spoke in a whisper. "Dan?"

"Hm?"

"A penny."

"Not worth it," he said lazily.

Or was it, he wondered. He was remembering the cold dawns with the frosty bite of fall when the sky was gray with the pallor of death and he was coming out of the sun, sweeping in to the attack. In the back of his mind he heard the voices of all the men who had flown his wing and who had gone down under his orders with the last smile or the last curse.

So it is always, if you listen to the music of the band. Down the street it marches and the little boys follow in a search for glory that is not there. Not ever there. And then the band is finished and you realize that even your soul has gone on ahead of you, to wait for you in the memories where old men live. So it is too late now and you go on, plodding after your own soul, and you do it alone, all alone, because there are no soft and fragrant girls in the high skies where your soul has gone. So the music is flown, the flowers gone, no violins, and you know a sweaty flight suit is a damned poor badge of glory.

"Perhaps I have found it after all," Belden mused aloud.

"Found what?" she asked.

"I'm not sure," he lied. He was thinking perhaps he had found his soul again and Hawkins had been right; every man deserved a second chance at salvation.

"When you think like that you go away from me," she whispered.

"There are places like that," he said. "Places you can't ever go. Well, maybe I can stop going to them in a little while."

Lori Morlaix heard that. But she didn't hear the roaring of the engines and the dead men's voices that stirred the worn pennants. She didn't hear those voices as she leaned over and kissed Dan Belden on the lips.

He watched her tenderly a moment, then raised his eyes to the night sky. A few puffs of cloud shone in the moonlight and the city's lights bounced with a hard brilliance. How do I say it? he thought. How do I say there are things I still have to do? Men who depend on me. I have a rendezvous to keep with a man named Lee somewhere out of sight to the north. He may be waiting for me now. So how do I say what is to happen next? And even then this problem remains— you have the glory of your youth and I am walking close upon middle-age. There is a thing here to be considered; when I am finished in the sky, where is the market for old fighter pilots?

"Things will work out," he said.

She nodded with satisfaction. "Doesn't it ever scare you?"

"Doesn't what scare me?"

"Oh," she said, "the way other men look up to you. Depend on you somehow. The others always seem to be waiting for you to tell them something."

He laughed easily in the night. "They don't depend on me. I'm just another cog. I'm the one who depends on them."

"Sometimes you confuse me," she confessed. "But I think that's because I never knew anyone like you before. You're very special, Dan."

He ran his fingers lightly across her face. "Don't always believe your eyes, Lori. Too often they tell you what you want to be told.

I'm no different from the rest. Just lived a little longer than some of them."

She made a small sound and turned to him. He saw a tear sparkle in the corner of her eye.

"Kiss me, Dan," she breathed. "Kiss me, my darling."

Belden took her in his arms and kissed her with a great gentleness. And even as he did so his mind told him: Go slowly here; find your way carefully. This is something new to you and it is something worth living for. In your trade you cannot count on the future because there may be no future. When life becomes too dear, then caution enters your bones and, in this business, an excess of caution can mean your destruction.

Seated alone at the far end of the bar, Ray Hawkins ran his palm along the back of his neck where the pain had been coming again. It was no worse than before, but it came with greater frequency now. It started in his neck and spread into the shoulder muscles and lately he had felt the knife-sharp pain in his chest.

He smiled ruefully to himself. When you considered it dispassionately, there was almost an element of humor in the situation. Here he was, sitting at this bar, surrounded by young men—fliers and soldiers and sailors. All of them wondered, with deep concentration, about their mortality. They wondered how long their luck would hold and if they would be alive next year on this date. And, if not, then how would the ending come to them? Hawkins was very sure of this because a long time ago he had wondered in the same manner.

He had no need for this sort of contemplation now. He was fully aware that his luck had run out and left him with death in the back of his neck and in his lungs. He had accepted this, and now he beckoned the bartender and ordered another drink.

Chapter
VII

In the November days the fighting in the rice paddies and in the jungles to the north increased in tempo. Vietcong guerrillas maintained their steady penetration from the sanctuaries in Laos and they came treading lightly down the Ho Chi Minh trail. Under the cloudless November skies the villages and hamlets were attacked and the atrocities continued unabated. Village chiefs were disemboweled in the village squares and young men were marched off in the night to be trained in another philosophy of life.

In Saigon there were murmurs of unrest as greedy men watched for an opportunity to enhance their personal ambitions. In the headquarters of government and in the embassies, men grouped around tables until late at night, their brief cases open and their eyes troubled as they consulted the sheaves of paper spread before them.

To the city's Tan Son Nhut airport, hard-eyed strangers came. They came unobtrusively, climbing down from MATS C-54 cargo planes or disembarking from the jet airliners that arrived from every port on earth. These tanned strangers carried little in the way of personal belongings, perhaps a battered val-pak or a worn suitcase. They were men in their thirties, calm and unemotional, and they looked out on the world with an ironic amusement. Soft-spoken, they talked only among themselves as they watched with expert eyes the long rows of Air Force jet fighters parked on the far side of the field.

Whenever a jet liner took off, their glances would follow it until the plane was lost to sight.

They spoke in quiet tones to the information officer at the airfield and then they reported singly, or in pairs, to a certain colonel at General Pham's headquarters. Transportation was arranged and in a matter of hours they had arrived at the Morlaix plantation and had reported to Dan Belden.

Their coming, it was thought, caused no undue furor, nor did anyone of note even realize they had come and had so quietly disappeared. Their passports had been inspected and if anyone wondered for a moment at this influx of rubber salesmen for the Morlaix company, he made no mention of it.

General Pham's Minister of Defense, a small, intense man, received reports from his secret agents, however. He grew thoughtful for a time and then made an appointment to meet a certain party at the junction of two lonely roads three miles outside Saigon. To this courier he imparted information which was to be relayed to his brother in North Vietnam. The Minister of Defense felt a satisfaction each time he sent information north because he knew he was whittling away at the already weakened underpinning of General Pham, a man he detested utterly and whom he intended to replace. He was not fully aware of any military significance in the information he had imparted. How much of value was there in the knowledge that hard-eyed strangers had come to join the man Belden at Robert Morlaix's plantation? Well, he had done what he could; it was up to his friends in the north to evaluate the information.

With a sense of accomplishment, he bade farewell to the courier and climbed into his limousine and ordered the driver to return him to his office. The driver had traveled three miles or less when he found himself facing a squad of riflemen standing at the ready in the middle of the road. He turned to find the Minister of Defense staring out the window with a look of naked fear on his face. A short, slight officer walked up and opened the rear door of the car.

"A fine night, eh, my friend?" General Pham murmured.

The Minister choked back a sob of terror.

"I am not inclined to ruin the interior of a good automobile," Pham said. "Please get out."

The Minister, his limbs locked in a paralysis, was unable to move, so Pham emptied a .38 revolver into the Minister's head. So much for traitors to the state!

On the rutted, winding road that led through the paddies to the Morlaix plantation gasoline carriers lumbered in the dark of night. Following them, moving cautiously along the road, wary for guerrilla attack, came heavily guarded ammunition carriers and trucks loaded with live and practice bombs and the heavy, cylindrical tanks used to carry napalm, that terrible jellied gasoline that sears and burns with unbelievable ferocity.

And during this time there was angered talk in the bars where the young Air Force pilots gathered and in the wardrooms of the aircraft carriers prowling the waters of the China Sea. Radar operators stationed along the 17th Parallel had reported increasing jet fighter activity in the sky high above North Vietnam. The pilots wondered why they were not allowed to test their immortality in combat. The MIGs seemed to taunt them as they waited for the order to scramble.

So the days wore on and in the muggy heat tempers frayed and the sense of futility gathered and expanded like the hot air within a balloon until all of South Vietnam was seething with a silent suffocation. The peasants found themselves torn between fear of their government and fear of the raiders who came quietly in the night. They cursed both sides. The soldiers cursed their superiors because of futile forays into paddies and jungles where the enemy was only a fleeting shadow and then was gone. The superiors cursed the generals and the politicians, which is what most military officers do when they cannot find an answer for a thing themselves.

For three weeks Dan Belden waited for a turn in the weather. Each morning he watched the sky, hoping for a sign of a weather front, a sanguine report from a pilot returning after a training flight in one of the eight Skyraiders that now lined the parking apron.

But the weather, obstinate bitch that she ever was, refused to turn. Bright and cloudless days with only slight overcasts at intervals. So Belden shrugged and continued the work of shaping a squadron from the human ingredients which had come into his hands from all corners of the world.

From dawn till dusk the Skyraiders flew, and then on into the night. The soldiers General Pham had sent to set up a perimeter around the Morlaix plantation watched with admiring eyes the crazy Americans who flew off into the distance with such monotonous regularity and with such apparent dedication.

Sometimes, high above their fortifications, the soldiers could watch two Skyraiders twisting and weaving, climbing and diving, turning in circles so tight that slight contrails whipped from the wingtips, the engines protesting as the planes were thrown into every conceivable maneuver while the pilots practiced the most basic fundamental of the fighter pilot's trade—the dogfight.

Of course it was preposterous to assume that any of them would dogfight in a Skyraider. The AD was made for bombing, not defying laws of aerodynamics in the scramble of a melee. But after a man has been flying transport planes or lumbering freight carriers, he has forgotten some of the tricks of remaining alive in the sky. He must renourish his instinctive reactions and he must become acclimated again to hanging upside down on his seat belt; he must learn again the art of flying by the seat of his pants so that, when the chips are down and the guns are spewing live ammunition, he will not have to pause in the fight to confirm where he is, what he is doing, and in what attitude his airplane flies. He must feel all this in a split second and react accordingly, throwing the stick correctly even as he retards or advances the throttle and eases pressure on the rudder, while at the same time striving to bring the pip on his gunsight into proper alignment on the enemy plane. All these things must be accomplished in the time of a heartbeat if he is to remain alive to fight another day. So, whether or not the Skyraider can survive in a dogfight, it nevertheless affords a much better means of practicing the trade than sitting on the ground with a book that relates how other men have done it.

A few miles from the plantation large white circles had been painted on the ground. Continually the Skyraiders peeled over and came down in screaming dives or in flatter glides and dropped their water-filled practice bombs or napalm drops.

Farther south, over the water area where the delta fell off into the sea, the planes would make their gunnery runs against a towed target banner. Again, the Skyraider with its minimal speed and lack of maneuverability could not in any way approximate the gunnery runs of a jet fighter. But the eye must become accustomed again to the target in the gunsight and must learn again to measure the distance remaining between the gun and the target as the plane hurtles in and closes the range until the finger tightens on the trigger. The mind must become reacquainted with the effect of the g-forces as the stick is pulled back and the body presses down into the seat and the blood is squeezed from the brain, leaving only a grayish, filmy curtain before the eyes.

In the huge main house of the plantation the pilots poured over the handbooks of the F8 Crusader until late in the night. There were manuals, too, on the art of subsisting in the jungle, the myriad ways in which a man can make his environment less deadly. Escape routes were traced in case luck ran thin over enemy-held territory. But, at the bottom of it all, Belden sought the first signs of squadron integrity, which come only with a complete confidence in ability, and with the respect finally accorded by one man to all the other men with whom he will fly and fight in the sky.

Belden's days became more enjoyable when Lori, airily spurning her father's denials, moved to the plantation and set herself up as house-mother to fourteen hard-bitten, cynical fighter pilots. When Belden protested the danger, she reminded him aloofly that the plantation was *her* home and that he was merely a guest there.

And then one day the word came.

Belden was standing at a window in his office, a barren room in an abandoned barracks-type building carefully camouflaged under the trees adjacent to the landing area. He was scanning the list of men who had answered his call from every direction on earth, and he smiled as their names brought to his mind other places and years when all of them were younger. Shonnard and Dugan, who had scoured Korean skies with a laughing abandon that had made them both aces before they were twenty-three years old. MacGregor Kilpatrick and Don Corey, who had led fighter squadrons from the decks of the carriers in the freezing winter off Hungnam and Hamhung. Stoney Wildman and Bob Thayer and Lou Knight, who had won glory at Truk and Iwo Jima and Okinawa in World War II. They had gone on together and tried the crop-dusting game, and with magnificent unconcern had lost everything, and so had turned to the wild flying in the Texas oil fields. Now at last they were back where they had started, and if they should finish the journey here, it would be all right with them. Sam Dewall, that lean, quiet Texan who, trying to make a dead-stick landing at night in a charter DC-3, had smashed into a treetop and so killed nine passengers, one of whom had been his wife. Sam didn't smile much any more, but his skill in the air had not lessened. And those two close friends of more years than Belden cared to remember, Sid Carpenter and Del Crandon, who had left behind the luxury of a successful flying school to learn if what they had once been had gone away from them forever. Ten men had answered Belden's summons and he nodded with satisfaction. He could not have been more pleased with the men with whom he would challenge the odds in this sky they had all come to investigate.

Now a voice sounded over the radio receiver set up in a corner of the room. Belden crossed quickly to it.

"Viceroy from Royalty." It was General Pham's voice. The General had installed the radio at Belden's request, to afford a direct line from the field to headquarters in Saigon.

Belden spoke into the mike. "Viceroy here. Go ahead."

"Dan," General Pham said, "there is a friend of yours here with news I believe will delight you."

Dusane's voice grumbled over the radio. "Where the hell did you dig up a call sign like Viceroy?"

Belden chuckled. "I stole it from you. Twenty years ago."

"I remember," Dusane said. "Listen, Dan. My weather people report a front moving down fast from the northwest. Nothing big, but a lot of low stratus with rain and mist. Sounds like it might be what you wanted."

A smile creased Belden's face as he looked across the room at Bates, leaning back in a chair with his feet perched on the desk.

"Where is she now?"

"She passed the Burma-Laotian border last night. Moving this way and spreading out a bit into Thailand."

"How bad can we expect it?" Belden's voice held a note of exuberance.

"Christ!" Dusane grunted. "How bad do you want it? It's down on the deck. Rain and drizzle and mist and any other kind of crap you can think of. Visibility ought to be about two feet. That satisfy you?"

"Ask General Pham if his men are ready to go to Lao Bao and Ban Me Thuot."

"You sound like you're throwing up. Hold on one."

Belden grinned at Bates and held up a thumb in a victory sign.

"Dan"—General Pham's voice came over—"we have done even better. The men are at Ban Me Thuot and we have taken high ground adjacent to the Laotian border near Lao Bao. Understand this clearly, Dan. The enemy base is *exactly* twenty miles from the homer site on a direct course of two-six-five. I say again. Two . . . six . . . five. We estimated the distance from our own aerial reconnaissance and from Admiral Dusane's high-altitude photographs. You can be sure of it. In addition, there will be another homer in the mountains west of Tam Ky. You should pick it up forty-five minutes out of Ban Me Thuot. Do you have that?"

"I sure as hell do. Thanks, General."

"Dan." It was Dusane's voice again. "What's your zero hour?"

"Will we be socked in tomorrow at first light?"

"Should be. The whole area ought to be zero zero."

"Then we'll launch at 0400. It's a hell of a long flight."

"How many planes?"

"All eight," Belden said. "Smoke, you and General Pham make a big thing out of grounding all aircraft. I want the newspaper guys to know that everything is on the ground. I don't want *one goddam plane* flying tomorrow."

"We've already attended to that," Dusane said. "You talk to me like I'm an ensign instead of three stars."

"Well," Belden said with a laugh, "after tomorrow you just may be an ensign again."

"I'll be talking to the Old Man tonight," Dusane said.

"Tell him to hold his breath," Belden said.

"Will do. And Dan"—there was a slight pause—"good luck, old friend."

Belden replaced the mike and turned to Bates.

"Break out the maps, Batesy," he said quietly. "Alert O'Toole to load bombs and napalm. Full ammo. All pilots in the ready room at 0200. Only eight will fly, but I want them all there."

"I'll attend to it all," Bates said.

He got to his feet lazily and had started for the door when Belden's voice stopped him: "Batesy."

Bates turned back and held Belden in a grave glance. "Yeah, Dan?" There was no humor in his voice now.

Belden started to speak, then hesitated. Finally he merely said, "I'm glad we're together on this one, Batesy."

A slow grin came over Bates's solemn features. He nodded and said, "Better get some sleep, Dan; 0200 comes mighty early."

After Bates had gone, Belden turned to the window and looked out at the night sky. He felt the stir of excitement in his guts again and suddenly the night air smelled good to him. He glanced at his watch: 1930—7:30 P.M.

Well, he thought, it will be time soon for another mission. No great fight here, no glory road to travel, just a sneak attack on a lousy base across the Laotian border. But it's something that has to be done. And it has to be done by eight guys who have come across the world to give it a fling. Christ, I wish to hell those faint-hearted bastards back home could be here to see what some Americans are really like. Well, we'll carry the fight for them and I hope to God they get off their dead asses and realize what is needed over here.

From out on the flight line he could hear O'Toole's voice intoning orders, and shortly thereafter there was the stutter of starting engines as the planes were turned up for engine checks. A few minutes later the last engine choked into silence and O'Toole's voice bawled for the gas truck for final fueling.

Belden finished his cigarette and flipped it through the open window. Well—he sighed to himself—it's time to hit the sack. The ball opens in a few hours and who would dance with a man with pouchy eyes?

At 0200 the ready room was a scene of subdued anticipation. Men sat relaxed in heavy leather chairs and sipped coffee as their eyes studied the maps on the wall and the information chalked on the blackboard at the front of the room. When they spoke, they did so in low voices, their eyes revealing nothing.

On the walls hung the flight gear and the gaily colored hard helmets with the radiophones attached. Oxygen masks hung by the gunbelts and parachute back-packs were spread over empty chairs. An

112

occasional voice spoke unemotionally as the pilots watched Bates write on the blackboard.

"That weather really socked in during the night."

"Christ. I nearly busted my ass walking over here."

"Somebody will have to lead us out to the runway."

"What runway?"

A voice chuckled. "O'Toole is putting lanterns out for take-off."

"What if we can't see the lanterns?"

"Take off on your directional gyro."

"Jesus."

Bates smiled as he listened to the voices. In the area on the blackboard lined off for weather information he wrote: Visibility horseshit, wind 195, 10 knots, mist and drizzle. In the area set aside for flight components he wrote: Flight leader, Belden, then added the names of the other seven pilots who would fly the mission—Kilpatrick, Bates, Corey. Second division, Anders, Wildman, Hawkins, Dewall.

"God damn it, Batesy. What about me?" Dugan complained. The others who would remain behind chimed in with various remarks of displeasure. Bates faced them with a spurious solemnity.

"It seems," he said, "we have an overabundance of heroes this morning. All of you are too old to be heroes. Do you all have a death wish?"

They looked toward the door as Belden appeared and walked to the front of the room.

"All right, guys," Belden said. "We will go over the flight plan for the five hundredth time. It may bore you, but it may also save your lives. I promised your mothers I'd bring you all home safely, so please bear with me."

The aircraft, Belden told them, were loaded with napalm and 500-pound demolition bombs. The flight would be made under strict radio silence unless an emergency arose in which case a special high-frequency channel had been installed in the airplanes.

Take-off would be at 0400 and once airborne the vector would be 045 degrees until they picked up the homing beacon at Ban Me Thout, a leg of the flight that should take approximately forty-seven minutes at an air speed of 180 knots indicated. After passing the beacon, they would fly due north for sixty-seven minutes, at which time

113

they should pass the radio beam at Tam Ky. Then a vector of 300 degrees for fifty minutes and they would pass the homer near Lao Bao.

"Now here," Belden said, "is where we make points. As soon as the direction-finding needles swing, we start timing. We fly for *exactly* six minutes and forty-five seconds on a heading of *exactly* two hundred and sixty-five degrees. At that time I will issue one order—bombs away—at which time you gentlemen will bang every armament switch in your cockpits and shitcan the entire load. I estimate it will take us twenty seconds to cross the area of the base, so if we are at all lucky, our stuff should hit somewhere in the breadbasket. They have an ammo dump somewhere in that base, and if we hit the damn thing, I will donate to every man in this squadron a fifth of the best booze in Morlaix's liquor locker. They also have a gasoline dump they use to refuel trucks they capture from our people and it would be nice to cream that too."

"Dan." Hawkins held up a hand. "What about Red radar along the border?"

"Well," said Belden, "I'll tell you. We'll go in at a reasonable altitude because we won't be able to see a goddam thing, so maybe they'll pick us up. I don't think they have radar-controlled guns up there, but if they do, then I suggest you all make out your wills."

"How about getting back here?" Bates asked. "It won't be any easier than getting out."

"There's a homer here. I don't have to tell you how to use a homer. Hit the homer and fly three minutes on a reversal course. Make a procedure turn and come back in on a heading of one hundred and eighty-five. The field is two minutes from the homer at one hundred knots indicated air speed. For a man of your vast experience, Batesy, it should prove a simple matter."

"So is walking on water when you learn how," Bates grumbled.

"The arresting wires are in place, so we should have no trouble getting on the deck," Belden added. "This is due, of course, to my exceptional foresight."

"One thing, Dan," Anders said. "If the weather lifts and the MIGs come down, have you any suggestions for such a contingency? I ask this only because, by your own admission, you are so much smarter than the rest of us dumb bastards in here tonight."

"If such a situation arises," Belden said, "I suggest that all of you start to pray. Incidentally, do you want to live forever?"

"I have considered it," Bates admitted judiciously. "The prospect has its attractions."

And now, as the hands of the clock set high on the wall moved slowly toward the appointed hour, they talked in quiet voices of other mornings like this and other friends who had moved away from them, victims of the inexorable odds of the business they had chosen.

And so they waited.

And Storm Ryerson waited too. He sat in the living room of Ralph Yeager's suite in the Mayflower Hotel and twisted his hands nervously as he consulted his watch.

"It's about that time, Ralph," he said to Yeager. "I feel as nervous as a kid going into his first whorehouse."

Yeager nodded. "I talked with the President this morning. Officially, he claims to know nothing about this."

"And unofficially?"

"He's as nervous as you are. He doesn't have any more idea than we do what the outcome of this will be."

"Whatever it is," Ryerson stated, "it can't be any worse than the way things stand now. The President is aware of the intelligence reports on the Chinese move next year. Sooner or later, regardless of the political consequences, he'll have to provide the massive intervention we're going to need. Christ, I wouldn't want to be in his shoes."

"Maybe not in yours either," Yeager said dryly.

"Ralph, I didn't tell the President one thing. I should have, I suppose, but I thought I'd wait and blame it on the results of Dan's mission."

"What the hell are you talking about?" Yeager was plainly puzzled.

Ryerson grinned broadly. "General Pham is going to move north across the Parallel within forty-eight hours."

"What?" Yeager was disbelieving.

"That's right. He's going to carry the fight north."

"Good God, Storm. He'll be massacred."

"He won't move far. Just across the Parallel and he'll hold a line just within North Vietnam." Ryerson's voice was eager. "Don't you see, Ralph? This, together with Belden's job, is exactly what we want."

Yeager shook his head. "What does Pham do after he gets north of the Parallel? He's wide open for annihilation."

"He'll wait and see what the Chinamen do. If they move troops into North Vietnam—and so far nobody expects them to—then Pham will hold where he is and let them come to him. If they don't come, he may try to push toward Hanoi. Whatever he does, nobody will be able to ignore it, anyway. *Something* has got to happen and that's what we want."

"You're starting a new war, Storm."

"The hell I am. I'm trying to see we don't lose this one."

"You really think we've got another Korea, don't you?" Yeager's voice displayed neither approval nor disapproval.

"I sure as hell do," Ryerson stated positively. "That's exactly what I think we've got. I don't like it any better than you do, but we're stuck with it. The only thing is, if we don't do something, we're liable to end up with a lot worse situation than Korea ever was. We're liable to get our asses shoved right out of Vietnam and into the ocean."

"Who else knows about Pham?"

"Me. You. Belden."

Yeager let his breath whistle softly past his teeth. "Well, if I go down, at least I'm going down in good company."

"It won't come to that, Ralph," Ryerson said. "So Pham moves north a little way. We don't like it, but what can we do about it? There's no one else to take Pham's place right now. And Pham knows he has to do something or his own people will throw him out, stand him against a wall, exile him. He really hasn't a hell of a choice in this matter."

"Thank God I can go back to my oil wells." Yeager smiled. He lifted his glass. "To success, Storm. And the men who are trying to buy it for us."

Ryerson smiled back. "I'll make reservations for us at the Old Sailors' Home."

Lori stood silently in the darkened hallway and watched Belden shut the door to his room.

"Dan." She spoke very softly.

He saw her move toward him, a dim figure in a night robe, her hair pulled back severely and her face pale in the gloom.

"It's an early hour for young ladies to be up," he said.

"I couldn't sleep. You knew I wouldn't."

"It's not a good morning for sleeping," he said equably.

There were things she wanted to say, her heart cried them, but she knew they would be left unsaid. He stood before her, tall and strong in the darkness and she heard the soft sound of his laughter.

"You're happy," she said in amazement. "At a time like this you're laughing."

"Yes," he said. "I'm happy. I feel like a kid again."

"Why? Because you're going out tonight to do something that kids are supposed to do?" There was anger in her voice. "Because you're flying out to take chances that kids are supposed to take? Does that make you happy, Dan? Does that really make you happy?" Tears stung her eyes and her voice broke.

"Here now," he whispered. "Take it easy. I understand."

"Do you?" she sobbed. "Do you really understand? I wish you did."

"This is a thing beyond you, Lori. It's a thing I have to do."

"Of course you do. Of course." She stamped her foot. "Damn you, Dan Belden. Go on out and fly your silly airplanes in the dark and rain. Be a hero and feel young again."

She turned and Belden heard her sob. Then her door slammed shut and he stood a long moment in the darkness. Why, he wondered, in forty years have I learned not one damn thing about women?

Chapter VIII

NOVEMBER
1964

At 0345 Belden faced his pilots in the ready room. There was no exuberance here such as characterized the ready rooms of the aircraft carriers. The men in this room had all been down the long trail and there was no more youthful jubilation left in them. Only a dry and arrogant certainty that no men living could do their job quite as well as they. In the hard-boned faces there was only a wry acknowledgment that they were all growing old in their trade.

All Belden said was, "It's time to go, guys."

No words. Merely the nodding of heads. No smiles. No jokes. Just the pat on the shoulder or a hard handclasp. Perhaps the memory of a hundred other times like this. Maybe "General Quarters" sounded in their minds.

It was pitch-black outside and they could feel the mist on their faces as they walked toward the dark silhouettes standing aligned and waiting. Then one by one they climbed into the cockpits. Adjust the seat and slip the shoulder straps over and into the seat-belt buckle. Make certain the rudder pedals are satisfactorily adjusted because you are going to be sitting in this tiny seat for well over five hours.

In his cockpit Belden flipped his primer switch several times. He saw the dim figure of O'Toole standing by his port wing, a fire extinguisher ready in his hand. O'Toole raised a hand with a thumbs-up, signaling all was ready for the start. Belden nodded and flipped the starter switch and manipulated the mixture controls to auto lean and then to auto rich. The great engine stuttered twice, then caught, and the flames shot back along the fuselage from the exhaust stacks. O'Toole unplugged the auxiliary starting unit and moved on to the next plane as Belden felt his plane shudder slightly under the force of the huge, spinning metal blade. He studied the phosphorescent dials staring at him from the instrument panel. Fuel and oil pressure, cylinder-head temperature; uncage the artificial horizon because on this hop you will never see the ground and that tiny instrument will be of paramount importance. Now plug the radio connection into your headset and close the cockpit canopy because the rain and mist are running down into your eyes. Belden looked back over his shoulder and saw the exhaust flames of the other planes streaking the darkness of the night. He stepped hard on the brakes and ran the throttle all the way to the stop. The great engine answered with a mighty roar and the plane strained against the brake pressure. Belden pulled the throttle back until the RPM gauge indicated 2,000 revolutions and then he flipped his magneto switches, checking for proper magneto operation. There was a slight reduction in RPMs as each magneto assumed the full load for a brief moment. Then the switch was returned to "both" and Belden pulled the throttle back to the idle position. His hands manipulated deftly in the blackness of the cockpit and he set his control tabs to the proper setting for take-off with a full load. O'Toole had already removed the chocks, and now Belden advanced his throttle, moved out of the parking apron, and turned hard right to taxi to the take-off area. One by one the other planes moved out after him, their exhaust flames scarring brightly against the night.

Belden swung into position and through his windshield he could see the lanterns O'Toole had set out to mark a straight path down the cleared area. Since this was to be a formation take-off, Belden pulled a few feet down the runway to allow the other planes to assume their positions. Kilpatrick moved in tight on his right wing. On his left Bates was only three feet away and on Bates's left Corey was drawn in tight.

In weather as foul as this it would be impossible to effect a rendezvous after take-off, therefore Anders and his wingmen had assumed position on the number four man of Belden's division and now all eight planes were positioned for a single-formation launch.

As Belden slowly advanced his throttle, his plane inched forward in the darkness and his attention was focused on the line of lanterns ahead. The speed increased with more throttle added and now all eight planes were under full power, each flying tightly on the plane next to him. Their eyes were riveted on the wingtip lights of the plane they were flying on. Only Belden dropped his glance down to his instruments and noted his air-speed indicator. He eased back ever so lightly on the stick and the plane lifted off the ground. The others were with him all the way and now the hands reached down and flipped the landing-gear levers to the "Up" position, the throttles were retarded and the RPMs were set in accordance with climb configuration. Belden glanced at his watch. Off the deck at 0400. He looked over his shoulder and saw the other planes' exhaust flames stretched away from him in a stepped-down echelon. On his right wing, Kilpatrick hung in tight, a few feet away.

Belden turned to a heading of 045 degrees and settled back for the long flight to Ban Me Thuot.

Forty minutes later the first faint signal from the homer came through their radios. They were still in the thick weather and visibility was less than a hundred yards in the misty rain. Belden noted that his Automatic-Direction-Finder needle had not as yet responded to the radio signal.

Three minutes later the ADF needle quivered spasmodically and then jerked itself into a position pointing at the twelve-o'clock position on the dial. Belden was directly on course. The formation flew steadily in the smooth air.

At 0447 the ADF needle swung 180 degrees and now pointed at the six-o'clock position on the dial. They passed over Ban Me Thuot in the thick mist and turned due north for the second leg of their flight.

Sixty minutes later Belden heard the signal at Tam Ky. He flew in such a manner that the needle pointed to the three-o'clock position and thus he passed Tam Ky several miles to its left. The first signs of morning were evident now and he looked out at the formation and could see the other planes through the grayish haze of clouds in which they were flying. So far so good. Belden turned to a heading of

300 degrees. He took a computer from his flight-suit pant-leg pocket and quickly manipulated the dial, checking for the final time to insure that his air speed and distance from the homer near Lao Bao to the enemy base in Laos were correctly designed to result in a hit when they dropped their armament in the blind. He rolled a minute amount of back trim on his elevator control and began a gradual climb through the sky. They were over mountainous territory now and these clouds could very well be filled with rocks. He looked out and watched the other planes close in as their power settings were corrected for the climb. There was no sound other than that of the muted roar of the engines and the whistle of the wind outside cockpit canopies.

Eight men—Belden smiled to himself—sneaking in to bomb an enemy base at Laos. Eight guys on instruments in weather that even ducks wouldn't fly in, going in on a place they would never see. There should be a moral in this someplace, he thought, but I'm damned if I can make it out. He cracked the canopy open and let a breath of fresh air into the cockpit. His back muscles were cramped and he tried to stretch in the close confines and laughed as he realized it was impossible. He peered directly above him and noticed the lightening of the sky and the thinning of the mist. His altitude was 6,500 feet.

He flew with a light, delicate touch, maintaining control of his plane with tiny pressures of his fingers on the stick, always watching alertly the artificial-horizon dial and insuring that the wings of the miniature airplane were exactly level with the line on the dial which corresponded to the true horizon. He turned his head and grinned at Bates off his left wing and Bates responded with a half-salute and a brief flashing of teeth.

The formation droned steadily onward, eight sets of hands gentle and sure on the controls as the pilots placed all of their trust in the man leading them. Below them the mountainous jungle passed unseen in the murky weather.

Belden's watch read 0635 when he heard the first faint tone of the homer set up near the Laotian border. He looked out at Bates and motioned with his hand, indicating he was turning slightly to starboard. The entire echelon formation bent gently to the right and Belden watched the needle point slightly left of the twelve-o'clock position. He flew on and the needle dropped down toward the ten-o'clock position. Belden gestured with his hand again and they turned to the left and were now inbound for the homer site on a course of 265 degrees, the exact course they would fly past the homer and dead-on for the enemy sanctuary twenty miles within Laos.

Visibility had increased somewhat with the coming of daylight and the planes slid out and took a wider interval to allow for manipulation of controls and armament switches when the attack was made. The tone of the signal was louder now and Belden reached for his radio-volume control and dampened the tone to a soft "bleeping."

The mistiness had condensed into a spattering rain and their windshields revealed a flat, dull expanse of gray overcast. Belden turned his eyes back to his artificial horizon. His watch read 0640 when the ADF needle quivered and swung 180 degrees and they passed over the unseen homer below them. He eased forward on the stick and the formation went into a shallow glide, losing altitude slowly and maintaining a steady 180 knots air speed as the throttles were inched back to accommodate this flatter angle of attack. His eyes darted restlessly around his instrument panel. He must fly *exactly* six minutes and forty-five seconds on this heading of 265 degrees, and then, all elements of fortune being equal, he would pickle off his armament and the load would fall through the sky and hit directly on the supply base 2,000 feet below.

The other planes took an even greater interval, and moved forward until they were almost flying in a line abreast of Belden. The smoothness of the flying was gone now as the pilots moved about in the cockpits, arming their bombs and making ready for the attack. Belden checked his altitude again—1,800 feet—then leveled off and pushed on an inch or two of throttle to hold steady at 180 knots.

Below them on the ground puzzled eyes swept the murk and men wondered who might be airborne in weather such as this. Probably someone lost up there in the thick soup.

Belden watched the second hand on his clock move toward the appointed moment. He checked his arming switches with a fleeting glance. He scanned his directional gyro and his compass and they held true on 265.

Then the second hand on his clock touched forty-five seconds. He spoke into his radio mike: "Foray Leader. Bombs away."

That was all. From the undersides of the eight aircraft the deadly bombs dropped away almost reluctantly, as the pilots' hands pickled them off in succession. The planes flew steadily on course and the falling armament was necessarily spread across the terrain below as the planes sped by at three miles per minute. Last to fall were the cigar-shaped napalm tanks with the terrible jellied gasoline. They tumbled through the sky without grace, ungainly and wicked with their loads of fiery death.

Belden had started his reversal turn when the first repercussions came to him. As first there was only a slight jarring as the bombs hit somewhere below. He was in a tight 45-degree bank when one of the bombs hit the ammunition dump. The resulting concussion almost threw Belden's plane on its back and then the dim murk was lit by an eerie glow that turned the rainy sky into a multicolored spectrum. A second blast followed and Belden was thrown upward and his head hit against the cockpit canopy. He cursed silently and fought to bring his plane back under control.

There was a third blast and below them an amber glow seemed to rise and ebb and rise again. Belden looked off his port wing and saw Sam Dewall in the last plane wildly trying to counter the extreme buffeting. He bit off a curse as he saw that a section of Dewall's tail section had been torn away.

Screw radio silence, he thought. "Sam, this is Dan. Are you in trouble?"

In his cockpit, Sam Dewall had no time to answer that query. He had felt something hit his tail section and immediately thereafter his plane had started to buffet. God damn it, he thought, we must have been closer to the deck than we realized. Debris must have flown up and got me in the ass end. He moved his stick tentatively, but the buffeting continued.

The formation was turning now and Dewall, on the outside of the turn, started to slide under to shorten his radius of turn. He looked above him and saw the underside of Hawkins' plane move slowly across his windshield and then he was almost under Wildman's plane, standing in the sky on his wingtip, his plane in a 40-degree bank.

At that moment the controls went slack in Dewall's hands. The pressure he was holding caused the stick to flap uselessly back into his lap and the nose of his airplane bucked up suddenly. With a hoarse shout he jammed the throttle forward, a maneuver that might have thrown his plane away from the rest of the formation and out into the clear. But Sam Dewall had forgotten in his moment of crisis that Wildman's plane was directly above him.

With the added throttle Dewall moved forward several feet and climbed just enough in the sky so that his cockpit canopy came up under the propeller of Wildman's plane. With a horrified clarity, Dewall saw what had happened and chopped his throttle all the way back to the idle position.

But it was too late.

Aware of the change of air pressure as Dewall's aircraft hung beneath his plane, Wildman, puzzled momentarily, exerted a small bit of back pressure on his stick, rising six feet in the turn. This maneuver saved Wildman's life, but it did not do the same for Sam Dewall. As Wildman's plane rose, Dewall skidded under him and forward just far enough so that the spinning metal slab of Wildman's propeller chopped down viciously into his cockpit canopy. Dewall had perhaps a split second in which to regret his mistake, then the great metal blade smashed the glass of the canopy and thudded into Dewall's head even as Wildman's back pressure pulled the two aircraft apart.

Belden heard Wildman's hoarse shout over the air: "Jesus Christ. I hit something."

Belden straightened out of his turn and looked back to see the shattered canopy of Dewall's plane sliding down out of sight into the rainy mist.

"Sam," Belden shouted. "Sam."

There was no answer. Sam Dewall was dead at the controls as his plane slowly rolled over on its back. The heavy nose fell through the invisible horizon and the Skyraider went into a vertical dive that continued all the way to the ground.

Wildman had pulled out to one side and was testing his controls, deciding how badly he had been damaged. His eyes flicked to his RPM gauge and saw the needle holding steady at 2,000 RPM, even though he could hear clearly the roughness of the laboring engine.

"You hurt bad?" Belden's voice called.

"Wait one," Wildman replied.

The other planes moved in on Belden, allowing Wildman a little extra room in the sky as he checked out his engine function. Slowly he ran his throttle forward to the stop, watching carefully his RPM gauge and his manifold-pressure indicator. Then he retarded the throttle all the way and finally moved it back into cruise configuration and called Belden on the radio.

"This is Stoney. I've got a rough engine, but she checks out okay. My prop took him in the canopy." There was a dismal knowledge in Wildman's voice.

Now Anders spoke across the sky. "Any chance he made it?"

"No," Belden answered slowly. "He didn't make it. The prop took the canopy and"—he hesitated a moment—"everything else with it."

They were silent then, the seven planes holding tight formation as they flew homeward. The tally was added in each mind and all of them would live with it on the long flight back to the base. They had had another encounter with the inexorable odds of their business and none of them felt more than a bitterness that a friend had to die. It was something all of them lived with and, in the final analysis, was there a more satisfactory way for a flier to die? Dewall knew his last split second of living as he sat in a cockpit, his hands on the familiar controls and his mind flashing over the problems confronting him. At the end there had been no last wail of despair, only a remorse that he was dying due to a freak accident and perhaps also to a slight manipulation of the throttle that had not served its purpose and so had contributed to killing him.

The formation passed the homer at Lao Bao and took up a heading of 120 degrees magnetic.

As Belden and his flight headed toward the Tam Ky homer, Colonel Lee Cheng flew a routine patrol at 45,000 feet just south of the city of Hanoi. They were far above the weather and at that altitude the sun bounced brightly off the wings of the eight MIG fighters as they circled lazily on an indoctrination hop. Lee had received new pilots in his command and he was breaking them in on the new MIGs. They had come down from Lungchou as far south as Hanoi, and only now did the inclement weather show any signs of breaking. To Lee's west there was a single crack in the overcast and looking down he could see the faint outline of a mountain crest. To his south, stretching toward the 17th Parallel, the entire sky sloped downward in a flat expanse of overcast until, in the far distance, he could see a single clear area about fifteen miles wide splitting the sameness of the leaden blanket of cloud. He loosened his shoulder straps slightly and slid down in the seat, stretching his legs before him with a sigh. He was considering leading his fledgling pilots through a tail chase to test their acrobatic proficiency when a voice crackled in his earphones.

"Eagle Leader. This is Hanoi radio." There was an urgency in the voice.

"This is Eagle Leader," Lee replied.

As he spoke, Lee gestured with his right hand, indicating to his wingmen to tighten up the formation. The MIGs slid swiftly into line, tucking in tight so that the formation assumed a taut appearance, and Lee held them in a bank toward the south.

"This is Hanoi radio. A raid has been carried out by enemy planes on the base west of Lao Bao in Laotian territory. Heavy damage has been inflicted."

Lee was dubious. "In this weather? Check your reports, Hanoi."

The voice repeated. "The base was attacked by Skyraider aircraft. One of them crashed east of the base on withdrawal. They attacked in zero zero weather conditions."

Lee straightened on a due south heading. "Do you have orders for me?"

"No, sir," the radio operator replied. "We just received word ourselves."

"I will take station at forty-five thousand feet north of the Parallel. Alert our radar stations."

Lee nodded his head forward emphatically, signaling his pilots to add throttle.

The voice from Hanoi came to him again: "Eagle Leader. We have an early report from a radar station on the border. Unidentified blips moving southeast from Lao Bao at six thousand feet. The weather is zero zero."

Lee replied, "This is Eagle Leader switching to radar station frequency."

He looked back and saw his formation bunched tightly and now he called, "Afterburner."

The hands flipped the throttles outward on the quadrants and the great engines roared into afterburner as the MIGs flashed southward toward the 17th Parallel.

Belden could see the weather front lessening in intensity as he flew southeast. The sky above him was lighter now as the sun strove to pierce the rainy overcast through which they had been flying since 0400. Despite the loss of Dewall, he knew the job had gone well this morning. Lady Luck had smiled on the rest of them, even if she had neglected Sam Dewall. He looked down to consult the map spread out on his lap.

He knew he might cut off a considerable distance on the return trip if he bore more to the southeastward and slid along the edge of the Laotian-South Vietnam border. But to do so he would necessarily fly too far westward to pick up the homer at Tam Ky and thus the long leg from his present position to Ben Me Thuot would have to be flown in the blind and over rugged, treacherous territory. He decided to adhere to his original flight plan.

Thirty minutes after Belden had passed over the Lao Bao homer, homeward bound, he was ninety miles from the border and just south and west of Hué. At this point his formation flew out of the overcast and into brilliant sunlight. Belden ascertained immediately that this was only a single break in the front and estimated the distance to the wall of cloud at the other end of the clearing to be about eighteen miles. Well, he thought, we can afford to fly in the clear for six minutes. He inched his throttle forward because even six minutes in the clear on a mission such as Belden's was six minutes too long.

As the Skyraiders burst into the clear weather, a radar operator north of the Parallel picked them up on his scope. He called Colonel Lee, who had covered the two hundred and ninety miles from Hanoi south to the border in exactly nineteen minutes.

"Eagle from Watchdog. The enemy approaches one hundred and fifty degrees from you. Altitude six thousand feet on course one hundred and twenty degrees."

Lee flew due east along his own side of the border, his eyes scouring the sky below him and to the south. If the enemy stayed in the cloud formation, he would never find them. His only chance lay in that their course would bring them into the clear area, if only briefly. From this altitude Lee could see a hundred miles in any direction. He decided he would risk official censure and move a little way south of the 17th Parallel. He headed in the direction of the clear area of the sky, losing altitude as he came down to 25,000 feet. He was still well above the top of the weather front.

Belden was halfway across the clear space and might well have made it into the cloud formation ahead without Lee ever having spotted him had not Wildman's engine taken this exact moment to react in anger. Wildman spit out a curse as the engine started to vibrate in its mountings and a heavy black pouring of smoke erupted from the cowling. He pulled his throttle back and called on his radio: "This goddam thing has a bellyache, Dan."

Wildman's plane lost several hundred feet of altitude as he tried to put out the fire in his engine.

It was the pouring of black smoke that Colonel Lee saw against the grayish background of overcast cloud. Had it not been for the smoke, he would never have seen Dan Belden's formation. As it was, his eyes were passing lightly, fleetingly, over the entire expanse of southern sky when he saw Wildman's plane and then all the rest of the Skyraiders.

He did not waste a moment. He was already in a steep dive when he called to his flight: "This is Eagle Leader. In the clear area to the south. Seven enemy planes. One smoking. Initiate attack and select targets of opportunity."

Lee knew well the Skyraiders would be away from him if they could make it to the cloud sanctuary only a few miles ahead of them.

Belden and Bates simultaneously spotted the contrails of the MIGs. Lee was coming down from behind and to one side—from the seven-o'clock position on Belden—and as Belden watched in his rearview mirror, he could see the slat of the dive brakes emerge from the undersides of the MIGs as they sought to slow down for the kill on the slower Skyraiders.

Belden had a decision to make and he had to make it in the tenth part of a second. He had two choices. He could whip around in a reversal turn and present the guns of his flight to the MIGs, or he could barrel straight ahead for the sanctuary of cloud just a short distance in front of him. He was unconscious of it, but past decisions crowded into his mind and were instantly sorted out and discarded. He held steady on course for the cloud bank. If they turned back into the MIGs, they might never make it to sanctuary. They might all go down in flames under the MIG guns.

"Stoney," Belden called, "can you make the clouds?"

"Six of one, half a dozen of the other. I don't know."

Belden saw the other Skyraiders under full power ranging out in a line from him. Slightly behind was Wildman's plane, keeping up, but still trailing the black smoke.

Lee came down and level and into extreme range. He knew he had only seconds left. He raised his nose and the pip of his gunsight was thirty miles above the lead plane in the Skyraider formation when his finger squeezed the trigger and his shells arced across the intervening sky.

"Full balls, guys," Belden spoke calmly into his mike. "We're almost there."

"God damn it." Bates's voice was cheerful. "I hate to run from these bastards."

"There'll be another day," Belden replied. The first tracings of mist appeared on his windshield as he approached the cloud sanctuary. Belden turned his head and saw the tracers from the MIG guns lacing the sky and falling away below him.

Then Wildman spoke unemotionally in a flat voice. "This bastard just froze on me."

Three hundred feet below Belden, Wildman's plane glided into the mist of the front, its propeller frozen still, a ludicrous metal slab appearing totally out of place on the snout of the Skyraider.

Lee ranged up, still holding his trigger down, and then turned sharply away as the last Skyraider disappeared into the front. There was no conceivable advantage to be gained from following into the inclement weather. Before Wildman's plane had entered the front, Lee had seen the propeller freeze and he knew that, if nothing else, he had at least caused the Skyraider to exert full military power in its flight and had thus indirectly been the cause of the plane's destruction. Because it was a certainty that no emergency landing could be effected over the mountainous terrain looming below in the encovering weather. He took up a northerly heading as his flight joined up again, pointing his nose skyward and roaring up above into the bright sunlight.

Belden was on instruments as he called Wildman. "Stoney. Bail out. I repeat. You're over friendly territory. Hit the silk."

The other pilots could hear a chuckle in Wildman's voice. "I find little cause for gaiety in this situation. I am leaving now. Keep your fingers crossed."

There was silence again and Belden said, "Move in tight, gang. We're headed home." He banked gently to the right and flew on a southerly heading, waiting patiently now for the first signal from the Tam Ky homer beacon.

When Stoney Wildman had watched his propeller jerk to a stop, he had admitted to himself that he had known ever since Lao Bao that his wounded engine could not withstand application of full military power for any length of time. And so he accepted the inevitable bail-out without undue trepidation. This was not the first time he had bailed out of a stricken airplane.

He calmly set about his preparations. First he checked his air speed and altitude—180 knots and 6,000 feet. He held the stick steady, maintaining that altitude as he unbuckled his seat belt, freeing it and the encumbering shoulder straps, which he shrugged aside. Then he cranked open his canopy and threw his helmet and radio connections out into the windstream. He checked again to ensure that his parachute leg straps and chest strap were all securely fastened. He made a slight tightening adjustment of his leg straps as he remembered the cautioning words of a long-forgotten instructor to the effect that loose leg straps might well de-ball a man when the chute jerked open.

Now Wildman put his plane into a shallow dive. He focused his attention on his altimeter and air-speed indicator as he realized that, without a functioning engine, his gyros would not function either. Then he pulled the stick back slightly and pointed his nose skyward in the dense weather. The air speed dropped off rapidly as his altimeter climbed. When the air-speed needle touched 120 knots, Wildman rolled the plane over on its back with a quick manipulation of the stick to the right hand side of the cockpit. He centered the stick when he judged himself to be upside down and then, with all the strength he could muster, he jammed the stick as far forward as it would go. The resulting aerodynamic reaction threw the inverted nose of the plane upward and hurled Wildman out of the cockpit with the force of six negative g's. He counted to four, very slowly, and then reached with his right hand and yanked the ripcord handle. He had time for one deep breath before he felt the first tentative bite of the straps and then the hard, neck-snapping jerk as the chute blossomed above him. He looked up and grinned at the billowing canopy spread over him and listened to the whistling sound his Skyraider made in the distance as it screamed down to destruction. He could hear the dull thunder of the blast when the plane hit and the gas tanks exploded. Then he sat back in the harness and waited for the ground to come up and meet him.

Captain Tran Minh and his guerrilla group had been on the trail since first light. They were on their way to the tiny village of Hon Bat in the high central mountain area of South Vietnam for the purpose of levying taxes in the form of provisions. Until late last night there had been a patrol of South Vietnamese infantry in the village, but Minh and his men had made a feint at another village four miles to the north. Now the South Vietnam troops had gone there and, when they returned, the Vietcong would have supplied themselves from the acquiescent villagers and would have disappeared into the wet jungle.

They were topping a small rise when they heard the whine of the diving Skyraider. Minh waited expectantly until he heard the distant sound of the crash. He thought it had come from directly ahead of him, so he called his men together and spoke quietly as he ordered them forward in a spread skirmish line at twenty-yard intervals. He placed himself at one end of the line and his second-in-command, Xuan Nonh, at the opposite end.

They moved forward silently, their rifles at the ready, their bare feet making only soft swishing sounds in the damp grass. Minh was anxious to find the pilot of this airplane because he had lost a certain amount of face when the Americans had published the picture of the two Skyraider pilots standing in the village waiting to be executed. His superiors had wasted a few words with Minh and he understood that his position with the command was precarious indeed. He and his group were bound for the southern plains area and a mission which had not yet been revealed to them. But the highly secret modus operandi indicated it was one of great importance. What a manner, he thought, to embark on this important mission. The capture of an enemy pilot would gain much face for him, would wipe away the disgrace of his censure and perhaps turn the blame for the execution of the two American fliers where it belonged—on Colonel Lee Cheng.

They slipped down a steep slope and started a slow climb up another crest. It was slow work, moving across this tortuous terrain. Minh shivered slightly in the cold rain and moved out another few yards until he could barely see the man on his left inching his way up the heavily tangled rise.

Stoney Wildman crouched in a thick clump of jungle grass and wiped the action of his .38 pistol with his handkerchief. He had been fighting this goddam jungle for an hour and had no idea whatsoever where the hell he was. He had landed in the branches of a small tree and it had taken only a few minutes' work with his knife to cut himself loose. He had dropped the few feet to the ground unhurt save for several scratches on his face where the tree branches had scraped him. Using the small compass attached to his parachute harness, he had made his way in a southeasterly direction.

He finished wiping the action of his gun and replaced it in his shoulder holster. He had started to move quietly out of his hiding place when he heard the sound of something moving through the jungle. He tensed, hardly daring to breathe and his hand went to his pistol again.

He waited in silence, his heart beating heavily, and took a deep breath to calm himself. He nestled back farther into the thicket and lay flat along the ground until only the top of his head was visible above the jungle growth.

He saw the man emerge about twenty-five yards away. The figure appeared suddenly out of the dense jungle and paused, the head cocked in an alert posture. Wildman cursed to himself as he saw the black cotton shirt and drawers and the floppy hat made of entwined reeds.

God damn it. A Vietcong.

He watched as the man moved slowly toward him. How many of them were there? Was he certain they were the enemy? Might they be only farmers? "Quit bullshitting yourself, Stoney boy," he said to himself. "That's the enemy out there and if you will remember, there was the picture of those two Navy guys getting clobbered in a clearing not so long ago. So you have a choice, Mr. Wildman. Give yourself up and take your chances, or give it all you've got and get away from these skinny bastards." Wildman slid his knife out of its scabbard and with the other hand withdrew his pistol. His legs tensed, ready to spring.

Captain Minh moved cautiously, alert to some unnamed danger. He could hear nothing in the jungle silence except the chirping of some small bird and the gentle sound of the rain on the jungle roof. He stopped and let his eyes pierce the dense growth ahead. He swept his glance around the perimeter before him, wondering if he should call to the man on his left who had moved ahead a short distance and whose quiet sounds were lost now under the soft patter of the rain on the foliage.

Wildman watched Minh from his cover. He had heard the sound of Minh's soldier passing farther over in the jungle and he decided to use his knife for this. Quietly, he slid his pistol back into the holster.

There was no fear in Stoney Wildman now, only a grim certainty of what he must do. The man paused for a moment, then moved toward Wildman again. He was only ten yards away now and Wildman could see the young face under the broad-brimmed hat.

For crissake, he's only a kid, Wildman thought.

He reached beside him on the ground and picked up a small broken branch.

Minh had moved to within five yards of Wildman when he heard the sound of something in the brush to his right. He turned quickly in that direction, his knees bending slightly and his gun coming to his shoulder.

Wildman had tossed the branch and had leaped almost simultaneously. Minh was half-turned away from him when Wildman's arm circled the thin neck and his knife flashed upward from behind and took Minh in the liver. Wildman felt the body jerk spasmodically and he moved his hand up and covered the enemy's mouth. He

133

wrenched the knife loose and struck again, driving upward with all his strength and twisting viciously as he felt the blade sink deep. He felt a gurgle against his palm and then suddenly a sharp pain as Minh sank his teeth into Wildman's hand. Instinctively Wildman jerked his hand away and a loud, dying groan escaped from Minh's lips, bubbling and frothing in a spray of blood.

The sound was still lingering on Minh's lips when Wildman slashed once across the thin throat and threw the body from him. He started to run into the heavy undergrowth in the direction opposite from that in which he had heard Minh's soldier move.

He had about fifteen feet to go when Xuan Nonh stepped from cover on the opposite side of the small clearing and fired twice with a U.S. .30-caliber carbine.

Wildman thought: Oh for shit's sake, as he felt the bullets slam into his back. He felt a dull ache and a sudden dizziness and he knew he was falling. His face pressed into the mud of the jungle floor and with a great effort he rolled over and fired his pistol. It seemed the pistol weighed a ton in his hand and his eyes were already dimming in death as the pain welled up into his throat and he choked on his own blood.

The last thing Wildman ever heard was the echo of his pistol shot reverberating in the fetid air.

Two hundred and fifty miles to the south, Belden and the returning members of the flight dropped out of the overcast and onto the landing area at the plantation. They bounced forcefully on the uneven strip and then their tail hooks caught the makeshift arresting wires and the planes screeched to a halt.

It was 0946 in the morning and they had been airborne, almost continually on instruments, for five hours and forty-six minutes.

Chapter
IX

Lori stood by her window at 0400 and watched the planes take off into the rain-driven night. She could see the flickering flames from the exhaust stacks and she stood motionless until the last of them had disappeared into the darkness. As she turned away, she felt a sudden, fierce loneliness and she shivered although the room was warm. She paced restlessly a few minutes and then she dressed hurriedly and went down the long flight of stairs and out into the wet night.

She drove the carryall through the black murk and parked outside the long barracks building that served as the flight operations center. She entered quietly, her hair wet and gleaming under the dim lamps burning above the entrance.

There was an utter silence all about her, the silence that comes to a great stadium at night when only the shouts of the ghosts are left. The other pilots had returned to the main house and she was alone in the building. Her footsteps echoed hollowly as she walked to the ready room. She paused at the door, trying to make herself believe she could hear the strong voices of the men who had flown off into the night. But there were no voices and she laughed at herself, feeling childishly defensive. She sank back in a seat and shut her eyes and pretended she could hear the sound of Belden's plane approaching from a distance.

She did not hear O'Toole open the ready room door and move

down the aisle to the coffee table at the far end of the room. When he rattled a cup and saucer, she opened her eyes and saw him pouring a cup of coffee. She watched him in silence, remembering the warmth in Belden's voice when he had told her about O'Toole and a war of twenty years ago. The rugged-looking man had spoken to Lori only once, but despite the somber face she had seen the eyes twinkle and instinctively she had liked O'Toole. He was wearing his battered Navy cap, denim trousers, and a worn flight jacket still sodden from the rain. He took a sip of his coffee and scalded his tongue.

"Sonofabitch!" he complained aloud. Lori chuckled and O'Toole, surprised, turned to her.

"Miss Morlaix. What are you doing down here?"

She shrugged. "I think you call it 'sweating it out'?" She spoke it as a question.

O'Toole nodded. "It is a thing we all do in this business." He raised his cup. "Coffee, miss?"

"Thank you."

He poured another cup and brought it to her and then sank tiredly into the seat beside her.

"It's a night," he said, "when even the birds walk."

"Did they have to go?" she asked. "Did they really have to go?"

He did not look at her, but studied the opposite wall with intense interest. Finally he said merely, "They had to go." He brought his glance around to her. "They always have to go. In this business it is an undeviating truth. The clock moves to an appointed hour and they have to go. Does that make sense, Miss Morlaix?"

"Not very much," she answered honestly.

"I suppose not," he said. "I rarely speak well when there is something I really want to say. Well, perhaps I've been around men like that too long. Thirty years is a long time."

"What was he like?" Lori asked.

O'Toole was puzzled for a moment. "Who?"

"Dan," Lori said. "When he was young."

"Like all the young ones," O'Toole said. "Immortal. Invulnerable. They're all that way when they're young. None of them think they can lose then. It's a gift they all get for a little while. It's taken away from them too soon."

"He didn't lose," she said. "He won't ever lose."

"We can hope so," O'Toole said. "But the gift has been taken away anyway. They all lost it years ago. They watched too many friends go down. That's the only way you lose the gift. You have to live and watch the friends go down."

She sipped her coffee and watched the strong profile staring ahead with a pensive soberness. Strangely, O'Toole's somber melancholy gave her spirits a lift and she felt a sudden warmth for this craggy man.

"I like you, Mr. O'Toole," she said impulsively.

His face softened under her words and, for the first time, she saw him smile broadly.

"That's kind of you, Miss Morlaix," he said. "I'll take your words with me wherever I go."

"And," said Lori, "I think I know what you mean about the gift they all have lost." When O'Toole said nothing, she asked, "But will he . . . they . . . be as good without it?"

"Perhaps better," O'Toole said in a thoughtful voice. He turned to face her. "I'll tell you something, Miss Morlaix. Do you know what we've got out there in those Skyraiders tonight? There are eight legends out there in the rain and the dark. Eight men whose names are known wherever flying men gather, wherever flying men meet or speak. You can't find a man who wears wings between here and Pensacola who doesn't know of them and where they've been and what they've done. They've written the book that other men fly by. They've spent their lives doing it and no one spends his life doing a thing without getting pretty good at it. So when the gift was taken from them, they were already past the point of no return. Instead they had something else—a skill and proficiency so finely sharpened that nothing could take it away. That's why they're better now perhaps than they were when they were young." He shook his head perplexedly. "I wish I could tell it better."

She smiled. "You tell it well enough, Mr. O'Toole."

He watched her eyes carefully. "You would ask me another question?"

"I would," she said.

"Well," O'Toole said, "it's a good night for questions."

"I think you already know," she said.

O'Toole lit a cigarette and examined the glowing tip of it before

137

he spoke. His eyes squinted and when he answered his voice was soft and musing, almost as though he were speaking to himself and she was not sitting next to him in the quiet ready room.

"I'm not your man, Miss Morlaix. I haven't seen Belden in nearly twenty years. Oh, I've heard of him along the way, heard the stories that all of them tell when they drink and remember. Sometimes I think most of their lives are spent in remembering." He took a deep drag on the cigarette and let the smoke trail gently from his mouth. "When he was young, he looked much as he does now. Not so hard, maybe. But the eyes were the same, and the quiet laughter in them. He was one of the few that truly heard the bugles in the sky. All of them say they do, but most of them are only pretending. When I knew him, we were both younger and he was an officer and I was enlisted, and so the barrier was there which is the way it has to be. But there is no barrier anywhere on a dark morning when you strap a man in a cockpit and he goes out to fight and perhaps to die. No barriers at all. So I came to know him better than most men merely in the few minutes I stood on the wing of his plane and wished him good luck. Because I could read his eyes then and at a time like that you come to know a man better than his wife ever will."

He paused and she asked, "Was he ever afraid?"

"The first time perhaps. Most of them are then. But it didn't last."

"Go on," she said. "What did you find in his eyes?"

"Like I said. Bugles in the sky, and more important than that, an acceptance of the inevitable."

"I'm not sure I know what you mean."

"There is a defeat for all of us, Miss Morlaix," O'Toole said. "It starts with our first breath. How many people"—he smiled briefly—"do you know who have lived forever? All of us put death out of our minds, but it is there nevertheless. Someday each and every one of us will lie under the cold ground, our eyes closed forever and our brains empty. No one can elude that. When a young man can see this and understand it and accept it, he becomes a little special. And whether he knows it or not, he has acquired a philosophy of life that in some cases stands him in very good stead. In the case of flying men it is a great good fortune."

"Who wants to live forever? Is that what you're saying?"

He touched her hand lightly. "We all do. It's only human. But to

138

realize we aren't going to, that is the thing. It could possibly lead to recklessness, which in Belden's case might have killed him long before this. Or it can lead to an absence of fear, which is the reason he is alive to fly out there tonight in this preposterous weather."

"You are making him sound indestructible. I like that."

"I didn't say that," O'Toole said, shaking his head. "There is one thing over which none of them have any control at all. It is their luck. When that runs out, nothing can save them. Nothing can save any man when his luck runs out. And one thing I have learned; no man makes his own luck. Some of them say they do, but it's a lie. The luck is there or it is not there. It's as simple as that."

"I want his to last forever."

He smiled at her. "What is your question that I haven't answered?"

She shook her head wordlessly.

He stuffed his cigarette out in the ash tray set into the arm rest of the chair. Well, O'Toole, he thought to himself, what do you tell the young lady? How do I tell her I have no answer for her? How do I tell her that to some men a knowledge comes with a certain time of life? At some precise time in their lives they realize that they have already lived more years than are left to them. They have passed the halfway point and it is downhill from there on in. When a man realizes he has fewer years left than he has already lived, it can do something to him, and what it does is not always pleasant to behold. I would bet that Belden will never change. But I am not in the betting business and so how do I answer this lovely girl sitting next to me tonight?

"You are in love with him, aren't you?"

She nodded.

"He is a very lucky man." He paused a moment. "Does he know?"

"He knew from the beginning." Watching her, O'Toole thought he had never seen such a desirable woman. "I guess I'm not very devious," she said with a smile.

"And Belden?"

"He's put up some kind of barrier. I can feel it, but I don't know what it is. His age, perhaps."

O'Toole nodded. "Perhaps. But there is another thing that Belden

139

himself might not realize. There is a thing he has to do. I know this."

She was disconcerted. "What thing?" she asked.

"He has said nothing of a Colonel Lee?"

"No."

"Belden has an appointment to keep," O'Toole said quietly. "At forty thousand feet up there." He gestured toward the north.

"Colonel Lee?" she said in a puzzled voice.

"A Chinese flier. Belden fought him in Korea. It was never finished."

"That sounds ridiculous."

O'Toole shrugged. "Maybe it is. But such things are important to men like this."

"I think it's ridiculous," she said angrily. "How would he know?"

"Lee has the Red fighter outfit up on the Chinese border. It was in the papers when those Navy jets were shot down."

"How would he know Dan was here?"

"Maybe he doesn't. But then again, maybe he does. It doesn't make any difference. They'll fight again."

There was a cautious note in her voice. "Dan will win?"

"I have no doubt of it," O'Toole said.

Suddenly Lori no longer wanted to talk about this appointment of Dan Belden's in the sky. Just as suddenly she felt a fierce enmity for a Chinese colonel whom she did not even know.

"You still haven't answered my question, Mr. O'Toole."

"Will you get Dan Belden? Well, Miss Morlaix, I will say this. Dan is the world's greatest jackass if you don't."

"That's not an answer."

"I don't have one. You want to know how you can smash down that barrier? Just be there, Miss Morlaix. Be there when Dan needs you. And he will need you. He won't know it, but he will. He has made the trip alone long enough. Soon now it will be time to climb out of the cockpit for good. It is a lonely step down from that cockpit for the last time and perhaps if he saw you there waiting for him, he wouldn't fight it so hard."

"Mr. O'Toole," Lori said. "I don't think you're being altogether honest with me."

"I," O'Toole admitted, "am one of the world's greatest liars. This is

140

a failing I have been unable to subjugate." He lit another cigarette. "Sometimes the truth isn't the answer to a thing. Does that sound upside down?"

"I'm not a child, Mr. O'Toole." Or am I? she thought. She was aware of the words O'Toole had not spoken and she knew that beyond the heart, which could not always be trusted, there were difficulties which could not be overcome simply by saying: "I love this man." What she wanted this man next to her to say was: "I have known Dan Belden for twenty years as well as one man may know another. He is the man for you and you are the woman for him. Never mind the disparity in your ages, never mind a lot of other things, and don't trouble your mind over the future. It will all work out and you and he will walk hand in hand down the pathway of your years in sunlight and happiness." This is what she wanted O'Toole to say, but instead he answered her in a fatherly voice.

"It hasn't been so long since you were a child though. Don't try to grow old too quickly. When you arrive there, you will wish you were back again at your beginnings. I have found this to be so."

"You sound like my father," she said.

"Pay no attention to me, Miss Morlaix," O'Toole said with a grin. "I am an old man and tonight my bones ache with this awful weather and with the waiting."

She covered his hand with hers for a moment and suddenly he wanted very much for this girl to find her happiness.

"What time will they be back?" she asked.

He glanced at his watch. "A long time yet. The flight will be at least five hours." He let his gaze move around the cluttered ready room. "It's always like this when you're waiting. Sometimes you swear you can hear their voices laughing as they wait for the 'Pilots-Man-Your-Planes.' You can almost see them sitting hunched over the acey-deucey boards, their brows furrowed in concentration, but what they are really concentrating on is the first clack of the teletype machine that will tell them they're on their way again." He drew a deep breath and turned his eyes to Lori. "When the message comes, you see them change before your eyes. The years pile on their faces and around their eyes comes a look of some sort of wisdom. Because where they're going, you can never go, and what they're going to do, you'll never be able to do. It's not always a pleasant thing to watch."

"But when they come back," she said persistently, "they're the same again."

"They don't all come back, miss. Not always. And then there's the empty chair in the ready room, exactly like all the other chairs except it appears to be ten feet tall and big enough to seat a giant. No one will use that seat until a new man comes along and he is assigned it. Soon after that it will be forgotten." O'Toole allowed himself a small smile. "But remember, we're speaking of ordinary pilots. Not legends."

Lori nodded and leaned her head back against the rest. It was nice talking to O'Toole because it was evident that he loved Dan, in his fashion, as much as she did. It was a beautiful thing when two strong men felt such a bond between them. Women, she decided, could never know such friendship and she wondered why. She was pondering this weighty problem when her eyes slowly closed; her head fell to one side, and she went quietly to sleep.

O'Toole walked to a chest standing against the far wall and from it took a woolen blanket with U.S. NAVY stenciled on it. Carefully he unfolded the blanket and draped it over the sleeping girl. He stood and looked down at her, his face shadowed in the dim light.

Her soft breathing caught at O'Toole's throat as he stood there and watched her loveliness and thought his own thoughts. For suddenly he needed that thinking—for permanence—as some men needed their families or their God or their money. Forty-eight years old, O'Toole, with thirty of them under his belt on the high seas. The thinking brought back the girls of his youth, this one and that one, and suddenly it was plain in his soul that no girl he had ever known could measure up to this one and if he had it to do over again he would wish for a daughter like her. But it was too late for that, so he wished her luck and added a wish for Belden's invulnerability too.

He flicked off the light switch and stood in the darkness, hearing her breathing over the sound of the rain splashing gently on the roof. His watch read 0445 and he estimated Belden would be passing Ban Me Thuot in two minutes.

Lori came awake to the touch of O'Toole's hand. For a moment she was startled by the strangeness of her surroundings and then she smiled at O'Toole.

142

"I must have dozed off."

"It's morning, miss," O'Toole said. "The planes are coming in."

Lori got to her feet and moved to the window. The heavy weather still hung over the field and it was raining harder now. The tops of the low-hanging clouds were only a few feet above the ground and from the underside of the grayish, sodden mass, small streamers of heavier condensation fell to the earth like so many hanging ribbons. Above, somewhere in the midst of the blinding cloud mass, she could hear the steady droning of the planes' engines. She noted that it was 0940 in the morning.

Through the window she saw O'Toole hurrying out toward the cleared area that served as a runway. He was clad in a full-length raincoat and parka hood. Two other men joined him and they trotted toward the center of the runway area.

There was a different sound to the engines now. The planes had separated and were flying singly. They passed directly over the field at fifteen-second intervals, the individual engines roaring for a moment and then fading away to the north as a new engine sound built up from the south. She strained her eyes against the flat gray overcast, trying to catch a glimpse of the planes, but there was only the steady rain falling and forming in puddles out on the dirt runway.

She was watching the north end of the field, her fists clenched tightly, the knuckles whitening, when the static from the radio in the other room abruptly ceased. There was a momentary pause and then Belden's voice came over the air, calm, unemotional: "Foray Leader. Over the homer inbound."

Belden was past the runway's edge when he dropped into the clear. Lori watched the Skyraider's nose ease up and she could hear the sputtering of the engine as Belden chopped off the throttle. The plane leveled out a few feet above the ground and another voice came over the radio. She recognized Kilpatrick's Texas twang: "Foray Two. Over the homer inbound."

Belden's plane flew a third of the length of the runway before it succumbed to the final tug of gravity and settled gently on the puddled strip. A giant cloud of spray was thrown outward as the plane touched down and careened through the small lakes of water like some maddened animal. Then the tail hook caught the arresting wire and the heavy plane was jerked abruptly to a halt. Immediately

143

O'Toole was racing onto the field and disengaging the wire. Almost before he had finished, Belden had poured on the throttle again and was turning off onto the taxi strip. Even as his plane cleared the runway, Kilpatrick was dropping down out of the clouds, taking his cut, and leveling off to the accompaniment of Bates's low-pitched voice: "Foray Three. Over the homer inbound."

And that is the way they came home. Out of the clouds by the grace of an artificial horizon, an air-speed indicator, and a tiny needle on a dial that always pointed to home. One after another they dropped onto the runway, caught the wires, and taxied off just as the next man came down. Lori counted them as they came and after the sixth plane had landed she frowned. There had been eight of them, she thought. She turned and looked at the blackboard in the ready room and noted the flight composition. Eight had gone out and only six had come back. Who were the missing? Maybe they landed at Danang. Perhaps they ran short of gas, or maybe they are just late coming back. She watched the planes taxi up and swing into the parked position; the great metal propellers slowed and finally jerked to a stop as the throttles were retarded and the mixture controls were yanked back into idle cut-off.

Out on the rain-pelted flight line O'Toole jumped up on the wing of Belden's plane. O'Toole knew after the sixth plane caught the wire that all had not gone well. Now he watched Belden's tired face as he helped him slip out of the parachute harness and shoulder straps. Belden's flight information was still written on his knee pad. He angrily tore the sheet of paper off the pad and threw it out into the wind and rain. He looked up at O'Toole wordlessly.

"Mr. Wildman and Mr. Dewall," O'Toole said. It was not a question.

Belden nodded. "They have gone away from us for a while, O'Toole. We may get Wildman back. He bailed out."

"They had the radar-controlled guns?"

Belden shook his head. "Mid-air collision over the target. I don't know what the Christ happened."

He stepped out on the wing and O'Toole cranked the canopy closed. And that is what I was telling the young lady just a while ago, he thought. It happens to the very best of them. When the luck runs thin, there's nothing on God's earth can save you. No man makes his own and when it's gone, there's nothing to do but bite down on the nail.

Lori heard their footsteps coming down the corridor to the ready room and she noticed the silence with which they came. When Belden saw her standing there, his face openly revealed his surprise.

"Lori. What are you doing here?"

O'Toole's voice answered for her. "She's been here since 0400."

The others smiled at her and began shedding their wet flight clothing. Suddenly embarrassed, she started to leave the room. Belden, busy hanging his holstered pistol and cartridge belt on a hook, turned to her: "Got the carryall?"

She nodded.

"Wait for us," he said. "We'll ride back with you."

Not a word about the men who had not come back. Not a word concerning Wildman or Dewall. Were they going to pretend it had never happened?

"Who has the key to Stoney's locker?" Bates asked unconcernedly.

"I have," Hawkins answered.

"Let's break out the booze when we get to the house," Anders said.

Belden nodded. "Why not?"

They continued the business of divesting themselves of the flight suits and helmets and now they spoke of Wildman and Dewall as though the two men were there in the room with them. Lori stood by the door and listened in bewilderment.

"Anybody see them collide?" Hawkins asked.

"I saw Sam go into the overcast," Belden said. "His canopy was shattered. The prop must have taken him out."

"He was fighting that sonofabitch all the way into the turn," Bates observed. "Bucking like a bronco. When that ammo dump went, it must have thrown something up into his empennage."

"Lousy break," Macgregor Kilpatrick said.

Hawkins, his face drawn and very pale, was shrugging into a flight jacket. "Think Stoney got out?" He asked the question in a tone that was almost disinterested.

Belden spoke to Hawkins, but his eyes were on Lori.

"Maybe," he said. "Depends on the ground elevation where he bailed out. That and a few other things."

"Like guerrillas?" Anders asked.

"Like guerrillas," Belden said.

Belden moved to the bulkhead and took a gaily painted hard-helmet from a hook. He inspected it a moment as the others watched. Then he handed it to O'Toole.

"Sam had an extra helmet, Larry. Take it out and get rid of it."

"I can't understand Sam trying to go into that turn if his tail was shot up," Hawkins observed. "Why didn't he get out of the damn thing?"

"Maybe his control wires went," Belden said. "Whatever it was, he must have had a reason."

"Well," Bates said, "his reason had fatal results."

Belden crossed to the portable radio apparatus and flipped a switch. "We'll see about Stoney now."

There was static for a moment as the set warmed up. Then Belden picked up the mike and spoke.

"Royalty from Viceroy. Royalty from Viceroy. Go ahead, Royalty."

A few seconds later General Pham's voice came over the air.

"This is Royalty. Go ahead, Dan."

"Viceroy here," Belden said and now there was a note of weariness in his voice. "Mission completed successfully." He paused. "We lost two planes. One pilot dead for sure and one bailed out. Do you have any information for me?"

The General's voice came slowly and with a hint of anger. "Yes, Dan. One of our patrols found Wildman a few minutes ago. He was dead. Shot in the back. They're bringing the body in."

There was a silence in the ready room as Belden let his breath out in a tired sigh. The others stared at the floor or at the ceiling, avoiding each other's eyes.

As Lori watched them, she was aware of an almost visible effort on the part of each of them to remove any trace of emotion from his face. Bates made a great production of lighting a cigarette. Hawkins rubbed his hand slowly across the back of his neck. Anders and Corey displayed an intense interest in the number of cartridges remaining in their ammo belts. No one spoke and the silence was thick enough to touch.

"The dirty bastards," Belden said to no one in particular. He spoke into the mike again. "Any reports from Laos?"

146

It was Smoke Dusane's voice that answered. "Dan. This is Smoke. Hell yes, there are reports from Laos. You really creamed the bastards. They've been yelling on the radio for two hours. When are you coming down here?"

"Tomorrow," Belden said.

"Good. I'm going out to the Task Force today. Christ only knows what Washington will do about this. They've got the proof with that Skyraider that crashed."

"Frankly, Smoke," Belden said, "I don't give a good goddam right now *what* Washington does."

"Yeah," Dusane said. "I don't blame you."

"Smoke," Belden said. "We'll fly the Skyraiders down tomorrow. I'll want to talk to you about those fighters. I don't care what kind they are, but I want some fighters."

"And I," Dusane replied, "would like a new set of bowels, but I don't have any."

"Can you swing it?"

There was a brief silence. "I can swing it, Dan. You come down tomorrow."

"Thanks, Smoke." There was a grin on Belden's face. "See you tomorrow." He replaced the hand mike and stood rubbing the back of his head.

Lori held her eyes on Belden until he looked up and noticed her. "I'd forgotten you were here."

"You wanted a ride," she said.

Belden's glance passed over the men standing in a group before him. Suddenly they were all grinning at one another. Lori was aware that she was witnessing something that O'Toole had tried to tell her and had failed. This was a part of Belden's life into which she could never intrude. She was not at all sure why they were grinning at each other when two of their friends had just died, but back of it somewhere was Admiral Dusane's promise to find some fighter planes for them. This was a very simple thing and she thought she should understand, but she didn't.

"Well," Bates finally said, "I believe that Stoney and Sam would appreciate it if we drank their booze."

"I agree," said Anders. "And after we have finished this excellent whiskey and have surfeited ourselves on outrageous war stories bordering on the unbelievable, I intend to hit the sack and sleep for twenty-four hours. This has been a most trying morning."

Already, Lori thought, they have accepted the deaths of their friends and they can joke about them. Or are they only pretending because they know that other friends will die before they are finished out here? Perhaps their way is the best after all.

"The carryall is out in back," Lori said. "I'll cook breakfast at the house."

"Good whiskey, good friends, and bacon and eggs," Bates announced. "What else is there?"

They filed out of the room and walked back to where the carryall was parked. They piled in as Lori started the engine and drove slowly down the flight line toward the dirt road that circled the field and led to the main house. Belden sat beside her and she could feel the hard muscle of his arm as it circled her shoulders. When she glanced at him and found him watching her, she turned her head and touched her lips lightly against his hand.

As they passed the parked airplanes, gaunt and ungainly in the wetness, she noted the two sets of empty chocks lying haphazardly on the ground, useless and forlorn-looking as the rain formed small puddles around them.

A few hundred miles to the north, Xuan Nonh savored the authority which he had bestowed upon himself with the death of Captain Minh. Now that he had become a captain, Xuan was unpleasantly surprised to discover that a captain's hunger was in no way different from the hunger experienced by a lieutenant or, for that matter, a corporal. He led his ragged band in mountainous country toward a tiny village where Captain Minh had intimated they would receive important orders. The terrain was exceedingly difficult here and Xuan gasped for breath as he fought his way through the tough elephant grass toward a mountain pass that would lead to the small clearing where the orders would be waiting. He wondered if there should be some special manner in which he should act now that he was in command of the detachment. It crossed his mind that he might already have made his first mistake as a captain. He had intended to bury the American flier's body, but his scouts had reported a squad of South Vietnamese infantry moving on their position, so he had left the body in the underbrush and had piled dead leaves and branches over it. Xuan shrugged and told himself it was too late now to do anything about it.

He held his rifle beneath his arm as he stepped out of the heavy growth at the edge of the clearing. There was no sign of life in the village, but he knew he was under observation. He turned and gestured his men ahead, then walked into the village square.

From behind the line of huts at the end of the square, he saw a slight movement and then a small, emaciated man appeared and stood quietly regarding Xuan. The two studied each other for several moments before Xuan motioned his men to follow and moved toward the other man.

"You have them?" Xuan asked when he faced the stranger.

"Have what?" the man asked. He was still watching Xuan carefully.

"My orders," Xuan said. He looked around the village perimeter, wary of an Arvin trap. If the squad that had been reported by his scouts had had word of this meeting, they might conceivably have skirted the mountain pass and come up on the village from the rear.

"I have no orders for you," the man said. "I don't even know who you are."

"This is Captain Tran Minh's detachment," Xuan said.

"I see no Captain Minh," the man replied and Xuan knew this was his man.

"He is dead by the hand of an American pilot. His throat cut."

"Ah!" the man murmured. "You have proof of this?"

Xuan raised his carbine until it pointed at the man's mid-section. "This is my proof."

The man said nothing, so Xuan rammed the bolt on the carbine home.

"I don't trust this one," one of Xuan's men said.

"Silence," Xuan ordered, not turning his head. "This is our man. He has been described to me by Captain Minh." This was a lie, but he wished to test the man.

"I never met the Captain," the man said and Xuan nodded.

"Now I know you are my man. We passed through Lao Bao last night."

149

The man inclined his head, but nothing more. Xuan prodded him in the stomach with the carbine.

"I have killed once this morning. I don't mind doing it again."

"Your name?"

"Xuan Nonh. *Captain* Xuan Nonh. A soldier of the liberation."

The man said nothing and Xuan decided he would have to kill him. It must have shown in his eyes because the man suddenly said, "All right, Captain. Follow me."

Xuan motioned to his men to stay back and he followed the skinny man into a large hut under the umbrella of jungle growth. Inside the hut there was nothing but a straw mat on the floor and a bulky object against the wall over which a tarpaulin was placed. The man turned to face Xuan: "You are a cautious man, Captain."

Xuan nodded. "I intend to remain so." He inclined his head toward the tarpaulin. "What is that?"

"In a moment, Captain. First, let me apprise you of a few things. There will be trucks here in a short while to transport you south."

Xuan was plainly puzzled. "Trucks? I have never ridden in a truck."

"You will now. Your mission has suddenly assumed a degree of urgency."

"I don't even know what my mission is."

The man walked to the tarpaulin and jerked it away. Xuan caught his breath as he saw the four 81-mm mortars standing against the wall. A smile split his face and just as quickly was gone.

"The Americans attacked the base in Laos this morning. Somehow they managed to find it in zero visibility and inflicted considerable damage. In itself the base is unimportant. For morale purposes and for propaganda we must strike back immediately. You will take your men south, Captain, to the Bien Choa air base."

"Bien Choa?" Xuan's voice was disbelieving. "That is only a few miles outside the city of Saigon."

"Does it worry you, Captain?" the man asked in a faintly condescending tone. "We can find other volunteers."

"Soon," Xuan said in a low voice, "you will try me too far."

The man appeared not to have heard. "The trucks will take you as far south as is practical. From there you will infiltrate as best you can. The range on these mortars is two miles maximum. I suggest you attempt to close within a mile before you set them up and open fire."

"Do you have maps?" Xuan asked. "And the enemy. Do they not have a perimeter set up around the field? How far from the base itself?" Already his quick mind was probing ahead, seeking out the bits of information he would need to complete this mission successfully. Xuan had never gone to school in his life, but he was a better soldier than many a military-school graduate. He had been taught in the hardest school of all.

The man scoffed. "Perimeter? The enemy has a perimeter, of course. Only it has holes in it you might drive through in the trucks themselves. You will infiltrate with little difficulty. It may, however," he added dryly, "be somewhat more difficult to get out."

"And my target?" Xuan had no interest in the dangers of escape.

Now the man laughed outright. "They have their jet bombers, the B-47s, parked in rows along the runways. Their small propeller planes too. There is also a barracks on the field. These will be your targets. You will send two men forward dressed as farmers. They will carry a small radio and will direct your mortar fire. They will be considered expendable. After your attack you will withdraw as quickly as possible, keeping to cover and working west before you turn north. Their helicopters will search north, I have no doubt."

"It would seem foolish of them to leave their planes parked where we can reach them," Xuan said.

"It is hard to believe the stupidity of the Americans at times." He looked again at the mortars. "You have men capable of operating the mortars?"

"I do," Xuan said. "You have food?"

The man nodded.

"Good," Xuan said. "Then my men and I will eat. After that we will discuss the operation of the mortars. Then we will sleep until your trucks arrive. After that we will go south and destroy the American planes on the runways at Bien Choa."

There was a garden behind the main house at the plantation. At the far end was an open patio over which a portable roof of canvas had been drawn. Lori and Belden stood behind the bar mixing drinks while the rest of the men spoke in solemn tones as they told her of ridiculous feats they had accomplished in the sky. They used their hands in impossible juxtapositions to describe maneuvers which they invented as they spoke. There was a warm feeling of camaraderie and Lori basked in its glow, feeling a certain glory in their acceptance of her.

She was aware that Dan was watching Hawkins with a worried frown on his face. Hawkins' face was an unhealthy grayish color and the deep lines around his mouth and under his eyes had grown more pronounced during the past weeks. He was sipping at his drink and smiling at something Bates had said when a spasm of pain swept over him and he could not hide a grimace as the agony seared deeply down the side of his neck.

Lori touched Belden's arm. "Is something wrong with Hawk?"

She could not fathom the look in Belden's eyes. "Stiff neck maybe," was all he said. He handed her another drink and then moved down the bar to Hawkins.

"You look like hell, Hawk," Belden said. "You all right?"

Hawkins shook his head. "My malaria's acting up."

"You never had malaria in your life," Anders said.

"Maybe it's my hernia then."

Belden spoke carefully. "Maybe. Want to talk about it?"

Hawkins said, "I haven't been sleeping well. That's all."

The pain today was worse than before. It had been better for a little while, but today it was worse than it had ever been. He had deliberately refrained from taking any of the pills the doctor had prescribed for him. He had not wanted to dull his senses in any manner and thus impair his flying proficiency. But the ache in his neck had moved down below the heavy shoulder muscles where it lay like a hot iron and caused a sharp pain whenever he drew a deep breath. It was too soon, he knew, for the real trouble to begin. That was weeks away at the earliest. So he would bear with it a while yet and he would know when it was time to put an end to it. He decided that tonight he would take one of the pills and see if this goddam pain would go away from his neck and back and then perhaps he would sleep again.

He followed Dan's glance down the bar to where Lori stood laughing with Mac Kilpatrick and Don Corey.

"I'll tell you something, Dan," Hawkins said reflectively. "From the depths of my wisdom. There is not as much time left as you may think. There is not as much time left as any of us might think. Don't waste it. And don't waste that lovely girl. You'll regret it if you do."

"You're sure as hell burdened with weighty thoughts," Anders said.

No, my friends, Hawkins thought. But I am dying and a dying man see some things more clearly than a living man. I've cleaned up the odds and ends of my life and I've said good-bye to my loved ones. So for all practical purposes my life is already finished. Nothing remains now but the ending. There's no longer any reason for me to dissemble. I can say what I think and feel with abandon because there's really nothing left in life for which I give a goddam.

The sound of the voices grew louder as the day wore on and the levels in the whiskey bottles slowly dropped. They spoke gravely of preposterous matters while the liquor grew warm in their bellies.

"I remember the day I sank the *Ise*," Bates started to say.

"*You* sank the *Ise?*" Corey interrupted. "It so happens that *I* sank the *Ise*. I happen to have a Navy Cross to prove it."

"Half the Third Fleet got Navy Crosses for sinking that mother. Know where she was when the war ended? Tied up at the dock at Kure Naval Harbor."

"Well, anyway, as I was saying. I came out of the sun at a hundred thousand feet . . ."

"Are you aware that I am the only man in the history of aviation to snap-roll to a carrier landing? Looking back on it now, it was really not too difficult. You see . . ."

"And so the ship called me on the radio. 'How many of them are there?' they asked. I made a quick calculation. 'About three hundred,' I reported. 'How many of you?' they asked. 'Two,' I replied. 'Do you need help?' they said. 'Hell no,' I told them. So I came around in a high side attack and . . ."

"I like them, Dan," Lori said. "They're so different."

"How would you know?" Belden smiled. "You never met anyone like them before."

"Let's walk," she said.

He took her hand and they slipped out into the garden. There was a small stone seat under the shade of a large tree in one corner. The rain had stopped some time ago and now the sun was visible, moving toward the western sky in the wake of the afternoon. They sat down and Lori looked around with a childlike appreciation.

"This was my favorite place when I was little," she said. "I had a tiny hut built up in this tree. It was the place of my secret heart and I never let anyone come here. I would take my favorite doll and sit for hours, cross-legged on the floor of the hut, and dream what it would be like when I was grown up and a lady." She looked up at him. "Where were you then, Dan?"

Belden was thoughtful a moment. "Flying airplanes somewhere. And dreaming what it would be like to be a child again, sitting on the floor of a hut built into a tree overlooking a garden."

He felt the pressure of her fingers. "It was mine, all alone," she said, "and I was sure that no one could ever find me here. I could be anyone—anything—I wanted to be. I could be a great lady at court —a queen with her entourage—I could be a movie star or an heiress. And sometimes, when I grew a little older, I would dream of the man I would love someday." She kissed his hand lightly, her lips feathery as they touched. "I don't have to dream any more, Dan," she said frankly.

"Don't stop dreaming, Lori," murmured Belden. "It's the most precious gift you have."

She nodded and hugged his hand to her breast. He could feel the warm swelling there as she shut her eyes in a quiet ecstasy.

"Dan," she said abruptly, "tell me about Colonel Lee."

"What do you know about Lee?"

"Mr. O'Toole told me."

"Mr. O'Toole talks too much," Belden said mildly.

"Please, Dan."

He gently disengaged his hand and put his arm around her. She dropped her golden head on his shoulder and he could smell the sweet fragrance of her hair. He felt an overwhelming tenderness for this girl, a tenderness compounded of vast respect, compassion, and a sudden hardening of desire. That such loveliness could be offered to him confounded his mind. He brushed his lips across her hair and his hand tightened on her shoulder.

154

"You already know if O'Toole has told you. Lee is a Red Chinese colonel I'm going to kill. I knew him impersonally in Korea. We fought there, but it was never finished." He was silent a moment. "It will be now." There was a note of finality in his voice.

"Does he know you're here?"

"I would guess so. It was no secret when I came." He chuckled. "How badly does your father really need rubber salesmen? I think Lee knows."

"He'll try to kill you too." She spoke with a trace of anger.

"That's the name of the game," Belden said.

"That's all it is to you?" she asked. "A game?"

"Not this time," he said. "Lee killed those two jet pilots from the *Concord*. Strafed one of them in his parachute. No"—he shook his head—"it will be no game this time."

She was silent then until he finally tipped her head up and looked into her eyes. He could plainly see the love shining there under the hint of tears. Her eyes searched his face and she traced a finger lightly over his features as a blind woman might seek identity.

"My darling, my darling, my darling," she whispered.

Her hand moved over a white slash of scar that ran across Belden's temple, a faint, jagged mark that ended high on his cheekbone.

Belden took her in his arms with a great gentleness and her lips softened and parted as they met his and he could feel the warm searching of her mouth as her arms tightened convulsively around his neck. His big hand was gentle as it moved down to her breast and she moaned softly against his lips.

Try as she would she could not control the quick gasp of pain as his hand moved on her breast and she writhed in a sudden agony of desire and hunger. Her breath quickened and her mouth opened wide under his and she surrendered herself completely to the erotic craving.

When she thought she could no longer stand the intolerable, sweet, unceasing agony, he pulled back and stared down at her, his eyes narrowed in some ponderous concentration.

She stared back at him with widened eyes, shivering uncontrollably. She tried to still her breathing, but it caught in her throat and she swallowed with difficulty.

"God damn it," Belden breathed.

She said nothing. A tremulous smile lay on her lips as she rose, pulling him to his feet. They stood there together, watching each other gravely and without words, their hands clasped tightly as they spoke the language of the eyes.

Then she turned and led him into the house and up the stairs to her bedroom.

Lori shut the door quietly behind her and then turned and placed her back to it and watched Belden across the room. And now it was he who appeared defenseless and childlike. He stood there, tall and powerful in the rays of the sinking sun, and he looked like a little boy. His big hands opened and closed nervously and a frown crinkled his forehead.

Suddenly Lori laughed because she was no longer apprehensive at all. As is usually the way in a bedroom, the woman had become the master.

"What's so funny?" Belden asked.

"You are. You look like a naughty boy." She laughed again. "Why, Dan, I believe you're nervous."

"Well, God damn it . . ." he said exasperatedly.

She came to him slowly, holding his eyes with her own. He turned and drew the curtains, leaving the room in half-light. When he looked at her again, she was sitting on the edge of the bed, her skirt and blouse lying on the floor at her feet. Her eyes were very wide now and even from a distance Belden could see the strong beat of her heart.

"Lori," he whispered.

"Hurry, Dan. Hurry, my darling." Her voice was lost in the dusk as Belden reached for her.

And then their eyes spoke and their hands spoke and as they did so the sky darkened and the stars appeared and through a slit in the curtains the starlight came and in it Belden saw her beauty in its fullness. It was the whole beauty of Woman in the ecstasy of giving, selflessly, completely. Belden saw it and knew it by the ancient means and meanings. He was entwined in it and locked with it and became a part of it.

And then as full dark came, the rain began again and the lightning. When Belden felt Lori arch her body and heard her shrill cry of rapture, the might of the elements only reflected his own. The pouring rain became a symbol of a more procreant flood and Belden knew in that moment that the rain could never fall again out of any sky, without bringing a remembrance of this joining with his love.

Chapter X

DECEMBER
1964

They had disembarked from the trucks many days before when the terrain had become impossible for the vehicles. Then in the night hours they had continued south, moving slowly and with great caution, bivouacking during the day deep in the brush and out of sight of the prowling Arvin patrols. They bestowed great care on the 81-mm mortars and the weapons were kept out of sight when they entered a village to force provisions from the reluctant inhabitants. Xuan had his maps and at night he studied them with diligence, marking trails which would offer the least possibility of an encounter with enemy troops. More than once he forced himself to refuse an engagement and run away, turning his back to his enemy.

Couriers from Hanoi had contacted him during his move southward. The American attack on the base in Laos had been the deciding factor in this attack on the enemy airfield at Bien Choa. Also, Xuan knew, Chinese air squadrons were massing near Lungchou above the North Vietnam border. Xuan was aware that Colonel Lee had violated South Vietnam air space when he came down after the raiders the day of the Laos raid. Perhaps Lee had made a mistake at that time; perhaps not. Xuan was not in a position to deliberate. He thought perhaps it all went back to that morning in the clearing when they had executed the two American fliers. After that came the blow at Laos. Then Lee's violation of air space, now the attack on

158

Bien Choa. The war was picking up in tempo, Xuan knew. Who was behind it all did not interest him. What interested him just now was the successful completion of his mission.

He sat on his haunches and watched the sun lower toward the distant mountaintops to the west. From his place of concealment his eyes measured the angle of the sun and he judged darkness would come within the hour. He had pinpointed his position and he knew that less than six hundred yards directly in front of him was the perimeter of defense of the complex at Bien Choa. If he was to be caught, it would be within the next hour or two. He hoped fervently that the intelligence reports concerning the laxity of security around Bien Choa were accurate.

He rose and moved back into the brush where his men waited patiently, grouped around the mortars and the cases of shells. Xuan knelt and fingered the heavy mortar shells in an open case and wondered if the humidity might have affected the firing mechanisms. He knew little of such things, but the importance of the mission was not lost on him. He glanced again through the heavy undergrowth and the sun was almost touching the mountains now.

He gestured and two soldiers came to him. "You will leave now," Xuan said. "Scout to the perimeter and no farther. Return within thirty minutes." The two men nodded and disappeared into the jungle.

Xuan moved a distance away and sat by himself. He was nervous tonight and strangely he felt the need of a woman. He listened carefully, but the only sound in the jungle was the rustle of some crawling thing as it moved in the bush. Xuan let his thoughts move back to that morning in the clearing when they had killed the two Americans. The thinking of Colonel Lee had been good, Xuan decided. But no one could have known that the American jets would take a picture that morning and that Lee's execution of the fliers would serve only to produce a retaliation by the Americans. The blows were coming faster now, by each side, and Xuan wondered where it all would lead.

Twenty minutes later his scouts returned.

"They are there, Captain," one man said. "Camped just off the trail. Eight soldiers and an American sergeant. They are cooking dinner."

Xuan nodded and got to his feet. He motioned at the weapons and shells and when the soldiers had picked them up, he led the way toward the enemy's perimeter.

Six hundred yards away a U.S. Army sergeant named Harry Crawford ate his rations with distaste. He had been scheduled for relief two nights ago, but someone had fouled up at headquarters and now he was sitting here in this lousy jungle, eating beans and pressed ham out of a sour-tasting tin dish. He had had a date with a Saigon whore for tonight and his mind taunted itself with erotic visions of what might have been if he had not had to remain in this cruddy goddam forest. He spat violently as a bug flew into his mouth and with a curse he threw the remnants of his meal on the ground and walked across the tiny clearing to the wall of the jungle. What the goddam hell, he thought. I wonder what ass-backward second john got the idea to set up a perimeter way the hell down near Saigon. The bastards would never dare come this far south and, if they did, they couldn't get close enough to the airfield to threaten it anyway. He lit a cigarette and wondered what it was like tonight back in San Diego at the Grant Hotel.

Twenty-five feet away from Sergeant Crawford, Xuan Nonh crouched in the darkness. Crawford was only a faint shadow to Xuan, a darker form against the first darkness of the night. He laid a finger on his lips as he looked back at his men and spoke in a low whisper: "Move out in a line of attack. Quietly."

As low as Xuan kept his voice, its sound rustled in the stillness and Sergeant Crawford looked up, alert for a moment, as he heard what he thought was a night bird waking.

Xuan's men silently, stealthily, took position within the covering of the jungle, rimming the tiny clearing where the troops were eating their dinner. There was a small fire burning in the center of the group and the flickering light displayed the Oriental faces grinning as the idle conversation flowed. Xuan moved five steps closer to the Sergeant.

Studying the impenetrable blackness of the tangled growth, Sergeant Crawford thought he saw a shadow move. He squinted his eyes and the shadow was gone. He decided he was tired and he had seen no shadow at all. He drew deeply on his cigarette and wondered if his relief would be on hand in the morning. A twig crackled in the underbrush and he looked quickly into the night and thought he saw another shadow move.

"Tran," he called, "throw some more wood on that fire."

This goddam duty is enough to drive a guy screwy, he told himself. Wandering around in this goddam jungle. And for what? Ain't a thing gonna happen way down here. Why, Christ, I could be in Saigon in fifteen minutes.

Xuan was flattened against a large tree on the edge of the clearing. He could see clearly now the figure of the American Sergeant. He drew his long knife slowly from its scabbard and dropped into an apelike, crouching position. He moved another five feet and now he was in the open, but covered by shadows which had not yet been dispelled by the flame from the wood being tossed on the fire by one of the troopers.

Crawford finished his cigarette and ground it out under his heel. He looked once more into the recesses of the jungle and then turned to walk back to the fire. He felt a wiry arm slip around his neck, shutting off his incipient cry. He twisted violently and grasped the small hand under his neck. Then he felt a white-hot explosion just under his chin and something thick and rough boiled into his throat with a searing agony. A hand clapped over his mouth as the heat rose up in his throat and the torrid pain dissolved into a warm flood that gushed from his nostrils as he felt his body slipping to the ground.

"Aieeee!" Xuan Nonh screamed silently to himself. "It is done." In a low voice he called into the night. "Kill them all."

His forty men erupted from the brush and fell on the startled troops around the fire. The enemy had no time to defend themselves and Xuan saw the flashing of knives in the firelight and he heard the bubbling groans as men died under those knives. In a matter of seconds all was silence around the campfire and the shadows danced on the sprawled bodies.

"Into the brush with them," Xuan ordered.

They were inside the perimeter now and the lights from the air base bounced off the low-hanging clouds. Xuan moved with great care and he left segments of his command posted behind to cover the line of their retreat.

He moved through the heavy growth for a distance of a half-mile and stopped in an area that had been someone's former campsite. He sent two of his men ahead to scout the edge of the airfield. From another man he took a small portable walkie-talkie. Unbidden, his men set about to mount the mortars in a firing posture.

Fifteen minutes later a voice came over his walkie-talkie.

"Land of our fathers." The voice spoke the password. "We are in position, Captain." The man's words were whispered.

"You have the targets in sight?" Xuan asked.

"Aiee! Many big bombers and fighters and also many smaller planes with the metal blades."

Xuan spoke to the men operating the mortars. "We will do this thing quickly. Are you ready?" They nodded and Xuan waited while the man sighting the weapons adjusted the range to one and one-half miles.

"Open fire," Xuan said.

With a great *whoosh* the first shell burst from the muzzle and sped across the sky. Quickly, a second followed and a third. The loading was done with practiced dexterity and six shells had been fired before the first report came over the radio.

"Down fifty. Two hundred right. Down fifty. Two hundred right."

They could hear the distant explosions as the shells hit. The man adjusted the range speedily and the shells went on their way again.

"Down twenty-five. Down twenty-five." The range was lowered twenty-five yards.

"On target. On target."

"Keep them going." Xuan ordered.

There was an orange glow from the airfield that lit an angry sky. Detonations reverberated through the jungle as gas tanks and ammunition piles exploded.

"On target. On target." The scout's voice was jubilant. "Many planes burning."

Xuan spoke unhurriedly into the walkie-talkie. "The personnel barracks."

"Two hundred right. Two hundred right."

More shells *whooshed* across the sky and in the distance there was a steady *thump thump thump thump* as they smashed into the barracks.

162

"The barracks are burning," the scout reported. "The whole field is in flames."

Xuan waited until the last of the ammunition had been expended. Then he spoke into the radio. "Return to base. Follow the line of retreat. We are moving out." His men disassembled the mortars and moved back in the direction from which they had come. As Xuan came last, covering the rear, he saw the helicopters flying out from Bien Choa on a northerly heading.

Passing the spot where they had ambushed the perimeter guards, Xuan stopped a moment and finished the warm food on one of the tin dishes lying on the coals.

Two hundred miles southeast of Saigon the Seventh Fleet cruised at 15 knots on a course of 270. The planes on the flight deck of the *Concord* were spotted for launch. High overhead a Combat Air Patrol from the sister carrier *Ardennes* flew in lazy circles and left on the blue blackboard of sky a wide, sprawling series of contrails, which were rapidly spread by the wind in the jet stream at 35,000 feet.

On the flight deck the handling crew moved forward to land a helicopter on the elevator. The clumsy-looking craft approached from the port quarter and hovered noisily as the pilot waited for the deck crew to push the last jet fighter forward to leave a clear area for the landing. The chopper picked up speed until it flew parallel with the huge carrier, then it slipped sideways and hovered a few feet above the landing circle, flying at exactly the same speed at which the carrier was traveling. With a slight bump it settled on the deck. The chocks were quickly shoved in place and the rotor blades coughed to a stop.

Vice Admiral Dusane, standing on the flag bridge, watched the landing and smiled as he saw a familiar figure jump down from the chopper to the flight deck. The figure wore plain dungarees and a beaten flight jacket and perched on the back of the head was a battered chief petty officer's cap with the insignia removed.

"Have that man brought to my sea cabin," the Admiral ordered his Officer-of-the-Deck.

"Aye, aye, sir."

The Admiral turned and entered his sea cabin, a Spartan room with only a desk and a chair and small bunk set against the bulkhead. He twirled the dial on his desk safe and when the door swung aside, he withdrew a half-empty bottle of whiskey. He placed the bottle on the desk and took two glasses from the cabinet above the washbasin.

A voice spoke from the door. "That's against regulations, sir."

"O'Toole," Admiral Dusane remarked, pouring the two glasses full, "this is not ordinary whiskey. This is medicinal whiskey and is to be taken only when something is wrong with your nerves." He handed a glass to O'Toole. "You look nervous as hell today, O'Toole."

O'Toole accepted the drink. "I should be nervous, sir. I've been living in the jungle with a bunch of maniacs." He sipped the whiskey appreciatively. "This is fine medicine, sir."

Dusane gestured O'Toole to a chair and then seated himself behind his desk across from the grizzled ex-Chief.

"That was a hell of a job Dan did in Laos."

O'Toole nodded. "Costly too, sir."

"Yeah." Dusane sighed. "It always costs something." After a moment he said, "What's this I hear about Dan getting married?"

"That's right, Admiral. The young lady long ago made up his mind." O'Toole smiled as he spoke.

"Christ, O'Toole. Dan is forty years old."

"Well, sir"—O'Toole spoke in a dry tone—"with some luck he may have a few years left to him."

Dusane grunted. "I keep forgetting that you and I passed forty a long time ago."

"Long enough, sir," O'Toole agreed.

"I hope he can make it work."

"We all do, Admiral. Dan doesn't make many mistakes."

The Admiral rose and poured another drink into O'Toole's glass. Then he walked to the porthole and stared at the sky for a few moments. When he turned back, there was a look of spurious bewilderment on his face.

"O'Toole." The Admiral shook his head in consternation. "You won't believe what has happened out here. You simply won't believe it."

"Probably not, sir."

"Honest to God, O'Toole, it staggers the imagination. Would you believe me if I told you my maintenance department has run into a series of malfunctions in our new F8 Crusaders that defy the efforts of Seventh Fleet engineers to repair them? Now would you believe that?"

"I would," O'Toole said solemnly, "if a Vice Admiral told me to."

"I have twenty-four F8s aboard and *exactly twelve of them have to be surveyed*." The Admiral stressed the words with an assumed disgust.

"That's a hell of a situation, sir," O'Toole said.

"I simply do not have room on my hangar deck for those downed airplanes. They clutter the place up. I may even have to shove them over the side."

"It seems a waste, sir," O'Toole said gravely.

"Unless, O'Toole, you might be able to find a parking place somewhere ashore until such time as I can get a Chance Vought man out here."

"You've already got a Chance Vought man aboard," O'Toole said.

"I do?" Dusane appeared surprised. "Well, what do you know about that?"

"Nothing, sir." He offered his glass. "I believe I'm getting nervous again, Admiral."

The Admiral refilled the glass and said, "Well, then. Suppose you go down to the hangar deck and take a look at those planes. They're parked aft. Chief Merchant is with them. You might talk to him."

O'Toole downed his drink and stood, his hat held respectively in his big hands. "Thank you, Admiral. For the whiskey. It is seldom I drink with flag rank. If I may mention another thing, sir. We need a maintenance crew."

"Talk to Merchant about that."

O'Toole slapped his cap smartly on his head and saluted. He was at the door when Admiral Dusane said, "O'Toole."

"Sir?"

Dusane smiled warmly. "Tell Dan I wish him luck."

After O'Toole had gone, Dusane refilled his own glass and replaced the bottle in the safe. Then he stood at the porthole and watched the activity on the flight deck as the crews prepared for the afternoon launch. Since Lee had come down across the Parallel to get Belden's raiders, Dusane's pilots had been patrolling along the border and along the limits of international waters in a vain hope that they might intercept and tangle with the MIGs should the occasion present itself. But Lee had not come down again and American planes were still prohibited from crossing into North Vietnam to look for him. The restraint on his pilots was a constant source of irritation to Dusane. His reverie was interrupted as his aide entered with the news that Admiral Ryerson's plane was a hundred miles out from Saigon.

Dusane grinned at the news. If the Old Man was here, then something was surely destined to hit the fan. His spirits lifted as he thought of the tough old bastard steaming into Saigon and roaring like a wounded bull at the inefficiency and procrastination which characterized the American efforts in that politically oriented city.

Four decks below the flag bridge O'Toole edged his way carefully through the confusion of massed airplanes crammed onto the hangar deck. He swore as his head cracked against a wing in the dim light.

He was still rubbing his head when he ducked under a wing and came upright at the aft end of the ship. Peering around, he caught sight of a familiar, bulky figure, in indescribably dirty coveralls, working industriously on the landing gear of an F8 Crusader. He moved quietly to a position behind the laboring man and watched in silence for a few moments.

"You're going to foul that gear up beyond all recall," he said quietly.

A grease-smeared face peered up at him. "For Christ's sake, gang," the voice declared. "We got a goddam civilian aboard this ship." The man scrambled from beneath the plane and offered a begrimed hand to O'Toole, who took it with reluctance.

"Merchant," O'Toole said painfully, "I thought I taught you a long time ago not to work on a bad landing gear without propping the airplane up. You want to get squashed or something?"

"When I need advice from a civilian, I'll ask for it," Merchant answered with an element of disdain. "How the hell you been?"

"Lousy," O'Toole said. "I'm probably getting malaria."

"Tough shit," Merchant said. "What're you doing out here?"

"You know what I'm doing out here."

"Well, yeah," Merchant said. "But I'm not supposed to."

O'Toole gestured at the aircraft surrounding them. "These the planes the Admiral was talking about?"

Merchant nodded. "These are them."

O'Toole shook his head in despair. "Your English is still abominable. I thought I had you in pretty good shape when I left."

"You did, Irish. I'm the leadin' Chief now."

"It's a wonder there are any planes flying," O'Toole said as he inspected the aileron surfaces of one of them. He cocked an eye at Merchant. "The Admiral said to ask you about a maintenance crew ashore."

The burly Chief rubbed his hands with a rag. "What you need them for?"

"For Dan Belden," O'Toole said.

"How many?"

"Fifteen. Good men or nothing at all."

"All I got is good men," Merchant said. "This a volunteer mission?"

"Yeah. But remember something. There's plenty of whiskey ashore and maybe a girl or two if they get lucky."

Merchant nodded. "You said Dan Belden?"

"Dan Belden."

"That's good enough for me. When you want them and where?"

"Right now if you can get them."

"I already got them. Had them last night after I talked with the Admiral."

"Well, what the hell was all this conversation about?"

"Just wanted to be sure. Now I'll get these things ready for launch and then we'll go below and pack my gear."

"Well, I'll be damned," O'Toole said. "You're coming too?"

"What else? The Admiral said this might be important." Chief Petty Officer Merchant clapped a heavy hand on O'Toole's shoulder. "You can tell Dan we'll give him the best we've got."

One hundred and twenty-five miles due north of the 1500 position of the Seventh Fleet an unarmed United States Air Force RB-66B reconnaissance jet flew on a course intended to intercept the airfield at Danang. The pilot was an apple-cheeked twenty-three-year-old. His name was Lieutenant Don Gordon, and he had been flying aircraft for almost two years. He considered his proficiency vast and at this moment was cursing the contrary wind that had blown up from the north and caused him to hold a heading of 340 degrees magnetic, almost 50 degrees to the right of the course originally plotted to bring him into Danang. The wind must have reached a velocity in excess of 75 knots, he decided. Below him the waters of the China Sea reflected the afternoon sunlight and in the distance the first faint outlines of the coast of Vietnam were visible as light smudgings on the horizon.

Briefly Gordon wondered why the air was so smooth if the wind was of such velocity. This thought occupied his mind only for a second before he turned his attention to flying this bear of an airplane. He was an uncomplicated young man who took a tremendous joy in flying, but whose tender years necessarily limited his aerial experience.

Thus he was in no way to blame for being unaware that his radar had been jammed by the Red Chinese and that he was flying a course that would take him unhesitatingly into North Vietnam at a point some thirty miles north of the 17th Parallel.

Gordon had been briefed on Soviet jamming devices, in particular on the device the Air Force called the "Pied Piper." But no one entertained the slightest notion that the device was in the hands of the Red Chinese. It was a Russian innovation and until recently the Russians had been more than reluctant to offer aid in any form to the Chinese Communists. Gordon could not possibly have guessed, even had he been far more experienced than he was, that his radar signal had been deliberately blacked out and a Red Chinese signal substituted. There was no vagrant wind at 35,000 feet this day. He was flying a true course down the false radar beam that would lead him to his destruction. Had he had the benefit of more flight hours in the area in which he was flying, perhaps he might have recognized certain terrain features that would have alerted him to his false course. But Gordon had never flown to Vietnam before; in fact, until one week ago, he had never been west of Hamilton Air Force Base in San Francisco.

Now he turned to his co-pilot and said, "Call Danang and get the wind on the deck."

A few moments later a voice from Danang came over the air.

"Ceiling and visibility unlimited. Wind one eight zero, ten knots."

Jesus. There must be a 180-degree wind shift. Well, at least the wind on the ground was okay. Gordon had never landed an RB-66B in a violent wind and he was not overly anxious to do so now. He eased forward trim tab on his elevators and the nose of the RB-66 lowered slightly; the air-speed needle began to climb as the plane accelerated.

"Get clearance for twenty-five thousand feet," he said to the co-pilot.

The clearance was granted and Gordon leveled off at 25,000 feet, his plane in cruise configuration. He squinted through the windshield where the sun was lowering, causing a blinding glare from the water almost five miles below. The shoreline was closer now and he could see the mountains looming far to the west through the hazy mist. Around him the sky was clear and a brilliant blue. There was nothing perilous or inimical in this sky that might threaten his well-being. Through his earphones he could hear the voices of the pilots flying the CAP from the *Concord*. He found it hard to believe that this land mass coming toward him was filled with countless numbers of desperate men who were trying their utmost to kill one another. Actually, Gordon had never truly considered the possibility that flying was anything other than a pleasurable pastime and a magnificent way in which to make a living, so he was totally unprepared for what was about to happen to him.

Colonel Lee Cheng circled slowly at 47,000 feet with a flight of eight MIG-21 fighters. In the thin air the control surfaces responded less acutely to the pressures exerted on them, so Lee's flight strung itself out in a loose, almost haphazard formation. He had been in contact with a coastal radar station for ten minutes and was aware that the American plane was being misdirected into North Vietnam. He smiled to himself as he turned the volume control on his radio receiver up just a trifle. His formation was flying precisely thirty miles north and twenty miles west of the 17th Parallel where it hits the Vietnam coast on the eastern seaboard.

He swept the sky out to sea with his hard eyes, straining for the first glimpse of the American bomber. He had not been informed what type aircraft the enemy was, but the radar station had relayed to him the inbound vector of the bomber and its estimated air speed.

Several days previously General Soohoo had informed Lee of the plan for decoying the enemy north of the Parallel. Soohoo had seen no reason to include Peking in his plan, so when the stray enemy planes were destroyed, Peking would believe it was deliberate violation of air space on the part of the enemy. This was exactly what Soohoo wanted Peking to think. The General's plan to escalate the war had already had some success. He had managed to have six additional squadrons of MIGs assigned to the Lungchou area from the Air Defense Command across the straits from Formosa.

Now Lee called the radar operator nine miles below. "Watchdog from Eagle Leader. Are you tracking?"

"Affirmative, Eagle Leader. Enemy approaches on course three hundred and forty magnetic. Altitude twenty-five thousand feet, air speed five hundred miles per hour."

In the cockpit of the RB-66 Lieutenant Gordon was in the process of committing an unforgivable error. On the radio panel was a small toggle switch that was of paramount importance to the young officer, although he was unaware of this. It was his IFF, Identification Friend or Foe, actuating switch. Had this vital piece of metal been thrown to the "On" position, Gordon's future would probably have been much brighter. This device sent forth a signal to the radar stations south of the Parallel that would have identified Gordon as a friendly, had the switch been on. As it was, Gordon's blip on the friendly screens was only a blip, without the identifying radio signal, and thus without identification, Gordon was presumed to be the enemy.

Gordon had forgotten his IFF completely because he had never turned it on. There had been no need for it until he had approached enemy waters. This oversight would have disastrous results for Lieutenant Gordon. Because all American and South Vietnamese airplanes had their IFF switches taped to the "On" position, when Gordon's blip appeared on the friendly scopes it was, of course, misconstrued.

"Enemy aircraft approaching on course three thirty. Estimate landfall twenty miles north of the Parallel." The report was made by a station located fifteen miles north of Hué.

Eight U.S. Air Force F-104s wheeled north from the sky above Danang and headed for the border. Since they had no intimation of an emergency, they left their throttles in cruise setting.

Gordon had decided to maintain altitude until he spotted Danang visually. He was still on traffic-control frequency having not, as yet, switched his radio to the tower frequency. He passed over the coastline and felt a slight premonition as he searched the ground below, unable to see the sprawling runway at Danang.

Colonel Lee got his final vector.

"Eagle from Watchdog. Enemy over the coast. Twenty miles due east of you at twenty-five thousand feet." Lee was on his way, his throttle rammed against the stop, before the transmission had ended. He did not go into afterburner because he wanted the enemy plane to be well within the definable borders of North Vietnam before he initiated his attack.

Lee saw the RB-66 long before Gordon saw the MIGs. Gordon and his co-pilot had their heads buried in the cockpit, earnestly consulting a map of Vietnam, as Lee and his flight passed them on a reciprocal heading.

"The enemy," Lee barked out. "Below at three o'clock. Swing behind and come down in high side runs. Bracket after completion. Eagle Three take the left side. Do not acknowledge."

Lee was already rolling over and letting the nose of his plane come down through the horizon. Then, as his speed built, he eased the nose up slowly and centered the enemy plane in his sights. He was far out of range, but he held the bomber on the inner sight ring and came down in a medium angle of dive. He was unfamiliar with this particular type of American aircraft and he did not know what armament, if any, might be stationed in the tail section to provide a stinger. His first pass would be merely a high-side run from astern. There would be ample time later to make a longer, sustained attack.

Forty miles south of the RB-66 the F-104s hurtled north. It might as well have been four hundred miles for all the good it would do Lieutenant Gordon.

Lee grunted and squeezed the trigger on his control stick. The shells vomited from the muzzles and streaked the sky, curving slightly downward and forming a shallow arc as they approached the target. He saw a small piece of the fuselage tear away in the high wind. He closed with a grim and relentless determination, his guns firing in short bursts as the enemy loomed ever larger before him. He was only two hundred yards from his target now and passing directly astern as he eased an infinitesimal amount of left aileron on his controls.

When at first Gordon heard the sound of Lee's guns, he thought he had thrown a turbine blade. He had only started to curse when blood erupted from his co-pilot's mouth and sprayed out over the map which Gordon held in his lap. With a horrified awareness he watched his co-pilot's eyes roll up into his head until only the red-streaked whites were showing. The body quivered as though in an awful chill and, as it slumped forward, Gordon saw the gaping hole torn in the back. Blood spattered the cockpit and dampened Gordon's flight suit as his heart thumped with triphammer blows. Without looking out of the cockpit, he shoved the controls full forward and firewalled his throttles. The RB-66 screamed downward through the sky.

"Jesus!" he cried to his radar controller. "Somebody's shooting at us. Get on the horn."

"Mayday, Mayday. Mayday." The radar controller's voice was constricted with terror. "This is Air Force Seven Thirty-five. We are under attack. We are under attack. Mayday. Mayday. Mayday."

Twenty miles away the flight of F-104s swung to the east and paralleled the border. Major Jack McKellar, the flight leader, watched the contrails to the north slashing a line of silver down the sky as Lee's plane came down on its attack.

"Danang control," McKellar called. "Friendly under attack north of the Parallel. Request permission to intercept. Go ahead." To the formation packed in tightly off his wingtips, McKellar said, "Charge armament."

Lee had passed the RB-66 and was climbing ahead for altitude to initiate his second attack. The rest of his planes came down with implacable deadliness, their tracers marking crimson veins through the thin air.

Gordon swore bitterly at his lack of caution as he thundered toward the deck, the air-speed needle already past the Mach One marking on the dial. The plane shook with an unceasing vibration at this speed in excess of the speed of sound. The control column pulsated in his hand and he hunched over as though to make of himself a smaller target in the cockpit. He had been an utter fool and he knew it and there would be a toll to pay before this day was done. He looked wide-eyed over his left shoulder and saw two MIGs flashing in at him, the red eyes winking at him and then elongating into red threads floating across the interval of space and disappearing just as they came to him. He heard a solid *wham* as something crashed into his rear section and his instrument panel quivered until the dials blurred in his eyesight.

His radar man's voice shrieked wildly. "Mayday for Christ's sake. Any friendly plane . . . we are under attack. We are under attack. For Christ's sake." His words were more a prayer than a curse.

Major McKellar still cruised south of the Parallel. Danang control had not yet answered his transmissions. He still watched the contrails away to the north. They were closer now as the RB-66 clawed for the border and sanctuary and the MIGs followed, all guns flaming.

"God damn it, Danang control," McKellar shouted into his mike. "Do I get permission to intercept?" There was no answer and the rage in McKellar grew. He was goddammed good and mad and had been even before the MIGs went after the RB-66. McKellar had stifled a simmering anger ever since the wire services had come out with the picture of his kid brother and a man named Miller standing before an execution squad in an unnamed village in South Vietnam. Now he waited with a vast impatience as his finger massaged the trigger on his stick in a gesture of hopeful anticipation.

Lee was down again, coming out of his high side run with dive brakes extended and feeling the drag effect on his plane as the airspeed needle drew itself down and rested on 550 knots on the dial. He did not sweep past as before, but hung there unmoving, glued to Gordon's tail as if by an invisible steel filament.

Gordon was running out of time and he knew it. In his rearview mirror he saw the MIG on his tail and closing. His altitude was now only 2,000 feet and he had no more depths of sky through which to flee. Ahead of him he could see contrails forming high above where the F-104s were coming down. Only he did not know they were F-104s. Had he been aware that McKellar was coming down, perhaps

173

he might not have made his final mistake of this dismal day. He watched in his mirror as the MIG settled in closer and he judged precisely when Lee's guns came into range.

At that moment Gordon did the only thing he thought was left for him to do. He pulled back strongly on his stick and the RB-66 soared up into the first half of a loop. There were numerous reasons why this maneuver was a poor choice. Not the least of these was the fact that he had never before attempted a loop in an RB-66. It was an unfortunate time and place in which to attempt his first.

McKellar was only five miles away now and he could see the MIGs and their target. He still waited for orders from Danang. He was putting his thumb on his transmitter button when Danang control came over the air.

"Random Leader from Danang. You are ordered to remain south of the border. I say again. You will not cross the border. Acknowledge."

"For Christ's sake," McKellar shouted. "They're shooting down an RB-66. Eight MIGs. I'm going after the bastards."

Another voice, this one heavy with authority, came over the radio. "This is Colonel Henricks here. You will *not* violate North Vietnam air space. This is an order, Major." There was a slight hesitation. "I don't like this any better than you do, McKellar," the Colonel said bitterly.

"Shit!" McKellar roared, in direct violation of Air Force regulations.

Gordon had reached the vertical now and was screaming directly up into the sky. His air speed dropped off rapidly and approached the stalling point, in his present configuration and power settings about 125 knots. Gordon started to pull onto his back too late. He eased toward the inverted position when he had dissipated too much of his air speed, so when he pulled back on the stick, the entire aircraft shuddered and the nose pitched violently for a moment. Then the plane fell off on the right wing and slowly mushed down through the sky. Gordon swore harshly as he jammed the control column all the way forward and banged the left rudder all the way to the floor boards. It took a second for the controls to bite into the air and receive an aerodynamic reaction. It was all the time Colonel Lee needed.

Lee in his MIG had seen the RB-66 pull up into the beginning of a loop and had shaken his head in disagreement with Gordon's manner of thinking. It was a stupid maneuver under existing circumstances and Lee made the most of the stupidity.

He swept up after Gordon, his throttle halfway retarded on the quadrant. He allowed the enemy plane to draw away from him on the vertical climb and he saw the other plane shudder and heave in the air as it stalled, then tumbled slowly over until its nose fell toward the ground. It was then, at a moment when the RB-66 was totally defenseless and out of control, that Colonel Lee jammed his throttle forward, opened fire, and flew up the pathway of his tracers. It was a no-deflection shot in the vertical-climb position; he merely held the trigger down and the majority of his shells found their target. He saw the enemy plane shed fragments of fuselage and tail assembly and there was a puff of black smoke from the left engine air-intake duct. Lee held his fire in one continual burst and released his trigger pressure only when he flew past the RB-66 at a distance of fifteen feet. He moved his aileron to the left and came over in a wingover roll; he pointed his nose toward the ground, regaining the enemy in his gunsight but out of range.

The last of Lee's shells had ruined Gordon. He stared with dismay at the stump of his right wrist where his hand had been. Horrified, he glanced at the floor boards and saw the bruised hand lying there, terribly blue for a moment, then turning pure white as the fingers curled into a claw. His chest had been torn away and he wondered in his brief and final moments why there was no pain. His eyes stared ahead through the windshield as the ground rose to meet him. It came very fast, he thought, and the last thing he ever saw was a small hillock that suddenly covered the entire windshield.

McKellar saw Gordon's aircraft explode when it hit the ground. There was a bursting blossom of black smoke and debris and then a curl of purple flame that mushroomed into a blazing pyre. Rage was hot within McKellar now and the memory of his brother and of the men who had died in the Skyraiders the day Belden flew out was with him and suddenly McKellar no longer gave a good goddam for restrictions or orders or anything else.

"We're going after the bastards," he called to his flight. He banked steeply to the north in the direction of Gordon's burning plane. The other 104s obediently followed, going into afterburner and screeching a cry of vengeance across the sky.

Lee saw them coming and called to his flight. "Rendezvous, Eagle flight. Return to base." The MIGs raced northward, away from the fight. Lee knew only too well that his ammunition and fuel were critical. He intended to offer no advantage to the enemy. There would be another day.

When McKellar saw the MIGs hightailing it north, a measure of sanity returned to him. He might catch the bastards, but to do so he would have to fly well into North Vietnam, possibly all the way to the Chinese border, a prohibitive distance in his present fuel state. He had turned back to the south when Danang control called him on the radio.

"Random Leader from Danang. Radar reports you have crossed the Parallel. I say again. You have violated North Vietnam air space. Acknowledge, Random Leader."

McKellar waited a few seconds. Then he said laconically into his mike, "That certainly is tough shit, Danang. You are fucking able right I violated air space."

It was Colonel Henricks' voice. "McKellar. Return to base. You are under arrest for disobeying orders. Do you receive? Over."

McKellar sighed in his cockpit. "I receive, Colonel. For Christ's sake, I receive. Only you're talking to the wrong guy. Talk to that pilot of the RB-66 if you can."

Then McKellar reached out and switched his radio to the "Off" position. He had had enough conversation for one afternoon.

Chapter
XI

At the far end of the strip at Danang airfield there was a former French Air Force barracks. It had long been ignored by the units on the field, due to its inaccessibility and the paucity of maintenance facilities in the area. The entire space had been ringed by a barbed-wire fence that had succumbed to the elements and had rusted and broken along its length. There was also a makeshift hangar, lopsided and dilapidated, about fifty yards from the barracks building and near to the pock-marked expanse of cement that served as a parking apron.

One morning in January the occupants of Danang awakened to find the run-down corner of the field undergoing a renovation. The barbed wire was being restrung, carpenters worked industriously on the broken boards and windows of the old hangar, and the barracks was already occupied by unidentified civilians, close-mouthed and taciturn, who turned away curious onlookers with curt disdain.

On the parking apron stood twelve glistening new F8 Crusader jet fighters, all without markings of any kind. The planes were fully configured for combat: four 20-mm cannon in the noses and the underside of the wings racked for the deadly Sidewinder missiles.

Gas trucks appeared as if by magic and parked in the fueling area. Ammunition supplies were stored carefully in ramshackle buildings adjacent to the barracks. Crates of spare parts were stacked before the hangars and covered with heavy tarpaulin.

Over all was an air of secrecy. Men came and went about their business with a total disregard for the activities of the rest of Danang airfield. Two rock-faced men in battered Navy chief's caps supervised the work within the boundaries of the barbed-wire fence. The others on the field pondered the air of quiet proficiency that lay over the entire operation. Without the usual confusion that accompanied the setting up of a squadron, the strangers, with a minimum of effort, transformed what had been no more than an eyesore into an efficient operating area.

The Commanding Officer at Danang, chagrined because he was unaware of the identity of the newcomers or the source of their considerable supplies, consulted the top-secret dispatch orders he had received from the headquarters of General Pham. He shook his head in perplexity. In more or less desultory language he was told to mind his own business and not interfere with what the dispatch referred to as the "operations of Squadron X Ray."

At night in the Officers' Club bar, the young Air Force pilots were puzzled as the civilians kept to themselves unless they chanced upon an old acquaintance. In such cases the word was passed quietly, heads nodded in acquiescence and the probable cause for the presence at Danang of Squadron X Ray remained a moot question. But the young men heard the names and like all young men, they wondered.

"Belden. Seems I heard the name somewhere."

"Christ! You mean you don't know who that guy is? Listen, friend, he wrote the book."

"Belden. Dan Belden. Good God! I thought he hung up the wings a hundred years ago."

"We tangled with him up there this afternoon. That sonofabitch must have been born in an airplane."

"You hear who the other guys with him are? Listen to this, you guys. Bates, Anders, Hawkins, Kilpatrick, Corey . . ."

"Jesus."

"Sort of old, aren't they? They go back to when I was a kid."

"Further than that, sonny. Like I said. They wrote the book."

The days and nights wore away and Squadron X Ray came to be an accepted addition to the operations at Danang, although no one as yet was certain of the reason for its existence. Belden watched his men lean down from the strenuous flight schedule, watched their eyes harden as they approached that pinnacle of expertness toward which they all aimed. Old abilities were remembered, refurbished and nurtured carefully and all of them found that the years had not dulled the myriad skills with which they had written their page of glory.

Each of them found that memory retains more than the sharpest images, the violences, the dramatics, the incongruities. If you go back far enough toward your beginnings, you will find again the skills of your youth, dim in the back of your mind but waiting to be called up again, waiting for the nerve ends to reacquaint themselves with the delicate touch, the reflexive action. Quiescent in a corner of your mind you will find the old lessons learned on the flying fields of Kansas or in the skies of the South Pacific. They are there and to the fighter it is only a matter of desire to call them up and then you were what you had been in your youth and what you had been all your life and would be until you died.

And as Belden told himself that at last they were as ready as they would ever be, and wondered what chance would present itself to engage in combat in the air, Colonel Lee came blasting down again.

On the tenth day in January another inoffensive RB-66 was drawn off course by the radar-jamming devices of the Reds north of the Parallel. In a situation identical with that which befell Lieutenant Gordon the unwary reconnaissance plane was lured fifty miles north of the border and Lee destroyed the RB-66 and the men in it.

Again a flight of 104s was within striking distance of the scene of the action and again they were prohibited from crossing the Parallel and engaging the MIGs. The flight leader of the 104s, this time a gregarious lieutenant colonel named Pat Murphy, replied to the order to remain south of the Parallel with blatant disrespect.

"Danang tower," Murphy called. "Have received your order. Go fuck yourselves."

But Murphy did not intercept the MIGs. Lee was away again, leaving behind the twisted, blackened wreckage of the RB-66 and the echo of silent laughter in the sky.

And there now occurred on the airfields of South Vietnam and on the aircraft carriers of the Seventh Fleet, a series of events that in any other war or in any other set of circumstances would have been incredible.

It all started in the BOQ at Danang where Major Jack McKellar and Lieutenant Colonel Pat Murphy were confined to quarters while court-martial proceedings were instigated against them. Both McKellar and Murphy were exceptionally popular men whose flying skills were respected by their subordinates and superiors alike. The murmurs of discontent soon blossomed into bitter curses of anger at the injustice being visited on the two officers.

There were quiet conversations in the BOQ, and voices argued heatedly late into the night. A division of Navy fighter pilots, stranded overnight at Danang, joined in the discussions and carried word back to the pilots in the Fleet. McKellar and Murphy, of course, had no part in the conversations because they were confined to their quarters until their courts-martial convened to try them because they had wanted terribly to fight an enemy who was killing one of their own.

In the ready rooms the feeling of unrest and dissatisfaction spread. The stories of the RB-66s and the Crusaders were told and retold and youngsters newly come from the training fields in the States were puzzled at the air of rebellion that infected the flying men in South Vietnam. They had come west with bright dreams of glory, thoroughly indoctrinated in the past honors of their service and they all had visions of the pennants waving and the blare of martial music in the air. But they had found disillusionment where they had thought to find grandeur, and debasement where they sought distinction. They were not unlike the small boy who has been punched in the nose and is dragged away by the teacher before he has struck his first blow and thus is not at all certain that he would have measured up had the contest been allowed to continue. In a stranger manner, all of them felt their personal honor had been impugned.

The date of McKellar's court-martial was set. February 1.

On the twenty-sixth of January ten pilots of Fighter Squadron 146 based at Danang reported to the flight surgeon in sick bay. They had identical complaints. Each of them, strangely enough, suffered from sharp pains in the lower part of the back near the end of the spinal column. They waited patiently while the flight surgeon kneaded and probed and finally injected a shot of cortisone into each back. Naturally with such devastating pain the pilots could not fly and were grounded.

The next morning seventeen pilots from the squadron adjacent to 146 on the airfield reported to the same flight surgeon, this time with complaints of severe pain in the *upper* part of the back where the large shoulder muscles ridge the shoulder blades. The flight surgeon shook his head, employed his needle again, and grounded the seventeen sufferers. There was absolutely no medical proof available to substantiate or disprove the validity of the supposed complaints. A sore back is probably one of the few ailments of the human species that a doctor has to accept as valid on the word of his patient. It will not show up on an X ray and it causes no protuberances or discolorations in the afflicted area. When a man says he has a sore back, only God can call him a liar.

Aboard the carrier *Concord* fully three-quarters of the Crusader fighter squadron came down with a stiffness in the central region of the spinal column. One pilot stated categorically that an epidemic of encephalitis was under way and it would probably be only a few days before the whole damned Task Force came down with it.

There was logic in his reasoning because the next day a sister squadron on the *Ardennes* was suddenly beset in the same manner. Exactly 90 per cent of the pilots experienced crippling spasms in the area near the tail bone and were grounded indefinitely.

Absolutely no one was deluded by these supposed paroxysms of agony, but it is a known fact that any pilot has one final prerogative left to him when everything else is gone. He cannot be ordered or in any way forced to fly an airplane when he deems himself physically unfit to do so. And who would be so foolhardy as to fly a jet fighter with a stiff back?

On the twenty-ninth of January 80 per cent of the available combat pilots in the Seventh Fleet and on the airstrips of South Vietnam were grounded.

For all practical purposes the military aviators in Southeast Asia were out on strike.

"This is the goddamnedest sit-down strike in history," Admiral Smoke Dusane said to Storm Ryerson. The two men were sitting in the operations barracks at Danang airstrip.

"Who the hell can blame them?" Ryerson asked. "Christ, Smoke, they have to stand by and watch their buddies shot down in cold blood and they can't fight back. How would you feel?"

"Lousy," Dusane admitted. "That's why there'll be no courts-martial in the Seventh Fleet. If their backs are sore, it's all right with me." He cocked an eye at Ryerson. "This is what you wanted, isn't it? What does Washington have to say?"

"They're shook, Smoke. They're really shook. They're re-evaluating their policy now and I think we're on the right track. I still can't figure"—he shook his head—"what Chinaman up there is working for the same thing I am. That commie Frenchman who writes out of Hanoi says that Lee is leading the MIGs on these flights, but Lee's only a colonel. There's someone back of him with more rank than that. And working against Peking's policy too."

"More power to him," Dusane murmured. "And now would you mind telling me why you're here at Danang and why you sent for me?"

"I'm here on that RB-66 investigation. It's ridiculous. I don't have to investigate. We know that kid was lured north on a phony radar beam and then Lee jumped him. They had it figured and they knew we wouldn't let our guys cross the Parallel after them. Well, one of these days we'll fool the bastards and maybe that day isn't so far off."

"Oh?" Dusane said carefully.

"As for your second question—why you're here—I'll let Dan answer that."

"I would assume," Dusane remarked dryly, "that the shit is going to hit the fan again."

"You assume correctly." Ryerson grinned. "Only this time"—his grin faded—"it's going to be a hell of a lot hairier than that raid on Laos."

"Well," Dusane said, "I hope to Christ we're doing the right thing. I hope all this works and that we aren't left with egg on our faces."

"There's something else you don't know. Something that absolutely precludes our giving up now. You'll find that out, too, when we see Belden."

"One more thing, Storm. Why didn't General Pham move north after Dan hit Laos? He was all set for it."

"Partly my fault," Ryerson said. "We learned the Chinamen didn't have the troops up north that we thought. The move wouldn't have sucked them down and that's what we wanted. All Pham would have done was stick his neck out and lay himself open to air attack. We wouldn't violate the Parallel to help him and so we decided to wait. But he's going north. And pretty damn soon too. He has to and you'll know why in a little while."

"Well, no matter what. We've done pretty well so far. I noticed those new Air Force fighters out on the line. Too damn bad all the pilots have these terribly sore backs. How many new planes came over?"

"Seventy-five. And we've got a regiment of Marines in bivouac near Saigon. And a whole damn division standing by at Okinawa. Three more aircraft carriers are at berth in Pearl Harbor. Things are moving."

"Then this new thing with Dan and his men is important?"

"Smoke"—Ryerson spoke heavily—"it may be the most important fight you and I ever saw."

"Well now," Dusane said softly. "Can I have a piece of it?"

"I wouldn't be surprised. You might lose those three stars."

"Well!" Dusane sighed. "We'll go down together, old friend. My only hope is that there is a place set aside somewhere for dishonored Admirals."

Dan Belden leaned on the railing of the porch on the upper deck of the converted barracks and studied the runway activity at Danang. Only a few cargo transports lumbered around the landing circle and slowly came in for their landings. The jets were parked in silent rows that stretched to the far end of the field. An ominous sense of desolation had settled over Danang. It reminded Belden of the aircraft graveyards in Arizona after the war. He had seen them parked there, silent and empty, stretching as far as the eye could see, row on row of fighters and bombers, mothballed against the weather and time, ghosts of another day.

He flipped his cigarette over the railing and watched the sparks flicker in the dusk. Then he went inside to where Hawkins sat on the edge of the bed.

Hawkins grinned up at him, the grin stretching the taut skin on his ravaged face. "Daydreaming, Dan?"

"A little." Belden sat on the other bed, facing Hawkins. "Hawk, there's something you want to tell me?" he asked.

For a moment Hawkins did not answer. When he did, it was in the tone of a man who had made a weighty decision.

"I'll show you something, Dan," he said.

He rose and moved to his val-pak lying in a corner. He rummaged in the bag and then handed Belden a small bottle. Belden glanced at the writing on it and handed it back.

"You know what I've got?" Hawkins asked.

"I knew it a long time ago, Hawk. You look like a handful of bones stuffed into a skin sack. Why the hell the big secret?"

"I thought maybe it wouldn't come badly until later." Hawkins forced a grin back to his lips. "It's worse every day. I may not last."

Belden gestured at the bottle. "Those things help?"

"Not too much any more. At first they did."

"Yeah," said Belden. "Well, there's only one answer. We'll fly you back to the States and a good hospital. Maybe there's——"

He broke off as Hawkins slowly shook his head.

"Not that way, Dan. I made up my mind a long time ago. This is where I want to go out. This way. Not in a bed fading away to a shadow lying on a white pillow like a death's head." He saw the doubt clouding Belden's eyes. "I'm okay for a few weeks. Maybe a month. After that I won't have the strength."

"Christ, Hawk!" Belden said futilely.

"How about it, Dan. Will you go along with it?"

"That's a stupid question, Hawk. I'll go along with anything you want. You fly my wing from now on."

"Thanks, Dan. Thanks for everything," Hawkins said in a low voice.

Bates spoke from the doorway where he stood with Anders. "That's a lousy goddam trick, Hawk. Keeping your old buddies out in the dark. What the hell."

"Eavesdropper," Hawkins smiled.

"One thing," Anders said decisively. "There won't be any embarrassment about this. There doesn't need to be. Okay. So Hawk is on his way out. Hell. We all are. One day or the next. What's the difference in a few lousy years? That's the way it will be from now on around here."

"That's the best speech you've made in twenty years, Cort," Belden said.

"You bastards," Hawkins said huskily. "You bastards."

"Well," Bates said solemnly, "if this guy is going to cry all over the place, I guess we might as well go over to the club where Admiral Ryerson has promised to spring for dinner. Eat some of those pills, Hawk, and we're on our way. And for Christ's sake, wipe your eyes. The Air Force will think we're a bunch of crybabies instead of the inscrutable legends I've been telling everybody we are."

"We'll keep this in the family," Hawkins said. "The brass would throw me out in five minutes if they knew."

"One thing," Belden said. "Your family?"

Hawkins nodded. "It's been attended to, Dan. Don't worry about it."

"That's good enough for us," Belden said.

"If somebody asks me why you look so goddam bad," Bates said, "I'll tell them you caught a bad case of the clap from that waitress at the club. Now let's go eat some free chow."

They joined Storm Ryerson and Admiral Dusane at the bar in the Officers' Club. It was early in the evening and only a few Air Force pilots were scattered around the room, speaking in quiet voices and with the ever-present juxtaposition of the hands.

"You look like hell," Ryerson said to Hawkins.

"My ulcers," Hawkins said. "I got them in Korea flying under a hard-nosed bastard named Ryerson."

"What are you drinking?" Dusane asked.

"Double whiskies," Belden said.

"How's Lori?" Ryerson asked.

"You're the spymaster around here," Belden said. "Suppose you tell me."

"She's fine," Ryerson smiled. "When are you getting married?"

"April," Belden answered.

"That's a good month to get married," Hawkins said.

"As good as any, if you have to do it," Anders added.

"By the way, Dan," Ryerson said, "when are you giving Pham back his ADs?"

"Not yet," Belden answered. "One more thing to do with them."

"May I remind someone," Dusane interjected, "that those ADs belong to *me*. Not to General Pham. It took a lot of paper work and skulduggery to steal them from the Navy. I think somebody ought to tell me what the hell is going on around here."

"Smoke," Belden said, "we're going to hit Hanoi."

"Why not Moscow?" Dusane snorted facetiously.

"You may have something there," Bates said.

"Are you serious, Dan?" Dusane asked. He turned to look at Ryerson.

"Don't look at me," Ryerson said. "This was Dan's idea."

"They'll stand you against a wall. That's what they'll do." Dusane faced the others. "Are you all crazy?"

"Slow down, Smoke," Belden said. "We've got reason. We're getting Lee to come down and fight. We're finally going to get to the bastard and the only way we can manage it is to hit Hanoi."

Dusane thought about this a moment and then nodded to himself. "Maybe," he said softly. "Just maybe it would work. Go ahead, Dan. Tell me more."

"I'm sending four of the ADs from the plantation up to Hanoi in darkness," Belden said. "They'll hit the airfield just outside the city just before daybreak. If I know Lee, he'll be down like a pissed-off panther. The ADs will head east for the coast at full balls and try to get inside international waters. Lee will be right on their asses. He'll get to the ADs sooner or later, but when he does, he'll find eight Crusaders waiting for him."

"Christ, Dan," Dusane said. "He'll have you on his radar?"

"No he won't." Belden shook his head. "A half hour before first light we'll launch from here. We'll stay on the deck and well out to sea and head north with the throttles against the stop. I won't go for altitude until I get a call from Kilpatrick. Their radar won't touch me at fifty feet. When Mac gives me the word, we'll go into burner and be at forty thousand feet in a couple of minutes."

After a moment Dusane said, "You know, Lee just might have fifteen or twenty MIGs up there with him. Maybe I'd better have a Combat Air Patrol up there somewhere. It might be a damn good idea."

"Suits me, Smoke." Belden smiled. "But no one goes after Lee. That one is mine."

Dusane inclined his head. "This could be a real Donnybrook."

"Which brings me to another thing," Ryerson interrupted. "Time may well be running out on us. That's what makes this fight of Dan's so goddam important." Ryerson lowered his voice, although they were an isolated group in the room. "We've got our reports from the underground in Peking. That blitz offensive is set for July or August. They've already started to move air squadrons and infantry divisions down from the Formosa area. We've only got a few months left."

"They know this in Washington?" Belden asked.

"Hell yes," Ryerson replied. "But they won't get off their asses and do anything about it. Maybe they think it's all a rumor. How the hell do I know? All I'm sure of is that we've *got* to be ready by July or August."

"That makes this flight of yours sort of special, Dan," Dusane mentioned.

"It has to be," Ryerson said. "This could be a suicide mission for Kilpatrick and his ADs."

"Well," Belden said, "we can hope not." After a moment he added, "It has to be done anyway."

"When do you go, Dan?" Dusane asked.

"Day after tomorrow," Belden answered. "And I'll tell you something, Storm. If Lee comes out and we meet him, I fully intend to fight that bastard all the way back to his base if I have to. I'll respect no sanctuaries or borders or any other damn thing. Okay?"

Ryerson nodded. "Okay, Dan." He turned to the others and raised his glass. "Let's hope we have the time we need, gentlemen."

It was 2000 and fully dark when the armada of new MIG fighters came into the landing circle at Lungchou. They came in a V of Vs, thirty-five of them, and they broke off sharply, expertly, maintaining precise intervals of space as they strung out on their downwind leg, their navigation lights gleaming brightly in the clear air. The voices barked sharply over the radio in the tower where Colonel Lee stood and watched them land.

Lee's grim face broke into a rare smile as he saw the planes wheel sharply into line on the parking apron. These were not novice pilots in the new MIGs. They were the finest fighter pilots the Republic had to offer. Lee had picked each of them after meticulous and discriminating investigation and he knew that he now had as expert a fighter command as was available in Asia.

He turned to the tiny figure of General Soohoo standing by his side. "We will move south to Hanoi at daybreak, sir," he said respectfully.

The General nodded. "Very good, Colonel. You will inform me when my headquarters are completed."

"I will, sir." Lee pointed to the planes stretching along the parking area. "We are winning our private battle with Peking, sir. We have a fighting force now. We can engage anything they throw at us."

"If they do, Colonel. If they do."

"They will, sir. I'm certain of this. Belden will not sit back and accept dishonor. I have ground it into his face the past weeks. He lost two Skyraiders in the attack on Laos. Then the Crusaders we decoyed north. And the reconnaissance aircraft we lured with the false radar. All this eats at him, General. He will come out fighting. I'm sure of it."

"Four additional squadrons are undergoing readiness inspections at Canton," Soohoo said. "We can expect them within a month, perhaps two. Sometime this spring fifty divisions of infantry will move down to this area, ready to move across the border in August. By that time we must demoralize the Americans. When we hit them they will fall back against the sea and then you and your squadrons will have them as so many clay pigeons."

"You heard the broadcasts regarding the attitude of their pilots?" Lee asked.

"I did," Soohoo replied. "Mutiny already and we have not even struck our first blow. Perhaps the Americans do not have the heart for fighting this war."

"I would not count on that, General," Lee said slowly.

"We will find out," Soohoo said. "Now come. We will brief the new pilots and drink a final toast before you go south to Hanoi."

Far to the south, Captain Xuan Nonh and his men bivouacked in the muddy delta country southwest of Saigon near the tiny village of Khanh An. A few yards removed from his men, who slept secure within the cover of an isolated region of trees and heavy undergrowth, Xuan consulted a set of written orders which had been delivered to him by courier that afternoon. He grunted with pleasure as he learned that he was to move north again. He was infinitely weary of operations in this country where Arvin patrols were so numerous. He thought of the high, cool mountains in the north and perhaps of a promotion that awaited him if he lived to reach them. But there was a thing he must do first. He moved a few feet nearer to the carefully camouflaged fire that burned weakly in a small indentation dug into a ravine wall. He spread his well-worn map out on the ground beside him.

Tomorrow they would cross the Mekong River and set a course to bypass Saigon. Xuan calculated it would take him a week, possibly ten days, to cover the distance to Hon Quan. He would take no unnecessary chances and he would travel with utmost diligence. He would live to see the cool mountains again and he would pause on his way to devastate the plantation at Hon Quan. Intelligence reports had indicated to his superiors that the troops garrisoning the Morlaix rubber complex had been seriously depleted to reinforce roving patrols in the field. His orders were to level the entire area after wiping out the troops holding the scanty perimeter around the makeshift airstrip.

His eyes gleamed in the weak firelight as he refolded his map and tucked it under his shirt. As it does with some men, the killer lust had seeped into Xuan's bloodstream and it sang now as he thought of the carnage he would wreak at the Morlaix plantation. He would kill. He would burn. Rape. Ruin. Leave nothing but smoking debris and a wail of terror in the night.

Chapter
XII

Belden stood on the flight line at Danang and watched O'Toole and Merchant supervise the final fueling of the eight Crusaders. Beside him were Storm Ryerson and Admiral Dusane, huddled within their raincoats, the misty wetness running in rivulets down their cheeks.

"Christ, what a night!" Dusane grumbled. "Will this damn weather screw you up, Dan?"

Belden threw his head back and squinted at the blanket of cloud cover. "It won't bother us," he said. "It may give Mac and the ADs a little trouble."

Belden looked out again at the aircraft standing on the line, the light from the parking lanterns glistening on the wet cockpit canopies. The planes looked bulky and unwieldy, resting their thick bodies on the slender struts of the landing gears. The unfolded wings looked too small to lift the massive weight of the airframe. The wings themselves were movable, capable of being adjusted to a greater angle of attack to afford increased lift and a lower landing speed. He could see the deadly snouts of the four twenty-millimeter cannon studding the nose sections. One of Merchant's men was busily loading the belts of tracer and high explosive incendiary shells. Belden glanced at his watch—0245. Mac Kilpatrick and his men should be launching within fifteen minutes.

"He's got six hundred miles to fly," Belden said. "Three hours and twenty minutes to the target. He'll hit them at 0620, fifteen minutes before first light."

"What are his chances of getting in undetected?" Ryerson asked.

"Pretty good." Belden shrugged in the darkness. "He'll try to stay between the deck and the lowest cloud layer. He might get lucky and find a couple of hundred feet of clear air. Otherwise he'll go by his radar." He turned to face the older men, the hard planes of his face accentuated by the shadows and the wetness glistening on his cheeks. "He's got to stay low or they'll pick him up on their scopes. The closer to ground level, the better off he's going to be." He glanced at Dusane, "You're going out to the fleet?"

Dusane nodded. "I'll be on the bridge when you make your tally-ho." He paused. "I have a sixteen-plane Combat Air Patrol up this morning."

The flash of Belden's grin was lost in the night. "Thanks, Smoke," was all he said, but there was warmth under the words.

"What time will you leave?" Ryerson asked.

"We've got two hundred and fifty miles to go. We'll launch at 0550," Belden replied.

Dusane nodded solemnly, as if in accord with a ponderous decision. "It will give you ample time," he said.

The voices of O'Toole and Merchant carried through the murky air in a hollowing echo of mild curses. The huge gas truck with its load of kerosene was only a lumpy shadow against the lighter color of the aircraft.

"I had a dream last night," Belden said with a smile.

"Ah!" Dusane nodded. "You were in flames and you were bailing out and at the last moment you discovered you had left your parachute behind." He chuckled because he had experienced this dream himself.

"No," Belden said, shaking his head. "I was on Lee's ass and I couldn't catch the sonofabitch. I had her at full balls and in burner, but he was drawing away from me and I was shaking my fist at him and using all the four-letter words I ever learned."

"You'll catch him today," Dusane said.

"I can hope so," Belden said.

"You'll carry Sidewinders?" Dusane asked the question.

"We only have eight. One to a plane," Belden said. "That's

enough. I never considered heat-seeking missiles too adaptable to air-to-air fighting between fighter planes. They're all right with the bombers."

"What's your line-up?" Dusane asked.

"I'll lead with Hawk on my wing. Bates and Anders the second section. Corey takes the second division with Shonnard, Dugan, and Thayer. Mac Kilpatrick takes the ADs in with Knight, Carpenter, and Crandon."

"Quite an all-star team," Ryerson mused.

"There'll never be another like it," Belden said. "Not in this war or any other."

"Agreed," said Dusane. "And I'd like to suggest that we go inside out of this abominable rain and drink some hot coffee. I'm sure O'Toole and Merchant can get the fuel into the tanks without our expert guidance. Besides, my nose is running."

"It happens to all of them, Dan," Ryerson said as they turned toward the operations building. "They get near retirement age and their noses start to run. An affliction indigenous to three-star Admirals."

"I'm nervous," Dusane said. "My nose always runs when I'm nervous."

"What the hell are *you* nervous about?" Ryerson said. "It's Dan who's going to fly."

"I'm nervous about my three stars," Dusane replied. "I have a feeling someone may try to take them away from me after this morning's work."

As the three men sipped coffee in the ready room, on the deck above them Ray Hawkins sat at a desk where he had spent several hours composing a letter to his wife, Janet. He had been amazed at the difficulty he experienced when he tried to set down in writing what was so plainly evident in his heart.

Now he read again the stilted phrases, then he slipped the letter into an envelope, scrawled Belden's name on it, and stuffed the letter into his val-pak, where it would be discovered when Belden inventoried his effects. He filled a glass with water at the washbasin and swallowed three pills from a tiny bottle, which he replaced in the cabinet. He stared at himself in the mirror over the washbowl and noted the angry veins lacing the whiteness of his eyes. The pain was becoming intolerable and it no longer localized itself in his neck and upper back. With each beat of his heart a fiery agony pulsated over his entire upper torso. A deep breath caused him to grunt with pain and sudden movement dizzied him. His strength was going, too, and his knees felt watery, as though something was drawing the vigor out of his muscles through a hole in his leg. In the mirror his face was an old man's face, the skin stretched tautly over the cheekbones and sinking in at the corners of his mouth, which was only a slash of torment against the ghastly whiteness of his flesh. From under his eyes two heavy lines ran down his cheeks to the muscle-ridged line of his jaw. He stared at himself and thought he looked like nothing so much as an old skull that had been disinterred after its owner had been dead ten years.

He uncapped a whiskey bottle standing on the dresser and took a long drink, grimacing as he sought to hold it down. He knew liquor could never make him drunk again, so he took another. It was strange, he thought, to be standing in this silent room with the sure knowledge in him that he would never know this exact time of day again. He laughed softly to himself because he felt as though some great, imponderable weight had been lifted from his shoulders. He looked down the length of his body and hated it as a man hates a shrunken and rotting thing. He forced himself to look upon his plight with the prejudiced eye of the man who has convinced himself that his good fortune holds strong. He was going to die quickly, in an instant of time, and the terrible pain would die with him. His ugly body would disappear, trailing its blackened hulk down the sky that he loved so well. This was the only way to go. With good friends saluting as he fell. Not in the fetid bed, wrapped in soiled bedsheets. And it could have happened before. He might have died in a thousand other places under circumstances far less pleasant. Hell. He might have killed himself falling up a stairway at home.

He placed the whiskey bottle on the desk in Belden's quarters and then he went below to the ready room.

"Kilpatrick should be launching now," O'Toole said to Merchant. They stood together by the last Crusader on the flight line, supervising the end of the refueling operation. "I keep telling myself we had those ADs running like a Swiss watch."

"We did. Relax," Merchant said. "We worked over those bastards till six o'clock last night. Whatever else happens, those goddam airplanes will fly." He glanced briefly at the sky above them. "Jesus, I wouldn't want to be going out in this crap. Not even if I was back at Pensacola and all it was was a night navigation hop."

"Forget it," O'Toole said. "You aren't going out anywhere in this crap. Neither am I and I'm ashamed to admit I'm glad about it."

O'Toole reached into his pocket and withdrew a small bit of medal that caught the light of a parking lantern.

"What you got there?" Merchant asked.

"A medal," O'Toole said. "A St. Jude medal." He held it up on its length of chain and Merchant glanced at it.

"St. Jude medal?" Merchant asked.

"The Patron Saint of Hopeless Cases," O'Toole said. "I've carried it a long ways."

"Ever do you any good?"

O'Toole regarded Merchant with a pained expression. "I'm here. I would guess it has."

Merchant followed as O'Toole walked down the flight line, climbed up on the wing of a Crusader and opened the cockpit canopy. He leaned in and carefully draped the medal around the throttle quadrant. Then he shut the canopy and dropped lightly to the ground.

"It's not good to trade your luck," Merchant said.

"He'll need it more than I ever will," O'Toole said.

"That's Belden's plane?"

O'Toole shook his head. "No," he said. "That's Mr. Hawkins' plane. I think he will find comfort in St. Jude this morning. I hope so."

"He's sure as hell a sick-looking guy."

"I think it will be over soon," O'Toole said gently. "I think he'll be all right soon." He shivered in the night air and turned the collar of his raincoat up about his neck. "And now let's get the hell in where it's dry and perhaps I might stumble on an old bottle of whiskey that I misplaced a few hours ago."

The minutes before a combat mission are precious because they may well be the last moments of time in which a man can remember the things that have made him. In the ready room at the Morlaix plantation the four Skyraider pilots of the attack mission had consulted their memories, sorted out the souvenirs of their pasts that they wished to take with them, and had then turned their attention to the plotting boards on their laps.

Macgregor Kilpatrick finished writing the flight information on the blackboard and turned to face the three men with whom he would fly out to attack the airfield at Hanoi. He assumed a spurious air of grave solemnity.

"Well, there it is," Kilpatrick said. "We've got six hundred miles to fly to reach the target. Three hours and twenty minutes. We will stay on the deck all the way."

The others nodded and made quick notations on their plotting boards.

"We will be on channel eight for purposes of communication," Kilpatrick continued, "but let's keep it quiet unless someone runs into an emergency. All radar units will be kept in continual operation."

"Only two of the planes have radar," Lou Knight advised.

"I am aware of that," Kilpatrick said dryly. "Just trust in your old dad here and I will get you there. One thing, however . . ." He paused a moment. "There are mountains to the north of us and these mountains have large gorges and crevasses and other nasty things in them. Some of these passes and gorges and things have dead ends and I advise all of you to stay out of them unless you've learned how to back up an airplane. I say this in case we might, through some childish mistake, become separated."

"That's very interesting," Sid Carpenter said. "Though hardly conducive to a high state of morale. Tell me something. If I lose you, and supposing I have not as yet learned how to back up an airplane, do I continue to the target in the blind or do I return to base?"

"You do neither," Kilpatrick said. "You pull back on your stick and you climb above the weather and head for Danang in the clear. Circle until the weather clears. By that time the rest of us who have not been so amateurish as to get lost will probably be there to take you by the hand."

Carpenter nodded with a wry smile and started to shrug into his Mae West. "I suppose," he said laconically, "we can expect the MIGs by the time we reach the coast?"

"More than likely," Kilpatrick said evenly. "We will drop our loads and head down the Red River. I assume you will all be able to follow the Red River to the sea because it's the only large river in the whole damn area. This Red River"—his tone was didactic—"is not to be confused with the Red River in the great state of Texas. That is a different river altogether. If I had more time, I would give you all a lesson in geography."

"But you don't have more time," Del Crandon broke in. He slipped his .38 pistol and cartridge belt over his shoulder. "It frightens me to contemplate the dire results should Dan Belden be five minutes late or we should be five minutes early."

"Belden will be there," Kilpatrick said positively. "When we head down the Red River, we will spread out in two sections about a quarter of a mile apart. If the MIGs get to us, go into a weave and keep heading down that river. Let's hope we get out to sea before they find us."

Lori Morlaix was waiting as they filed silently from the ready room. She put a detaining hand on Kilpatrick's arm.

"It's too early for you to be out here, Lori."

"I had to, Mac. I had to," she said simply.

"I know," Kilpatrick said. "You'll get used to it."

"Mac"—she spoke softly in a beseeching voice—"don't let anything happen to him. Take care of Dan."

Kilpatrick laughed with a genuine amusement. "I'm afraid you've got the wrong guy, Lori. *We're* counting on *him* to take care of *us*." But he saw the terror far back in her eyes. "It's nothing to worry about. Everything will be all right. Believe this, Lori."

"It isn't that simple, Mac. I can't believe it's all that simple."

"Isn't it?" Kilpatrick smiled. "This isn't something new to us, Lori. To any of us. Other men get up in the morning and get on a train and go to the office. We get up and go out and bomb Hanoi and fight the MIGs in the sky. So it really is rather simple. Try to understand and you'll be all right." He glanced at his watch. "See you later, Lori."

She watched him move into the mist until he was only a shadow climbing into the cockpit and the voices of the others were mere unintelligible murmurings coming to her out of the murk. A few moments later the engines stuttered and the flames flashed from the exhausts and then all four propellers were spinning in great crimson-tinted medallions. The mechs whom Merchant had left at the field jumped down from the wings and removed the chocks. Then they stood back from the planes, two red night wands lighted in their hands. They signaled the ADs out of the chocks and the engines' sound rose in pitch as the Skyraiders moved, sluggishly at first, then faster, and Kilpatrick led the way down the taxi strip to the take-off spot. They wheeled into position, forming a four-plane division on the runway. To Lori, they were only a handful of flames spurting in the darkness. The engines shrilled to an ear-piercing roar and the ADs moved down the runway as one plane, each pilot jockeying his throttle to maintain precise position on the exhaust flames of the plane on which he was flying. They accelerated to take-off speed that way, not deviating so much as a foot from their predetermined position.

They were airborne at 0301 hours and Kilpatrick flipped his gear lever and the wheels tucked into the wheel-wells of the Skyraider. He throttled back and set a course for the northeast. As his compass needle steadied on 030, he looked back and in the hissing drizzle of the night he saw the licking tongues of the exhausts holding in close to him, flying tight off his wingtips as the planes droned steadily on a vector for Hanoi.

Two hours later Macgregor Kilpatrick passed abeam of the Tam Ky homer. At this point he checked his exact mileage against the time he had been airborne and came to the conclusion that he was flying in a no-wind condition. This deduction was in accord with his pre-flight navigation, but Kilpatrick was only human and could not possibly have had the slightest premonition that the vagaries of fortune were at that moment conspiring against him.

Far to the south, near a small island named Poulo Condore, the calm surface of the sea was rustled by a light breeze, which at first only rippled the water with no more significance than the whisper of a zephyr through tall grass. But the ripples persisted and nourished themselves into swells which moved northward as rolling waves heralding a wind of considerable velocity. In itself this wind possessed no importance whatsoever and it was doubtful it would ever reach

20 knots of motion. But it directed itself due north and this fact would culminate in appalling results for Macgregor Kilpatrick and his flight.

The Skyraiders were twenty minutes past Tam Ky when the wind came from behind them and gently brushed them along through the sky. Since an air-speed indicator only reacts to the wind coming from in front of it, from the force of the onrushing wind hitting the Pitot tube, there was no possible way—with the exception of utilizing prominent landmarks—to deduce ground speed, by which Kilpatrick could become aware of, and estimate, the increase in his speed over the ground.

With the advent of the tail wind, of which they were all unaware, the flight of Skyraiders would reach their target approximately nine minutes before their estimated time of arrival.

Belden finished his briefing at 0530. The pilots were on their feet, rummaging through their effects and strapping various articles of flight gear to their bodies when Belden had one thing more to say. The murmuring of voices stilled as he rose to face them in the ready room.

"If this was a long time ago," he said with a smile, "I suppose I would stand here and give you guys instructions on how to react in the various sets of circumstances we might run into up there this morning. As things stand, I think that would be sort of presumptuous of me. Nobody alive can tell any one of you how to conduct yourself in a fight in the sky. That's why you're here this morning. Frankly, I almost feel sorry for those Chinese bastards. The book says we ought to stay in two-plane sections no matter what happens. It worked for us quite a while ago, but I'm not sure it will work this morning. We're not flying Hellcats any longer. So take it as you see it. We'll probably be outnumbered, but we've been that way before. As a matter of fact I doubt if we'll run into anything up there that we haven't run into before someplace or sometime. That's the best part of going to a fight with a bunch of old men. Nothing new can happen to us."

He scratched the back of his head and, before continuing, looked slyly at Storm Ryerson, who sat quietly in the back of the room.

"About twenty years ago I sat in a ready room like this and listened to a tough old bastard give me the word before my first mission. He told me something I've never forgotten. He said that in every war the resources of any country can be considered in the shape of a spear. The shaft is back home in the States and the spearhead is the whole shebang of men and guns and planes and ships that go out to conduct the war. At the very tip of the spearhead are the men who fire the guns, who come into contact with the enemy. Everything else is secondary to the guy who pulls the trigger. He will win or lose the fight. Well, this morning it seems that out of this whole mish-mash over here a handful of old men are going to shoot the guns. I think we ought to be pretty proud of it. That old bastard who told me that is sitting in the back of the room. Maybe he has something immortal to say. How about it, Storm?"

"No speeches this morning, Dan," Ryerson said in a loud voice. "Only good luck to all of you." He cleared his throat and added, "I don't think we'll see your like again. That's all."

"All right, then," Belden said to the men. "Let's get out to the planes and check them over. O'Toole will give us the 'start engines' at 0545."

Belden waited as they filed out, conversing in quiet monotones of matters entirely divorced from this thing they were about to do.

"Hell. The Dodgers have a lock on the pennant this year."

"You've got three to one on that."

"Koufax will win twenty-five this year. Wait and see."

"If I don't stop flying these Mach Two airplanes, I may not be around to see *anything*. I feel like Casey Stengel playing with the Little League."

"That is a poor but precise figure of speech."

Finally they had all gone except Hawkins, who remained seated until the sounds of their voices had faded. Then he rose and approached Belden. "Well, Dan," he said, "my thanks for everything." He extended his hand.

"You're sure about this, Hawk?" Belden asked in a low voice.

Hawkins nodded with a slow grin. "Don't think I haven't given it considerable thought. It's not a thing you do lightly."

Belden shook his head with a feeling of futility. "God damn it, Hawk. I'm sorry. It doesn't sound like much, but take it for what it's worth."

"I do, Dan. And let me tell you something. A true friendship is the most precious thing a man can have. Remember this."

"Anything you want me to do—after?"

"I left a letter in my suitcase addressed to you. There isn't much."

"Janet and the kids," Belden said. "I'll do what must be done for them."

Hawkins inclined his head. "I know. It makes it easier, knowing that." Suddenly a broad grin split Hawkins' ravaged face. "What the hell are we so solemn about? Consider it and you'll see I'm the luckiest bastard alive. Christ, how I hated to think of dying in a bed. So let's go, Dan. Let's go out and meet the MIGs somewhere to the north."

"One thing, Hawk," Belden said.

"Anything."

"When you go, don't take Lee with you."

"Hell, no. He's all yours, Dan." He offered his hand again.

"So long, Hawk," Belden said.

"So long, Dan."

Hawkins turned and walked away, leaving Belden with a shadow of regret on his face. As Belden followed him from the ready room, he stopped by the blackboard where the flight composition was chalked in large letters and drew a heavy horizontal line through Hawkins' name. So simply did Ray Hawkins move away into the mists of memory.

Belden taxied out at exactly 0548. The heavy-bodied F8s that followed him were identical chunks of shadow moving in dark majesty down the taxi strip until they passed and the fierce furnaces of flame could be seen in the tail pipes.

They took off in two-plane sections. Belden and Hawkins raced down the strip under full power, the great flames shooting out from the tail pipes to mark their progress like twin torches moving away at an unbelievable rate of speed. Belden eased off the deck when his air-speed needle touched 130 knots. The plane lifted softly, easily, and Belden eased on a slight amount of forward elevator trim tab to hold the nose down and remain below the blanket of overcast. He flew directly ahead for exactly forty-five seconds and then began a gentle turn to the left. He pulled back the throttle and maintained a steady air speed of 300 knots. Behind him the others launched and took a bearing on his wingtip lights and began their turns when his plane was at the eleven-o'clock position from them. As Belden and Hawkins sped on their downwind leg, Bates, Anders, Corey, Shonnard, Dugan, and Thayer moved to meet them, tightening the radius of their turns in such a manner as to point their noses at a spot ahead of Belden's section and thus arrive at this rendezvous simultaneously. Belden was abaft his take-off spot when the last Crusader swung expertly into position at the tail end of the echelon formation.

It was 0550 when he banked to his starboard and headed out to sea.

At the exact moment that Belden passed the coastline east of Danang, three hundred miles away Colonel Lee Cheng led the last formation of new MIG-21s into the landing circle above the jet strip at Hanoi. He had with him eight planes which he had picked up at Lungchou. With the addition of these new arrivals Lee now had sixty-eight fighters under his command. He broke off and came into his downwind leg as the tower turned on the runway lights, illuminating the landing area 1,000 feet below him. Behind Lee the other MIGs spread out in an orderly line of winking wingtip lights and he led them down past the ninety in an orderly, precise pattern of continuous touchdowns.

As he flashed over the end of the concrete strip he noted the camouflaged revetments where the planes for the morning patrol were parked. He decided he would take the flight himself this morning. It would be a good opportunity to let all the new men fly and from the air he could watch their procedures and aerial techniques. He felt his wheels bump gently on the runway and he began to ease pressure on his brakes, gently pushing against the tops of his rudder pedals as he slowed and then turned off onto the taxi strip.

The Line Chief was waiting respectfully as Lee nestled into the chocks and cut his engines. He opened his canopy as the man jumped up on the wing.

"How many planes are going on the morning launch?" His voice was coldly impersonal.

"Twelve, Colonel."

"Are they ready?"

"No, sir. We're still loading ammunition."

Lee climbed out of the cockpit. He had a single order for the Chief. "We will launch thirty planes at 0700. I expect them to be ready to go at 0645. Is that understood?"

As Lee walked to his operations office, it was 0555 and Dan Belden had reached a point fifteen miles at sea. The Crusader formation swung to a heading of 340 degrees, a course that would direct them to an area just off the coast of North Vietnam where the Red River emptied into the South China Sea.

Macgregor Kilpatrick and his flight of Douglas Skyraiders had been airborne for three hours. Kilpatrick squirmed in his cockpit and cursed the sensation of numbness that was afflicting his ass bone. Through his windshield he could see the ground ahead clearly despite the faulty light that only now was edging up the blackness that had rested so resolutely on the horizon for the entire duration of the flight. His eyes were goddam good and tired from staring at the radar scope and he would be pleased to see the Black River, which he estimated would pass under his wings in about ten minutes. When he passed the Black, he would be thirty-five miles from Hanoi. The Black emptied into the Red twenty miles west of Hanoi and Kilpatrick had elected to make his attack from the west, facilitating his withdrawal on a continuing course out to the open sea. He was taking his map out of his flight-suit knee pocket when Carpenter's voice came to him over the radio: "Mac from Sid. There's a river coming up."

Kilpatrick strained his eyes ahead and saw the snakelike bend in a river of considerable size. Well, he thought, the bastard who drew this map must have been drunk because there shouldn't be any river where this river is.

He studied his map in the dim light from the instrument panel and compared the sharp bend to the northward in the Black River with the sharp bend in this unmapped river below him. He glanced at his watch and swore. For Christ's sake—0600 and I'm over the Black. I need no computer to advise me that I'm ten minutes ahead of schedule and so I picked up a tail wind somewhere back along the way, a tail wind that I definitely did not need.

With the realization that he was passing the Black, Macgregor Kilpatrick had a simple decision to make. He could delay his arrival through the expedient of circling lazily in the sky until the ten minutes had been suitably expended doing nothing. In this case, if his flight had been picked up by enemy radar—and there was at least a fifty-fifty chance that it had been—the MIGs might already be launching from the strip at Hanoi. On the other hand, if his Skyraiders had not been sighted by radar and continued on in to the target, they would arrive at the rendezvous point and find Belden still ten minutes away. The MIGs would have those interminable ten minutes in which to shoot Kilpatrick's ass out of the sky. "God damn," Kilpatrick said to himself. "I have a choice of busting my butt either way. Stay here and let them come after me and clobber me. Or go in and give them ten minutes after the attack to do the same damn thing. Well, at least I can get to the target if I go in."

The Skyraiders held steady on course and passed the Black River at 0601.

Belden's Crusaders were flying at 88 percent of power, the Mach needles touching the figure .9 and the air-speed needles resting on 600 knots. The planes held to a minimum altitude, skimming over the water with blinding speed and leaving behind them long streaks of eddying turbulence on the ocean's face. They were well north of the 17th Parallel when Belden called to the flight: "Move out in line abreast and check your guns."

The F8s moved out and forward from the echelon formation and soon were strung across a wide expanse of sky. The sky was suddenly, briefly, scourged with red lines of tracer and the *pom pom pom* of the twenties sounded over the muted engines' roar. Then all was silence again and the aircraft slipped back into formation.

"Two four-plane divisions," Belden ordered.

Bates and Anders moved as a section onto Belden's left wing, Bates's nose section nearly touching the right wingtip of Belden's plane. Across the scant interval of space, Belden could see the oxygen mask hanging to the side of Bates's face and the white flashing of his grin.

"It's nice to know you're so happy this morning," Belden called.

Bates held up his left arm in the cockpit. "You know what they say." His voice was laughing. "If you're left-handed, you owe the Devil one day's work. Well, I am left-handed and today I'm paying off."

Belden nodded and turned his head to scan the eastern horizon where a new day was struggling for birth. There were intermittent breaks in the overcast now and he could see small spaces of pale sky overhead. He touched his stick gently and climbed three hundred feet.

It was 0612 when Kilpatrick sighted the runway at Hanoi through the predawn mists. He had contemplated trying to contact Belden on the radio, but abandoned the thought when he reminded himself that at extremely low altitude the radio range was decidedly restricted. The only way in which he could have contacted Belden to tell him of the change in his ETA would have been to climb to altitude and that would have alerted every radar station in the area.

The other pilots spotted the airfield when Kilpatrick did, and without direction they spread out in a line abreast and flipped their bomb-arming switches and turned the gunsights up full bright.

"One pass only," was all Kilpatrick said.

When they were three miles from the end of the runway, Kilpatrick pulled back on his stick and the four planes pointed their noses at the cloud cover and climbed rapidly to 2,500 feet. One mile from the field, they leveled off and then nosed over into a glide toward the target.

The four Skyraiders came down out of the first shade of morning and brought their sights to bear on the parked airplanes aligned in neat rows forty yards off the runway. They came with a sudden roar out of the misty drizzle and held their points of aim until they reached 650 feet. Then the bombs fell away like black droppings from some monstrous birds. Their planes were pulling up and away even as the bombs hit and burst the morning wide open in a series of gigantic, burgeoning billows of flame and debris that soared into the sky as though some giant hand had thrown them in anger at the attacking aircraft. All along the rows of parked planes the bombs burst with deadly accuracy. Looking back over his shoulder, Kilpatrick tried to count the flaming MIGs dying on the flight line. He stopped counting when he reached nine. Then he wheeled away,

dived down close to the ground, and swept across the steaming paddies to the muddy waters of the Red.

"Full balls," he called. "Let's get the hell out of here."

With throttles firewalled and prop controls at full low pitch, the
ADs skimmed the surface of the river as the pilots watched with
narrowed eyes in the rearview mirrors for any indication of a chase.

Three minutes after Kilpatrick had passed over Hanoi, Colonel Lee
led the vengeful MIGs from the runway. The Skyraiders had approached from the west and so had been unaware of the planes
parked in the large revetment which had its camouflaged back to any
western approach. Kilpatrick and his men had destroyed ten of the
enemy fighters, but Lee still had fifty left. Thirty of them were in the
process of taking off or taxiing to the strip when Lee's wheels left
the ground and he called to his flight: "No rendezvous. Head for the
ocean at minimum altitude."

He did not know why he was certain the enemy planes were on a
course for the ocean. He only knew that in their place he would never
have considered flying back inland where their presence would be
recorded by every radar station between Hanoi and the border. He
threw his plane into afterburner and screamed toward the Red
River.

Lee's ground speed was in the supersonic range, nearly 13 miles
per minute. Kilpatrick's Skyraiders plodded through the sky at 3
miles per minute. In this unequal contest there could be but one
victor. Colonel Lee made visual contact with the ADs when he was
six miles behind them. He had climbed to 1,000 feet altitude and he
saw them against the backdrop of the muddy waters of the Red. The
bombers had divided their division into two two-plane sections
which paralleled each other as they strained under full power to
reach the open sea.

"Attention," Lee called into his mike. "Four enemy propeller aircraft over the Red heading for the beach."

Behind him his MIGs went into afterburner and whistled a scream
of warning to Kilpatrick's lumbering Skyraiders.

In his cockpit, Carpenter, leading the second section, saw the
enemy first. Lee was only a slight smudge of darkness trailing across
the sky in Carpenter's rearview mirror.

"Mac, this is Sid. Bogie on our tail. Coming like hell."

Kilpatrick and the others saw Lee then. Their reactions were instinctive and without conscious volition. They pushed over and lost 100 feet of altitude, affording the enemy no space in which to make a low-side attack.

"Watch them," Kilpatrick called. "Break on command."

Lee closed from the rear at 780 miles per hour and so had time for only a short no-deflection shot before he had sped past his target and was pulling up and away. His relative speed was far too great to allow him to bring his guns to bear accurately and the Skyraiders escaped unscathed from the first attack.

"God damn that ten minutes of time," Kilpatrick swore in his cockpit. Six hundred lousy seconds and they might cost us all our asses this morning. He watched Lee carefully as the MIG swung wide and high above them. His eye flicked back to the mirror again and he saw other MIGs closing on his tail. He waited a moment and then called, "Break."

The two sections banked violently toward each other; the pilots held hard back pressure on the sticks and the Skyraiders wheeled in a vertical reversal turn, presenting their guns to the oncoming MIGs. Kilpatrick opened fire when far out of range because he knew he must complete the entire turn before Lee was down again behind him. He saw his tracers fall short and raise spouts of water in the river. The MIGs were firing now and closing at a tremendous rate of speed. Their tracers passed over the Skyraiders and then Kilpatrick and his men were continuing their turn and were again headed down the Red as Lee swung down in a flat-side run.

The MIG came from the port side and level and flew directly at the formation. Not until it seemed the planes would collide did Lee open fire and then he had time for only a two-second burst. The majority of the shells passed under the AD formation, but one shell did not. It slammed through the engine housing of Del Crandon's plane, destroying a vital oil line, caromed off the heavy mounting, and passed through on the other side. The oil spewed out over the hot engine and black smoke billowed from the Skyraider as the windshield filmed over with the errant fluid.

Crandon opened his cockpit canopy before he realized the foolhardiness of his action. He was far too low to bail out and the draft from the inrushing wind caused a tongue of flame to lick from the floor boards. As the flame reached hungrily into the cockpit from the left side, Crandon reacted instinctively, moving his right hand away from the flame. Since his right hand was holding the control stick, the plane went immediately into a sharp bank and turn to the starboard. Crandon was flying only nine feet away from Sid Carpenter, so there was absolutely no time in which to remedy his mistake.

Del Crandon's propeller chewed off eight feet of Carpenter's wing before Crandon was aware that he had struck the other plane. The aerodynamic reaction to the sudden disappearance of eight feet of wing flipped Carpenter over onto his back at an altitude of 70 feet. Before forward pressure could be applied to hold the inverted nose up long enough to attempt to roll the plane to the upright position, the Skyraider flew into the water upside down.

Del Crandon never saw his friend die. When Crandon felt his prop chop into Carpenter's wing the flames were already licking up around his face and neck. He yanked his throttle all the way back thus separating the two stricken aircraft. Then he exerted back pressure, trying to climb for sufficient altitude to allow him to bail out. But Crandon's time was up, and the brightest smile that Lady Luck could ever summon would not help him this morning.

He had reached only 800 feet of altitude when the pain from the searing flames became unbearable and he actuated his ejection lever. With the advanced techniques of aircraft ejection, an altitude of 800 feet is usually sufficient to assure survival. But not if, at the moment of ejection, the unbearable heat causes the pilot to move the stick to the right side of the cockpit, rolling the plane over to the inverted position in its climb. In such an event the ejection mechanism will shoot the pilot out of the cockpit, but it will shoot him *down*, not up. Such was the case with Del Crandon and his body hit the water before the parachute even trailed.

He died just twenty seconds after Sid Carpenter.

Kilpatrick and Knight did not see their comrades go. They were too busy flying evasive maneuvers against Lee and his MIGs. Somehow they twisted and turned and flew under full military power for what seemed an eternity. Then they passed the beach southeast of Ninh Binh and were out over the open sea.

Belden had started his climb when he estimated himself to be four minutes from his intended rendezvous with the Skyraiders. He had no way of knowing that, because Colonel Lee had ordered thirty planes readied for the morning flight, Kilpatrick had already been under attack for five minutes. He intended to climb to 20,000 feet, but had reached only 10,000 when he saw the two ADs desperately struggling for survival. In an instant his trained mind sorted out the possibilities and then he spoke into his mike.

"Tallyho," Belden called. "Twelve o'clock on the water. Ten miles."

He held his altitude and flew directly over the planes fighting on the deck. Lee did not see Belden and the Crusaders, nor did any of Lee's men. Early light is treacherous and with two helpless ADs to attack, who would waste precious time staring overhead?

"We'll come down from behind," Belden called. "Get rid of your missiles first." If ever the heat-seeking Sidewinders were to be of avail, it would be with a no-deflection rear-end shot straight up the MIGs' tail pipes.

Belden flew two miles past the MIGs and then rolled over and came down in a split ess, a maneuver similar to the last half of a loop.

The MIGs, intent on the destruction of the helpless Skyraiders, did not see the F8s swinging down behind them. Belden came in fast and level from directly astern. He picked the first MIG that entered his gunsights and held it steady there until the wingspan of the enemy plane filled two of the mil rings and then he fired his Sidewinder. With a spitting hiss, the missile blasted from under his starboard wing and flashed across the intervening space. From Belden's viewpoint it seemed to hover in its flight, almost hesitantly, much as though it was reluctant to find its target. Actually it flew unerringly and found its mark in the flaming tail pipe of the MIG. There was a slight puff of smoke from the rear of the stricken plane and then suddenly the plane was no longer visible anywhere in the sky.

Belden looked to the side and saw Hawkins flying parallel with him. Then Hawk's missile flew and Belden followed it on its way. He saw the Sidewinder score another direct hit and two MIGs were finished in the first ten seconds of battle.

They swept up in a steep, almost vertical climb, reaching for alti-

208

tude because they knew they would get no more cold-turkey chances like the one they had just completed. Behind them the other Crusaders fired and followed in the climb. The MIGs had been alerted by Belden's fire and now the enemy took evasive tactics. The Sidewinders, unable to cope with the sudden changes of direction, fell harmlessly into the ocean below.

Belden circled at 15,000 feet and the flight joined up in echelon. He watched across ten miles of sky and saw the MIGs rising to meet him. Down on the water three enemy planes remained to terminate the affair with Kilpatrick's Skyraiders.

"Dugan. Thayer," Belden called. "Go down and help Mac."

Without acknowledging, the two F8s peeled off and dived steeply for the deck. Belden turned toward the MIG formation ten miles away.

It was 0630 when the battle was finally joined. The two formations flew down each other's throats. Lee and Belden flew the point on each formation and they opened fire at precisely the same moment, trading their lines of tracers as the range closed. They passed each other port-to-port and Belden saw the crude dragon painted on the MIG's tail.

With a great shout he pulled back sharply on his stick and sent his Crusader winging vertically in a soaring climb as he batted his throttle out and then forward. His afterburner roared as the rate of climb indicator touched 20,000 feet per minute. Even as he climbed, he strained to see behind him, to fasten his gaze securely to Lee's plane and not let it get away from him.

He came out of the climb in a rolling chandelle, hanging almost motionless as his eyes probed the surrounding sky for his enemy. He did not have to look too hard. Lee was not running today. He had chosen Belden even as Belden had chosen him. Lee had effected an Immelman turn and now he and Belden once again flew down the mouths of their respective guns. Later it would be hard to decide if either man took evasive action at the final moment. Neither believed he did. But in the last fractional moment there appeared three feet of intervening air between their wingtips; then they were past each other and climbing to turn and come back to the fight.

The entire sky was a confused pattern of flashing streaks of tracer bullets and twisting, diving aircraft. Lee had twenty-eight airplanes and Belden had eight after the first pass. There would be far fewer when it was ended.

Hawkins broke away from Belden when he saw Lee move to meet them. A MIG was climbing steeply from below and directly in front and Hawk jammed his throttle to the stop and pulled his nose up to follow the enemy plane. He came into the vertical and held there, his nose pointing straight up at the sky and the MIG securely trapped in his gunsight. He went into afterburner and closed in the vertical climb. He was still out of range when the MIG pilot, perhaps out of inexperience, perhaps out of fright, perhaps from sheer stupidity, moved his throttle with a sudden, jerky motion and the engine flamed-out. Moving the throttle with sudden, spasmodic motions is a cardinal sin when flying a jet aircraft, especially at high altitudes. The MIG was at 20,000 feet when he jerked his throttle abruptly. He lost the fire in his tail pipe and with it all efficiency in his power plant.

Hawkins saw the flame wink out and his tortured face grinned as he opened fire. The MIG stalled in the vertical-climb attitude and the plane fell off sluggishly on the left wing and turned slowly over in a floundering movement that presented its belly to the arcing line of Hawkins' tracer and high-explosive incendiary shells. Hawkins watched the tracers eat into the heavy belly of the MIG, pounding relentlessly into the unprotected underside until a piece of fuselage tore away in the high wind, a trickle of gasoline escaped, and then there was a great burning pyre mushrooming and tumbling downward. He did not pause to relish his conquest, but rolled out of the climb and over onto his back, holding momentarily in the inverted position with the slightest forward pressure on the stick. He came out of afterburner as he let his nose fall through the horizon and the plane accelerated rapidly in a dive.

Bates and Anders came to the fight three seconds after Belden. They were slightly higher than Belden had been and so had underneath them a thin layer of cloud, which had been invisible in the first light. Bates glanced down and saw a division of four MIGs pass him on a reciprocal course before moving under the meager tier of stratus. Anders was on Bates's left and on the inside of the turn as Bates slapped the stick hard to port and so Anders moved ahead and took the lead as the Crusaders whipped around and down on the enemy rear.

"I'll take the second section," Anders called.

"Roger," Bates replied. He slid out slightly and moved level with Anders. They came under the cloud platform and found their targets four hundred yards ahead. Anders dropped a few feet of altitude and they came up behind the MIGs from directly astern and below. This is a position in which it is patently impossible for an enemy to see you if he holds to a steady course and does not turn or weave in the sky. Anders realized this. Consequently, when he pressed his trigger, the MIG in his sights never knew that he was dying early in the morning, fifteen miles off the mouth of the Red River. A jet aircraft has one fatal idiosyncrasy. It is more or less a flying gas tank and if the fuel, for any reason, floods the area of combustion in the after section, nothing on earth can prevent the destruction of the plane. The MIG blew up in a split second and Anders flew through the flaming wreckage with a joyous laugh.

Then two MIGs, flying in close section, wheeled down behind Anders and Bates. They slid down from the eight-o'clock position and Bates saw them in his mirror.

"Behind us, Cort. Two coming in fast."

"Roger," Anders replied, watching the enemy in his mirror.

"Fly straight and level," Bates called. Anders thought he heard Bates chuckle. "You'll play decoy this morning, Cortney."

The MIGs ranged up behind, confident of two easy kills. And now, you sonsabitches, thought Bates, see how this sticks you at 0630 in the morning.

Bates popped his speed brakes as Anders threw his plane into a vertical bank. Anders moved away from him and Bates climbed 500 feet. The climbing maneuver together with the extending of the speed brakes caused Bates to lose 50 knots of air speed in six seconds. He watched the MIGs slide underneath him and turn to follow Anders. He retracted his speed brakes, threw his plane into afterburner, and came down on the tails of the enemy. The MIGs opened fire on Anders as Bates closed on them from the rear, spraying his shells at random across the flight path of the enemy aircraft. He was only one hundred yards away from his target and 90 percent of his shells went home. He held the trigger down with a grim determination and came out of afterburner to hang there, holding precise distance from the MIGs until both target planes erupted in flame and fell apart in the air.

Anders' voice came laughing back to him: "I thought for a minute you were going to be late, Batesy." They joined into section again and climbed for altitude.

"I'll be a sonofabitch," Macgregor Kilpatrick swore. "I believe that shitty ten minutes of time is going to kill me."

Three MIGs were on the attack and Kilpatrick and Knight were flying only the remnants of their Skyraiders. Both planes had been shattered by MIG guns and were remaining airborne only through the skill of their pilots and by the Grace of God. When Carpenter and Crandon had gone down, the number of guns the Skyraiders were able to turn into the attacking MIGs had been halved. With only the guns from one AD to face at a time the enemy cast aside caution and bore in to attack with a disdain that infuriated Kilpatrick and Knight. Shreds of Knight's tail assembly flapped in the wind and the engine of Kilpatrick's plane, as a result of eight direct hits by the MIG shells, hacked and spit in complaint. At full power both planes were unable to exceed 200 knots.

Dugan and Thayer broke up the MIG attack by the simple expedient of flying directly into their formation with all guns blazing. Each Crusader took on a MIG in individual combat. Since the odds were disparate, there remained one MIG uncontested and he followed on Kilpatrick's tail, firing short, continuous bursts. At this point, had Knight turned away, leaving Kilpatrick to his uncertain fate, he might have lived. But Knight turned hard at the MIG, bringing his futile guns to bear even as he felt his entire aircraft shudder violently. His eyes flicked over his air-speed indicator and he saw the needle quivering near the stall line. His badly damaged control surfaces were unequal to the demands presented to them and faltered in the multiple g-turn. The shuddering became more violent and the Skyraider snapped in the opposite direction and twisted into a spin. Knight jammed the stick forward and stamped on the opposite rudder, trying desperately to bring the plane out of its uncontrollable state. He might have accomplished this had he possessed 500 feet additional altitude. He did not have 500 feet additional altitude, so he watched the ocean rush up to meet him, feeling completely futile as his controls flapped uselessly in the cockpit. He died in a great spray of water that cascaded outward from the orange blossom of flame that burned fiercely on the surface of the sea.

Kilpatrick died regretting that lousy ten minutes of time. He died without fear, but with regret and with a certain anger for himself and his mistake. He was still trying his best to fight the MIG, turning hard until his eyesight dimmed under the g-forces, when the MIG guns winked close on his starboard side near the four-o'clock position. The last sounds Macgregor Kilpatrick ever heard were the shells slapping at his fuselage, then moving into the cockpit. The last sight his eyes ever saw was his own blood spraying the windshield. He felt no pain and his eyes were closed forever when his plane hit the water.

The main body of the fight had resolved itself into a restricted space of sky where eight Crusaders and twenty-four MIGs now fought in wild melee. Neither side sought sanctuary. On the part of Belden's men, it was a matter of courage, determination, and gallantry. On the part of Lee's men, it was only common sense. When the odds are twenty-four to eight, the opponent with the twenty-four would be out of his mind to break off the fight.

Above the main body of the conflict, Belden and Lee fought each other with every trick that had been assimilated in two lifetimes of fighting in the sky. The years that had gone under the wings of both of them had their stores of knowledge plumbed until it seemed no other maneuver could evolve from the furious, twisting, snarling aircraft. The sky was split asunder by the great screaming of their engines and by the staccato slamming of their guns. They fought from sea level to 30,000 feet and back again. They tried to kill each other in vertical climbs and in terminal velocity dives. They held the triggers down in eight g-turns when the vision of both men was restricted to a hazy film under the pull of the gravity.

In this battle there was no admiration of one man for another; there was nothing but an acknowledgment on the part of each that he was meeting a master at his trade. Belden remembered the skies over Majon-ni, Hungham, Pyongyang. Past victories came back to him from Wake Island and Truk and Okinawa. And Lee remembered how it had been high over the wintry wastes near the Yalu River.

In his cockpit Belden glanced at his fuel gauge and knew this fight could not continue interminably. He had two hundred and fifty miles to fly to Danang. Lee had seventy-five to Hanoi.

Belden soared high in a wingover roll, holding hard pressure on his bottom rudder and pulling the nose swiftly downward as he hung at the top of the maneuver. Lee was just starting his climb far below, confident he had finally managed to get on Belden's tail. Belden laughed aloud in his cockpit because that was exactly what he hoped Lee would think. He let the nose fall on through and swing toward the water far below. Lee's MIG was only a tiny spot in his gunsights, climbing at a steep angle of attack.

Belden's speed was necessarily extremely slow as he came out of his wingover and into his dive. The air-speed needle was just passing 150 knots when he rolled 180 degrees onto his back and shoved the stick forward, exerting *negative* g-force and effecting a climb in the *inverted* position.

Lee had seen Belden's wingover and had smiled grimly with the realization that his adversary had committed an unpardonable error. He started to come out of his climb, rolling into a banked position and letting his nose come down to the horizon, when he saw the Crusader start down at him. He intended to hang there in a nearly stalled position, holding his place in the sky until his opponent flashed past in a steep dive. Then Lee would go into afterburner and sweep down behind the enemy and thus insure the kill.

Lee waited for Belden's plane to flash by, but it did not come. Belden remained high above in inverted flight, watching Lee from the upside-down position. Since Lee could not hold his plane in its attitude forever, he had to continue on through and into a steep glide. Belden saw this from 3,000 feet above and split-essed down after the MIG.

He had employed one of the most ancient frauds in the fighter pilot's handbook and it had worked. He came down swiftly with his altitude advantage and when the range closed he opened fire. Lee felt the MIG shiver, then shudder as the twenties crashed home. He twisted his plane violently, but Belden was glued on his tail, held there tightly by the four streams of tracer that poured from the nose of the F8. Belden held the trigger down with a grim determination, his eyes narrowed with the effort and cold as a gravestone as he waited for Lee to die.

The Chinese had no altitude below him with which to play and so he had only one direction in which to go to escape Belden's deadly guns. He roared into a steep climb and Belden grinned as he followed. The pressures from his anti-blackout suit swelled against the vital arterial points on his body as he went after Lee, presenting obstructions to the flow of blood from his brain and thus enabling him to maintain visual contact with the enemy plane. He followed in a steep climb, his altimeter winding like the second hand on a watch as he swept past 15,000 feet closing.

A mile away a Chinese pilot named Tsien saw Belden following the MIG up the sky. Tsien was a dedicated young man who fought with ferocity if not with a great deal of skill. He cut across the sky and zoomed up after Belden.

Tsien was on Belden's tail and directly astern when he opened fire. Fortunately for Belden, Tsien was inexperienced and fired when far out of effective range. But he was coming on, his speed far greater than Belden's, which was diminishing under the climb conditions. Tsien might well have ranged up and destroyed Belden and his Crusader had not one thing remained in the sky to provide Belden salvation.

It was Ray Hawkins barreling down the sky with the great pain welling in his chest. Hawkins had been certain that the time would present itself this morning. When he had seen the MIG fasten itself to Belden's tail, he knew the time was now. From an altitude advantage he had come down, building speed before he swung behind Tsien's MIG. His eye measured the distance between his plane and the enemy's and Hawkins knew he had only that much space in which to live. He was in afterburner with the throttle full forward when he called Belden on the radio: "Dan. This is Hawk. Keep after your target. I'm taking this one off your tail."

Belden saw the MIG behind him then. Tsien had closed to firing range and his shells began to hit the Crusader. So Dan Belden had a choice to make. He could take evasive action and get that goddam MIG off his ass, or he could hold steady on Lee's tail and blast him out of the sky. It was a measure of his resolution to destroy Lee that he elected to ignore Tsien and leave himself open to destruction. He followed Lee and never took his finger from the trigger, shutting his mind to the *thunking* of the shells battering his plane.

Hawkins came up through the sky on his final run. He held Tsien's MIG in his sights and at the end did not even trouble to hold the trigger down. He had no more use for guns or bullets. In the last moment of his existence Ray Hawkins whispered his wife's name.

Then he flew directly into the tail pipe of Tsien's MIG. At the end there was only the growing sphere of flame from the MIG's tail pipe covering his entire windshield.

Belden saw Hawkins die and somewhere deep inside of him there was a sudden ache—and then it was gone. He turned back to Lee again, but Lee had taken advantage of the momentary lapse on Belden's part and was away from him, hurtling across the sky to join his squadron in the melee. Belden cursed and followed him.

The fight was fourteen minutes old and nine MIGs and three Crusaders had fallen from the sky. Corey had died and had taken two of the enemy with him. He had come out of the bottom half of a loop to find himself flying head-on at a section of two MIGs. The enemy spotted Corey at the precise moment that he spotted them. The opposing aircraft flew down each other's throats, each side holding hard to its line of flight. Whether or not Corey or the MIGs, at the last second, tried to avoid a collision, no one would ever know. If they did, they waited a fractional moment too long and collided head-on in a gigantic detonation of fuel and spattering debris.

Belden had re-entered the fight looking for Lee. But other aircraft intervened and he realized he had lost his opponent. Just then a MIG came vertically into his sights, clawing for altitude. Belden pulled his nose up abruptly, aiming at a point 200 feet above the MIG, and opened fire, holding the stream of tracer steady until the enemy flew through that particular space of sky and exploded. As he rolled his nose toward the horizon, he heard Anders' voice: "Dan, this is Cort. I'm over the beach. Got about eight of these bastards cornered here."

Belden and Bates answered the call and streaked westward where a smaller swarm of planes were entangled in a weaving pattern at 8,000 feet.

Anders saw them coming, but he had time for only a quick glance before his attention was focused again on his adversaries. He was fighting eight against one and he admitted he was a silly sonofabitch ever to get himself in this foolhardy position. A MIG came across Anders' sights from his right and he threw his stick hard left and booted the rudder, jerking his nose around to the flight path of the MIG and spraying the entire sky through which the MIG had elected to fly. The enemy plane found Anders' bullets and it heaved once in the air; a wing tore away, flame gushed from the after section and the airplane broke in half and fell toward the ocean.

Bates and Belden rammed into the MIGs attacking Anders and each got a kill on the initial pass. Bates downed his with a 45-degree deflection shot when his target rolled over to split-ess out of range. Belden flew up behind his and saw the canopy fly off in a spray of splintered glass. The pilot ejected, his body hurtling upward and separating from the seat almost directly in front of the attacking F8. Belden thought he could see the face of the enemy as he sped past, but he knew this was impossible. You never see the man you kill in this business, he thought. Perhaps it is better that way.

As Belden and Bates continued through the MIGs and swung around to return to the attack, Colonel Lee came down on Anders from directly above. Under ordinary circumstances Anders was a match for any man living in this particular type of combat. But today he was fighting six MIGs at once and a man can direct his attention to only a given number of the enemy.

So Anders did not see Lee swooping down and when Lee opened fire in a vertical dive with a full 90-degree deflection, Anders did not even see the tracers lacing down at him. In the fury of a dogfight a man rarely looks directly overhead.

The first and only inkling Anders had that this morning held the stink of the grave for him was the numbing blow that clubbed his right shoulder and sucked the air out of his lungs. For a moment he wondered what had happened and then the rush of wind on his face alerted him to the shattered canopy. Only then did he look down at the ruin that Lee's shell had made of his body.

His right shoulder was a soggy, bloody mass with a white splinter of bone sticking out through the cloth of the flight suit. The shell had gone on through the shoulder, ripping a great gaping hole in Anders' right side. His eyes squeezed shut in agony and he dimly thought to himself: I've got to get out of here. He coughed and a glob of blood choked out of his mouth as he bent over in the cockpit, his shoulder straps biting into his wounds. His plane slowly swung 180 degrees and eased into a nose-down attitude and on a southerly course.

Belden was after Lee with flaming guns. Bates hung back, allowing Belden to drop away from him; then he moved onto the tail of two MIGs which came after Belden. The deadly daisy chain strung downward through the sky.

Bates selected the first MIG to center in his sights and followed him down to 1500 feet where his bullets took away the tail assembly of the Red plane, which continued unswervingly into the water. Bates barely missed accompanying his victim, pulling out of his dive at an altitude of 200 feet.

Belden, again on Lee's tail, hung there relentlessly. He fired in sporadic bursts now because he knew his ammunition was critical. He had not seen his Crusaders fall, not all of them. He knew that MIGs were going down, but in the wildness of the fight, he had no idea of the odds that remained against him.

Shonnard had gone down under the combined fire of five of Lee's planes. He had taken two of the MIGs with him on the trip. This left four Crusaders in the sky to fight fourteen MIGs. Lee had lost sixteen planes in the brief encounter. And it was not finished yet. Dugan and Thayer took on two of the MIGs that had killed Kilpatrick, and Thayer sent his flaming to oblivion. The odds now stood at thirteen to four.

Lee employed every ruse he had absorbed in his fifteen years of flying, but to no avail. Belden hung to his tail with implacable intent. He had ranged up to within forty feet of Lee's tail pipe and his shells were smashing into the MIG continually. Suddenly Belden cursed aloud as his guns went silent.

"Sonofabitch," he shouted.

He had expended all of his ammunition. He pounded the side of the cockpit canopy in frustration. Ahead of him Lee flew on a westerly course that would take him out of the fight and back to Hanoi. For the first time in his life, Lee, unaware that his opponent had emptied his guns, was running away. Watching the Crusader in his rearview mirror, he saw Belden turn away. Only then did he turn back and climb toward the fight again. Deep in his heart Lee knew he had been spared by the grace of a depleted ammunition can.

As Belden looked around for the rest of his flight, he experienced a sinking sensation in his gut. Away toward the south he saw a lone F8 flying low along the water, smoke trailing in spurts from its tail pipe. Anders was making the greatest effort of his life to remain conscious until he could get back to Danang. The blood continued to pulse out of his awful wounds and the odds on Anders diminished by the heartbeat.

As Belden re-entered the area of the melee he saw two Crusaders taking on four sections of MIGs. As he watched, Bates scored with a high-side run and the MIG fluttered downward until the wings tore away. Bates continued over onto his back, pulled through in a split ess and out of the fight. Dugan and Thayer were surrounded by the milling MIGs and Belden was still a mile away when he saw both the Crusaders falter, trail dark smoke for only a moment, and then disappear in twin balls of flame that seemed to spring from their aft sections and move forward along the fuselages. Even as he cursed, he saw two MIGs roll over on their backs, hesitate, then plunge vertically toward the water. Dugan and Thayer had taken company with them when they went.

The odds now stood ten to two and Belden knew he could no longer continue the fight. He was preparing to call Bates and order him to return to Danang when a voice rang down the sky: "Crusader Leader from Jehovah One. I am ten miles from you and closing. Eight F8s and eight F4s. Hold on."

Belden saw them coming. He saw them coming down from 30,000 feet, their contrails streaming in jumbled patterns along their paths. Sixteen fighters from Smoke Dusane's Seventh Fleet on their way to pick up the fight.

"I doubt if I'll ever see such a beautiful sight again," Bates called. He might have been lecturing a class of cadets at Pensacola.

"Join up, Batesy," Belden called as he swung in a lazy turn.

Lee and the MIGs saw the Navy coming too. They had no stomach to take on sixteen fresh fighters, so when Dusane's men screamed in to the attack Lee and his pilots were barreling for sanctuary. They had only fifteen miles to go to reach a landfall. They made it safely, but Lee came back with only one-third of the pilots with whom he had flown out.

"Go after them, Jehovah Leader," Belden shouted into his mike. "I'm out of ammo."

"Sorry," Jehovah Leader replied with regret. "I've got orders to stay in international waters." He paused. "God damn it to hell," he added.

Bates slid into position off Belden's wing and only then did both men realize the extent of their losses that day. Belden looked down and behind, hoping with a forlorn hope that he would see Crusaders climbing to rendezvous. But all he saw below him was the open sea, mottled here and there where a plane had crashed and a man had died. Some of the planes had been Crusaders and more had been MIGs. On the ocean's calm surface there was no indication which had been which.

"Crusader Leader from Jehovah. One of your planes was headed for base. Hit pretty badly and smoking."

"Thanks, Jehovah," Belden said. "We'll be heading back now."

"I sent a division to escort him home," Jehovah Leader said. "His side number was one three two. Jehovah out."

Belden knew 132 was Anders. Well, we might salvage something from all this, he thought. Christ, but that was a fight. I had that bastard Lee and he got away. He ran away, the sonofabitch. Well, I'll get him next time if there is a next time. It occurred to him that out of the twelve men he had sent out that morning only two were returning. Anders would make three, but if Anders had left the fight his damage must have been critical.

They left behind them a sky that was as quiet as a graveyard at dawn. There was no trace of the deadly battle that had been waged there, no last whispering echo of the final curses and the last bitter words. That is the way fights end, not in a great final roar of thunder but with the silence of eternity stealing over all. At the end there is nothing but peace left in the place where men died.

Belden and Bates flew home in silence, each burdened with his own thoughts and his own farewells. That they had won the fight was perfectly clear. But was two out of twelve an excessive price to pay? It seemed altogether possible. In these moments of loneliness they did not consider the ultimate results of the attack on Hanoi and the fact that Lee had come down to international waters. What they considered was: There was no piece of the sky left that Hawkins, Kilpatrick, Corey, and all the rest had not left signed with their honor. They flew along in silence, their minds delicately attuned, listening intently for the first faint echo of the sound that they knew would come to them. Steadily they flew, their wingtips nearly touching in the bright rays of the rising sun. Behind them came the Navy jets in proud formation, but far in front Belden and Bates flew alone, leaving their contrails behind to mark their passing. Two out of the twelve that had formed the tip of the spear that had been cast.

It came so dimly at first that they thought perhaps their minds were deluding them.

Then it came louder and they heard it plainly.

They heard the sound of bugles in the sky.

Cortney Anders was dying as he approached Danang airfield. His strength had left him and it was only through superhuman effort that he managed to control the aircraft as he came low over the strip and up into the break. The great wound in his right side no longer pumped the arterial blood; the pressure from his heart merely leaked a red ooze down onto the floor boards. The runway was a hazy blur in his eyes as he turned downwind and with a great exertion pushed the landing gear lever to the "Down" position. The dials on his instrument panel swam dizzily before him and he could not bring them into focus. His right arm hung uselessly at his side and he flew the plane with his left hand, leaving the throttle unattended.

He turned his head weakly and saw indistinctly where the runway ended and merged with the flat expanse of the rice paddies. It took all his strength to push the stick to the left and bank into his crosswind leg.

There was a great pounding in his ears and a sense of something thick and heavy stuffing his gullet. He squinted at the instrument panel, but the dials moved and converged and then separated again in a constantly changing pattern. He raised his head and saw the runway ahead of him, an opaque strip of filmy whiteness splitting his windshield. The wind rushed through his shattered canopy and tore at the raw edges of his wounds.

Anders was nearly lined up with the strip, almost out of his last

221

turn, when his air-speed needle dipped below the stall marking line on the dial's face. He felt a sinking sensation as the great plane faltered in the air. Anders took his left hand from the stick and pushed the throttle forward, but it was too late.

The Crusader hung quivering in the air 50 feet over the end of the landing area. The shaking grew more violent and then the plane bucked up its nose and flipped over onto its back. With the loss of all aerodynamic efficiency, the F8 plowed its nose into the dirt just off the runway and burst into a ball of purple flame.

"Christ!" The tower operator's voice came to Belden and Bates as they approached the field from the north. "An F8 burning at the end of the runway. Alert all crash crews."

The red-crossed ambulances and the heavy-duty crash trucks raced out on the field and Belden saw them congregate around the fiercely flaming wreckage.

"Danang tower," he called. "What was the number of that plane?"

"This is Danang tower. That aircraft was F8 number one three two."

Cortney Anders was high above Danang, so high that he thought he could see all the world stretching out before him. The wind had stopped blasting through the shattered canopy and the pain of his wounds was gone somewhere into the distance. Ahead he could see endless spaces of high towering cumulus clouds, their great crenellated heights blazing white in the sun. Over a distant echoing of bugles he could hear the sound of countless voices singing.

A million miles below, Belden and Bates touched their wheels lightly to the runway and rolled past the smoldering wreckage.

Cortney Anders laughed in the face of the warm breeze coming with a sweet fragrance into his cockpit. His heart sang as he flew on and on into the rays of the morning sun. Higher he went, and higher, until all the universe was below him and the great surging of his engine carried him at last out of sight and into the sanctity of the high places.

Chapter
XIII

APRIL
1965

The true value of Belden's engagement with Colonel Lee was not immediately discernible. It takes time for democracies to move. When Belden and Bates returned from the fight off the mouth of the Red River, the immediate reaction was one of cautious approval. The outraged cries from Hanoi at the bombing so successfully carried out by Kilpatrick and his Skyraiders were countered by equally outraged accusations that Lee had violated international waters.

General Soohoo's plan for escalating the war worked admirably according to design and, unknown to the General, fitted in perfectly with the design of Storm Ryerson. Peking added four more squadrons of MIGs to Lee's roster even as they stationed ten infantry divisions south of Lungchou and within ten miles of the North Vietnam border. These movements were accurately reported and three aircraft carriers moved out of Pearl Harbor to join Smoke Dusane's Seventh Fleet.

Back in the States the draft boards quietly increased their quotas and National Guard regiments prepared for a call to active duty. A paratroop division in Georgia was placed on twenty-four-hours notice. Four troop transports were pulled out of mothballs and activated in record time. At Camp Pendleton in California, the civilians in the area noted with some puzzlement the long lines of truck convoys moving out of the camp in the early dawn and heading in the direction of San Diego or perhaps San Pedro, the embarkation points on the West Coast. Ships sailed in the first light and moved past Point Loma and out to sea on a westward heading.

In Vietnam a careful optimism replaced disillusionment. What had been missing in the Vietnam war was a certain *esprit* that fighting men remembered from World War II and the Korean war. There were no songs sung and no tales of heroism had emblazoned the headlines of the papers back home. Because there had been so little of glory to be had, there had been even less of it to employ as a means of building a sense of urgency into the war. When you fight a war without a sense of urgency, you are like a man swimming in a pool filled with glue. You may struggle mightily, but you are not going anywhere but down. There had been no clear-cut goal for which the soldiers might strive and so they had marked time, waiting for their tours of duty to end, living out their combat on the fringes of the fighting, and wondering with some bitterness why the hell nothing ever happened. What none of them realized was that what was missing was the pride that comes with accomplishment in battle.

When Belden beat the MIGs, the pilots, for the first time, found this sense of pride and with it the urgency began to come to them. They looked to the north now with an eager light in their eyes, as if they were counting the hours until they, too, would find the enemy high in the sky and challenge him in mortal combat. They began to think: Well, what the hell, maybe we're out here for something after all.

The courts-martial of Major Jack McKellar and Lieutenant Colonel Pat Murphy were postponed until the eighth of February and then were canceled altogether. When the senior officers perceived the burgeoning *esprit,* they knew that this was a time for heroes. McKellar and Murphy were the closest thing to heroes the military had.

On the ninth of February, after the word of the courts-martial cancellations had been disseminated around the airfields, there was a descent on the sick bays by a horde of eager fliers, who had discovered overnight that the mysterious pains in their backs had disappeared completely.

For the first time since the shelling at Bien Choa, the press releases concerning the war in Vietnam were not stashed away in some forgotten corner of a back page of the newspapers, but were splashed in bold print on the front pages.

In the ready rooms verbal orders were spoken by commanding officers. Not written orders mind you, because we still are not authorized to carry this war north. But listen carefully, young men. You will fly along the Parallel closely, fully alert, and you will wait *offensively*, not defensively, in the sky. You will fly along the edge of international waters, keeping carefully on the seaward side of that imaginary line. Perhaps Colonel Lee will come out again and in such a case, since that line is only imaginary, who is to say that you were actually on one side of it or another?

And as activity in the air increased, so did activity on the ground. Pham's soldiers, emboldened by reports of additional intervention by the Americans, drove the Vietcong back in the area southwest of Saigon. Garrison troops who had spent their military years without ever firing a gun or killing an enemy were pulled from their billets at the embassies and the villas. They were dragged away, handed a gun and bayonet, and all of them were sent out into the swamps and mountains to kill the Vietcong.

The same night that a report came in to Saigon concerning the Red Chinese divisions moving into Minchiang south of Lungchou in China, a Marine regiment north of Saigon moved out silently in the darkness. Three days later they were in battle positions along the 17th Parallel. The next day a convoy of troopships sailed past Cap St. Jacques near Saigon's harbor. Leathernecks of the First Marine Division disembarked under cover of darkness and moved into temporary bivouac near Tan Son Nhut airfield.

Old Korea hands murmured, "Well, finally it is shaping up again. It's the same situation, but this time we're not going to be caught with our pants down, so some General will have to tell us to stay in our foxholes and die."

One morning in early March, the Marine regiment near the Parallel came under strafing fire from a Red MIG. It was the signal that could not be ignored. The pilots waited for eight hours and then the word was flashed from Washington that American planes would henceforth be allowed to fly into North Vietnam in an offensive posture. A MIG pilot was so unfortunate as to be killed directly over the Parallel by antiaircraft fire. His plane crashed south of the Parallel

225

and his identification papers left no doubt as to who were flying the MIGs in North Vietnam.

The battle was joined the first day after the orders came through from Washington and so the situation that had existed in Korea years before pertained again. From Danang the jet fighters went forth daily to meet Lee and his MIGs in the skies of North Vietnam. But the sanctuary still prevailed and American pilots swore with frustration as their enemies flew across the Chinese border and found safety. Certain newspapers in the States decried what they referred to as "this monstrous act of cowardice in allowing the Reds a sanctuary," but their cries were lost somewhere behind the strange mixture of caution and daring that came with the rapid escalation of the war.

O'Toole and Merchant had repaired the two Crusaders in which Belden and Bates had made their fight off the Red River. Now they flew a two-plane section in the skies where Air Force and Navy jets went to battle in formations of twenty, thirty, forty. There were times when Belden would slide in behind the F-100s and the F-104s and there were other times when the Air Force, recognizing Belden, would join on him, so that he led the uniformed pilots to battle, much to the chagrin of some of the brass-bound senior officers.

General Pham did not cross the Parallel, but he did move north to within sight of the border. He sat there, within artillery range of the enemy, like some suppurating sore, and he waited. He knew he was taunting the enemy, almost begging them to move down from China and start something. The Americans now had almost 50,000 fighting men in South Vietnam, but Pham and Storm Ryerson knew that this was not enough. *Triple* the present force and there *might* be sufficient strength to fight the Chinese if the expected August offensive took place. More provocation must be supplied; the Americans must be *led* into massive intervention and they had to be led *now*.

And while men died in the rice paddies and fell from the high places, in the palaces of government other men lived and prodded and considered and deduced and ignored and accepted and argued and acquiesced, and finally rumors started from no one knew where and nourished themselves and spread until they came to be accepted as true fact despite their contradictory nature:

We're moving north in force.

226

We're not going to respect their sanctuary. They're going to let us go after the bastards.

We're pulling back around Saigon.

For Christ's sake. Why?

China threatens to send down ten divisions.

Screw the Chinamen. Let them send their ten divisions.

We're negotiating a truce.

We turned thumbs down on China in the UN.

Colonel Lee has four hundred MIGs up there.

Red China is going to get into the UN.

Colonel Lee has fifty MIGs up there.

General Pham is going across the Parallel.

They're going to sign a cease-fire.

General Pham is getting the shit kicked out of him.

We'll never sit down with those bastards like we did at Panmunjom. Christ, a year has gone by. Where did it go? I want to go home.

An English diplomat was sent to Peking for high-level discussions on the matter of ending the fighting in Vietnam. It was considered appeasement by many Americans, but this was not the case. The diplomat was in reality a top British Intelligence agent and when he returned, he did so with the confirmation of the August deadline for the Chinese blitz offensive. But even this stark news failed to warn sufficiently certain politicians in Washington. The intervention continued and supplies and men filtered continually into South Vietnam, but in nowhere near the amount that would be necessary.

Meanwhile the air war continued unabated and the pilots laughed because they had become inured to the Chinese sanctuary and, after all, they were fighting daily in the skies of North Vietnam. They figured that being allowed to fight at all was better than what they had been permitted before. And for Christ's sake, this was the only war they had, wasn't it?

By the first of April, Dan Belden had shot down twenty-three MIG planes. He did this with a minimum of publicity because his and Bates's status in this war was still obscured. Storm Ryerson and Smoke Dusane intimated that Belden and Bates might or might not be working on highly important matters for the CIA or Naval Intelligence, matters which could not be discussed at the present time.

Weeks passed and Belden searched the sky for Colonel Lee, but to no avail. Lee had implemented his squadrons and now there were three hundred and fifty fighters on the airstrips around Lungchou and Hanoi. Lee himself was writing his history in the air and by April he had destroyed twenty-one American aircraft.

Captain Xuan Nonh had not moved north to the Morlaix plantation as he had intended in the last days of January. Five times he had been forced into battle with General Pham's roving patrols, and five times he had escaped capture or death by the narrowest of margins. Twice he had been driven out of South Vietnam altogether and had been forced to take refuge over the Cambodian border. As the fighting up near the Parallel increased in fury, Xuan's superiors elected to pull him out of southwest Vietnam and the delta country. Pham had thrown a cordon of steel across the area where the Mekong River flowed through South Vietnam, forcing Xuan and his men to move into Cambodia and then turn north to follow a dim trail to the Parallel in the vicinity of Loc Ninh. It was in the last days of April that Xuan topped a small hill on the Cambodian side of the border. Thirty miles distant he could see a relatively unobscured valley where the Morlaix plantation stood. He had forgotten entirely his original plan to raze the plantation, but now that he was here, he decided not to forego the opportunity. He sent out reconnaissance patrols in the dark of night and they returned with reports indicating that the plantation was guarded by only a skeleton force of South Vietnamese troops.

Xuan decided to postpone the attack temporarily, until he could ambush an Arvin patrol and procure additional arms.

He and his men, who now numbered eighty-five, went into camp on the Cambodian border within sight of the plantation. Although the personnel at Morlaix's did not know it, they had exactly seven days before the murderers came down in the night.

On the same day that Xuan Nonh's scouts reported back to the camp, Dan Belden and Lori Morlaix were married by a French missionary priest in a tiny chapel on the outskirts of the plantation.

The ceremony was brief and simple and Storm Ryerson and Smoke Dusane and General Pham stood and watched as Robert

Morlaix gave his shining daughter into Belden's keeping. If they thought they could see the ghosts of twelve flying men standing by, why then it must have been so.

Belden would remember little of the ceremony. His mind wandered and passed over the long years of his life and he wondered if a man could say farewell, finally, to all of the things that had made him. As the priest intoned the words of the marriage service, Belden went back again to his beginnings, to a wind-swept field on the outskirts of Olathe, Kansas, and he and Bates were boys again, staring in awe at the old Yellow Perils parked on the flight line. The years passed swiftly through his memory as he scrubbed his mind clean with remembering and in a matter of minutes he had made the journey and the ceremony was over.

Outside, the plantation workers gathered in quiet groups to wait for the newlyweds to appear. Brown-faced and toil-worn, they whispered excitedly as the soft strains of organ music came from within the chapel. Inside, O'Toole and Merchant knelt in a pew, their calloused hands clasped before them as their lips moved to the strains of the lilting music.

And farther away, over the steaming rice paddies and swamplands, Xuan Nonh crouched on a hilltop with a set of binoculars and scanned the area round the plantation.

Outside the chapel there were the gestures of friendship, the warm handclasps, and finally, of course, Lori's tears.

"I don't blame you, Lori," Bates announced gravely. "I'd cry, too, if I married Belden. He snores."

She came to her toes and kissed Bates's weathered face. "We're all he's got, Batesy," she whispered. "Help me take care of him."

A shadow passed fleetingly across Bates's face and then it was gone. "I will do what I can, Lori. Perhaps it is all over now." There was no conviction in his words.

She understood. "No," she said slowly. "It isn't over yet. I can accept that now. But it will be soon."

"We can hope so, Lori," Bates murmured.

Lori turned to look at Belden, who stood with the other men a few yards away.

"Mr. O'Toole told me once," she said, "that Dan had something he had to do first. Some man named Lee."

Bates was silent a moment. Then he said, "Yes. There is the matter of Lee."

"And then?"

"Then perhaps it will be over."

Lori smiled brightly. "I'll think of it that way then. I'll think of it that way until it *is* over. I owe it to Dan."

Bates regarded her with a warm affection. "You've grown up to him, Lori. At first I thought you were too young, too perfect, without depth. I'm happy to say I was a hundred and eighty degrees out of phase. You were a child eight months ago at the Moana bar. You're a woman now and Dan needs such a woman. I'm glad for you both." Bates touched her hand and nodded his head. "Now"—his tone was light—"I'll go and drink great quantities of your father's excellent champagne."

The salon of the main house had been opened to the entire personnel of the plantation. Great tubs of ice held the countless bottles of champagne and on a long table there were varieties of hors d'oeuvres and cold meats. Two white-jacketed waiters circulated constantly with the trays of delicate champagne glasses brimming with the sparkling wine. Gay laughter sounded over the murmured hum of babbling voices.

Ryerson and Belden stood at the center of the room. Ryerson wondered at the hint of solemnity in Belden's eyes.

"Going on a honeymoon, Dan?" he asked.

"Not for a little while, Storm," Belden replied.

"You did the job for me, Dan. Almost, anyway. I'm grateful."

Belden smiled. "Almost, Storm?"

"We've done what we had to do. It almost worked. We've got fifty thousand men over here now. Five hundred airplanes. It's a hell of a lot better than what we had eight months ago. But there are only four months left until August, Dan. The Chinamen will come down then and I don't think we'll have enough to stop them."

"Four months is a long time," Belden said.

"Christ!" Ryerson said bitterly. "Why can't politicians understand? Sometimes I think they're chosen by a reverse selection of brains. I'm going to tell you what I think and I hope to hell I'm wrong. I think the people back in Washington believe we've got enough out here to keep the Chinamen from coming down. I think they'll settle for a stalemate. I think they'll shoot for another truce and I know goddam well they're wrong. I believe those silly bastards may well rescind permission to cross the Seventeenth Parallel and good Christ, Dan, if we can't hurt Lee in the air up there, when they do move down in August, they'll have air superiority and everything else going for them."

"Well," Belden said slowly, "maybe we can manage to hurt Lee in the air no matter what they rescind. Don't worry your mind with it, Storm. None of this has happened yet."

Robert Morlaix joined them as Ryerson asked, "Is Lori coming back to Saigon?"

Morlaix answered. "Not yet, Storm. She's remaining to close up the house. General Pham informs me he will have to remove the last of his men before long. I think the General plans to cross the Parallel soon."

"More power to him," Ryerson stated.

"Dan," Morlaix said, "when do you go back to Danang?"

"Day after tomorrow," Belden said. "Lori will go to Saigon by helicopter before Pham's troops pull out. I don't like it this way any better than she does, but right now I have no choice."

Morlaix smiled. "You have many years ahead of you, Dan. Do what you must first. There will be time for the other things."

"All my life," Belden said reflectively, "I've been able to handle responsibility. It never bothered me before. Now I'm a little scared."

Ryerson chuckled. "Most brand-new forty-year-old husbands are."

"You'll get used to it," Morlaix advised lightly. "We all have to, sooner or later." He looked across the room and saw his daughter making her way toward them. "She's matured since she met you, Dan. She's a woman now."

Belden might have been speaking to himself. "You can say that again."

Lori came up to take Belden by the hand. "If you will excuse an old married couple, I think we'd better speak to some of the other guests." She smiled at her father and Storm Ryerson. "And please look happy. I'm so happy myself that I want everyone else to be that way too."

"Blessings on them both," Ryerson said as Lori and Belden moved away.

"A thing puzzles me," Robert Morlaix said. "Dan has done the job he came out here for. You've got your escalation. Now he has found something that can change his life. Why doesn't he give it up now? Why doesn't he quit?"

Ryerson thought about this a moment before he answered. "Two reasons, Bob. Lee's air force up there hasn't been hurt. The MIGs can mean the difference in winning or losing for them. We may not have the stuff we need by August and if Lee is unhampered, we're done in. Then too, there is the matter of Lee himself. Don't forget that Dan lost ten friends off the mouth of the Red River."

"Vendettas are for children," Morlaix observed.

"Not always," Ryerson said. "It depends on the business you're in."

Much later that night, long hours after the guests had departed and the last of the champagne bottles had been tossed aside, Belden and Lori lay together in the large bed, under the ancient canopy. A wash of moon walked itself across the flatlands outside and dappled the floor just inside the open French window. They had made love with great tenderness and satisfaction and now Lori studied her husband as he lay on his back, his arms crossed beneath his head.

"This is a damnable thing," she said. "I'm happier than I've ever been in my life and yet I want to cry."

"It happens that way sometimes," he said lazily. "But cry if you like. Most of the world is crying in one way or another."

They were silent for a time and then Lori leaned over and kissed him on the lips. "You go away from me sometimes. I told you that once. Where do you go?" When he did not answer, she asked, "A minute ago . . . where were you a minute ago?"

He stared out the window and his voice was musingly mild. "Up north," he said, "they are getting ready to take off again. In a few minutes they'll be on their way and not all of them will be coming back again. I'd like to know *why.*"

She touched his hand and waited for his voice to continue because she knew he was speaking to himself and not to her.

"When you come right down to it, I suppose I know why Hawk

232

and Anders and Mac and Corey and all the rest of them died. They died because I asked them to. Now isn't that a hell of a thing to die for? I called and they came running and now they are all dead, dead and cold and gone forever and I lie here in a soft bed with a new wife and I am alive and they are dead." He shook his head. "It doesn't make sense. It isn't right."

"You miss them." She made the statement in a whisper.

Surprisingly, he said, "No. Not in the way you mean. I regret them, if you can understand that. If I missed them, I would be taking something away from their memory."

"Well," she said, laying her golden head on his shoulder, "you can go with them sometimes. As long as you come back to me."

"Once in a while, perhaps," he said. "Once in a while I will go with them."

"Can you find them?" Her voice was drowsy and her long lashes lay on her cheeks.

"I can find them," he said. He looked down at her and her breath was long and even in her sleep. A tender smile touched his lips as he thought: There are some things one knows with certainty even as I know you are my final woman. It is simple and direct and I'll never be so sure of anything again in my life. I can find them just as a man can find anything he loves if he looks hard enough. For the stuff that dreams are made of is unselfish stuff if the dreams are worth a damn, and ten men dying off the mouth of the Red River are the toast of the gods, and the ghosts of friends still fly your wing if you believe in wine and moonlight and the old songs the fliers sing.

There was a rustling sound from outside as some night birds made their way south. But Belden knew they were not night birds because he heard the sound of engines and he saw with surety the shadows of twelve planes move ghostlike across the sky.

A breath of wind swung the French windows and let a splash of moonlight dance across the room and rest lightly on the face of his wife. Belden watched her for a moment, feeling a great gratitude in his heart, and then he turned very quietly and kissed her on the lips.

Chapter
XIV

The rainy season had come, slowing down the tempo of the fighting in the air. The jets still launched daily from Danang, but the encounters were less frequent and oftentimes degenerated into deadly games of hide-and-seek in the heavy cloud formations. It became as though both sides were waiting for something; exactly what, neither knew. The Seventh Fleet sailed north after the enemy had made an attack on a destroyer division. Smoke Dusane was afforded a valid reason for initiating several slashing attacks along the coastal area both north and south of the Gulf of Tonkin. The actual damage inflicted was negligible, but Dusane's attacks sharpened the edge of the knife along which both sides were treading.

At Lungchou, Colonel Lee now had four hundred and eighty-five MIG fighter planes, the greatest single concentration of air power since the founding of the People's Republic. Unfortunately, he did not have enough qualified pilots to fully man his complement of aircraft. Approximately half of his fliers had been blooded well in the skies to the south, even as had the pilots of his enemy. The almost fatal afternoon on which he had met Belden seemed a long time ago and he had nearly put it from his memory. The conflict all about him was taking shape and resolving itself exactly as he and General Soohoo had foreseen. The increments which had been added to his fighter command had astounded even Lee. And it appeared the Americans would not push the necessary manpower and equipment into South Vietnam in time to affect the August offensive. Lee knew he would be able to provide air supremacy and, in the opinion of the high officials in Peking, this made the August offensive a certain victory. General Soohoo had risen high in the circles of the top command and his power was destined to grow even greater. Lee was aware that he would rise in power and position along with the General.

Then, on the fifth day of May, Dan Belden killed General Soohoo Mu Thik.

One of General Pham's advance patrols, operating far to the north, had intercepted a radio transmission to the effect that Falcon would take off from Lotus, destination Hummingbird, at 0900. It was only 0700 when this apparently innocuous information reached the desk of Pham's personal intelligence officer.

Two weeks earlier a Red Chinese pilot had crash-landed three miles south of the Parallel. On his body was found a small notebook containing the code appellations for air-to-air and air-to-ground radio communications. It was at that time that General Soohoo's luck began to run out. This code enabled Pham's men to deduce that General Soohoo-Falcon would depart Lungchou-Lotus at 0900 hours for Hanoi-Hummingbird. So easily was it done. There would be an escort of eight fighters with the General and the trip was short enough so that it would entail no undue hazards to the most important man in the Red Chinese Air Force.

General Pham consulted with Storm Ryerson and it was 0730 when they decided to call Dan Belden at Danang airfield.

Bates watched Belden as he crossed the last name from the typewritten list that lay before him on the desk.

"That's the last of them," Belden said, pushing the paper away. "I thought I was through writing letters like these."

"You're never through. Not until someone writes one about you." He glanced at Belden. "You're restless, Dan. Maybe this waiting is getting us down." Bates lit a cigarette before he continued. "God knows, I've been doing some thinking about this."

Belden smiled. "We've always understood each other, Batesy. You're thinking of me. Not yourself."

"Who says so?" Bates was properly indignant. He crossed the room and sat on the edge of the desk. "You know, Dan, I am beginning to think of a woman in Palm Beach named Helen Mabry." Bates was silent a moment. "I may never find it so good again."

"You'll find it again. She'll be there. You'll go back and she'll be there."

"Will I, Dan? When? You know something?" Bates frowned. "I thought it was getting stale. Back there in Palm Beach everything was flat. I don't think so any more. I begin to think maybe flying a goddam Grumman Goose at a hundred and twenty knots over that blue water to the Bahamas is not so bad a way to spend a lifetime at that. Every night I could come back to Helen and her eight million dollars and what the hell is wrong with it?" His eyes lighted with a sudden thought. "You know something else, my friend? You'd like it too. You can do worse than consider a partnership with me flying from Palm Beach to the Bahamas. I'll even cough up the money to get us started." He nodded to himself. "Helen will never miss it."

"It's something to think about at that," Belden said half-seriously.

Bates studied his friend in silence. He stuffed his cigarette out in the ash tray before he spoke.

"We're useless as tits on a boar out here now," he said. "The guys are gone and there are only two of us left. We did what Pham and Ryerson wanted us to do. We brought this thing out in the open. Now what the hell good are we? Two middle-aged guys flying two F8s in the middle of a couple of hundred young kids who can do the job just as well as we can. I think we've squeezed all the best juice from the orange, Dan. It's time we went home."

"Soon perhaps," Belden said. "But not quite yet." He picked up the list of the names of the friends who were dead and scanned it a moment.

"We might stay here for ten years and never find Lee again," Bates said.

"You know better than that," Belden replied. "When Pham moves, no matter what else happens, Lee will come out with all he's got. He has to. It's only May and the Chinamen aren't going to come down until August. They can't afford to let Pham move north and dig in.

Lee is the best deterrent they've got." Belden spoke decisively. "He'll come out."

Bates took the paper from Belden's hand. He folded it and then methodically tore it into tiny pieces.

"They're gone, Dan. The way they wanted to go. Let's forget the vendetta. Lee will get his. Some twenty-three-year-old kid will fight him one day and the kid will get lucky or maybe Lee's years will tell on him and the kid will fly home a hero. Why not let it go at that?"

"You really think that's the answer?" Belden smiled.

"I'm not on trial here," Bates said. "You are. You've got something to lose now."

"And I'm grateful for it. How lucky can a guy get? But remember one thing, Batesy. Hawk and Cort and Mac and all the rest didn't truly want to lose anything either. But they did." He paused a moment. "No. There's one more fight waiting for us. We'll have to take it on."

"Ah," Bates made a sound of disgust. "The only two-man air force in the history of aviation."

"Perhaps they'll give you a medal for it," Belden remarked with a smile.

"What the hell would I do with it? I've already got a cigarbox full of them. I gave them to Helen Mabry to keep. For two reasons. I've got so goddam many of them I ran out of room on my chest. Also, it's an excuse for going back again. Not that I need one, mind you. But you never want a woman to know exactly how you feel about her. She'll think I just came back to get my medals again. This is ridiculous." Bates sighed. "They may prove to be of some use after all."

The radio set on the far side of the room broke into a burst of static that eased off as General Pham's voice came over: "Viceroy. This is Royalty. Are you there?"

Belden crossed quickly to the set and spoke into the hand mike: "Roger, Royalty. Standing by."

"Dan. This is General Pham here. I have important news. We have intercepted a Chinese radio transmission. General Soohoo is taking off from Lungchou at 0900 for Hanoi. He will have an eight-plane fighter escort. Can you intercept and destroy?"

"Why me? You've got the U.S. Air Force waiting to go. But the answer is hell yes, I can intercept and destroy."

"Then get at it. We don't want to send a large attack group. It might alert them and scare them back to Lungchou. Two planes might get away with it. Try to keep off their radar."

"Any idea what type of plane Soohoo's in?" Belden grinned at Bates.

"No. Perhaps you might get him when they land at Hanoi. And, Dan. Don't wait around to fight the MIGs. Get back here when the job is done. I need you for something coming up soon."

"Okay, General. We're on our way."

"Good luck, Dan. Royalty out."

Belden replaced the mike and slapped Bates on the shoulder. "You heard the man. Let's go kill the General."

Bates was already moving toward the map on the far wall of the room. He took a ruler and measured the distance from Lungchou to Hanoi.

"A hundred and ten, maybe fifteen, miles," he said. "Doesn't give us much time."

"We won't need it," Belden said. He was studying a weather report supplied them by the Air Force meterological officer at the field. Already his mind was probing the possibilities and framing a course of action.

"The weather's lousy," Bates advised from the window. "Build-ups northwest up to thirty thousand."

"The weather is delightful," Belden grinned. "Get O'Toole."

"You're getting old," Bates replied. "Your memory's going. You sent O'Toole with Lori to the plantation to help her close up. He left three or four Navy guys here."

"Well, get them on the planes. How many Sidewinders have we got?"

"Three, I think."

"I'll take them all. Full ammo."

"You'll take them all. What about me?" Bates's tone was wounded. "What am I going along for? The ride?"

"You, my friend," Belden said smugly, "are going to be a pigeon. A large, bald-headed, forty-one-year-old pigeon. Are you happy?"

"Thanks," Bates retorted dryly. "Helen Mabry may hate you when this is all over."

*　　*　　*

It was exactly 0820 when Belden and Bates taxied into take-off position at the end of the Danang runway. Directly overhead the sky was clear, but to the north and northwest towering thunderheads reached up to tremendous heights. The early morning sun bathed the upper halves of the formidable bastions in a jumble of pastel shadings, broken where the purplish shadows hovered over the entrances to the deep caverns that jutted into the boiling cloud mass. There was power in that beauty, awesome power beyond the ability of the human mind to conceive. The entire majestic bank stretched across fifty miles of sky, beginning in the west and moving its appalling bulk to the north where it finally thinned out into a high overcast.

"Danang Tower," Belden called. "Viceroy One for take-off with two. Direct Saigon. VFR. Over."

He deliberately gave the false information to mislead anyone who might be listening in on an enemy receiver. The VFR flight plan was to make certain that there would be no alarm when he failed to arrive at Saigon.

"Cleared for take-off, Viceroy One," the tower replied.

Belden glanced over at Bates sitting complacently a few feet from his left wingtip. He nodded once and advanced his throttle smoothly to the stop. The engine whined and then rose into a crescendo. As his power needle passed 90 percent, he leaned forward in the seat with an exaggerated motion, indicating to Bates that he was releasing his brakes and beginning his take-off role. The plane eased forward slowly and then began to pick up momentum as the great thrust of the engine exerted forward pressure. When his air-speed needle passed 100 knots, he looked out of the corner of his eye and grinned to himself as he saw Bates hanging tight, not more than two feet off his wingtip. The two planes raced down the runway as one, the two trails of exhaust smoke winding after them almost as a single plume.

They were off the deck at 0821, wheels up and the planes in clean configuration. They swung to a heading of 350 degrees, steering for the center of the mountainous front looming before them. Belden eased back on his throttle because he knew he had time to spare and no man spends more time than is absolutely necessary within the confines of a thunderhead. They shallowed out in their climb and held their air speed at 400 knots.

The minutes sped past and as they drew closer to the array of clouds, even minor patches of clear sky were obscured by overreaching claws of vapor emanating from the front. They were at 30,000 feet and the tops of the battlements were still thousands of feet above them. Belden took off more throttle and held his altitude, allowing his air speed to drop off abruptly. When a man intends to defy the power of the gods, he does not enter into the maelstrom at high speed unless he wants to tear his airplane into shreds. He enters it slowly and in a dirty configuration in order to cope better with the unbelievable forces he knows he will encounter. Belden moved his arm in a jerking motion visible to Bates, then dropped his landing gear. Bates did likewise and the sleek jets assumed a cumbersome appearance in the darkening sky.

Belden had flown a course parallel to the storm for several minutes and then had reversed course and come back, watching his time closely. He was still south of the 17th Parallel at 0840 when he turned head-on and entered the ferocious front.

Just before the black, heaving fists of cloud came at him, he lowered his seat all the way to the floor and turned his instrument-panel lights up full bright. He knew that Bates, in his cockpit, was performing a like operation. He flicked on his wing lights for Bates's benefit and then they were swallowed by the heaving phalanx.

Sitting low in the cockpit, Belden's attention was riveted on his instrument panel. His eyes never ceased moving. Artificial horizon, needle, ball and air speed, tail-pipe temperature. The dials jumped crazily before his eyes as the airplane was buffeted by gigantic winds. Belden was not tense, but he was very alert, almost as though he was waiting for something. He glanced at his air-speed indicator and pulled the throttle back another inch. In the inferno of the storm he could not hear the sound of his engine. In his earphones the radio stuttered with great spasms of boisterous static and he turned the volume control down.

Suddenly the two Crusaders rammed headlong into a solid obstruction. Belden grunted as he became instantly weightless and was jerked hard against his seat belt. He stared at the artificial horizon now, intent on keeping the wings level and the plane's nose on the horizon. A flash of lightning split the dark cloud mass, accompanied by a blasting cannonade. For a split second Belden was blinded, but then it passed. Had he not had the foresight to lower his seat and

240

turn his lights up bright, the blindness would have lasted appreciably longer.

The monumental anger of the storm increased and the planes were thrown about the inimical sky as two toys in a high wind. Belden knew he was passing through the center of the storm and the area of greatest turbulence. He glanced at Bates and smiled as he saw him fighting his plane to hold a wing position. In that moment of crisis he felt an admiration for Bates's flying ability. Another long, jagged blade of lightning glared in the sky and the rumble of deep thunder shook the airplanes. It seemed that all the fury of the elements was crammed into this particular little chunk of sky. A vicious downdraft hit the aircraft and the pilots shoved throttles forward and held back stick and so maintained their altitude. Belden fought the storm with practiced skill and as he did so, he found time to be grateful for at least one thing. No radar set on earth could pick up two airplanes flying in a sonofabitch of a storm like this one.

Finally, after they had battled the beast for what seemed a lifetime, the anger lessened and they could hear the sound of rain smashing in torrents against their windshields and along the sides of the planes and at last they could even hear the noise of their engines.

The black, murderous intensity of the sky lightened and Bates swung out twenty yards and wiped his forehead while shaking his head in wonder at such titanic power.

Both pilots were utterly amazed when they glanced at their watches. They had been in the fury of the storm for thirty minutes on a course of due north. According to their pre-flight navigation, they should break out of the front at 30,000 feet and ten miles due west of Hanoi.

They held their altitude and resumed a cruise setting on their throttles. The boiling puffs of black cloud gave way to lighter layers of thick mist and the turbulent air smoothed out as suddenly as it had stormed up. Belden turned 10 degrees to his right and flew out into a hazy sky that was overcast at 38,000 feet but clear below. Off his starboard wing he saw the long strip of the Hanoi airfield. He immediately began a steeply banked turn to his port and called Bates: "We'll circle here on the edge of this beauty. They won't pick us up on their scopes. Keep your eyes peeled, pigeon."

Bates grunted an unintelligible reply and the two planes maintained a continuous, tightly banked circle on the very edge of the storm.

General Soohoo's private plane was a converted Russian Ilyushin bomber. The insides had been torn out and refitted with plush seats and a decor that would have done justice to a Texas oil millionaire. The plane had taken off from Lungchou at exactly 0900 and after an uneventful flight was approaching the landing pattern at Hanoi at 0920. The pilot called Hanoi tower for landing instructions when he was still eleven minutes from the field. He was told that he was cleared to land; he was the only plane in the pattern; ceiling and visibility were unobstructed. The pilot let down to 2,000 feet and continued his initial approach into the pattern. He told the tower he estimated arrival over the field at 0931.

An aide went to the rear of the plane where General Soohoo reclined on a heavily cushioned couch. The aide imparted the landing information and the General decided to attend to his private functions before they landed. Accordingly he repaired to the well-appointed lavatory situated at the extreme tail of the plane.

Belden and Bates swept by the face of the storm front and headed outward in their circle. They had gradually descended until they flew at a steady 10,000 feet. Both men had armed all gun and missile switches and their gunsights were turned on. They spotted the enemy simultaneously. General Soohoo's plane was clearly visible approaching Hanoi from the north at a low altitude. Slightly behind and a few thousand feet above the Ilyushin flew two four-plane formations of MIGs.

"Tallyho," Belden said softly into his radio.

"I got 'em," was all Bates said.

"Okay then," Belden said. "You know what to do."

Bates broke away from Belden and his voice came lightly over the air. "Here goes your pigeon." He peeled off and swept downward, building up great speed as he turned toward the runway at Hanoi.

The eight MIGs flying escort for the estimable General Soohoo had no premonition that enemy fighters were on the attack. This mission had been considered a milk run of short duration with absolutely no threat of danger. The flight leader, a young captain of considerable experience, watched the General's plane as it swung into its downwind leg. He heard the pilot report to the tower that he had entered the pattern and was approaching his base leg.

Bates was past Mach One, the speed of sound, as he came out of his dive, leveled off at 4,000 feet, and blazed in on the MIGs from their five-o'clock position. They had not seen him coming, so he closed unconcernedly and opened fire when out of range. He was flying up his tracers when the MIGs noted the crimson streaks of the shells flashing past them. Before they had time to take evasive action, Bates was within range and his sights were centered on the rear four-plane division. He held his trigger down and sprayed his shells from left to right with gentle pressures on stick and rudder. Two MIGs exploded into balls of flame and then Bates was past them and climbing steeply with his great speed. The MIG leader threw his plane into a steep bank and searched the area to the rear for more of the enemy. When he found nothing, he wheeled back and went into afterburner, calling to his flight to follow, and then pulled steeply into a 45-degree climb after the rapidly disappearing Crusader.

Belden had come down on the deck as he saw Bates swing in behind the MIGs, so when the enemy leader looked to the rear, Belden was already below him and lost to his vision against the background of terrain. Belden saw the six remaining MIGs go up after Bates and he called over the air with a jubilance in his voice, "We've got 'em, Batesy. They're on your ass."

Bates's reply was sardonic. "That's pleasant news. I'm heading for the thunderhead."

"Roger," Belden said. "I'll be with you as soon as I attend to the General."

The familiar scene was in his gunsight again as he came behind the Ilyushin. The wingspread of the bomber filled the entire outer ring and the MIGs had gone after Bates, so Belden sat there and held his position and thought to himself: This is easier than shooting tin cans off a backyard fence. He moved a little closer and glanced to check his switches.

General Soohoo was in a most indelicate position in which to die. He was having some difficulty with his gastric functions and was in considerable distress when he heard the sound of Bates's guns hammering away at the MIGs. There was nothing he could do about it at that precise time.

Belden laughed softly as he let his armament go. The Sidewinders blazed briefly in the gray sky, arcing out and down into the engine area of the Ilyushin. Simultaneously he pressed his triggers and the four cannon in the nose spit fire at the target. The Ilyushin never had a chance. The engines went at the same time as the gas tanks, exploding out of their mountings and ripping the front half of the plane away.

The rear half of the bomber careened through the sky like some amputated monstrosity. So General Soohoo died going to the toilet and with his pants down. This may not be the accepted manner of departure for a soldier, but it is quite as terminal as any other.

Belden saw the Ilyushin break apart and he turned away in a high g-climb toward the southwest and the protection of the front. He was at 27,000 feet in less than ninety seconds and he was scanning the sky ahead, looking for Bates, when he heard a laughing voice in his earphones: "The General died at dawn. Or shortly thereafter. I'm on your wing, Dan."

Belden looked and Bates was hanging in position again, tight off his wingtip.

"Where'd your playmates go?" Belden asked.

"I lost them in a hunk of cloud back there. Let's go home."

"Roger," Belden said. He smiled in his cockpit because the job had been done and he and Bates were going home again. He reset his artificial horizon, turned off his arming switches, and bored back into the thunderhead. He flew higher this time, just skirting the very peaks of the giant escarpments and the turbulence was negligible. He no longer gave a damn if they were picked up by enemy radar. No one could get to them now.

He looked over at Bates and held up his thumb and forefinger in the timeless gesture of victory. Then he sat back and let the tension ease out of his bones. Bates did the same and they droned on through the highest places, weaving gently as they picked their way along the jutting topmasts of the storm. Below them men had died in a quick, fierce flurry of fire, but that was all. It had been done before and men would do it again before the day was over. They listened to the strong singing of their engines and felt the quick response of the controls as their hands and feet exerted featherlike pressures on stick and rudder. The oxygen was clean and good coming out of their masks. So they sat that way. Listening. Far back in the sky it started first as a mere tugging at the memory.

They listened closely over the rushing of the wind along the canopies.

And then they heard it. They heard it together in the same second of time.

The sound of bugles in the sky.

Late that same night the story was released to the wire services. It created the same furor that had attended the shooting down of a Japanese admiral in World War II when, by the breaking of a secret code, the flight plan of the Admiral had been deduced and a flight of P-38s was waiting for him. Radio broadcasts of the incident were monitored in North Vietnam and Colonel Lee knew who had shot down the General. Because Lee had not been on the flight himself, he suffered no loss of face at the General's demise. But the pilots of the escort were court-martialed and executed within twenty-four hours.

The senior officers in Peking, having no suitable replacement on hand to take General Soohoo's place, elected to allow Colonel Lee to assume temporary command of the Air Force in the Lungchou area, although with no increase in rank.

Lee decided he would intensify his training program. Half his pilots were totally inadequate in aerial combat techniques. Lee, by this time, was fully convinced that the Americans would not escalate their forces in time to meet the August offensive. He was aware of the importance his air command would play in the coming battles. He saw no reason not to expect a relatively easy victory over the Americans, providing his men were well indoctrinated in this highly specialized business they had undertaken.

In the vicinity of the Morlaix plantation, Xuan Nonh listened to the reports of his reconnaissance patrols. Six days had passed since he had arrived at his present bivouac. He had ambushed a small enemy platoon and now had ample arms with which to carry out his plan. His scouts were reporting that the small company of men who had remained as guards were making preparations for departure.

Strangely, for some time now Xuan had had a feeling of disquiet.

At night he let his mind wander and he found himself going back again to that morning in the clearing when he had executed the two American pilots. Somehow he was certain that after that morning, after the echoes of the rifle shots had died away, his life and his fate were inextricably bound up with the events of that early dawn. Just how this was, he did not know. But in some manner or other, everything had begun at that time. He wondered how the death of two Americans in a quiet village yard could influence his destiny.

He knelt in the darkness and with a small twig sketched diagrams in the dirt, outlining for his squad leaders the plan that had taken shape in his mind. With definite knowledge of the number of men who would be left to resist the attack, the offensive would be quick, incisive, carried out in darkness, and there would be no survivors among the personnel at the Morlaix plantation.

Tomorrow night at dusk they would move in.

Chapter
XV

MAY
1965

General Pham's men moved in the night and during the following day, passing swiftly over the 17th Parallel in force. The terrain was intolerable, high mountains and narrow, winding passes, and the rate of advance was necessarily slow. If some of his troops slipped to the west and moved north through Laotian territory, it was done stealthily and in the furor no one heeded the outraged cries from Vientiane.

The Vietcong's guerrilla tactics were of no avail in halting the aggressive infantry action and Pham had established his lines ten miles within North Vietnam before sufficient forces could be mustered and sent south from Hanoi to resist him.

Even as he was doing this and Smoke Dusane's Seventh Fleet hit at coastal installations, in Saigon the Communist-infiltrated Buddhist movement rioted in the streets and fought the soldiers with knives, bottles, and bare fists. Pham ignored the strife in Saigon and paused to take breath before smashing on northward. In the United Nations angry voices were raised and indignation flourished to the cries of "imperialism and aggression."

United States Air Force and Navy fighters flew in the skies over North Vietnam, wary and alert for the enemy who did not come. Lee held his powerful squadrons on the ground at Lungchou under orders from Peking. Ten divisions of Red Chinese infantry moved

247

down to the border. These movements of the enemy were accurately reported by Dusane's recco planes and the two U.S. Marine regiments came out of the lines and moved forty miles to the north, backing up Pham's front-line troops.

Overnight, so it seemed, the war in Vietnam had slipped on the sharp edge of the knife and now was precariously straddled along the razor-sharp blade.

Belden and Bates had flown three hops that day in company with a section of F-100s based in an adjacent hangar. They had flown all the way to the Chinese border without making contact with the MIGs. It was 1700, five o'clock in the afternoon, when they wearily discarded their flight gear and mixed a drink in the ready room.

"Why don't they come up after us?" Bates asked as he threw his helmet into a chair with a snort of disgust. "They've got so damn many MIGs parked up there I couldn't begin to count them."

"Relax," Belden told him. "They'll come out."

"Yeah." Bates stretched luxuriously. "When's Lori coming back?"

"Tomorrow." Belden studied his drink reflectively. "Tell Merchant I want the planes painted tonight."

Bates frowned. "What the hell for?"

Belden might not have heard the question. "I want the South Vietnam insignia on them. The shield in red and orange with the black circle and the white star. We're going to fight under somebody's colors even if we can't fight under our own."

"This is a hell of a time to worry about paint jobs," Bates complained.

"Time's running out," Belden said succinctly.

"Would you mind explaining that? I'm sort of stupid today."

Before Belden could answer the radio sounded across the room.

"Viceroy from Royalty." It was General Pham's voice.

"Go ahead, Royalty," Belden said into the mike.

"Dan. This is General Pham here. My congratulations on General Soohoo."

Belden grinned at Bates. "Nothing to it, General. He just ran out of altitude and information simultaneously."

"Dan." Pham's voice was serious. "A question. Is your wife at the Morlaix plantation?"

"Yeah. She and O'Toole are due to drive into Saigon tomorrow. Why?"

"Can you get her out of there tonight?"

"I suppose so. There's an Air Force Cessna 310 I can borrow." His hand tightened on the mike. "Is she in danger?"

"She may be," Pham replied. "We have reports of a guerrilla band in the vicinity. I've pulled most of my men to the north and left only a handful around the plantation. I've ordered a patrol in company strength to move there as fast as they can. But they won't get there for several hours. If there is danger, it may come tonight. My movements across the Parallel may trigger a counteroffensive by the Vietcong. I think to be on the safe side you'd better get her out tonight."

"Okay, General. My thanks."

"All right," General Pham said. "And, Dan." He spoke carefully. "I wouldn't waste any time if I were you."

"Roger from Viceroy and out," Belden said. He turned to Bates. "Okay, Batesy. Let's haul ass."

They had moved up at dusk and now studied the plantation from a distance of one-half mile and through a heavy screen of foliage. The sun was gone behind the western mountains and in the dim light there was no sign of life around the main building or in the surrounding brush. Far to the south a farmer trod laboriously with his tired oxen at his side. He was the only living being visible.

Xuan Nonh crouched with his arms resting on his knees. He remained in this position until he saw a light appear in a window of the house and then he grunted in satisfaction. He had men out on either side and on the point at a distance of only a few hundred yards from the scanty perimeter set up by the remaining South Vietnamese soldiers. Xuan's eyes narrowed in anger as he remembered the radio transmission he had received that morning, describing General Pham's attack. He had been recalled to the north, so he knew he could waste no more time. Tonight he would destroy the plantation, perhaps taking prisoners, perhaps not. It depended on what he found down there. As for the woman his scouts had reported, he would use her as he pleased. His hand moved and rubbed slowly on his crotch and he felt a stirring in his loins. He turned his head to find his second-in-command watching him nervously.

Xuan took the heavy .45-caliber pistol from its holster and snapped the barrel back, injecting a cartridge into the chamber. He flicked the safety on.

"Soon now we will go down. Remember one thing. Tell your men. The woman is mine. Afterward she may be yours. Is this clear?"

"Yes, Captain," the man replied.

"The men understand the plan? All of them?" The question was unnecessary. The men had been briefed daily for a week.

"They are ready, Captain," the man said.

They spoke in hushed voices. "I don't like this," Xuan said. "If they are moving north, there may be patrols coming this way. We must be gone quickly." The other man nodded in the darkness.

Xuan turned his attention out into the night, watching and waiting with calm patience. He felt the movement in his loins again and took a deep breath, letting it expel slowly through compressed lips. The night would go well. The fighting would be brief and there would be time to loot and eat and take this pale woman with the golden hair. Then they would move back across the Laotian border to safety and move north to join the fight across the Parallel.

From the gathering gloom ahead a light flashed briefly. Once. Twice. Three times.

The man touched Xuan's arm tentatively. "The men have taken their positions, Captain."

Xuan nodded. His hand caressed the barrel of his gun, and he wondered if he would feel regret when he killed the golden woman. He had never killed a woman before. For a moment his mind lost itself contemplating the various pleasurable methods in which this might be accomplished.

He turned his eyes to the other man. "They are not expecting the attack. The big house will be unguarded. I will take five men there. The rest of you will destroy the troops on the perimeter."

"There is the American," the man said.

"He, too, is mine," Xuan replied.

Xuan glanced at his watch, his proudest possession, which he had removed from the wrist of a dead American Special Forces officer after an ambush near Ben Cat. The time read six-thirty as Xuan rose to his feet and holstered his pistol.

"We will go now. Quietly."

Four miles northwest two hundred South Vietnamese infantry under the command of an American Major moved toward the Morlaix plantation at double time.

There was the fragrance of flowers in the garden as Lori sat in her favorite chair and listened to the heavy footsteps of O'Toole as he finished the last of the packing inside the house. The silence was heavy enough to slice, out across the fields and into the heavy growth of trees. She felt a certain sadness at leaving this familiar garden for what she sensed would be the last time. Her childhood had bloomed here and here also it had died. In this house she had married the man she loved and now she was leaving it forever to follow him wherever fate decreed. She was sad, but with a nostalgic sadness, not regret. She turned to find O'Toole standing in the entrance, his big shoulders filling the doorway. He wore his dungarees and battered Navy cap and there was a pistol holstered at his side. His worn face creased into a smile as he approached Lori.

"That's about the last of it, Mrs. Belden."

"I can't get used to being Mrs. Belden," she admitted with a smile. "And what are you grinning about, O'Toole?"

"I just talked to Dan on the radio. He's on his way here now. We'll be leaving tonight." His face assumed a pained expression. "So all that packing and crating was for nothing."

"Leaving tonight?" She was puzzled. "Is something wrong?"

"Not a thing, miss."

"You're lying to me, O'Toole." She studied him with a grave attention. "You don't have to, you know."

The expressions of concern and affection passed over O'Toole's crooked features as small shadows. All during this day he had felt a sense of uneasiness. He could not put his finger on it, but he had felt this way on a December morning at Pearl Harbor just before the dive bombers passed over Diamond Head.

"If we're going tonight, why have you been packing everything in the house?" she asked.

"We'll be back for it," he said. "In a few days perhaps." He did not tell her that the sounds she had heard had been the uncrating of a heavy box of submachine guns and ammunition which had been ordered long before, when her father had first taken alarm at the Vietcong infiltration. He had wiped one of the guns clean of its coating of cosmoline and had inserted a full drum of ammunition.

"Are they coming tonight? Is that what you won't tell me?" she asked in a calm voice. "I'm not a little girl, Mr. O'Toole."

"No," he smiled. "Not any more." He paused. "A guerrilla band is reported around this area someplace. It's only a rumor, but Dan doesn't want to take a chance. He wants us out of here tonight."

"All my pretty things? My wedding gifts?" She stamped her foot angrily.

"That's like a woman," O'Toole reflected aloud. "When the earth finally shudders in the last cataclysmic rumble, they will think only of their pretty things." He shook his head. "You may bring only a suitcase, miss. The plane is a small one. I will go to operations and arrange for the lighting on the strip. Please hurry."

O'Toole hurried out to his jeep and quickly drove the half-mile along the bumpy dirt road to the makeshift operations building, deserted and forlorn now in the darkness of evening. As he switched off the bright headlights, he breathed a sigh of relief and thought to himself: Now why should I be so certain that men were watching me during that short drive? I'm getting old and nervous, I guess. He carried the machine gun with him as he went inside to gather the runway lanterns.

Six hundred yards away from the main house, Xuan Nonh watched O'Toole disappear in the dusk. He followed the streak of the headlights until they winked out across the field and then he motioned to the five men behind him and they crept quietly through the tall grass.

According to Xuan's scouting reports there should be a post of ten men guarding this approach to the plantation. He did not intend to attack until the rest of his men had opened fire across the field. There was the possibility that a command post had been set up within the house, in which case he might run into heavy opposition in this area of the attack.

Crawling on hands and knees, the six men made no sound as they wormed down a slight decline and came to a halt in a shallow gully. They sat motionless for nearly five minutes. Around them crickets chirped and there was only the sound of the wind rustling the tree branches and the high grass. The moon slipped behind a solitary cloud and the forms of the crouching men became nothing more than angular chunks of blackness in the gloom.

Xuan glanced at his watch and noted the time. It was exactly 1850 and his men should be in position across the field within two minutes. One of the men shifted in the dark and the cracking of a twig startled the others. Xuan smiled to himself at the sound of indrawn breaths. He watched the large house standing against the almost invisible horizon and across the lighted double windows on the second floor he thought he saw a shadow swiftly pass.

Belden and Bates were ten minutes out from the plantation at 1850. The cockpit interior was blacked out except for the faint luminescence from the instrument panel. They had not spoken during the flight from Danang other than the necessary curt commands and replies at take-off and climb to cruising altitude. Belden had plotted his course by dead reckoning, since he knew the homer site at Morlaix's was inoperative now. He had assumed a no-wind condition and had flown a direct course, gambling that the weather would hold and he could find the plantation by moonlight. His face was etched in hard planes by the instrument lights, deep shadows lying on his cheeks and along the grim line of his mouth.

Bates lit a cigarette as he peered ahead through the windshield, trying to pick up a visible landmark. He drew deeply and exhaled the smoke, then placed the cigarette between Belden's lips. Belden nodded his head as his right hand eased back on the twin throttles set in the center of the engine operating quadrant. He had maintained excessive power during the flight, allowing the cylinder-head temperatures to approach the danger mark on the dial, and if his calculations were correct, he should be able to pick up the plantation within a few minutes. As he eased forward on the control wheel, the nose dipped toward the ground and the altimeter began to unwind.

"Nearly there, Dan," Bates murmured. "I'll try O'Toole on the low frequency."

Belden inclined his head and leveled off at 1500 feet. Below them the ground was intermittently splashed with moonlight as the moon played cops and robbers with some high stratus cloud formations. At low altitude the sky was clear and visibility unlimited. When they

253

had become airborne at Danang they had been able to see fierce flashes of flame to the north as the big guns worked along the Parallel, but here in the south there was nothing below them to indicate that men of contrasting beliefs stalked each other in the rice paddies and jungles with murder in their hearts.

Bates had been calling in vain, trying to raise O'Toole on the radio. He replaced the mike and turned to Belden. "No answer from O'Toole. Maybe they've already left."

Belden shook his head. "They wouldn't leave at night. He must be with Lori." Belden thought a moment. "Keep trying to raise him." Beneath the calm tone there was a touch of anxiety. Bates heard it and laid his hand lightly on Belden's shoulder.

"This is nothing, Dan. Just a flight in the moonlight on a summer night. That's all it is. Nothing to sweat, boy."

Belden's mouth relaxed into a smile and he glanced at Bates. "We've taken them before, haven't we, old friend? How many more will we take?"

"Many more, Dan," Bates said softly. "When Helen Mabry buys us our airline in Florida, I'll show you sights at night over the strip of water between Palm Beach and West End that you won't believe. It's a nice thing to think about. And who knows?" He shrugged in the dim light. "It may even come to pass."

They were silent as the seconds passed and Bates studied the navigation data written on a knee pad and consulted his computer. Finally he put the computer aside. "Five minutes out, Dan."

O'Toole had placed his runway lanterns with great care and had returned to the operations building where he turned on the radio set and waited for it to warm up. The feeling of apprehension was stronger in him now and he listened in the silence of the deserted ready room. The stray gear that had been left behind by the pilots when they went to Danang to fly out to glory and death had all been crated and sent away. All that remained to remind him that men had lived and laughed and cursed in this dusty room was some faint scribbling on the blackboard that on closer inspection proved to be the flight schedule of so long ago. O'Toole made out the faint tracing of the names: Belden, Hawkins, Anders, Kilpatrick, and all the rest. Dust covered the names now just as dust covered the men who had worn them. An old plotting board was stuffed into a wastebasket and high up on the wall of the room a heavy knife, of the type worn by the pilots, was stuck securely, the result of a practiced throw by a man who would never do it again.

The sound of static came over the receiver and O'Toole spoke into the mike: "This is Viceroy here. This is Viceroy here. Come in if you receive me, Dan."

"This is Dan, Larry. Go ahead."

"I've placed the runway lights. All is quiet here, but there's something bothering me. Don't ask me what it is because I don't know. But come in low and fast and without lights. Over."

"Are Pham's men still there?" Belden asked.

"A few of them. Not enough if those bastards come after us." O'Toole forced a small laugh. "Maybe we're just nervous tonight."

"Yeah. Well, you'd better get Lori ready. We'll haul ass without cutting the engines." There was a pause. "You're sure there's no sign of anything?"

"Quiet as a tomb," O'Toole replied. "Maybe that's what's bothering me. I don't even hear the night birds."

"Okay, Larry. We'll be in in about five minutes."

In the cockpit of the Cessna, Belden looked at Bates. "O'Toole's got the same feeling I have. Something stinks out here tonight."

Bates said nothing because he knew what Belden meant. It comes that way sometimes. Just before a big fight or a small fight that is dangerous enough or when the odds are bad enough, you become aware of a very peculiar odor. Sometimes it comes in the ready room where the pilots are in close proximity for the final briefing, but more often you meet it in the cockpit at the moment you hear a voice sound the tallyho and you wheel over in the sky to meet your enemy. To some men it is the smell of old flowers that have died a long time ago. To others it is the smell of dust blowing in a closed room with the heat turned up full. But the fighter pilots will tell you it is the smell of stale orange juice, sour and rotting.

In reality it is the smell of fear. Not personal fear, but a fear of failure or a fear for a comrade or sometimes merely for the success of the mission if it is important enough.

"Better get that popgun of yours ready," Belden said. He glided downward through the sky and leveled off at 500 feet. Bates reached

255

into the back seat and brought forward a submachine gun. He looked at it with a quizzical glance: "How the Christ do I shoot this thing?"

"Point it at somebody and pull the trigger," Belden said. "Open your window when we land. If they're down there, they may try to cream us in the final."

One hundred yards from the operations building where O'Toole was turning out the lights and getting ready to drive to the main house to pick up Lori, the level tarmac ended in a stretch of high grass and jumbled foliage. Along the edge of the level area Pham's troops had set up a camp from which were controlled several small squad-strength patrols that prowled the western 180-degree sector of the plantation. That it was a military blunder to set up a command post so near to cover had not yet been discovered by the young sergeant in command. But he would learn in a few seconds.

Xuan Nonh's men had moved within twenty yards of the command post without being detected. There were twenty men in this particular group. Thirty men were in a like position on the north end of the field and thirty-five men were ready at the south.

O'Toole was locking the door to the operations office when the entire area erupted into a crisscrossed pattern of flashing shells. The night was streaked and scarred by them and the silence was shattered by the muzzle blasts and the screams of dying men. It came so suddenly that for a moment O'Toole stood stunned. Then with a curse he turned and raced across the parking strip toward an empty gas truck. Bending low along the ground, he ran in a weaving line and took cover on the far side of the vehicle, crouching with the gun at the ready. He saw flashes of fire to the north as General Pham's men came under attack. To the south there was sporadic fire and the distant bawling of commands.

O'Toole's jeep was parked on the far side of the operations building and the shadows had partly hidden it from the view of the attacking Vietcong. He took a deep breath and sprang out of hiding, running for a corner of the building and the protection afforded there. Bullets kicked puffs of dirt around his feet and he felt a light tug as something brushed his sleeve. Then he was into the darkness of the shadows and only a few yards from the jeep. He paused and listened as the volume of firing intensified. He turned his head to the north and saw a faint licking of flame in the sky where Belden was dropping down toward the runway about a mile out.

After the first smashing terror of the Vietcong advance, General Pham's men, operating with exemplary co-ordination through walkie-talkie communication, drew back from their perimeter and slowly sucked into a circular line of defense well back from the brush and around the landing strip itself. They were dim shapes in the darkness and it was impossible to determine friend from foe. The lashes of the shells interlocked across the field like some Fourth of July celebration gone awry.

O'Toole, straining his eyes in the blackness, saw several dark shadowy figures emerge from the obscurity of the trees and race toward his position. He raised his weapon and waited until the figures were almost upon him. Then he held the trigger down in a long burst that cut the attackers down to a single man, who managed to hurl himself on the ground immediately in front of O'Toole. The burly ex-Chief stepped to one side as the Vietcong rolled toward him and as the man tried to get to his feet O'Toole put the muzzle of his gun against the man's ear and blew his head away.

Now he backed away, watching the dim shades of the perimeter, and climbed into the jeep. He heard the engine come to life and he wheeled away in a skidding turn and headed for the runway. The exhaust flames of Belden's plane were closer now and lower in the sky as the plane settled toward the end of the landing area.

O'Toole came to the new perimeter, set back in the open area of the field. He stopped the jeep and got out and joined with Pham's men as they moved in a yelling mass to meet the enemy hand to hand. The Vietcong had come silently the last few yards and Pham's men had waited, lying low along the ground. When the enemy's shadows loomed directly above them, they rose with great cries and man met man in a fury of flashing steel and stuttering gun blasts. O'Toole went in firing, holding the gun in one hand and flailing away with his ten-inch knife with the other. A red moment of fury. Steel and flesh and hot lead with the black lash of frenzy to whip it.

And the enemy drew back as silently as they had come. They fell back to cover and the long blasts of fire began again. Men dropped on both sides and writhed on the ground, or died and did not writhe at all. But Pham's men fought the numbers and the odds lengthened as his men went down. O'Toole led a squad in a raging charge to plug a gap in the thin line where the enemy had broken through and were moving toward the airstrip. He went into them head on, roaring like a mad bull and they fell back before the wild madness of his charge.

"Hold here," he shouted to a sergeant. "Draw in and hold here, God damn it." He thought he saw the flash of the sergeant's smile.

Now he saw the plane sweeping over the end of the runway and a hot stream of flame blasting from the window on the co-pilot's side as Bates gave his answer to the enemy. The wheels touched and Belden held the plane on the runway, its tail high, the throttle still on, maintaining speed as he raced away from the deadly perimeter. Not until he was in the center of the landing area did he chop off the throttles, let the tail settle, and come to a halt. He and Bates were out of the cockpit and racing for O'Toole before the propellers had stopped turning.

"All right, O'Toole," Belden barked. "Where is she?"

"In the main house," O'Toole answered, his face grimy under the sweat. "We'd best get there."

They piled into the jeep, Belden behind the wheel, O'Toole and Bates in the back, their guns already spitting fire out into the night. Belden roared onto the dirt road that circled the field. They were under enemy fire all the way and Bates and O'Toole faced it almost unconcernedly as they fired methodically at the muzzle blasts that came from the darkness all about them.

They came to the sharp bend in the road that was the halfway point and Belden felt the jeep skid as a bullet took the front left tire away. He fought the wheel as the vehicle skewered around, slid down a shallow embankment and came to rest pointing its front at the sky. The men were out of the jeep and moving into the wooded area behind them while the front wheels were still revolving. They paused and listened for a moment.

"No more time." Belden spoke sharply. "Bates, you cover our rear. O'Toole, you come with me." Bates nodded silently as the other two men disappeared into the brush. He held his position for fifteen sec-

258

onds and then began a cautious withdrawal toward the house, watching the area behind him.

Out on the field the perimeter began to tighten on itself as Pham's men continued to die under the overwhelming odds. They pulled into a circular line less than three hundred yards in circumference and prepared to die there. The Vietcong, assured of victory and not wishing to lose more men than was necessary, did not press their attacks, but contented themselves with drawing back to cover and picking off their enemy almost at leisure.

The South Vietnamese relief patrol was one mile from the field, moving at a steady trot and the American Major hoped to hell their arrival would be in time.

Xuan Nonh and his five men had moved when they saw the first flash of gunfire from across the plantation. In a single burst of fire they had killed the ten men of the post guarding the east approach to the field. The South Vietnamese infantry soldiers had been taken utterly by surprise and had not even had an opportunity to pick up their guns before they had been hit from the rear. One corporal managed to reach Xuan's men and, although he was already dying, he took one of the men with him as his finger tightened spasmodically on the trigger of his gun in his final death throe.

Xuan wasted only a moment looking down at the sprawled bodies of his enemy.

"All right," he said quietly. "Take position around the house. Cover all sides." He moved out running.

Lori had been packing a suitcase in her room when the fighting broke out across the field. The first thought that had come to her had been a simple though illogical one. She had thought: We are under attack, but it will be all right because Dan is on his way. She flipped the suitcase shut and spent a valuable few seconds fastening the straps. She surprised herself at the calmness with which she accepted the attack. She looked briefly around the room in the manner of a girl who is leaving on a vacation and does not want to forget even a trifle. Satisfied, she left the room and walked down the long hall toward the stairs.

Xuan Nonh had approached the house cautiously. He had opened the front door only a few inches and then had stood quietly, listening for a sound from within. He heard only silence and so he edged the door open further and moved a few feet into the main room. There were crates and boxes packed on the floor and sheets covered the furniture. This was the first time he had ever been in a house of such magnificence and he took a few moments to marvel at its size and at the paneled walls with the framed pictures hanging on them. He moved stealthily across the room to the foot of the stairs. From above, he heard the sound of footsteps and so he moved back against the wall out of the light. His hand slipped the safety off his gun.

When Lori turned to descend the final flight of stairs, she did not at first see Xuan Nonh watching her. She had taken three steps down when he stepped out of the shadows in front of her, his face enigmatical and his gun pointing at her stomach. She stopped abruptly, thinking at first that this was one of General Pham's men coming to help her to the jeep. But then she looked into the man's eyes and she knew. The suitcase dropped from her hand and she shook her head in disbelief.

"No," she said in a small voice. "Oh, no."

She turned with a cry of dismay and started to run back up the stairway, but Xuan leaped after her, thrusting his gun between her legs and causing her to sprawl on the upper stair. He grabbed her by the hair, pulling her head back as he pushed her right arm up behind her back. She was unable to scream. All that came from her mouth were strangled gasps of pain. And yet she continued to fight, kicking her legs and feet viciously and trying to squirm out of Xuan's steely grasp.

The pain in her arm and shoulder was unbearable as Xuan exerted pressure and inched the arm up higher on her back. She was bent backward almost like a bow when he felt her shudder and then go limp. He got to his feet, panting, and stared down at her. With one hand he grabbed her by the hair and dragged her unconscious body across the hall and into the bedroom. He placed his gun on a table by the door and hoisted the girl's body onto the bed where she lay sprawled, her arms thrown back and her skirt up around her thighs. Xuan watched her, breathing heavily from exertion and passion. He felt desire rising in him, swelling into his loins in a warm flood.

260

Perhaps she is fooling, he thought. Perhaps she is not unconscious at all. He grabbed her face in one hand and moved it back and forth; with his other hand he squeezed her breast brutally. She made no sound and he threw her back on the bed. Then he unfastened the button on her skirt and unzipped the zipper and pulled the skirt down from her hips and over her long, slender legs, leaving her clad only in her blouse, a brief garter belt and stockings. He would wait, he decided. He did not want an unconscious woman. There was time to wait until she knew what he was doing to her.

Outside he heard the volume of fire rise suddenly into a crescendo that echoed across the countryside. He thought that his men were closing in on the enemy. He could not know that the American Major and his troops had arrived at the field and surrounded the Vietcong and now had them pinned down in a murderous crossfire.

The girl moaned on the bed and her eyelids fluttered. Xuan moved a step closer, his eyes hot. Then her eyes opened; she saw him and opened her mouth to scream. Xuan grasped her by the throat, choking off the cry. She fought him with surprising strength and he tightened his grip until her eyes bulged. She twisted her head and sank her teeth into his hand. He cried in pain and swung his fist against the side of her head. She fell back again, stunned, only a soft mewling sound coming from her lips.

Belden had moved within thirty yards of the house unseen. He saw the Vietcong on guard before the main entrance and the other who patrolled the near side. Bates had moved around the other side with O'Toole. He was aware of the increased tempo of the firing and thought perhaps that Pham's men had arrived. No matter. He did not have time to wait. He moved out on his belly, crawling snakelike, in spurts of movement, always closing on the man who stood alertly near the doorway. Belden wanted to take them one at a time and so he had his knife in his right hand. He lay still, a mere shadow along the ground at a distance of ten feet from the man he was going to kill.

Suddenly the sound of firing blasted out from the far side of the building as Bates and O'Toole opened up. The guard turned his head in the direction of the gunfire and Belden was on him in a single leap. His knife moved once, swiftly and surely across the guard's

261

throat, and then Belden threw the body aside. He flattened against the wall as the other guard rounded the corner. Belden held his foot out and the man sprawled with a choked cry of surprise. Belden fell on him, driving the blade deep into the man's neck just under the right ear. He felt the warm blood spurt and wash over his hand and then he was up and running for the entrance to the house.

Lori was past tears and past screaming. She was conscious of an incredible terror and the horror of rough and alien hands on her body. She thought: This is unendurable and I will go crazy before this awful thing happens. She struggled, but her strength was leaving her and her efforts were nothing more than the feeble protestations of a child. She felt Xuan's fingers pulling at her garter belt and she tried to yell something, anything, that would make him stop. But her voice was only a croak and, as she struggled to rise, a brutal hand shoved her head back on the bed and then his body pressed down on hers.

Oh, God, please! she thought, and even as she did so she felt his weight lessen and then go away altogether and his terrible hands were no longer on her body.

Xuan Nonh would never know what made him look backward over his shoulder toward the door to the room. He had been intent on what he was doing when a strange sensation of uneasiness swept over him, as though someone were standing directly behind him. His heart stopped for a moment when he looked back and then he pushed himself slowly off the girl and stood rigidly and waited.

He had never seen such a terrible anger in a man's eyes. The man at the door was a big, brown-faced man and he held a gun in one hand and a knife in the other. The man stood motionless, his hard face expressionless. Only the eyes flared with something far beyond anger.

Xuan watched him alertly. At this time Xuan did not yet experience fear. He was a soldier, and a good one, and fear did not come to him easily. He thought perhaps he would die now, but the idea of dying was never very far from his mind. So it was with the eyes of a fighter that Xuan Nonh regarded Dan Belden.

Now he saw two other armed men come into the room. These were big men, too, and one of them wore a battered cap.

262

"Jesus," Bates breathed.

"He didn't make it," Belden said, never taking his eyes from Xuan. "I got here in time."

Bates slipped the safety off his gun. "You're sure?"

"I'm sure," Belden said.

Lori pushed herself up on the bed. "Dan," she whispered. "Oh, God, Dan."

Belden did not move from where he stood. "It's all right, honey. It's all right now."

Xuan knew his gun was eight feet away, lying on the table where he had placed it when he dragged the girl into the room. Now he made a swift play for the gun, diving for it with outstretched hands.

Belden moved with incredible speed. Xuan felt a heavy hand crash into the side of his head and he was hurled backward across the room and into the wall. He steadied himself and wiped a smear of blood from his mashed mouth.

He braced himself and stood defiantly. He was a soldier and he would show these American devils he could die like one. Let them shoot him down. Death only took a second of time.

But Xuan Nonh was not to die so easily.

"Take Lori down to the jeep," Belden said.

She had slipped into her skirt and now she watched her husband with an almost frightened glance.

"Dan," she whispered. "Dan, I'm all right."

"I know it, honey," he said. "But go along now. I'll be with you in a few minutes."

Bates thought that he never again wanted to see such a look in a man's eyes. "Go ahead, Larry," he said to O'Toole. "Take her below."

O'Toole nodded. "General Pham's men are here," he said to Belden. When Belden said nothing, O'Toole added, "It's all finished now. We can go home."

"Not yet," Belden said stonily.

Lori paused at the door. She spoke with trepidation. "What are you going to do, Dan? Nothing happened, you know."

Belden looked at her with evident surprise. "Why," he said in a patient voice, "he put his filthy hands on you."

Xuan watched the girl and the man leave the room. He wondered what they had been talking about. How they would kill him, probably. Well, he would handle it well. He managed to stretch a small smile across his lips.

"The bastard's smiling," Bates said.

"Not for long," Belden said. "Give me your knife."

With a puzzled glance Bates handed him the knife. "What for?"

"The way this sonofabitch is going to die, the least he deserves is a chance to fight for his life."

Xuan's eyes widened in astonishment as he saw the big man toss a knife across the room. It fell at Xuan's feet and he picked it up in bewilderment.

"You're a damn fool, Dan," Bates said. "Let's just shoot this bastard and go home."

"Wait outside, Dick," Belden said hollowly. "I'll only be a few minutes."

"I'll wait here," Bates murmured.

"Outside."

"Shit," Bates said. "All right then. Outside. About three inches outside."

Xuan kept his eyes fastened on the big man as the other one left the room. Neither man moved, holding their glances locked in a clash of pure hatred. Xuan felt a sudden coldness in his belly. For the space of three breaths he did not know what it was. But then it spread up his arms and down into his legs and he recognized it as fear.

The big man moved slowly toward him, moved lightly despite his size, the knife held negligently in a big fist.

Xuan moved back until his shoulder touched the wall behind him. He made a tentative move to his right and the big man merely took one step in that direction. There was nowhere in all the world for Xuan Nonh to run. Nowhere to hide in all the world. He swallowed as the bile rose in his throat.

Suddenly he knew he was not going to die like a soldier. He was not even going to die like an animal. A sound of desperation snored through his nose and he was not aware of it.

A sob tore at his throat and then with a thin wail of despair he lunged at the big man, his knife upraised.

Belden waited until Xuan's arm flashed down; then he stepped quickly forward, under the flashing blade, threw up an arm to block the blow and clamped down hard on the slender, almost feminine wrist. Xuan screamed as the bone snapped and the knife fell to the floor. Then a hard hand was holding him against the wall and another hand was beating his face back and forth relentlessly. There was no pain after a while, just the numbing shock as the heavy hands came at him. Through dimmed eyes he could see the big man staring down at him and he knew he would never find mercy of any sort behind those implacable eyes. His senses reeled and he sagged against the wall. He wanted to fall, to get away from those big hands, but they held him upright and continued to slam at his ruined face.

His hands plucked feebly at Belden's wrist, but there was no longer any strength in them. Finally his eyes closed behind the swollen, bloody lids and he slid slowly down the wall into a sitting posture.

Belden was breathing easily as he pulled Xuan's legs out and let the body sprawl on the floor. He waited several moments until Xuan regained a semblance of consciousness, then he knelt on one knee and cut the rope belt that held up the man's trousers.

Xuan glared up at him in horrified awareness. Somewhere in the recesses of his tortured mind a voice told him that this could not be happening. Not this. No man died this way. It was indecent for a soldier to die this way.

But Xuan knew he was going to die this way.

With all his will he strove to move, to resist, but he could summon only feeble, plucking gestures with his hands. There was no pain anywhere. Even his broken wrist no longer ached. Perhaps, he screamed to himself, there would be nothing to this, no pain or agony or anguish that would shrivel his soul in physical withdrawal. His legs twitched as Belden roughly yanked the tattered trousers from them.

As though from a great distance he heard the big man speak: "All right, you sonofabitch. You'll never have a need for this again."

Xuan did not know what the words meant, but neither did he have time to ponder them. He felt the man's hands moving on him.

Then Xuan Nonh's world dissolved in a blinding sheet of white agony that pounded and tore at his vitals with a torment that the human mind was not fashioned to conceive. It came in successive waves, rolling over his brain and leaving it limp and writhing like a crab plucked out of boiling water. The agony was a flash of blue-hot steel at first; then it was a rat gnawing at his crotch; then it became bubbling lead, molten and consuming, eating away at his very being. He screamed, but no sound came forth, only bubbles of bloody froth that passed his lips and dribbled on his chin. He screamed to a god he had long forgotten and he called on Buddha too. All this in silence. The knife bit deeper and something of his sanity rebelled.

He began to sing in a hoarse, dying voice. There were no words and no tune, only a chant that came from the bottom of Hell to accompany the unholiness of what was happening to him. His mind was gone now, lost somewhere in a red blaze of panic and flame, burned to a crisp by the unimaginable frenzy of the pain.

The notes fluted upward from his strained throat in some profane and frightful dirge from Hell. But it would not stop—the awful pain; it went on as his mind disappeared and all his reason and everything that was human in him until at the last he was only a sack of skin filled with useless bones and the blood bubbled quietly at the terrible wound.

Bates was waiting as Belden came out and shut the door quietly behind him. He said nothing as Belden paused and studied the floor with great concentration. Bates made a move to enter the room.

"Never mind, Dick," Belden said. "Let him rot there."

"I just wanted to spit on the sonofabitch," Bates replied.

"He's beyond that now," Belden said. "God damn his soul."

They walked together down the long hall and down the stairs and out into the night where the sound of the guns had stopped and where Lori and O'Toole waited for them in the jeep.

The American Special Forces commander introduced himself as Major Tom Kincannon. He was standing with Bates and O'Toole as Belden approached after getting Lori settled in the plane. Kincannon offered his hand to Belden with an engaging smile.

"Sorry we didn't get here sooner. This terrain is a sonofabitch."

"Glad you got here at all, Major," Belden replied. "How many of them got away?"

"A handful at best. We had them pinned down in a crossfire. Those that got away are hightailing it for Laos."

"There's a thing waiting for you up at the house," Belden said. "On the second deck, the first bedroom on the right. Do something with it."

The Major glanced at Bates. "Yeah. We'll take care of it." They were at the airplane now and Kincannon offered his hand to Belden again. "Let me give you one word of advice." He looked off toward the main house where a light still shone in the darkness. "You're a flier, so you're not supposed to know about these things." A slight smile touched his lips. "What you did tonight up there. Don't let it trouble your dreams. Believe me, we all do it. I know because I fight on the ground. Sometimes you have to do things you detest. Your soul demands it. Think of it that way and it won't bother you. Good luck."

"Thanks, Major," Belden said softly. "You'd be surprised how that helps." He shook the Major's hand again and then smiled at Bates and O'Toole. "You fly it home, Batesy. You fly the right seat, Larry. Me? I'm going to be busy in the back with a girl I know."

They climbed into the plane and Belden sank with a sigh into the rear seat and slipped his arm around Lori.

"Sorry I was so long, honey."

"Oh, Dan. We're safe. You made us safe."

Belden threw his head back and laughed with genuine enjoyment. "I guess Bates and O'Toole were along for kicks," he said.

"I've been doing it for twenty years," Bates affirmed with a sigh. "Just taking care of Belden."

They passed the end of the runway and were airborne and climbing up into the sanctuary of darkness.

"Dan?" Lori murmured.

"Yeah?"

"I knew I would be safe with you." He said nothing so she asked, "What did you do back in the house?"

"Got rid of something that was inside of me and that I don't need any more," Belden said.

"That's good," Lori said. "Kiss me, Dan."

Chapter
XVI

JUNE
1965

Colonel Lee came down with a bright white bone in his teeth.

After certain high-level conferences in Peking, it had been decided that General Pham's presence within the borders of North Vietnam was not to be tolerated. Secret intelligence reports confirmed that American forces in South Vietnam would not be sufficient to stand against the August offensive, especially in view of the anticipated air superiority of Colonel Lee's air command. In addition, Peking was fully aware that the augmentation of the Red Chinese infantry forces along the Sino-North Vietnam border had caused something more than consternation in Washington and in the other capitals of the free world. It was the unanimous opinion of the ruling hierarchy that the United States was not prepared to risk defeat in South Vietnam by backing General Pham in his wish to move toward Hanoi. There were now thirty-seven fully equipped infantry divisions on the border and this force was believed to be more than enough to bluff the Americans, at least until it would be too late to withstand the August invasion.

So the MIG squadrons in the Lungchou area swept down past Hanoi and slashed at General Pham's front-line invaders in a continuous series of close air-support missions. Lee began his operations on a summer day and, by first light, more than three hundred fighters were over the lightly defended perimeter defenses of the South

Vietnamese. After the first two missions had been flown, it became apparent that the American Air Force was not going to contest the sky north of the 17th Parallel. At first Lee regarded this phenomenon with some distrust, thinking that his enemy was trying to decoy him south. But as the hours passed and his planes smashed General Pham's troops with high-velocity rockets, air-to-ground missiles, and fierce strafing fire, he realized that something had occurred in the enemy high command that had left him unopposed in the sky.

What had happened was a complete stagnation of the thinking processes in Washington. When the Chinese moved their divisions in tremendous strength along the Sino-North Vietnam border and the reports of the strength of Lee's air command had been corroborated, faint hearts spoke loudly in the paneled offices of command and the American effort in South Vietnam paused momentarily, then ground to a halt. The specter of all-out war with China was too cataclysmic for some men to behold, so they backed away in indecision, demanding that the free world re-evaluate its stand in face of the obvious Chinese intent to escalate the war. They justified this ridiculous thinking by claiming they needed more information on American air strength and on American ability to hold air superiority in case of intensive ground warfare.

On that first afternoon the eyes of Pham's soldiers strayed to the sky where they knew they would see the welcome contrails of the F-100s and the F-104s. They looked out to sea and those soldiers near the coastal area could see the mighty warships of the Seventh Fleet steaming back and forth on slow patrol, their flight decks crammed with airplanes. But no missions launched from the catapults and for all practical purposes the Seventh Fleet might as well have been in San Diego harbor.

When the Air Force did not come, Pham's intelligence officers flew to Danang to discover the cause of the defection. They were told, rather shamefacedly, that orders had come from Washington to hold all aircraft south of the 17th Parallel. No one knew the cause for this preposterous order because the American fighting men in Vietnam wanted to fight and felt well able to win any contest in which they might find themselves.

And so while Colonel Lee's MIGs hammered unmercifully at Pham's troops, the long rows of jet fighters stood motionless on the parking apron at Danang. American pilots looked at the skies to the north and cursed bitterly and wondered why they had ever thought it an honor to wear wings.

Admiral Smoke Dusane roamed the confines of his flag bridge, spitting out words he had not used in twenty years, as he strove to understand the thinking in the higher places. At one point he paused to look down at the gold wings on his khaki shirt. Then he unpinned them and stuffed them in his pocket.

In a few short hours of a summer day the house of cards the Americans had built in Vietnam threatened to crumble. And it was due to a reluctance to stand decisively. Something was needed to prod the makers of decisions into taking the step that was mandatory in this hour of peril. But no one seemed to know exactly what would prod them.

General Pham somehow managed to hold tenaciously to his position. His troops were outnumbered but not outfought. Finally he was forced to withdraw, reluctantly, a foot at a time. He fought in the paddies and in the mountains and along the twisted trails. He fought the MIGs with pistols and rifles and sometimes his men in futile anger threw rocks at the enemy planes. But foot by foot he was pressed back until finally his thin lines held temporarily at a point two miles within North Vietnam. Pham thought perhaps he and his men would die here.

But time was running out and the house of cards continued to crumble.

Sam Tolliver was forty-four years old and he considered his job about as vital as an ingrown toenail. Not since he had been assistant laundry officer at Itazuke during the Korean War had he felt so categorically useless.

Tolliver was a public-relations specialist with the State Department, a position as ludicrous as that of a football referee with a club-foot. There was no possible manner in which he could approach his job with any but the most abject pessimism. However, he was an ebullient man and he attempted to search out the bright side to every situation with which he found himself confronted.

For several days he had busied himself lying to the foreign correspondents who dogged him relentlessly, asking always for the latest word from Washington. Of course there was no latest word from Washington, and if there had been, it would have been a mass of confusion and contradiction anyway.

Now, from a chair in which he lounged, he watched Senator Yeager and Storm Ryerson. Tolliver rubbed his hand tiredly over the back of his head and winced as he touched a tender spot where he had been struck by a rock thrown by a rioting student yesterday afternoon when the demonstrators had tried to storm the Embassy.

Tolliver sipped the last bitter dregs from his coffee cup and spoke in a tone of dejection.

"Mr. Ryerson, the Associated Press is outside. He wants to know what we're going to do about General Pham up north. I've got to tell him *something*." He made a gesture of hopelessness.

Ryerson flushed in anger. He actually didn't know what the hell was going to be done about General Pham. In addition, he had recently spent an unpleasant half hour with the Commanding General of the Marine forces in South Vietnam. The General had been understandably enraged when he received orders to pull back into a defensive posture and ensure that his Marines did not carry the fight to the enemy up north.

"What the goddam hell goes on around here anyway?" the General had bellowed in his parade-ground voice. "I didn't bring a goddam division of Marines over here to sit on our asses and let the Chinamen back us down. I've got a goddam good mind to quit. Resign. Say shit on it all."

Ryerson couldn't blame the hard-bitten marine. He was as disgusted as anyone else about the ridiculous mess. When Senator Yeager had explained the consternation, even the fear, prevalent in Washington, Ryerson had cursed the blindness and stupidity of his superiors. He knew damn well the United States *could* win the war in Vietnam. We *could* pour men and planes into the conflict in sufficient quantity to preclude the Chinese August offensive. We *could* beat Lee in the air and hold air supremacy. And now, just as General Pham carried the fight to the enemy, just as morale had taken a turn for the better, came this shameful withdrawal in face of the enemy's anger and apparent disregard for the possible consequences. Well, he thought, where the hell is *our* anger; where the hell is *our* disregard for the consequences.

271

Ryerson grunted sourly. "Tell the AP man that General Pham is probably going to die up north. Tell him that."

"I can't do that, sir," Tolliver said tiredly.

"No," Ryerson said, "I don't suppose you can. Well, tell him that, unless we stop Lee and his MIGs, we are going to be through out here. Tell him that unless we get off our asses and start to carry the fight to them, we might as well pull our troopships into Saigon harbor and start the evacuation. If we let Pham die up there, if we back down because the Chinamen have forty or fifty barefoot divisions eating rice on the border up there, if we let them get away with this gigantic bluff they're trying to run, then I think I'll resign from the human race. I think a lot of Americans may resign with me."

"Admiral, Admiral," Tolliver said softly. "I can't tell them that."

"Okay then." Ryerson glanced at Senator Yeager. "Then tell them I quit as of this evening."

"Storm," Yeager said, alarmed.

"That's right," Ryerson said curtly. "I've had it. If they don't want to win over here, then I can't do the whole goddam job by myself. Christ, Ralph. I thought you said the President was with us on this thing."

"He is, Storm. I know he is. But a decision like this takes time. You don't steam-roller Congress."

"But goddammit, Ralph. We don't have the time to waste. Time has run out. It's the middle of June."

Yeager was silent for a long time. When he spoke, there was a note of resignation in his voice. "Then pray for a miracle, Storm. Pray for a miracle."

"The miracle I'd like to see," Ryerson said, "is every one of our jet fighters flying north and fighting Lee in the skies of North Vietnam and China. The miracle I'd like to see is Lee blasted and beaten until their air power was absolutely negligible."

"Could we win it, Storm?" Yeager asked.

"I don't know," Ryerson said honestly. "I think so. But you never know the outcome of a fight until you go into it. We can't *talk* them out of the sky, for Christ's sake."

"Gentlemen," Tolliver interrupted. "This still doesn't tell me what to say to the AP."

"I told you," Ryerson said. "Tell him that Pham and his men are dying up there. They are dying because of indecision and cowardice in high places. A share of this shame belongs to me and to you and to Ralph Yeager and to every American everywhere." Ryerson's voice was angered as he finished speaking.

"All right then," Tolliver said as he rose. "I'll tell them that. It may cost me my job but what the hell!" His face suddenly lightened. "You know something, Admiral? I think I'd rather go down with you and keep my self-respect."

After Tolliver had gone, Storm Ryerson and Ralph Yeager spoke in low voices of a thing that still gave them hope, still offered some promise. It had to do with Dan Belden.

Only briefly had Ryerson had an opportunity of talking with Belden. At Danang, two days ago, he and Belden had taken a leisurely stroll around the air base. Ryerson had noted the lines of fighter planes, chocked and grounded, with their canopies shut tight against the wind and the rain. The only sound over Danang had been a muted engine roar as a lumbering transport took off to the south.

The two men stood smoking a final cigarette before Ryerson left for Saigon.

"Well, Dan!" Ryerson sighed, "I guess it's time you went home. I had high hopes for you and me. For all of us. They seem to have gone down the drain."

"Come on." Belden nodded out toward the gathering darkness. "I'll walk you to your plane."

They fell into step and moved slowly toward the silhouette of Ryerson's transport, parked near the main operations hangar. A few pilots nodded to Belden as they passed and somewhere in the distance there was the sound of a hammer ringing on resistant metal.

"Storm"—Belden's voice came softly out of the dusk—"I'm younger than you are and maybe I haven't forgotten some things that I learned." His chuckle came over lightly. "No offense meant. I mean that you seem to have forgotten something. We haven't gone down the drain. I think we're far from it. Maybe you and I are through out here. Batesy and O'Toole and some others. I know damn well Hawk and Cort and the rest are through. I regret it, but there's nothing I can do about them. Just don't forget one thing. Other guys will step forward. I don't know where they'll come from or how they'll get here, but they'll show up. They'll be like we were a long time ago. They'll take over and in the end we'll be all right. All of us. Here and back home. That's one thing I've always been sure of. No matter how bad a fight looks to the guy with the bloody nose, sooner or later somebody comes along who speaks the right word, gives the right piece of advice, and then the guy wipes the blood off his face and goes on to win."

He clapped Ryerson on the back. "So don't sweat it, Admiral. Sooner or later they'll see daylight back there in Washington. Someone will brush the cobwebs out of their brains and we'll be all right again."

"You really believe that, Dan." Ryerson did not speak it as a question.

A group of young pilots passed a few yards away and Belden's eyes followed them. "Somewhere in that group of kids," he said, "is another Smoke Dusane. Another Ray Hawkins or Cort Anders or Mac Kilpatrick. Those kids will get mad enough someday, get fed up enough someday, and when that time comes, they'll do what needs to be done. No political sonofabitch in the world will stop them. That's the way it happens, Storm. One morning they'll get out of bed and say, 'Well, by God, we've had enough of this. Let's go.' And that's how it will be done. I'm sure of it."

A smile flickered for a moment in Ryerson's eyes and then it was gone. "And you, Dan. What about you and Bates?"

Belden smiled. "I'll go where old war horses go after they are finished. I'll lie in the warm sun and play and laugh and love." He looked down at his friend. "Bates and I will be flying out of Palm Beach. Come and see us."

Ryerson nodded. "It sounds good. I'll probably do that. When will you leave?"

Belden whistled softly in the night. "Not for a while yet, Storm. Not for a while."

"I see." Ryerson cleared his throat. "How soon?"

"In a few days, perhaps," Belden said.

"What you have in mind is an admirable thing, Dan. But I'm afraid you'll gain nothing."

"No," Belden admitted. "But you don't want to leave a thread hanging either."

"Dan . . ." Ryerson wanted to say more, but decided against it. He offered his hand. "I'll see you in Palm Beach if not sooner."

"Sure, Storm," Belden smiled. "It's been a nice trip."

"Too goddam long though," Ryerson said. "Nothing foolish, Dan. Promise me that."

"Hell, old friend," Belden said gently. "I'll live forever."

In the Officers' Club bar at Danang there was none of the usual light banter and flying talk. The pilots stood silently at the bar or conversed in low monotones. Sometimes, when they caught one another's eyes, they would look away almost as though they were ashamed of some evil thing they had been party to.

Lieutenant Colonel Pat Murphy sat at a table with three squadron mates and traced idle patterns on the beaded surface of his whiskey glass. Murphy was an unhappy man tonight and he figured he would remain so as long as the Air Force continued to base him in Vietnam. Murphy had had a bellyful and he was not at all sure just who it was he was mad at.

He looked up as Major Jack McKellar slid into a chair at the table. Murphy eyed McKellar coldly.

"Hello, brother coward. Are you feeling as lousy as I am tonight?"

"I was," McKellar said pleasantly. "But right now I'm feeling a lot better." He grinned at Murphy.

"What's so goddam funny?" Murphy asked.

McKellar shrugged. "I just talked to my mech," he said.

"So what? Does he feel as lousy as I do tonight?"

"He just had a talk with O'Toole," McKellar said.

"Who the hell is O'Toole?"

"Dan Belden's mech," McKellar replied equably.

"Oh?" Murphy sat up in his chair and lit a cigarette. "I don't suppose this O'Toole had something to say that makes you so goddam happy tonight?"

"Well"—McKellar appeared to give serious thought to his statement—"this O'Toole said Belden and Bates are going north in the morning."

"Oh?" Murphy said carefully. "That's pretty stupid, isn't it? I

275

mean, after all, every damn plane up here has been grounded. We don't want to make the Chinamen mad, you know."

"Of course we don't," McKellar affirmed.

"Belden and Bates are going up there alone?" Murphy asked.

"There's no one else to go with them," McKellar said sadly. "They'll be outnumbered a hundred to one." He shook his head. "Too damn bad. They're pretty nice guys."

"Yeah. Too bad." Murphy carefully brushed the ash from his cigarette. "What time they going?"

"First light."

"Well," Murphy said, shaking his head. "It really is too damn bad. Those two guys going up there alone. Wish there was something we could do about it, Jack."

"I do too," McKellar said. "But orders are orders. You wouldn't want to get yourself a lousy fitness report, would you?"

"Hell, no," Murphy said. "It might ruin my career."

Other pilots had congregated around the table and were listening attentively. One young second lieutenant cleared his throat. "They must be crazy," he said.

"Yeah," Murphy said. "Crazy like we all were once. A long time ago. Makes me kind of happy to know we've still got a couple of crazy men left."

"Well," McKellar said, getting to his feet, "I just thought I'd let you know what O'Toole told my mech. It wasn't important, I guess."

The others watched Murphy as he rose. "Of course not," Murphy said. "If two wild men want to fly up north all alone and take on the whole Chinese Air Force, there certainly isn't anything we can do about it. Pray for them maybe."

"Wait a minute . . ." a young flier began.

"Now, now, sonny," Murphy held up a restraining hand. "Don't say anything you may regret. In fact, don't ever say anything in the Air Force that may someday be used against you. That's just common sense." He turned to McKellar. "Tell me, Jack. Is that friend of yours still in charge of the communications center?"

"Yeah. Why?"

"I have a brother-in-law flying off the *Concord*. I'd like to send the poor Navy bastard a message tonight. Think it can be arranged?"

"Sure," McKellar replied. He half smiled. "Your career could be going up in smoke, Colonel."

"That's very true, Major," Murphy said. "But perhaps I no longer am as anxious for a career as I once thought I was. Now let's go to your friend at communications and send my message. After that we will share a bottle while I reveal to you a plan that is simmering in my fertile brain."

Dan Belden lay quietly on his bunk, smoking and listening to the muted sounds from across the airfield. He had been to the meteorology office and had checked the weather for tomorrow morning. There would be early weather to the northwest, high build-ups up to 40,000 feet, but the front would remain stationary until late afternoon. Skies would be relatively clear over General Pham's beleaguered lines and the MIGs would be down in force. He stuffed his cigarette out in the ash tray and watched the burning ashes fade and disappear.

He rolled over and looked out the window at the bright, starlit night. He was conscious of a heaviness within him and he couldn't get back to Lori now; he couldn't touch her hand and hold her any more. In a few hours that slab of sky out there would be a wall between them, as wide as all the world and as high as any evening star. Because the MIGs were standing on the line at Lungchou and Pham's men huddled in their foxholes and waited for the red dawn of what could be their final day. There was no way he could reach Lori now, so he stared out at the darkness where the two Crusaders waited, their new paint jobs dull in the dim light, seeming to crouch on their haunches waiting for the first light flick of the starter switch.

It's the things you must do, Belden thought, without knowing exactly why. And you don't tally up the odds because the odds live only in the memories of the old men. The odds are for counting when the hair is white and the fingers tremble with the ague of old age.

Now he was alone in the night as he had always been. He shifted his weight on the bunk and listened to the squeak of the tired springs. He wondered if there was something he should do, but then he put the thought away. The secret things he had to say to Lori he had said poorly and in stilted phrases in the letter that lay on his desk. Christ, how many such letters had he written over the years?

O'Toole had come to him an hour ago with word that the planes were fueled, armed, and ready to roll.

"Thanks, Larry," Belden said. "Nothing now but to wait."

"Yes, sir. After you leave, I'll attend to your packing. We'll be leaving when you get back?"

"Yeah, Larry. We'll be leaving when I get back," Belden answered quietly.

"The little lady will be happy about that," O'Toole said.

"Sure she will, Larry."

"Dan"—O'Toole spoke hurriedly, as though in embarrassment—"after we're gone from here, it will be nice in Palm Beach. The hot sun and the water. We'll do all right."

"Sure we will. Someday, when we're old men, we'll sit in the hot sun and remember how it was at Danang."

"That's right," O'Toole said. He paused at the door. "One thing, Dan."

"Yeah?"

"It may not be as lonely up there tomorrow as you think."

Belden wondered now what O'Toole had meant by that. It was always lonely in the sky. It could never be otherwise because a man had only himself and his God to rely on.

He heard the faint sound of creaking hinges and sat up on the bunk as Bates halted in the doorway, a bottle of whiskey in his hand. They regarded each other for a moment, then Belden motioned Bates in.

"Sit down, Batesy," he said.

Bates sat beside Belden on the bunk. He handed him the bottle.

"Well," Bates said gently. "It's almost that time, Dan."

"In a little while," Belden said.

Bates sighed and shook his head. "We are damn fools. You know that."

Belden took a long drink from the bottle. "Damn good. Where'd you get it?"

"O'Toole scrounged it someplace. You know, Dan, I've been thinking."

"Spare me that." Belden chuckled.

"No," Bates said seriously. "I've been thinking that Lori would make a lousy widow. She's too young to wear black."

"I haven't thought of her in black," Belden said.

"Well, maybe you ought to." Bates took the bottle and drank. He wiped his lips on the back of his hand. "God damn. That's good booze. Why don't we pack up and go home?"

"We will. O'Toole will pack tomorrow morning."

"Is it absolutely necessary that you and I challenge the whole goddam Chinese Air Force? It seems a trifle foolhardy." Bates's voice was pained. "Christ's sake. Maybe Lee has fallen down a stair and killed himself by now. Maybe they put him against a wall when we killed Soohoo. Why go to investigate?"

Belden scratched the back of his neck as he sought an answer to Bates's question. Finally he said, "There has to be a last time for everything."

"Yeah." Bates nodded his head. "How did I get so lucky as to have this wonderful opportunity to kill myself?" He pursed his lips and uttered a shrill whistle of contemplation. Then he said, "Do we have any plan of attack?"

"Hell, no," Belden said. "We just fly up there and look for them."

"Well, that's simple enough," Bates said. "We just take off, two of us, and fly up there and look for three hundred MIGs to attack. It's really very simple and I congratulate you on devising such a starkly simple plan of attack. I think I will go to my room and cry about it."

After a while Belden said, "You know, Batesy, I've been thinking too. It might be better if you went down to Saigon and waited with Lori. There really is no reason for both of us to go up there tomorrow. Besides, it will be better for Lori if you're there."

"It will be better with Lori if *you're* there," Bates answered. "As far as flying off to get myself killed, I can do it quite as well as you can. So *you* go to Saigon and I'll go out and hunt for Lee. Stop talking foolishness. You sound like an ensign I knew twenty years ago."

Sitting beside each other on the small bunk in the darkened room, their shoulders touched as Belden drank from the bottle and handed it again to his friend. Such a simple thing as a touching of shoulders sent a flood of warming spirit through both men. There could be no sadness in either of them while they were together—lived together and fought and flew together. Each held for the other an affection beyond comprehension and, though both of them would have denied it, between them there was a shining bond of love that was as clean and pure as honor or glory or redemption itself.

For a moment each was aware of what the other was thinking and they did not trust their voices. At any rate, there was nothing that could be said of how they felt. Bates allowed himself an inward smile and slapped Belden's shoulder.

"Well," Bates said. "One more fight, eh, Dan? Then we go off to lie in the warm sun. Swim in clear blue waters and the only fighting we'll do is with the big marlin that come in the winter months when the rest of the world is freezing. You and Lori will live in a shack on the beach and Helen Mabry and I will live in a huge white stucco mansion that her husband willed to her. Who knows? I may even invite you up for Sunday dinner now and then."

He heard Belden's quiet laughter. "We'll be there before the week is out, Batesy. Just this one thing left to do."

Bates got to his feet, squeezing Belden's arm as he did so. "Sleep well, Dan."

He walked to the door and turned back to Belden, a puzzled expression in his eyes. "You know, Dan," he said, "I just thought of something. I don't think I'm going to be lonely any more."

"It's a good thing to feel at a time like this." Belden smiled. "I don't think any of us will be lonely any more." He paused. "Sleep well, Batesy."

Through the long hours of the night a golden-haired girl knelt at prayer at an altar in the Cathedral in downtown Saigon. She asked Our Lady's blessing on two men who were far away from her tonight and she gave thanks for the great understanding and honesty which had come to her and which she knew now were no small things to be held in a woman's heart, even for a little while.

Chapter
XVII

JUNE
1965

Belden came awake to the gentle nudging of O'Toole's big hand on his shoulder and to the shrilling of jet engines out on the airfield. Through the open window he saw the winking wingtip lights of a plane as it broke ground on its take-off roll. He rubbed his eyes and looked up at O'Toole's bulky shadow.

"What the hell is going on out there?"

"The Air Force are flying their jets down to Saigon," O'Toole said.

Belden swung out of the bunk and stood by the basin, splashing cold water on his face. O'Toole had left quietly and Belden could hear him bawling for Merchant. He dried his face with a heavy towel and shrugged into his khaki shirt and pants. Outside the moon turned the cloudbanks to the northwest a silvery white and the mounting banks of cumulus clouds fashioned great marble pillars in the sky. Overhead the sky was clear and studded with bright stars, but far in the distance there was an occasional flare of lightning and a faint rumble of thunder. He wondered for a moment if it was really lightning or thunder or if it could be the flashing of the guns where Pham and his men slugged it out with the enemy.

He moved down the silent corridor toward the ready room, the slight sense of depression he had felt when he awoke disappearing under the stir of excitement that quickened his step. He passed a window and saw O'Toole and Merchant out on the line plugging in the starting units and running back the canopies.

Bates was waiting for him in the ready room, a cup of steaming coffee in his hand. The two men said nothing as they climbed into their g-suits and donned the harnesses. Bates was whistling a discordant tune and Belden smiled to himself in the shadows of the room. When you came right down to it, what they were about to do was utterly ridiculous.

"The Air Force moved their jets down to Saigon," Bates observed.

"Well," Belden said, "it figured."

"Yeah," Bates said. He shook his head perplexedly. "For a guy who just got married you get the goddamnedest ideas." He frowned at his friend. "Tell me something. I may be dense as hell, but the very best I can come up with is odds of about two hundred to two. Now I realize"—there was a wry amusement in Bates's voice, "that we can't always have the best of it. It doesn't happen that way. But for Christ's sake, don't you think those odds are cause for at least a little alarm?"

"Perhaps." Belden smiled. "Be my guest. Alarm yourself for a while."

"Somehow," Bates said, "I sense an optimism in you. This is a ridiculous time and place for optimism. Would you mind lending me some of it? I think this would be a magnificent time to get optimistic."

"Optimism has nothing to do with it," Belden said. "We've *got* to go up there. It's as simple as that."

Bates understood Belden's thinking and clapped him lightly on the shoulder. "Sure, Dan. I'm getting old I guess."

"There were a lot of them," Belden said quietly, "along the way who didn't get old. They never had time. We owe it to them. All of them went thinking they were leaving something behind. Something bright and shining, Batesy. It would be a hell of a thing if they knew we backed off and there wasn't any more honor for people like us. It's a thing we bargained for in this life. So the odds have nothing to do with it. Either we have to go or we don't. You have to live with yourself."

"Yeah," Bates remarked in a dry tone. "For how long?"

"It doesn't matter. Don't think about it. It's out of our hands now.

282

Think of it that way and it won't seem hopeless. When something is inevitable, then the risk goes away."

"It doesn't help Lori any," Bates said.

"Well," Belden said, "if I didn't go, I'd never be any good for her again. Or myself either." His forehead creased as he sought the words he wanted Bates to hear. "But that isn't it. Lori hasn't anything to do with this. This is for the guys we knew and the promises we made all the way back to our youth. It's for the wings we wore and all the men who made the wearing of them worth a damn. It's for all the grand boasts we made at one time or another. It's because the last page hasn't been written in the book yet, and this morning we have to write it. Either that or go down the road wondering if we truly ever had what it takes or if we were really only little boys lying to ourselves all these years. Hell, you talk about optimism. That's not the word. I just feel goddam happy that I have the chance to go up north this morning. It's like a guy who knows he's dying and prays for a last chance to do something that might give truth and meaning to his living. We're getting a chance that other men pray for. So let's be glad we've got it. Forget the odds—they're irrelevant. We come back or we don't. Simple. At least this is our way of life and we have our chance to prove that we were what we claimed to be." He grinned at Bates. "Does that make any sense?"

"It sure as hell does, Dan," Bates said softly.

They were silent again, sipping at their coffee. It was warm in the room and they listened as the last of the jets moved away in the darkness, leaving only an echo of their passing. Belden put his cup on the table and in the half-light glanced at Bates and winked.

"Time for that walk," he said.

"Why not?" Bates shrugged.

So close were they in that moment that both men laughed aloud. Then they left the ready room, walking slowly under the binding weight of their flight gear. Their footsteps echoed hollowly in the silence. They moved out of the building and down a gravel walkway leading past a small fence that encircled the parking area. Belden glanced at his watch.

"A few minutes early," he said. He offered Bates a cigarette and they stood there smoking unhurriedly, casually deliberate. The tail assemblies of the two F8s stood out above the shadows of the buildings on the far side of the strip and their silhouettes were visible in the moon's light wash.

"Does Pham know we're coming?" Bates asked quietly.

"He knows," Belden replied.

The glow of their cigarettes briefly lighted their faces, casting hollow shades along their cheeks and under their eyes.

"Lonesome goddam place this morning," Bates murmured.

Belden nodded as his eyes scanned the sky to the north. It was growing paler now to the east as the first of dawn struggled to pierce the darkness. His glance moved across the horizon and then he tossed his cigarette on the ground and scuffed it out with his foot. O'Toole and Merchant waited patiently on the wings of the planes.

"All set?" Belden asked.

"All set," Bates replied.

They smiled at each other and their hands moved out and clasped.

"Good luck," Bates said.

"The last one," Belden said. "The last fight, Batesy."

Bates nodded and they walked to their planes in the darkness.

A few minutes later the tower operator at Danang heard Belden's voice come lazily over the receiver: "Danang tower from Red One. Taxiing out with two for take-off."

He saw the flames from their tail pipes licking at the night. The two Crusaders were at the end of the runway when the operator answered the call: "Red One cleared for take-off." Fully aware of where Belden and Bates were going, he added, "Good luck, you guys. The very best of good luck."

The planes were moving when Belden answered, "Thanks, Danang tower. Red One out."

From the tower it appeared that two streaks of flame were racing down the runway in the blackness. The first light had come at altitude, but on the deck night had not yet given way.

They were airborne and climbing at 0615. "Switch to Channel Eight," Belden called. A few moments later his voice came again. "We'll circle for altitude. I want them to know we're coming."

Belden sat relaxed in his cockpit, his hands caressing the familiar stick and throttle. The air was smooth this morning and the plane climbed steeply. As they passed 10,000 feet the sky was light enough so that he could see Bates's plane hanging tight off his wing. The navigation had been planned diligently and now there was nothing left but to reach altitude and check out the guns. Belden looked below and he could see the slash of the Danang runway beneath him, a light scar against the flat expanse of darkened terrain.

At 0630 Belden and Bates were at 40,000 feet and dawn had come. Belden signaled Bates to check the guns and for a second the twenties chattered nervously, almost as though they knew they would soon be contesting overwhelming odds. Briefly, Belden allowed an old man's thoughts to enter his mind and he considered the odds. In that moment he admitted to himself that his vendetta with Colonel Lee had lost its importance. He and Bates were here this morning, alone at 40,000 feet and vectoring north, because there had to be something of honor that could be salvaged from the shame. It could be stated simply: *Someone had to stand up and be counted or every man with whom Belden had ever flown—every man who had gone down under the gold wings or the silver wings—would have been the victim of a disgraceful hoax.* The ballads the fighter pilots sang, the brave stories told again and again around the bars and in the ready rooms, the epics of long dead heroes, all would be as ashes turned cold and the taste of the words in the mouth would be sour.

Belden had a debt to pay that had nothing to do with Colonel Lee. He owed it to the friends who had dropped away along the years; he owed it to Hawkins and Anders and to all the men who carelessly, with a laugh and a shrug, had climbed to the high places and then had crossed over, leaving behind only a memory of gallantry or a lettered mug standing on a shelf behind a bar somewhere so that their friends would never forget.

And Belden thought to himself:

And the idea of dying has nothing to do with it. Dying—what the hell is it anyway? A second of time when all that has gone before is forgotten. Your wife is gone and your life is gone and all your memories, but memories make a poor bank account anyway. There is a chance this morning up there. The hell with odds. There is a chance because, when everything else is gone, God always leaves a loophole.

I thought, at the beginning, when I first decided on this, that maybe I was throwing my life away, dying on purpose. Suddenly, I don't think so. I have my chance and Batesy has his.

The result is the thing. Not the effort that goes into it. If I can give hope to all the poor bastards on the ground that everything is not lost, is not given up, then whatever the hell this mission entails is worth it. They expect us up there this morning. They count on it with all their fighting hearts. If only two of us make it, then it is better than nothing at all.

This fight is against unbelievable odds but I never saw a fight yet that couldn't be won if all things went in your favor.

At 45,000 feet Belden came out of his climb and steadied his compass needle on 345 degrees magnetic. Bates moved out thirty yards on the wing and both men began to probe the sky ahead of them with sweeping glances.

For the last time they blasted northward for the fight. Two lonely planes in a lonely sky speeding out to take on the air might of a nation.

Colonel Lee had rendezvoused his squadrons at 0630. Three hundred aircraft carrying close-support armament milled in the sky above Lungchou. Lee swung southward and his legions strung out for fifteen miles across the heavens.

His orders had been briefly direct. No enemy air opposition was expected, so he would devote himself to the destruction of Pham's ground installations and lines of communication. Lee had been led to believe that with the obliteration of the enemy forces he might well expect to receive the General's stars of the late Soohoo Mu Thik. Two-thirds of Lee's complement of operational aircraft was committed to this early strike. The last one hundred and fifty of his fighters would be ready to launch at 1000 should another mission be deemed necessary. This was hardly conceivable, however, and it was considered probable that Pham's forces would be either annihilated or pushed south of the Parallel by nightfall.

Colonel Lee, flying at the head of his mighty armada, wondered at the strange sense of apprehension he experienced this morning. Some alien premonition tried to worm itself into his mind, momentarily bringing a frown to his face.

He was still well north of Hanoi when a Red Chinese radar operator fifty miles south of that city picked up Belden and Bates on his scope. For a moment the radar operator thought perhaps the two faint blips in such close proximity were merely some vagary of the sky at extreme altitude. It took him thirty seconds to confirm to himself that the blips were actually two enemy aircraft barreling north. He called Colonel Lee and reported this astounding fact with some disbelief.

"Their altitude and present location," Lee demanded.

"Eagle One. The enemy is at forty-five thousand feet, closing near the Parallel. I estimate their air speed at Mach One."

"Acknowledged," Lee replied. Well, two reconnaissance planes, he told himself. Covering the battle lines near the border to review the damage we inflicted yesterday. Perhaps I might get a chance at them.

Though Colonel Lee was not worried about the presence of two enemy aircraft in the air, the radar operator far below started to scan his scope with a degree of stupefaction. He shook his head and tried to confirm in his mind what his eyes were revealing to him.

Belden and Bates screamed over the Parallel at 0635, their gunsights up bright and their gun switches on. To the east the great expanse of ocean reflected the first of the sun's rays. To the northwest the great battlements of cloud formation hovered ominously, their peaks reaching above the two Crusaders.

In his cockpit Belden flicked his eyes over his instrument panel, expertly appraising each reading and recording it in his mind where it was confirmed and put aside. His nose wrinkled as he turned his oxygen off for the space of a breath and then turned it on again. He rechecked his tail pipe temperature, then turned in his seat and looked back in the direction from which they had come.

For the past few minutes a vague uneasiness had come over him, a feeling that he had forgotten something or that something had occurred of which he was unaware. He had experienced this sensation before, many times, when something was about to happen for which he had not prepared himself. It was not unlike walking into a dark alley at midnight.

He pressed his mike button and called Bates:

"Heads up. Something's wrong up here."

"Yeah," Bates replied. "I feel it too." Belden heard Bates chuckle. "Maybe it's that we're all alone and the sky is so goddam big."

Belden did not answer. The disquietude grew and his eyes

strained ahead through the windshield. They were past the Parallel and would be passing over Pham's lines in a few moments. Ahead there was no sign of contrails in the sky.

Colonel Lee was still one hundred and fifty miles away, flying a collision course for Belden and steering for Hanoi.

It was the contrails below him that caught Belden's attention first. He was swiveling his head from right to left, passing his line of vision through an arc of 180 degrees, when out of the corner of his eye he saw the streamers veining the sky below. He felt his heart skip a beat as he called to Bates: "Below at seven o'clock and climbing."

Both men saw them then. The contrails were climbing steeply and then the planes themselves were visible, stretching in a severe angle of attack, holding steady formation, so many of them that Belden could not count them.

Bates swung wide and took a position for a defensive weave.

"Hold it," Belden ordered. His eyes narrowed as he watched the oncoming aircraft. Then he began to smile and his heart sang.

"They're ours," he called across the sky.

The F-104s and F-100s swept level and held their formation off Belden's left wing. Beautiful in the morning sun, they held there, their wings glistening in the early light. Belden watched them as they inched in toward him and then they were holding just behind Bates and the length of their formation stretched back two miles.

Belden counted the four-plane divisions. Three . . . five . . . six . . . eight . . . Good Christ, there were forty fighters flying off his wing.

"Morning, Dan." It was Lieutenant Colonel Pat Murphy's voice laughing over the radio. "A nice morning for flying, eh?"

Belden found it hard to speak for a moment. His voice choked in his throat and he felt the unfamiliar stinging of tears at the corners of his eyes.

"You guys are heading in the wrong direction," he said into his mike.

"Well"—Murphy's voice danced across the sky—"I was always lousy at navigation. Suppose I just follow you this morning. Take me to China, Dan."

"They'll have your ass." Belden meant the high brass would throw the book at Murphy and his pilots.

"It's going to be worth it." Murphy's voice was jubilant. "This is Murphy out."

Belden grinned to himself and called, "We can give them a fight now."

It was Bates's voice that answered. "Better than that. Look at four o'clock low." Before Belden could look he heard Bates yell, "Yeeeooowww."

He turned his head to the right and looked down and saw the formation of F-104s moving up from his rear and slightly below. For a second he thought part of Murphy's flight had taken position on his starboard quarter. But then another voice sang out to him: "This is Jack McKellar with forty-eight F-104s. Like the good Colonel, I am lost this morning. Take us in, Dan."

Behind Belden now spread a great armada of ninety airplanes, their wings glinting in the morning sun as practiced hands guided them with swift, sure touches of aileron and throttle.

Belden felt a great surge of affection, an emotion bordering on love, for the unnamed men who had joined him at 45,000 feet. They had felt as he felt, that something had to be done to salvage honor in the sky. Their careers and their lives were the forfeits they were offering to pay.

Northward they flew and their air-speed needles passed the speed of sound. Holding taut on each other's wings, steel threads might have held them like that, rigid and still in the thin air, the whistling of the supersonic wind lost within the rumble of the great engines.

Then McKellar's voice came across to Belden: "Company, Dan. On the starboard beam."

The sun revealed the Crusaders coming down swiftly in a dive, leveling off behind and then sweeping up into position far out on the right wing of the formation. Belden said nothing as the Crusader leader maneuvered in and then held steady as he picked his slot.

McKellar called, "Welcome aboard, Navy."

"Wouldn't miss it for the world," the Crusader leader's voice replied. Then, "Dan. This is Tom Landry with thirty-six Crusaders. I've got a message from an old friend of yours." There was a pause. "Smoke Dusane says to tell you he wishes to hell he was here with you this morning. He can't come himself so he asked us to bring his greetings."

"Thanks, Tom," Belden replied in a low voice. "Thanks."

One hundred and twenty-six Americans flew north. Thousands of miles away in their homeland, bearded college boys tore up their draft cards and waved banners calling for a victory for the enemy. But here on a Southeast Asian morning, one hundred and twenty-six Americans flew north, and they split the sky asunder with the thunder of their coming, calling out a challenge that rushed through the wind ahead of them while old war cries sounded in their brains and they closed the distance that separated them from Colonel Lee and his MIGs.

Proudly they came through the high sky because pride welled up in each of them and they remembered the old names and places that etched themselves forever on the memory of fighting men. They heard ancient voices call the well-honored names and they thrilled to the sound. Okinawa and the Yalu, Iwo Jima and Anzio, Truk and Pearl Harbor and Ploesti; they heard Guadalcanal and Schweinfurt, Rabaul and Regensberg, and they heard the rubble crumbling in Berlin and Tokyo. All the voices of all the fliers who ever lived commended them and each heard it secretly and quietly in his own heart.

There it was. It belonged to them and to no other Americans anywhere at this particular time and place. No easy commitment, no flying lark over your own territory with the reserves to come up and help when the odds lengthened; no antiaircraft emplacements along the terrain to join you in the kill and cover your ass when you went in low. No. You'll watch that sort of fight from the sidewalk. If you go down, you'll die or accommodate yourself to walking three hundred miles through the rice paddies and mountains. You're out ahead this morning, all the way out ahead, on the tip of the spear, and if the shaft is weakened or bent, so much the less for your chances. And if you are a hero, no one will see it in the sky for a bright reward because the sky is choked full of heroes this morning.

"Spread out," was all that Dan Belden said into his mike. The planes slid slowly across and assumed a greater interval of space between them.

Ahead the sky was clear, but on their left the great pillars of the storm front loomed above them and now Murphy transmitted:

"Murphy here. I'll take mine and swing to the left and come in from the background of that front."

"Roger, Murph," Belden said. "Move out."

Murphy took his forty and they swung away, revealing the bellies of their planes in a steep bank and then they were lost against the multicolored face of the towering thunderheads.

They watched alertly for the enemy contrails, but ahead the sky was a steel-blue mirror and it was filled with the sound of martial bands and the marching of feet and they heard the bugles sounding over the horizon.

For some it was the last fight and for others it was the first. They came with their lips pressed tight behind the sucking oxygen masks and the smell of cooling gun barrels would fill their cockpits before the hour was out. Over the harsh red lines pressed into their cheekbones by the hard rubber edges of the masks their eyes swept ahead and were never still. The book was open and waiting for the stroke of the pen that would write their page of history on a summer morning at 45,000 feet on a day to be remembered.

The day one hundred and twenty-six flew out to meet the Chinese MIGs.

The battle? Well, it is recorded in the appropriate log books and it will be spoken of at times when there is a need for gallantry. When heroes are in short supply, they will talk about the fight south of Lungchou and of the men who carried it there from the airstrip at Danang. Carried it there at 45,000 feet on the bright wings of glory.

Lee knew the Americans were coming. The radar reports indicated only a large body of aircraft approaching on a northerly heading, but Lee knew with a certainty that today the fighters would come at him in force. He held his interception course and promised himself that if the Americans wanted battle this morning, he would be there to give it to them.

The fight started when the opposing forces were still thirty miles apart. When the closing speed is 1800 miles per hour, thirty miles is dissipated in one minute.

Belden saw the MIG contrails first as only the faintest tracings of color on the slate blue of the sky. He made his tallyho with the next breath.

"Tallyho," he called. "Dead ahead and level. Thirty miles." The thought passed through his mind that this was the last tallyho he would ever make.

Belden had eighty-six and Lee had three hundred. But Belden also had Pat Murphy and his forty screaming down from cloud cover on Lee's flank. Murphy had gone to 50,000 feet and skirted the cloud tops and he came down like some enraged falcon from the two-o'clock position. Lee, his attention riveted on Belden's formation ahead, did not see Murphy closing and so the F-104s and F-100s smashed at Lee's flanks and into his formation and chopped off the flank altogether and sent the MIGs milling wildly to meet the attack on their right.

Belden held steady as he saw Murphy strike home. He flew straight for the center of the MIG formation and in that instant of time when Lee was astounded by Murphy's attack, the MIG center cracked and Belden shrieked into it and the sky erupted like some suppurating pustule. The close-knit formations dissolved and the melee became general. Friend and foe twisted and intermingled in a crazy pattern of contrails that spread in the high wind and covered the sky with overcast.

Belden shouted aloud in his cockpit as he fired the first burst from his guns. He never knew if he found a target or not because he was suddenly by the MIGs and rolling high in a chandelle, turning to reverse his course, coming down again steeply, then leveling off as he came back to the fight. He picked the first enemy to cross his sights and he swung his nose hard around, pulling it on a line with the MIG and his tracers found home. The MIG heaved over once, righted itself in a side-slipping motion and then cartwheeled crazily until its wings cracked and then tore off and the fuselage tumbled downward.

The familiar exultation gripped Belden as the old skills proved themselves and he felt a gratitude that the artistry had not died. He grinned at himself in his rearview mirror and shouted again with the pure joy of the battle. Below him and in front a MIG came onto the tail of a Crusader, firing steadily and closing while the F8 twisted in a wild attempt to escape. Belden pushed over and came behind the MIG just as the enemy pilot, in his mirror, saw Belden approaching and rolled onto his back and pulled through. Belden was on top of him and rolling too, anticipating the MIG pilot's next maneuver. He anticipated wisely because the MIG rolled out and level just as he should have been going into the vertical part of his dive and Belden was there ahead of him, wings level and the trigger pressed down even as the Chinese pilot was congratulating himself on a clever ruse. The shells tore his head away before the congratulations had been fully delivered.

Lee had reversed course in a tight, low-speed turn. Just before the opposing formations had clashed, he had dropped his speed brakes and chopped his throttle back. He turned inside the rear echelon of Crusaders and before they could wheel into an opposite bank and get away from him, his guns were holding tightly to an F8. A gush of purple flame gasped from the belly of the Crusader and it was gone in an instant of time.

Man met man at 45,000 feet and one or the other died nine miles above the earth. They fought downward because dogfights are descending contests and the altitude diminishes as the planes fight for superiority of position. The battle spread over the entire expanse of sky as the melee developed, the great speed of the participants and their expansive radius of turn utilizing ten times the area of space that would have been needed by conventional aircraft. The engines drove the high-wind sound from the heavens and the throttles were moved with great care and not at all extravagantly because a jet engine responds to the minutest of touches at great altitude and any sudden movement of the throttle presupposes a flame-out and a sudden and complete absence of thrust. When your plane loses thrust in a dogfight, then you are dead, for all practical purposes.

Bates had lost Belden on the initial pass and had swerved deliberately into the middle of a swarm of MIGs, scattering the enemy formation and emerging on the far side with a MIG on his tail and another held securely in his gunsight. He had a heartbeat of time in which to make his decision. He could kill the man ahead of him or he could try to elude the man behind him. Discretion is the greater part of valor, he decided. He soared up into a half-loop with a roll on top, reversing his direction and watching the MIG in his mirror. "Come on, you bastard," he whispered. "Close on me." The MIG obliged and when it came almost within range Bates went into a split-ess and pulled out and into another half-loop, repeating the previous maneuver. This time, as he reached the vertical climb, he went into afterburner and held his nose steady, climbing directly up into the sky. Because he had initiated the action and knew exactly what he was going to do and the MIG pilot did not, Bates had considerably more air speed to squander in the vertical climb than did his enemy. Bates kept his eyes fastened on his mirror and he saw the MIG falter in its climb. The nose fell off and the airplane slewed sideways, then fell off into a slow spiral that heralded a spin. Bates grinned and rolled on his side, easing on bottom rudder pressure, pulling his nose down through the horizon and then he was diving after the spinning MIG. He caught it at 30,000 feet before the enemy pilot had regained control. With no emotion at all unless it was happiness, Bates opened fire at 600 yards and flew all the way down until the MIG exploded and he flew through the spattering wreckage.

Throughout the widening area of battle the streaming contrails interwove in graceful and delicate patterns. Men fought each other with a grim determination in some instances and with a surging exultation in others. There was no thought for sanctuary on either side and the minutes passed and the gas needles trembled downward unheeded.

"Murph. This is Jack. Three on your ass. Hold there and I'll come down behind."

"Roger. And hurry if you please."

"Six o'clock low. Ten of them milling. Spread out, Harry."

"Roger. Let's get 'em." A pause. "Christ but I'm hungry."

"A morning to create a good appetite. Three o'clock high. They're coming down in a high-side."

"Let the bastards come, Al. We're high cover over you. Hold tight."

"All right, Joe. They're into their runs. Watch it now. Break on command. . . . Ready. . . . Break!" The MIGs came, but Joe's radio had been shot out, so he did not receive the most important order he would ever have heard.

"Joe! For Christ's sake, Joe! Look out . . . they're behind you. Joe, God dam it, break. Oh, for Christ's goddam sonofabitching sake . . ." The voice trailed off.

Pat Murphy and Dan Belden were fighting six MIGs in a corner of the sky reserved for the unbelievable. Time after time the MIG leader thought he had the enemy cold. Time after time he started to grin as he or one of his men swung into position for the kill. But every time the other American would come from nowhere, guns blazing and slashing, and the MIG leader began to wonder what kind of devils he was fighting. Belden and Murphy got two of the enemy in a simple crisscross scissoring maneuver. Both had MIGs on their tails and were flying parallel when without a spoken command they both crossed steeply in a bank and covered each other's tail, their triggers held down as they passed, and they blew each other's assailants apart just as four Crusaders waded into the fight.

The fight did not wane as the minutes passed. Instead it increased in savagery and crescendo until it seemed the high air could hold no further bedlam. Young men grew old in a minute of time and old men grew young again. The pure, unadulterated rapture of mortal combat that honed their reflexes and abilities, they would not recognize until much later. That for this little while they had been given the capacities of the gods, they would not understand until later when the flame of killing had gone out of their eyes. But in these moments they fought with a divine grace and if some of them had to die, then that was the way it had to be.

For the writing of history does not come easily and if a man would know the ecstasy of victory in the deadliest game of all, he must be prepared to risk existence. The young men risked gleefully as they counted the MIGs that trailed downward in the sky.

They did not count the men that died in the MIGs because this is not the way it is done. The fighter pilots do not see their victims die. They are spared the blackened bodies pinned in the cockpits and the singed-beef faces with the mouths and noses gone. They will never know the sight of the skin sloughing off the arm in the soul-searing heat of the kerosene blaze and the legs writhing against the floor boards like grotesque baked potatoes. There is nothing memorable in hair burned to charcoal and flesh peeling away like old wallpaper as dying lips plead in vain, "Kill me, please. Somebody kill me." The medals are won on the count of planes sent down, the tumbling chunks of metal and fuselage and bits of engine components, not on the count of agonized screams and blood gushing from bowels. It is an impersonal war, the war in the air, unless you desire to torment yourself and dream too much at night.

Jack McKellar died because a ten-cent bolt on his empennage gave way at 40,000 feet. It seemed an absurd failure to result in such a final departure.

McKellar had blasted four MIGs out of the sky before his luck ran thin. He had come out of a tight six g-turn and was looking ahead of him for a target of opportunity when Colonel Lee came down on him from above and behind. McKellar saw Lee in his mirror at the same time he heard the MIG guns chatter. McKellar felt no premonition of disaster because he possessed a vast faith in his own ability and in his airplane. As Lee's reflection came into his mirror, McKellar expertly gauged the relative speed of the MIG and knew in a split second that Lee was not a novice and that his enemy had ranged up slowly. McKellar went into afterburner and threw his stick hard to the right side of his cockpit. It was then that Jack McKellar's heart skipped a beat.

His nose pitched upward as his actions actuated his aileron controls. Instead of screaming into a tight reversal turn, McKellar's airplane was in a bastard position in the sky, twisted around on its side yet without actually turning, the nose of the plane awkwardly hanging at a 40-degree angle of attack as his elevator controls refused adamantly to function. He hung there in the ridiculous posture for a moment or two and then cursed as he banged hard left aileron and the plane swerved into the opposite direction and assumed an identical attitude. He eased forward pressure on the stick as he brought the wings level and the nose fell to the horizon. "Good Christ!" McKellar swore. "I have no goddam elevator controls in this mother and there's a sonofabitch of a MIG on my tail, shooting the shit out of me."

Colonel Lee Cheng was not a man who killed dispassionately as most good fighter pilots do. He killed with a vicious satisfaction and if he could have watched his victims' faces, he would have done so gladly. Now he moved up on McKellar's helpless aircraft, checking briefly in his mirror to be sure that his own tail was clear. He smiled to himself as the enemy grew in his gunsight.

Jack McKellar had nowhere in all the world to go. He was condemned to fly straight and level due to the failure of that ten-cent bolt in his empennage.

McKellar felt Lee's shells begin their work on his after section. Jesus! He threw the stick back and forth in the cockpit, rocking his aircraft right and left in a sloppy, sluggish motion. It was to no avail. The shells pounded relentlessly closer and worked their way into the cockpit and McKellar died without pain, with only a great numbing sensation that started in his legs and almost instantaneously swept up over his whole body. His brain was the last thing to die and in the final split second, just before he stopped breathing, he saw a Crusader streak by on a reciprocal course.

Belden saw McKellar die, although he had no idea who it was. He saw the F104 trail a plume of black smoke and start a spiral downward and that was all he had time to see. Even as he swore, he was flashing by Lee's MIG and, as though the entire scene were exposed on slow-motion film, the two airplanes seemed to hang motionless in the air, floating past each other as in some dreamlike fantasy.

Belden saw the dragon painted on Lee's tail and he felt a great rush of anger. God damn it, his mind said to him. There the sonofabitch is and now he dies.

The anger receded as quickly as it had flared and Belden set about the business at hand. Even as he saw the dragon on the tail surface of the MIG, his mind was dashing far ahead of him and his hands and feet were actuating pressures on his controls. He came up steeply in a climbing turn, holding the back pressure on the stick and the aileron control and so his plane climbed and turned simultaneously until he was arcing over at the top nearly onto his back. He looked down and saw Lee climbing to meet him. With his low air speed he turned swiftly to confront Lee and flew directly down the MIG's flight path.

Both men felt it at the same exact instant and their minds confirmed it. It was as though a message flashed across the intervening space and sang some ancient song of warning. Suddenly they were alone in the sky, totally oblivious of the multitude of planes wheeling and milling about them; they were all alone in the whole world of the sky and one of them would die before this encounter was finished.

In his cockpit, Colonel Lee flew with that sense of disquiet that had come early that day growing stronger in him. He had never experienced it before. It had gone away when the battle started, but now it was back with him again as the Crusader came at him out of the background of blue sky. He was unable to name it for what it was, the knowledge—faint and ephemeral, hiding far back in the recesses of his mind—of death. But it crouched there in his brain and perhaps its presence dulled his capabilities minutely, just enough to take the fine edge from his precise art and kill him on a summer morning south of Lungchou.

Belden aborted his run before he had passed Lee, swerving sharply in a vertical bank and presenting, for a short moment, his underside to Lee's guns. He had anticipated this and so was ready when Lee pulled his nose through to get his guns ahead of Belden's flight path. As Lee's shells left his muzzles, Belden leveled his wings and in the same motion pulled up in a tight loop. Lee, already committed to his tight turn, was slow in following Belden's maneuver, so the MIG was far behind when Belden soared onto his back and from the inverted position looked down at the enemy plane just coming into the vertical.

"All right," Belden murmured. "Here we go, you sonofabitch."

He pulled harder on his stick, the arc of his loop tightened, and he came down at Lee with all guns blazing. He came on the back side of his loop, building speed while Lee was losing his, and his guns worked in continuous lines of fire, the red ribbons of flame stretching tautly from the Crusader's nose across the sky and into Lee's MIG.

In his climb Lee was vulnerable and he knew it. There was nothing to do but hope the American missed. Belden had only a short time within range, but he saw some of his shells hit and then he was into a climb again, all the excessive speed that he had accumulated in his dive working for him as he soared high and rolled out. This time he came level with Lee and slightly to one side. At the top of the roll-out his speed was again minimal and he used it to advantage. He banked steeply and before Lee was aware that Belden had come up on him he was behind the MIG and strapped on tightly, his guns blazing again.

By offering himself in a vulnerable attack posture, Belden had coaxed his enemy into an anticipated maneuver. When a man knows what his enemy is going to do a split second before the enemy himself knows, then the man has an insurmountable advantage if he is expert at his trade. The scant interval of time that Lee lost was enough for Belden to gain the advantage and now Colonel Lee Cheng knew he was going to die.

There was bright blue sky ahead of him as the knowledge that had been lurking in his brain walked out into the open. It should not have affected him much, one way or another. His was a stoic race and death was an inevitability that the Chinese accepted more readily than did other peoples in the world. So it was something of a surprise to the Colonel to learn in a breath of time that he wanted to live forever. His heart pounded and he experienced difficulty in breathing as he firewalled his throttle and went into afterburner. But Belden was behind him, hanging close and firing now in quick sporadic bursts. Lee whimpered into his oxygen mask. He tried to turn away, the last desperate gamble of a losing fighter, but Belden, no novice, was there again, turning inside and closing until he hung as if riveted to the MIG by steel braces, and this time all his shells went home.

Die now, bastard, Belden thought. Die now, you sonofabitch. I hope to Christ you go out burning.

Lee knew he could not get away. Never could he get away from the man hanging a few feet behind him. Terror rose in his breast and his eyes bugged in his head. There was a roaring in his ears over and above the stutter of his enemy's guns. The sky swam before his eyes and he knew the ultimate, paralyzing fear. A few seconds of time had transformed a coldly efficient fighting man into a frantic child crying out in the darkness. He had lost the power of decision and finally his hands left the stick and throttle and pounded senselessly against the sides of the cockpit.

The MIG withstood well the pitiless pounding of Belden's shells. Pieces of the airframe whipped away in the wind and screeching tracers ricocheted off the armor plating behind the cockpit to be lost somewhere in the sky.

299

Most men die as they have lived and their deaths have something of honesty in them. Lee had lived as a fighter and had done so with grace. He was unexcelled in his chosen profession until the end and he had done his killing with a great skill. His death should have been accomplished with the same measure of proficiency.

But Colonel Lee died screaming.

I'll end it now, Belden thought. I'll end everything now, this bastard in my gunsight, the long journey that has taken twenty years, the loneliness and the loss and all the rest. I'll end it all now. I've won my last fight and it's all over.

He slid a few feet behind Lee, hanging directly astern of the MIG. All his guns vomited point-blank and the tracers rushed into the tail section and over it and arced down into the cockpit. He saw the spray of glass from the canopy even before the smoke balled out of the tail pipe.

The screams came from Lee's mouth even before the shells hit him. It was a strange thing, but just before he died Lee thought of a small clearing in a forgotten village and two American fliers standing bravely before an execution squad. He was wondering at this thought when a 20-mm shell slammed into the back of his neck and tore out through his mouth, leaving a travesty of his head remaining. Lee never knew when his plane shuddered and erupted into flame, spurting orange and cobalt billows of smoke from the after section just before the explosion that hurled bits of the MIG through the sky.

Belden watched the MIG disintegrate and then nodded to himself and turned back to the fight. But the fight was over. The MIG pilots knew that Lee was dead. One pilot saw it and called his wingman, and the word spread through the sky as the combatants drew apart and watched each other warily. Fights end this way. In a given moment it is over—and one side has won and the other has been defeated. They do not fight to the last bitter end because there is the matter of fuel in the tanks and ammunition in the guns. The man-made increments are less durable than the human.

Lee had come out with three hundred, and another fifty had joined him during the fight. The MIGs rendezvoused less than seventy-five airplanes for the flight back to Lungchou. Belden brought back seventy out of the one hundred twenty-six which had gone forth. So fifty-six had died to destroy two hundred and seventy-five. The odds had been met and conquered by the selfless gallantry of men whose names would be remembered only by those who had fought with them on their last day.

But the page of history had been written as Belden's planes circled to rendezvous. Each of them knew it secretly and was proud.

They came into formation again south of Lungchou. The four-plane divisions swung in behind with a proud arrogance, only now there were not always the four planes. Here there were only two. And here, three. And there only one flew where four had been.

"A good fight." Pat Murphy's voice came across with a certain weariness. A moment later he said, "Hang in tight. Let's look good coming home."

Dan Belden led them back across the mountains and rice paddies at 30,000 feet. The sun was higher now in the east and below them the terrain was bathed in bright sunlight. They passed high over Pham's lines and soldiers stood and raised their guns overhead and shouted with hoarse voices because they had seen the contrails to the north and had watched the tremendous battle as distant spectators at some combat of the gods.

In his cockpit Belden removed his oxygen mask momentarily and breathed deeply of the familiar smell for the last time. It was an odor compounded of cordite, sweat, and hot oil, and over it the scent of kerosene. Belden wondered briefly if the smell would seep into his pores and his bones and become a part of him, so that he could take it with him now that it was over. He sincerely hoped so.

He looked over at Bates and grinned and then slipped the oxygen mask back on his face.

Well, he thought, I think we did it this morning. I think we battered that sonofabitch Lee and his squadrons so bad that any hope they had for air supremacy went up in smoke. I think we clobbered the bastards hard enough so that August offensive will be scratched off the boards. Maybe not, but I think so. They'll be screaming in Washington and Paris and London, but screw them all. We got lucky this morning, lucky because Murphy and McKellar and a bunch of their guys decided there was something to being an American after all. Let those bastards in Washington chew on that for a while. This time we really opened the door.

When you come to it rightly, there is only one way to go into a fight. You go in to win or you do not go in at all. This is a truism understood by fighting men, but unfortunately the decisions are very seldom made by the fighting men.

If we don't do something about it, Belden told himself, General Pham may well go down. Sooner or later they'll get to him, and then what the hell will they do for a leader? Some Buddhist sonofabitch will set fire to himself in the street, and before he stops stinking Pham will be through.

The Red bastards have all the best of it out here because none of us really understands the Oriental mind. It is truly different from our own, and we are interlopers in a place that was a million years old when we were still listening to the marching of the Roman legions.

He had passed the front lines now and was coming up on the Parallel.

It's like swinging your fist at a cloud of smoke, he thought. There just isn't any way to land a telling blow. But I'm tired of wearying my mind with it. My days are finished at this sort of thing. I've done the best I know how and I've lost good friends in the doing.

There was something I was searching for and I thought it was the thrill of youth I wanted again. I looked for the songs and the memories and a young man's ability to look on tomorrow and truly not give a damn. But all that went away from me a long time ago. It went down with the years and it left me when the knowledge came that I was on the downward side of the hill.

What would happen to Murphy and the rest? Nothing, Belden knew. Lee's Air Force had been slammed to defeat by a handful of men who would be heroes tomorrow, and who can discipline a hero? Any way you looked at it they had done only what honor demanded.

They were south of the Parallel now, holding in perfect alignment, the brightening rays of the sun glinting off the wings and along the polished canopies.

He pressed his mike button. "Heading down," he called.

"Take us home, Dan." Murphy's voice came to him quietly.

They followed Belden down, and where once they had known the name as a legend, now they felt they knew the man. For he had met the greatest challenges of the sky and in doing so had become the true professional. He was the cloth helmet and the old Hellcat fighter, the predawn rendezvous at Truk and New Guinea, and the frigid air high over the Yalu. The Pratt and Whitneys and the plotting boards when radar was still on the engineers' charts. He was of old days when glamour and glory came with the wings and the speed of sound was something in the comic strips.

They passed 20,000 feet and the strip at Danang lay tiny in the distance.

"Right echelon," Belden called and sixty-nine planes slid under and stepped down off his right wing.

Belden's hands moved automatically, turning off switches, selecting a radio channel, trimming his controls, but his mind moved away from him as he brought them down to Danang.

For now he knew how a man could partially control his fate. And he knew how to define the precise moment when the journey had ended.

Tell me now, Hawk, and tell me, Cort, and all the rest of you, since you have gone on ahead of me and thus are wiser now by far, did you find this truth before you left? Or did you know it a long time ago and merely hesitate to impart the information before you went away?

There is a manner in which flying men can influence their destiny. Since the essence of survival is in knowing when to quit, it then becomes a simple matter of determining when.

Belden leaned forward in his cockpit and eased the throttle back until the rushing wind muted to a whisper. He strained to listen and his eyes narrowed with the effort.

From far and away, from the farthest recesses of the sky, from out past all the stars and meteors and galaxies as distant as the mind of man could conceive, came only the sound of the wind calling as it swept past the timeless boundaries of space. He listened even more carefully now and he nodded as he realized this truth.

There were no more bugles in the sky.

For Dan Belden, when was now.

The huge Boeing 707 jet airliner waited patiently at the loading ramp at the airport outside Saigon. The rest of the passengers had gone aboard and now only a solitary group of people remained at the foot of the boarding ladder. It was dusk and the lights were going on in Saigon, casting their orange reflections against the low cloud cover coming down from the north. The heat of the day had given way to a cool breeze that held the smell of the mountains and the dampness from the river. O'Toole had gone aboard with the hand luggage and all that remained now were the farewells.

Lori stood on her toes and lightly kissed Storm Ryerson and Smoke Dusane.

"You'll come to see us?" she asked both of them.

"I'll be along soon," Ryerson said. "I'll want to land some of those marlin Bates talks about."

"And I," Dusane said, "will be going out on thirty shortly. Do you think you can find a billet for an old sea dog?"

"Of course we can." She turned to Belden and Bates and said, "I'll go aboard now and wait for you."

After Lori had gone, the four men stood quietly and smoked as they sorted their memories of the past twenty years. There was little left to say now that had not been said before.

"Well," Ryerson said, "I think you did it, Dan. This morning the President authorized a hundred thousand men over here within the next eight weeks. They have no Air Force now. You took care of that. Their fifty damn divisions will do them no good without air power."

"So the August blitz is off?" Dusane asked.

Ryerson nodded. "It has to be. Without Lee and his MIGs they couldn't make it go. By the time they can beef up their air power, we'll have enough to stand up to them. We're here to stay now."

"We'll carry the fight to them now," Belden said. "There was a big hump that we had to get over. A hump of fear and indecision. It's gone now."

Dusane said, "Well, these have been times to remember."

"It was a close thing," Ryerson agreed.

"Too hectic." Bates spoke with quiet meditation. "A man should have nothing more important on his mind than the hot sun, the blue waters of the Gulf Stream, and those goddam marlin shining on the end of a hook."

"I hope whatever is ahead of you two is good," Ryerson said. "I sincerely hope that."

304

"And I," Dusane added.

Belden ground out his cigarette. He offered his hand to his two friends. The clasp was warm and honest and much to be said was left behind the eyes.

"It's been a long trip," Belden said softly.

"It's not over yet." Ryerson smiled.

"Part of it is," Belden said. He glanced at Bates. "Ready, Batesy?"

"Ready, Dan." Bates shook hands with Ryerson and Dusane. "Don't worry about your boy here. I'll keep an eye on him."

"That's what I'm afraid of," Ryerson said humorously.

"So long."

"So long."

Belden and Bates walked up the boarding ramp and the two old men watched them go.

"If I had a trumpet, I'd blow it," Dusane remarked in a low voice.

"It would do no good, Smoke," Ryerson said. "They couldn't hear it."

"I prefer to think it isn't over for them," Dusane said. "That it will never be over for them. It would take something away from both of us."

The hatch to the plane was closed and the ramp was wheeled away. In a moment the engines whined and burst into life and the great plane began inching out of the chocks.

"Think of it this way, my friend," Ryerson said. His eyes brightened with his thoughts. "They've had the best of it. We have too. All of us have had it all the way. No matter what happens later, nothing can take it away from us."

They watched as the 707 wheeled into take-off position and began to roll down the runway. The flames from the engines were startlingly bright in the growing dusk as the throttles were opened wide and full power surged from the tail pipes.

The lights of the plane were dimming to the east and a silence had come over the field when Ryerson finally glanced at Dusane and laid a hand on his shoulder.

"We'll find your helicopter now, my friend, and fly out to your flagship tonight." They turned and started up the long walk toward the terminal building. "Then we'll drink some of your excellent brandy and stand together on the bridge in the darkness and remember our youth and the men who were a part of it. We'll get a little drunk and lie to each other and finally we'll sleep with no dreams at all unless they be of the hot sun and marlin dancing in the sea spray. Who knows? We may even find our youth again and speak in brave words of heroes we once knew."

About the Author

Richard Newhafer was born in Chicago and has lived in California, Florida, and Texas. He was educated at the universities of Notre Dame and De Paul. Mr. Newhafer was a Navy flier for fifteen years, both in World War II and in Korea, and won many honors including a Navy Cross, three Distinguished Flying Crosses, twelve Air Medals, and a Presidential Citation. He was a member of the Navy's jet acrobatic team, the Blue Angels. After the Navy, he flew in the Texas oil fields, and then in the Bahamas as a charter pilot. He is the author of *The Last Tallyho*.

About the Author